FEAR THE REAPER

THE REAPER SERIES, BOOK 3

TODD HOSEA

ISBN 979-8-9917874-0-6 (Hardcover)
ISBN 979-8-9917874-1-3 (Paperback)
ISBN 978-1-7357501-9-4 (Ebook)

First Edition: January 2025

ALSO BY TODD HOSEA

Steal the Reaper
Hunt the Reaper
Fear the Reaper

This one is for my sister, Shannon

ACKNOWLEDGMENTS

I am forever grateful to my incredible wife, Cindy. Your unwavering support and belief in me have been my greatest source of strength. Thank you for everything you've done to help bring *The Reaper Series* to life. I love you more than words can express.

To my family, friends, and—most importantly—you, the reader, thank you from the bottom of my heart. Your support, from purchasing this book and leaving reviews to offering words of encouragement, has been invaluable in keeping this dream alive. Thank you, thank you, thank you!

"Do not fear me for who I am. Fear me for what I can become."

- Unknown Author

PROLOGUE

Planet Earth
Satipo, Peru

Dr. Gabriel Vlachos leaned toward the closed-circuit television monitor, narrowing his gaze on Zoe, his new patient. On the screen, the teenager slept peacefully in a private room down the hall, blissfully unaware of his watchful eye.

As he observed her sleeping, a sense of satisfaction washed over Vlachos. All indications showed Zoe was a viable candidate. She had arrived three weeks earlier from an impoverished village in the Andean Highlands. After volunteering to undergo a comprehensive genetic screening process—as did every other fertile girl in the village—Zoe was the only female selected for a special medical procedure involving in vitro fertilization. If successfully impregnated and the embryo carried to full term, Zoe would receive 30,000 USD—roughly five years' wages in Peru—and return to her village safe and sound.

Zoe checked all the boxes for an ideal surrogate, and by all accounts, she was acclimating well to her new living arrangements at Mathias Industries. The last thing Dr. Vlachos wanted was to put undue stress on this mother-to-be. Miscarriages were common, so his staff went to great lengths to pamper Zoe. Fresh water, clean clothes, hot meals, and daily showers were just a few amenities now at her disposal; the spa treatments were her favorite.

Judging by how well Zoe was sleeping and eating, their efforts to make her feel comfortable were paying off. Despite the daily poking and prodding, Zoe counted herself lucky.

Yesterday, Vlachos heard her joke: "*I can't believe they're paying me for this!*"

Pleased with what he saw, Dr. Vlachos turned away from the CCTV and checked on the IVF incubator beside him. Using an embryoscope, Vlachos peered inside the incubator to a culture dish containing sixteen recently thawed human-cloned embryos. The embryoscope's time-lapse camera allowed the doctor to view each embryo's development in ten-minute intervals—at four hundred times magnification. Out of the sixteen candidates, one embryo stood out to him.

"Looking good, Number Four," Vlachos thought aloud, throwing props to the embryo he felt had the best chance of surviving to live birth once transferred to Zoe's uterus.

Hopes ran high that his team's next attempt at human cloning would succeed where past attempts had failed. Last year, they hit an unexpected snag with accelerated cell degeneration, which caused premature aging and death. Then, in a public relations nightmare, Dr. Vlachos's illegal experiments became public knowledge. Two cloned girls—and numerous dogs—were discovered at the Groom Lake facility in the United States. While his team had seamlessly shifted operations to Peru, pressure mounted from his employer, Edmund Mathias, to perfect the cloning process.

"Tomorrow," Vlachos muttered with a slight grin.

The embryos and his surrogate were ready. Fingers crossed, the in vitro fertilization would work. If all went to plan, Zoe would be well into her first trimester by the time Mathias returned from his trip to Challenger Deep.

Vlachos yawned heavily, the toll of 18-hour workdays evident in his weary eyes. Since Luna arrived, his team had been buzzing with excitement. Access to male and female Aiwan DNA was like early Christmas for his researchers. Their force enhancement serum had resulted from splicing human DNA with Earth-dwelling mammals, but Aiwan DNA opened up an entirely new realm of possibilities.

Despite the thrilling prospects, Dr. Vlachos had to focus on Zoe. The success of their current project hinged on mastering the cloning of a human before they could hope to create copies of Luna and Kypa—or even something altogether new. This step was crucial; without perfecting human cloning, the potential of Aiwan DNA would remain untapped. His dreams of groundbreaking biological advancements depended on his team's ability to navigate this delicate yet critical phase.

Rubbing his tired eyes, Dr. Vlachos decided to call it a night. As he rose from his chair and unbent his aching back, the entire facility suddenly rumbled beneath him. Startled, he dropped back in his chair and instinctively gripped the table with both hands as the tremor shook the walls, rattled test tubes, and caused the overhead lights to flicker.

Within seconds, the chaos subsided, restoring calm. The tremor had passed, but Dr. Vlachos remained motionless, waiting for potential aftershocks. As adrenaline coursed through his veins, his heart pounded loudly in his chest—a stark contrast to the stillness around him.

When no aftershocks came, he relaxed his grip on the table and turned to check on Zoe. Thankfully, she remained undisturbed. Dr. Vlachos dropped his shoulders and blew out a short exhale. Just as he started to collect his thoughts, the main power shut off, plunging the lab into complete darkness.

The backup generators kicked on immediately. Emergency lights flickered to life, and the computers began rebooting. For an instant, Dr. Vlachos believed they might be okay—until an ear-splitting alarm shattered the silence.

Darting a look at the CCTV screen, the doctor saw Zoe was awake, curled in a fetal position with ears covered and eyes squeezed shut.

"No, no, no!" Vlachos said in a panic.

He turned sharply to a nearby high-security blood storage refrigerator. Inside were a dozen glass vials that held the future of Mathias Industries. Six vials contained a yellowish compound known as Sampraviddha, meaning "enhanced" in Sanskrit. Mathias's marketing department had yet to come up with a catchy trade name, so Dr. Vlachos's team had adopted this temporary placeholder for their force enhancement serum.

The remaining six vials contained dark green blood samples from the Aiwans, Prince Kypa and Luna. These samples were critical to his research on their alien physiology.

Dr. Vlachos's gaze lingered on the vials, knowing the immense potential—and peril—within those fragile containers. In that moment of indecision, he faced a critical choice: move the vials from the fridge to a temperature-controlled transport box or check on Zoe. He chose the girl.

Bolting from his seat, Dr. Vlachos sprinted across the lab and threw open the door. The alarm echoed throughout the sterile corridor, and red strobe lights flashed from the ceiling. He winced from the skull-rattling noise as he looked right, then left, searching for his team, but the hallway was empty. He was the only person working at this hour. Everyone else was asleep four floors up, though they were surely awake now. Urgency gripped him; he needed to act swiftly to ensure Zoe's safety and secure their research.

Hurrying down the hall, Dr. Vlachos passed several windowless doors on either side. He ignored the pounding and shouting behind them as he made his way to Zoe's room. Sliding to a halt in front of her door, Vlachos quickly entered his security code on the keypad. The door unlocked, and he pushed it open to find Zoe still curled up on her bed in fright.

Despite the dimmed lighting, Zoe recognized Dr. Vlachos's silhouette in the doorway. Without hesitation, she leaped off the bed and crossed the room, thrusting her arms around his waist.

"Everything's alright," he soothed, gently patting her back while his mind raced to figure out their next move. With no time to waste, Vlachos said, "Hurry, put on your shoes."

Zoe retreated and quickly slid on her shoes. She then took the doctor's outstretched hand.

"¡Vamos!" Vlachos said, leading Zoe into the hallway.

They backtracked toward the lab. Zoe heard the unmistakable pounding and screaming while passing the other patients' rooms. Their pleas for help resonated through the heavy doors, sending chills down her spine. She pulled her hand free from Dr. Vlachos and slowed her pace, her expression filled with concern.

"What about them?" she asked, curious why they were not evacuating the others.

Dr. Vlachos stammered a reply, trying to mask his inner turmoil. The people behind those doors—if they could still be called that—were extremely dangerous and not to be set free under any circumstances, especially by an unarmed scientist in his late sixties and a teenage girl. It would take a team of guards to control just one of those test subjects.

Unfortunately, Dr. Vlachos had no time to explain this to Zoe. He knew the truth would only frighten her more and slow them down. Trying not to appear insensitive, the doctor put on his best poker face and lied through his teeth.

"It is best they stay in their rooms, at least for now," he attested, his voice as steady as he could manage. "I promise I will come back for them after I get you to safety."

Zoe hesitated, but the urgency in Dr. Vlachos's voice compelled her to move on.

As they resumed their hurried pace, the doctor silently prayed that the situation would not deteriorate further. Reaching the lab, the nameplate on the door read FORCE ENHANCEMENT DIVISION—EMBRYOLOGY.

"Gabriel!" came a woman's voice.

Dr. Vlachos rounded to find his colleague, Dr. Martin, approaching at a brisk jog.

"Sophia, thank God," Vlachos exclaimed, catching his breath and feeling a surge of relief at the sight of a familiar face. "What's happening?"

"I overheard the guards," Sophia replied, her voice laced with panic. "There's been an explosion in the east wing—everything is on fire."

Vlachos was stunned. The blast must have been massive to reach this far underground. And if the fire was as severe as it sounded, the lab and their research could be at risk.

Dr. Martin, meanwhile, exchanged a quick glance with Zoe and managed a reassuring smile. While they were not strangers, Sophia knew Zoe primarily as IVF-C122, the unique subject identifier assigned to Zoe upon her arrival. Out of instinct, Dr. Martin scanned Zoe for injuries and found none, a wave of relief washing over her. She had come specifically for Zoe, but seeing her safe with Dr. Vlachos was a significant comfort. Sophia, like Vlachos, understood the crucial role Zoe played in their work and shared in their collective sense of urgency to protect her.

"Sophia, you take Zoe topside," Dr. Vlachos instructed firmly. "I'll grab the vials and meet up with you shortly."

Dr. Martin nodded reluctantly, then took Zoe's hand. She tried to steer the girl away, but Zoe refused to let go of Dr. Vlachos.

"It's okay," Vlachos said, running his hand over her head and smiling warmly. "You will be safe with Dr. Martin. Now go. I will see you soon."

Zoe complied and took Sophia's hand. As soon as they departed, Dr. Vlachos entered his lab and went straight to the storage room. He retrieved a sturdy blood transport container from a shelf. The blue polyethylene container resembled the coolers used at youth sports events, but this one had a compressor that allowed it to keep temperature-sensitive products cool while on the go.

Hustling back to the lab, Dr. Vlachos unlocked the refrigerator using a keypad and carefully transferred the vials to the mobile container. Once finished, he closed the fridge and, for a split second, he considered removing the embryos from the incubator as well. Dr. Vlachos quickly discarded the notion. The embryos were fragile, and exposing them unnecessarily to contaminants in the air could do more harm than good. It was better to leave them alone and hope they remained undisturbed. He could always get more embryos. It was

Zoe and the DNA specimens that mattered most.

Sealing the container shut with a decisive click, Dr. Vlachos slung the shoulder strap over his head and made for the door. Outside, the corridor stretched eerily empty. The polished floors reflected the harsh red glare of the emergency lights, while the blaring alarm was a piercing reminder of the chaos that had erupted. Yet beyond it, he could still hear the desperate pounding of fists against reinforced steel doors. The test subjects screamed for release, their voices hoarse and raw with fear.

A sharp pang of guilt gnawed at him, but Dr. Vlachos knew there was no turning back. He could not afford to falter now, not with everything at stake. The mission had to succeed, even if it meant leaving the test subjects behind. Quieting his inner conflict, he hurried to the stairwell at the end of the hallway. His hand trembled slightly as he brought his ID badge to the scanner, the green light flashing an all-clear. The lock disengaged with a metallic clunk, and he pushed the door open. Without wasting another second, he began his ascent, the echo of his footsteps mingling with the distant cries below.

As Dr. Vlachos reached the exit to Sub-Level One, the door suddenly swung open, and a guard burst through, pistol drawn and eyes wide with adrenaline. Both men froze instantly, caught off-guard by the unexpected encounter before recognition dawned on them. There was no need for words; their tense silence spoke volumes. Dr. Vlachos stepped aside, his heart pounding, and allowed the guard to pass.

The guard double-timed his pace, racing up the steps to the main level. Dr. Vlachos followed at a distance, the sound of the guard's boots echoing off the cold, concrete walls. As he ascended, Vlachos picked up snippets of garbled radio chatter on the guard's shoulder-mounted radio.

"All units to the south wall. Repeat, all units to the south wall. We're under attack!"

The words sent a chill down Dr. Vlachos's spine. His mind reeled, struggling to comprehend the gravity of the situation. Who would do such a thing? Industrial espionage to steal trade secrets was one thing, but a full-scale attack to destroy the facility? It seemed unthinkable, yet the panic in the guard's movements told him this was no ordinary breach.

A sudden, icy fear gripped him. Whoever orchestrated this attack may be coming for the very specimens he carried. Dr. Vlachos knew he was in immediate danger, whether the perpetrators intended to steal or destroy the vials. The thought of losing his research and years of painstaking work sent a wave of nausea through him. Then it occurred to him: what if they wanted to capture or kill him because of his work? That idea made his feet move faster.

Reaching the main level, Dr. Vlachos stumbled into a scene of utter chaos. Terrified workers, many still in their night clothes, were herded out of the building and driven forward by security personnel. Local firefighters, their gear clanking with every step, pushed past him, making their way to the facility's east side.

Vlachos paused, trying to catch his breath amidst the commotion. His thoughts were a whirlwind of fear and uncertainty. He pushed through the crowds in the lobby and slipped out into the night.

Pausing at the base of the steps, he looked eastward, where a thick plume of black smoke billowed into the midnight sky. The acrid scent of burning chemicals and debris hung heavy in the air, stinging his nostrils and throat. Below the swirling smoke, red-orange flames licked hungrily at the dark night. The situation was worse than he had feared; the fire was out of control and spreading rapidly.

A fit of coughing overtook him, the rancid smoke clawing at his lungs. Instinctively, Dr. Vlachos tightened his grip on the storage container. With renewed urgency, he turned toward the main gate and joined the frightened crowd already surging in that direction.

Nearing the gate, the mass of people suddenly ground to a halt, the flow of movement stopping so abruptly that Dr. Vlachos nearly collided with the person in front of him. The crowd began to murmur, confusion and fear rippling through them like an electric current.

"Step aside!" came a harsh, commanding voice from behind. "Make a hole!"

Dr. Vlachos turned to see two guards muscling their way through the crowd as it parted reluctantly. Their faces were set with grim determination, and rifles held at the ready; muzzles pointed skyward.

Reaching the main gate, the guards lowered their weapons and took aim at something beyond. The night air exploded with the loud crack of gunfire, the sharp reports echoing off the surrounding buildings.

Dr. Vlachos flinched at the sound, his heart pounding in his chest. He watched in stunned silence, his mind racing as he tried to piece together what was happening. Was this another assault on the facility? Or had the attackers managed to breach the perimeter? The explosion, the gunfire, the chaos—it was all spiraling out of control, and for the first time, Dr. Vlachos wondered if he would make it out alive.

Panic swept through the crowd like wildfire. They instinctively recoiled at the sound of automatic weapons and reversed direction in a frantic rush away from the gate. Bodies jostled and shoved, desperate to escape the imminent danger, as cries of fear and confusion filled the air.

The crowd surged back toward the main building in a chaotic search for shelter, but something held Dr. Vlachos back, a morbid curiosity that rooted him in place even as the tide of humanity flowed around him. His instincts screamed at him to follow the crowd, to seek refuge from the madness, but he could not tear himself away. He had to know what was happening—who was responsible for this brazen attack and why they had chosen this night to strike.

Instead of joining the frantic retreat, Dr. Vlachos ducked behind a nearby golf cart, the vehicle offering scant but sufficient cover. Crouching low, he peered cautiously over the seats, his breath quick and unsteady. What he saw was beyond comprehension.

One vehicle?

Dr. Vlachos blinked twice, his round spectacles glinting in the flickering light. The guards were unloading round after round into a lone SUV—a Land Cruiser—that had somehow breached the compound's defenses and now sat vulnerable in the open field. The steady barrage of gunfire seemed disproportionate, almost absurd, against a single vehicle.

How could one vehicle cause so much chaos? Vlachos wondered.

His confusion deepened until his gaze shifted beyond the SUV. There, in the field, lay the smoldering wreckage of a military helicopter, its twisted metal frame partially engulfed in flames. Whoever had launched this attack was far more prepared and dangerous than he had initially realized.

Dr. Vlachos squinted, searching for any identifying marks on the helicopter's charred fuselage, but there were none. The lack of insignia only deepened his unease. It did not belong to the Peruvian Armed Forces or the national police—neither would dare operate this deep in cartel territory. Given Mathias's recent legal entanglements, this had to be the work of foreigners, likely the Americans.

But that still did not explain the lone vehicle.

Whoever was inside that SUV had to be incredibly brave or utterly desperate. The question gnawed at him, adding to the growing list of mysteries surrounding the night's events.

As the guards continued their relentless assault on the vehicle, Dr. Vlachos watched the escaping Land Cruiser serpentine its way across the wet field, up a nearby hill, and disappear onto the road leading to the airport. Once the mystery SUV was out of range, the sound of gunfire petered off, and an eerie silence filled the compound.

Dr. Vlachos remained crouched behind the golf cart. He could feel the tension in the air, thick and oppressive as if the very night held its breath alongside him. Nearby, the guards swept the area with the muzzles of their weapons, their movements cautious and deliberate, scanning every shadow for potential threats.

Moments stretched into eternity, and the silence was almost unbearable. Finally, with no immediate danger in sight, one of the guards lowered his weapon slightly and pressed a hand to the lapel mic of his tactical radio, his voice a low murmur as he communicated with whoever was on the other end.

"Control, this is Mike-Six," he said with a heavy German accent. "Main gate is clear, over."

More units around the facility followed suit, each reporting with the same message—no signs of enemy contact. The tension that had gripped the compound began to ease, and soon after, the all-clear signal cracked over the radios. The guards visibly relaxed, their rigid postures softening as they flipped the selector switches on their weapons to safe. The threat, it seemed, had passed.

Dr. Vlachos felt relief wash over him, the weight of fear momentarily lifting from his shoulders. He exhaled heavily, his breath coming out in a long, shaky sigh. Rising from his crouch, he allowed himself to believe, however briefly, that the danger was over. His eyes drifted back to the burning wreckage of the helicopter, now nothing more than a twisted mass of metal and flames. The sight was both horrifying and mesmerizing.

He squinted, trying to discern any further details in the wreckage that might explain who had attacked them and why. But before he could make sense of it, a voice cut through the haze of his thoughts, sharp and urgent.

"Dr. Vlachos!"

He turned around to find Sophia and Zoe running toward him, their expressions a mix of fear and relief. He broke into a hurried stride to meet them halfway.

"Are you alright?" he asked.

Dr. Martin nodded vigorously. "We're fine. Could you see what was happening? Who were they shooting at?"

Dr. Vlachos shook his head, exchanging an unspoken understanding with Sophia not to discuss it further in front of Zoe. As he glanced past his colleague, he noticed the entrance to the main building had cleared.

"It seems to be over now," Vlachos said. "Stay here with the others while I go inside to make sure the labs are safe."

Sophia nodded in agreement, her arm linked with Zoe's in a comforting yet secure embrace.

Adjusting the container strap across his chest, Dr. Vlachos re-entered the facility through the main doors. The lobby was undamaged, but an eerie darkness permeated the space, with only the soft glow of emergency lighting cutting through the shadows.

Navigating the dimly lit area, the doctor nearly tripped over two fire hoses, which he followed down the adjacent corridor. In the distance, he spotted firefighters battling a blaze. As he ventured closer, two guards suddenly emerged from a side room and stepped into the hallway.

The lead guard, a burly man with a shaved head, reacted immediately. Keeping his MP4 at a low, ready position, he thrust out his arm to block Vlachos's path.

"Hold up, Doc," he said, recognizing Dr. Vlachos from previous encounters. "It's not safe here. You need to go back and wait outside."

Vlachos stopped, but curiosity drove him to peer past the guards, trying to steal a glance at the efforts to fight the fire. "But what happened?" he asked. "Who attacked us?"

"You'll know when we know," the guard replied, though uncertainty tinged his voice. "Now, please, go back the way you came and wait for further instructions."

Undeterred, Vlachos persisted. "What about the fire? Is it spreading to the lower levels?"

"It's under control," the guard said, impatience cutting through his tone. "The fire chief says it's contained to the east wing. Now, you need to leave." He punctuated his words by raising the muzzle of his weapon toward the ceiling, a clear reminder of his authority.

The guard's gesture and finality in his words made it clear that Vlachos was not to argue further. He sighed in frustration and began to turn away. But as he moved, his gaze drifted through the open door to his right. There, Vlachos caught sight of Mr. Renzo's lifeless body, sprawled on a bloodied sparring mat.

The attack was inside the facility, too!

Curiosity got the better of him, and he inched toward the open doorway to take a closer look. The guard reacted swiftly, blocking Vlachos with his thick arm.

"Whoa, Doc, you need to leave," he said sternly. "I mean it."

Startled by the guard's forceful nature, Vlachos raised his arms in surrender. "I—I can help him," he stammered, pointing to Renzo.

Given the situation's urgency, the guard's patience was as thin as his tact. His gaze shifted to the metal container Dr. Vlachos carried. "What's in the case?"

Dr. Vlachos tightened his grip ever so slightly on the strap. "Nothing dangerous," he replied. "Just research samples."

The guard, first on the scene and still visibly affected by the discovery of Mr. Renzo's corpse, had spent several futile minutes attempting to revive the Chachapoyan. Eventually conceding to the inevitable, he notified his superiors of Renzo's passing. Though the prospect of resuming CPR seemed futile, a glimmer of hope flickered in his eyes.

After a tense moment, the guard relented and lowered his arm.

"I suppose it couldn't hurt," he conceded reluctantly, gesturing inside. "See what you can do."

"Thank you," Vlachos replied, straightening his lab coat.

Dr. Vlachos entered the darkened dojo; his thoughts focused on Renzo. The faint glow from the emergency lights in the hallway barely penetrated the shadows, leaving Vlachos blinded to his surroundings. Suddenly, his foot collided with something heavy on the floor. Startled, he looked down to discover a second corpse with vacant eyes staring blankly at the ceiling.

Vlachos grimaced at the sight of the dead man, but then his expression softened as he recognized him—Lalo, one of the facility's maintenance workers. He had a broken nose, and his face was smeared with dried blood. The puddle beside Lalo suggested that he had fallen face-first, likely dead before he hit the ground. The guards must have turned the body over.

As Vlachos scanned the corpse, something caught his eye—an object embedded in Lalo's neck. His curiosity piqued, he knelt beside the body, his brow knitted.

"Give me your light," he told the guard, waving him over urgently.

The guard complied, handing over his flashlight. Vlachos directed the beam onto the wound, revealing a small dart lodged in Lalo's neck. Carefully, he removed it and held it up for closer inspection. The skin around the wound was decaying, a clear sign that the dart had delivered a fast-acting toxin.

"That was Mr. Renzo's handiwork," the guard offered with a hint of admiration. "We think Lalo set off the explosion and was helping the prisoners escape."

Vlachos twisted around to look up at the guard. "What prisoners?"

The guard hesitated, realizing he had let slip more than he should have. Quickly, he redirected the conversation back to Renzo. "That's not your concern. Now, what can you do for him?"

Vlachos was smart enough to drop the subject. Yet, it was clear now that his research and the labs were not the primary target of the attack. The helicopters had come for someone, not something.

Luna was the obvious answer. Every government and entrepreneur on the planet would kill to possess an Aiwan, making an all-out assault on Mathias's compound more plausible. Yet, any reputable intelligence organization would have known Luna left with Mathias yesterday and canceled the mission.

Unless they came for someone else, Vlachos mused.

Parking that thought for later, he turned his attention to Renzo. Vlachos swept the shoulder strap over his head, slipped his arm free, and crawled to the Chachapoyan's side on all fours. He found the corpse as bloodied and bruised as Lalo. However, his first instinct told him Renzo had not died of a gunshot or knife wound; otherwise, he would be lying in a pool of blood. He also ruled out a poisonous dart, which led Dr. Vlachos to one conclusion: asphyxiation. Considering how Renzo's eyes bugged out, the Chachapoyan most likely had the life choked out of him.

Dr. Vlachos dropped his shoulders with a deep sigh. Renzo looked like a lost cause, but crazier things had happened. Seventeen hours was the world record for reviving a clinically dead person without any signs of brain damage.

"How long has he been like this?" Vlachos asked.

"We found him about thirty minutes ago," the guard replied. "He was non-responsive to CPR."

Vlachos nodded. "Out in the hallway is an AED and oxygen kit. Grab them," he instructed, pointing to the door.

The guard responded without question and hurried out the door. Meanwhile, Vlachos set the flashlight aside and unbuttoned Renzo's Wing Chung jacket, exposing his bare chest. Just as he finished, the guard returned toting a black, hard-shell case.

"Set it down," Vlachos instructed, then handed back the flashlight.

Opening the AED case, he removed a handheld Jumbo D oxygen tank and a clear plastic mask. After checking that the tank was full, Vlachos placed the mask over Renzo's nose and mouth. He then opened the valve to allow oxygen to flow.

Next, he retrieved the automated external defibrillator from the case. He placed both electrode pads on Renzo's chest and waited for the AED to analyze the Chachapoyan's heart rhythm. Sensing the patient was in cardiac arrest, the AED prompted Dr. Vlachos to press the delivery button.

"Clear!" Vlachos called out before delivering the first shock.

Renzo's body convulsed, but his heart did not respond. Wasting no time, Dr. Vlachos began CPR for the next two minutes. As soon as he finished counting off in his head, he rechecked the AED. The readout determined a second shock was needed. Dr. Vlachos delivered another, but still no response. He went back to administering CPR and repeated the process two more times. Before administering the fourth shock, he told himself this would be the last.

The final shock was delivered, but Renzo remained unresponsive.

Dr. Vlachos sighed, settling back onto his knees in quiet defeat. His gaze lingered on the lifeless body before him, but a small measure of solace softened the ache; he had upheld his Hippocratic Oath to the very end. Wiping the sweat from his brow, Vlachos's hand accidentally brushed against the case containing vials of force enhancement serum. He raised his eyebrows as inspiration struck. The serum might revive Renzo but could cause more harm than good in the long run. The rabid test subjects imprisoned in his lab were a grim reminder of that risk. Yet, it might give Renzo a fighting chance until Vlachos could perfect his formula.

"You did your best," the guard said. "You want us to dump the bodies in the jungle or send them to the crematorium?"

Vlachos ignored the question and sprang into action. He opened his carrying case, the yellow vials of force enhancement serum glistening under the guard's flashlight. He removed the black foam cushion from the lid, revealing a hidden compartment. Vlachos unzipped the pocket, retrieving the longest of three portable syringes, and clamped it between his teeth. With steady hands, he picked up a vial of serum.

Holding the vial in one hand and the syringe in the other, Vlachos bit off the needle's clear cap and spat it over his shoulder. He double-checked the beveled side of the needle's tip faced upward, then pressed it into the vial's rubber stopper. Like a skilled nurse, he knew this technique would prevent tiny rubber fragments from entering the syringe or contaminating the vial.

Vlachos extracted 0.25mL of serum from the vial and safely tucked it back into the case. Holding the syringe up to the light, he tapped it to bring any air bubbles to the surface.

The guard eyed the yellow substance warily. "What is that?"

"Not your concern," Vlachos retorted with a measure of satisfaction.

Next came the tricky part. Although intracardiac injections were nothing new to Vlachos, they were always nerve-racking. In his line of work, test subjects often flatlined during human trials, forcing him to administer heart injections with atropine. However, this was his first time using the serum in this manner, making him both cautious and morbidly curious.

Vlachos removed the AED pad over Renzo's heart, then walked his fingertips along the man's sternum until he located the fourth intercostal space between Renzo's ribs. Unlike in Hollywood movies, where the needle is dramatically slammed into the victim's chest, Dr. Vlachos was more surgical in his approach. Choosing his spot, he pressed the needle slowly into Renzo's chest and injected the serum.

Behind him, the guard winced as Vlachos withdrew the needle. He half-expected Renzo to bolt upright, but there was no reaction.

"Nothing happened," the guard remarked, stating the obvious.

"Not yet," Vlachos muttered, his voice edged with concern.

Replacing the AED pad over Renzo's heart, Vlachos activated the device. Prompted by the signal, he announced, "Clear!" and pressed the delivery button.

Renzo's body convulsed, his back arching as electricity ran through his body, then went slack.

Vlachos wiped his brow, watching and waiting for signs of life. When none came, he checked his watch, noting the time of death.

"Did he have family?" Vlachos asked the guard.

The guard shrugged when suddenly the AED beeped, detecting a heartbeat. Vlachos and the guard turned sharply in disbelief toward Renzo. Vlachos quickly leaned in and pressed his fingers to Renzo's neck, checking for a pulse. His brow arched with excitement as he felt a faint but undeniable rhythm—Renzo's heart was beating again.

"I don't friggin' believe it, Doc. You did it!" the guard nearly shouted.

Vlachos was also stunned by his success. Looking down at Renzo, he noticed the oxygen mask fog with each breath the Chachapoyan took. The doctor then jostled his patient and asked in a loud voice, "Mr. Renzo, can you hear me?"

Vlachos continued shaking Renzo, attempting to stir him from his death-defying slumber.

"Mr. Renzo, if you can hear me, I need you to open your eyes," Vlachos said firmly. "Mr. Renzo!"

Renzo's eyes suddenly shot open, and he gasped deeply behind his mask, startling Vlachos and the guard. His gaze darted in a blind panic, and he instinctively tried to sit up.

"Easy," Vlachos soothed, pressing his hands gently on Renzo's shoulders to keep him still. "You're alive."

He then waved irritably at the guard, signaling him to move his flashlight out of Renzo's face. Flustered, the guard redirected the beam, but this did little to calm Renzo. With a burst of adrenaline, Renzo pushed Vlachos away and sat up sharply. Vlachos recoiled, raising his hands in a gesture of peace.

Renzo blinked repeatedly, his vision clearing as he struggled to gather his bearings. Vlachos and the guard held their breath, watching intently to see what Renzo would do next.

Breathing deeply into the mask, Renzo locked eyes with Dr. Vlachos, searching for answers.

"It's okay," Vlachos said in a calming voice. "You're safe now."

Renzo glanced between Vlachos and the guard, each staring back at him with expressions of relief and amazement. Recognition dawned slowly; the vague familiarity of their faces had a calming effect, and the wildness in the Chachapoyan's eyes began to fade. He then turned his attention to his surroundings, a wave of relief washing over him as he realized he was in his dojo.

But then he saw Lalo's dead body a few feet away.

Traitor!

The events of the past hour flooded back. Renzo remembered delivering the poison dart that killed the maintenance worker. His gaze sharpened as he turned his head toward the door. He spotted the case holding his blowgun in the shadows, exactly where he had left it.

Then came the memory of his brutal brawl with the ex-North Korean operative, Choi Min-jun. Renzo stared unseeing into the distance, recalling their savage fight. Both had fought with relentless ferocity, exchanging blows without mercy. But in the end, Renzo had no memory of how the battle ended.

Jumping back to the present, he frantically scanned the room, searching for any sign of his opponent. But there was none.

In a flash of rage, Renzo tore the oxygen mask off his face. "Where?" he croaked in a raspy voice, then coughed. "Where is he?"

Dr. Vlachos gave him a curious look. "Who, señor?"

Renzo's eyes flared with a vengeful intensity, the name searing through his mind like a fiery brand. His muscles tightened, every fiber of his being trembling with rage. Through gritted teeth, he growled, "Min!"

1
ABDUCTED

Somewhere in hyperspace …

Captain Ava Tan was helplessly at the mercy of her captors. With her hands tightly bound behind her back, she lay on her side, unconscious. Her shallow breath barely fanned the bit of drool that puddled where her face was planted on the cold, unforgiving floor of a tiny storage room. Smythe's toxin had been potent. She had not moved since being hauled aboard the bounty hunters' freighter and tossed in this closet.

Oblivious to her grim surroundings, Ava's unconscious mind stirred at the edge of a distant sound, barely perceptible at first. A single twitch in her hand betrayed the faint intrusion. The sound persisted, gnawing its way through the haze of her drugged stupor, growing louder and more insistent with each passing second. It began to form into something recognizable—a bluesy guitar riff, the notes sliding languidly, joined by the thumping of a steady drumbeat. Gruff, smoky vocals reverberated through her aching skull like a phantom concert in the darkness, coaxing her toward the painful light of awareness.

"One bourbon. One scotch. One beer."

Of all the possibilities, Ava's subconscious chose George Thorogood and The Destroyers to rouse her from the depths of oblivion. She had no particular attachment to the band, though their infectious, boogie-blues music always tempted her to crank up the volume on her radio. The same could be said for the three types of alcohol mentioned in the iconic song—bourbon, scotch, and beer. She preferred something sweeter, like a glass of Moscato.

It was not the band or the drinks that carried special significance, but the song. As it echoed in her mind, Ava's mental fog gradually began to clear. Soon, the music was joined by a memory of laughing with friends around her kitchen table. They were back at her old apartment at Joint Base Lewis-McCord in Washington. It was the night she first met her soon-to-be fiancé, Captain Mark Jordan.

Mark was new to the base, having just transferred in to lead one of the Pararescue Jumpmen teams assigned to the 22nd Special Tactics Squadron. The team's outgoing leader, Captain Hinz, had invited Mark to the gathering at Ava's apartment to help him settle in. They arrived late at the party but did not come empty-handed. Hinz brought bottles of bourbon and scotch in each hand while Mark carried a case of cheap beer under his arm.

Captain Jordan's rugged good looks and chiseled physique immediately caught Ava's eye. She stood to greet her guests, nervously brushing her bangs aside. As their eyes met during the introduction, there was a mutual spark.

The night quickly escalated to a new level. Board games were swapped out with drinking games, and as the alcohol flowed, the chemistry between Mark and Ava sizzled with playful flirtation. But as midnight approached, the evening took an unexpected turn.

Hinz introduced a drinking game based on the Thorogood song, *One Bourbon. One Scotch. One Beer.* Already buzzed, Ava decided to join in. During the song, there are three times when Thorogood asks the bartender for one bourbon, one scotch, and one beer. Per the rules, players must down one shot of the bourbon, one shot of the scotch, and chug one beer before Thorogood asks the bartender for more.

By the end of the second round, Ava had hit her limit. She was three sheets to the wind after her second scotch and out of the game. As she stood from the table, the room began to spin, and she lost her balance, falling right into Mark's lap. They shared a playful laugh, but then a look of panic flashed across Ava's face as her stomach lurched.

Cupping her hand over her mouth, Ava stumbled down the hallway to the bathroom, where she spent the next twenty minutes praying to the porcelain god and puking her guts out. To his credit, Mark stayed at her side, holding back Ava's long black hair until she finished. That night might have ended in embarrassment, but it also marked the beginning of their whirlwind romance.

At the present moment, however, Ava was not feeling the love. Ever since losing that drinking game, she had phantom headaches whenever she heard that song. But nothing compared to the agony she was enduring right now, sprawled on the floor of the bounty hunters' freighter. Her brain must have dredged up that epic hangover as a way to pull her back to consciousness. When she finally awoke, it felt like she had been hit by a bus. Her body was weak, her head throbbed, and her stomach roiled—creating the perfect conditions for blowing chunks.

With one side of her face pressed against the floor, Ava moaned in anguish as she slowly cracked her eyes open. The overhead lights stabbed at her vision, forcing her to shut them tight. Even that small act sent her world spiraling out of control, triggering a wave of nausea. Violent dry heaves wracked her body, leaving her abdominal muscles aching. When her insides finally stilled, she felt fortunate that her stomach was empty.

Ava remained curled up on the floor, struggling to steady herself. She kept her eyes shut, taking slow breaths as she concentrated on the color black in her mind's eye. Kypa had taught her this technique to block out all sensory input, allowing her mind, body, and spirit to find harmony in the void.

Kypa!

Panic surged through Ava, shattering her fragile calm. The last time she had seen him was on Aiwa, on a white, sandy beach. He had been walking toward her, the Reaper looming in the background.

Ava's pulse quickened as she remembered being chased by a bounty hunter in the Aiwan jungle. The insectoid had pursued her ruthlessly, but she had managed to evade capture—most dramatically when she took to the air, soaring across a vast ravine as her nanosuit harnessed the wind to keep her aloft.

It was one of the most liberating experiences in Ava's life, but her freedom had been short-lived. The bounty hunter later ambushed her at the waterfall and marched her to a beach to trade her life for the Reaper. That was the last time she remembered seeing Kypa or her ship. The bounty hunter had sprayed her with a web-like substance secreted from his hand, and everything went dark after that.

Ava groaned in disgust, instinctively reaching for her face to wipe away the sticky residue. But her bound hands restricted such movement, sparking another wave of panic.

Her eyes flew open, only to be assaulted again by the blinding light that stabbed painfully at her temples. Ava writhed in agony, muttering a sailor-worthy string of curses. She then rolled onto her knees, forehead pressed to the floor, and began blinking rapidly to force her eyes to adjust.

The adrenaline rush kept the nausea at bay as a pressing sense of danger spurred her into action. Now fully alert, though her vision was still blurred, Ava lifted her head, surveying her surroundings. She was inside a tiny compartment, enclosed by cold, unyielding walls that matched the metal floor beneath her. The room was no bigger than the hall closet in her old apartment.

A prison cell?

Ava carefully rose to her feet, grimacing as every muscle protested. After being curled up in a fetal position for so long, her legs felt sore and unsteady, as if she had just endured a punishing leg workout at the gym and then had to descend a steep staircase to get to her car.

Using the wall for support, she straightened, which triggered another wave of dizziness. Stars danced in her vision, forcing her to pause, close her eyes, and collect herself. When the sensation passed, she cautiously opened her eyes and surveyed her cramped surroundings. The space was so tight that had her hands been free, she could have touched a wall on either side with her outstretched fingertips.

Realizing she was in grave danger, Ava's first instinct was to call for help. But until she knew more about where she was and who she was up against, there was no sense drawing attention to herself.

Ava faced the door. Spotting no door handle, she pressed her shoulder against it and shoved with all her might, grunting from the effort. But the door refused to budge. Only then did she notice the absence of hinges. Feeling foolish for not checking that crucial detail first, Ava rolled her eyes in exasperation.

"C'mon, Suntan. Wake up," she muttered irritably.

Ava eyed the compartment from top to bottom but found no sign of a control panel or service hatch. With no way out, her frustration mounted, intensifying the feeling of being trapped.

"Screw it," Ava growled, resigning herself to the fact that it was time to confront her captors. "Hey, let me out of here!" she shouted, the effort sending sharp pangs to her skull.

After a few moments, she paused and listened, her ear pressed to the door. There was no hint of movement outside, so she continued.

"Open the door!" she yelled. "Hey—"

Suddenly, the door slid open. Ava's breath hitched in surprise at the sight of the bounty hunter, Smythe, standing in the doorway. She backpedaled, heart racing, and bumped against the wall behind her. Feeling trapped, her fight-or-flight instinct kicked in. For a split second, Ava considered bum-rushing her captor, even with her hands tied behind her back. But that stupid idea was nixed when she glanced down and noticed the blaster in Smythe's hand, aimed at her midsection.

Swallowing the lump in her throat, Ava managed to ask, "What do you want with me?"

Smythe did not reply. He gave her a once-over with his beady, yellow eyes and sneered, then cocked his head slightly to the right and spoke to someone out of sight.

"She's alive alright," Smythe said in Basic. His blasé tone gave no indication if he cared whether Ava was alive or dead.

Ava remained oblivious to Smythe's words, wondering why her translator was not functioning. Instinctively, she attempted to reach for the nano-ring attached to her suit, only to be frustrated again by her bound hands.

The slight movement caught Smythe's attention, prompting him to swiftly raise his blaster to her face.

Startled, Ava froze, her eyes wide with fear, silently praying the bounty hunter would not pull the trigger. At that moment, the full weight of her situation hit her. She was now a captive aboard his ship—isolated, defenseless, and imprisoned. The bounty hunters had likely fled Aiwa, leaving her stranded in deep space, bound for an unknown destination somewhere in the galaxy.

Gort, Smythe's partner, appeared, and Ava gasped involuntarily. His frog-like features caught her off-guard. He stood upright on two skinny legs, clad in a grimy flight suit that clung tightly to his portly frame.

Together, Smythe and Gort formed a bizarre yet formidable duo. Their presence was imposing, and they held all the power in this grim scenario.

Ava's mind raced with one pressing question: *Why haven't they killed me yet?*

Her instincts suggested it had something to do with the blue crystal. Reggie's security protocols should have locked them out of the Reaper when they seized her ship. If that was the case, they might have taken her as insurance. She was the only one capable of overriding those security measures, which was probably why she was still alive.

Gort's sudden interruption broke Ava's train of thought, dragging her back to the immediate danger of her situation.

"Puny thing," Gort remarked, unimpressed by the human's small stature. "Can she understand us?"

"Not without this," Smythe replied. He retrieved Ava's nano-ring from his cloak, causing her eyes to widen as he handed it to his partner. "See what you can do with this."

"Sure thing," Gort replied, lifting the flimsy ring to examine it in the light. "Aiwan, huh?"

"Mm," Smythe grunted. "The suit keeps her hydrated but when the ring is attached, it can rearrange the nanites to provide additional protection."

Gort's mouth curled into a thin smile as he admired the ring's craftsmanship. He had always wanted to get his hands on Aiwan tech. "I call dibs on her suit when we're finished with her."

"Later," Smythe insisted. "We need her alive until we're certain we've deactivated all the fail-safes on her ship. How soon before Hiromi gets here?"

"A few days," Gort replied. "She still had to settle up with Kaji Clan." He shot Smythe an uneasy glance. "You sure about this, going against the syndicate?"

Smythe's uncharacteristic departure from their standard operating procedures did not sit well with Gort, mainly because his partner had acted without consulting him first. They both knew that crossing Grawn Krunig was essentially a death sentence. Yet, Smythe was no fool, and Gort trusted his partner must have a solid plan to attempt such a risky venture.

"Relax," Smythe assured him. "Something doesn't add up. I want to know how this ship defeated Krunig's fleet."

"We've never asked questions before," Gort reminded him.

"I know," Smythe admitted, "but I can stall Krunig and buy us some time until Hiromi arrives. She should be able to hack into the ship and find out what makes it so powerful."

Gort exhaled heavily. Hiromi's timetable did not help their cause, but if anyone could bypass the Reaper's security systems, it would be her.

"That's quite a gamble," Gort added cautiously.

"If Krunig grows suspicious and turns up the heat, we'll simply cut our losses and turn the ship over to him," Smythe reasoned. "But if my instincts are right, there's a lot of credits to be made … maybe enough so that this is our last job."

Gort nodded. It was the best outcome he could hope for. Besides, part of him was intrigued by the mystery surrounding the Reaper. It was the most interesting job they had taken on in a while—a welcome change from chasing down deadbeats for loan sharks.

"So, no luck bringing her ship online?" Gort asked.

Smythe shook his head in frustration. "We're completely locked out. Hiromi will definitely earn her pay on this one."

"Or blow us to pieces in the process," Gort said deadpan, then gestured to

Ava. "And what about her?"

"She's a feisty one, I'll give her that," Smythe conceded, reflecting on their chase through the Aiwan jungle. "But she's expendable. If we can access her ship, we'll dump her body somewhere. If not, we hand her over to Krunig along with the ship as an added bonus for the late delivery. Agreed?"

Gort recognized they were tempting fate but nodded in agreement. "I'll start working on this," he said, lifting the nano-ring. "Maybe I can disable the defense features so we can interrogate her properly."

Smythe was thinking the same thing. Retrieving a ration bar from a pouch on his gun belt, he held it up for Ava to see before tossing it to her. It bounced harmlessly off her chest and dropped to the floor.

Ava eyed the bar skeptically. It resembled a granola turd and smelled equally unappetizing. She wrinkled her nose in disgust.

"You expect me to eat this, bughead?" she retorted, her voice dripping with sarcasm.

Smythe ignored her comment and pressed the button to close the door.

"Hey—" Ava began to protest, then defiantly kicked the bar at him. It skidded into the corridor before the door slid shut.

Ava paused, listening intently, and then the overhead light flickered once before going out, plunging her back into darkness.

2
DELIVERANCE

Prototype II

Dr. Neil Garrett lay on his holographic bunk, staring blankly at the ceiling, his thoughts focused on Ava. Worry gnawed at him. Since her abduction, he imagined countless ways the bounty hunters might harm her—or worse, the horrors that awaited Ava if she ended up in the hands of the ruthless crime lord, Grawn Krunig.

Neil tossed in his bunk, sleep evading him. His heart ached for Ava, imagining the fear and isolation she must be enduring. Every passing second twisted his gut further, intensifying the dread of not knowing her fate.

A scene from his favorite movie, *The Empire Strikes Back*, flashed through his mind. He recalled when Princess Leia helplessly watched as Han Solo—or "Hans," as Ava liked to tease—was frozen in carbonite and then taken away by the bounty hunter, Boba Fett. It had always been one of the most poignant parts of the film for him. But that was just fiction. Ava was facing real danger, and if they had any chance of rescuing her, he and Kypa would have to risk everything.

The thought of facing actual combat made Neil's chest tighten with anxiety. His closest experience with battle had come from playing video games, which he was never any good at. Now, he possessed a real-life blaster and would be expected to use it.

If that time ever comes, he thought grimly as he rolled over onto his side.

In the darkness, Neil gazed at the gun belt on the floor. The overhead lights were off, but a warm, blue glow filled the main hold, streaming in from the cockpit as they traveled through hyperspace. The soft light reflected off the glossy handgrip of his weapon, casting faint shadows across the cabin. Neil wondered if he possessed the courage to use it.

He wanted to believe so. But as he stared at the blaster in the stillness of the darkened cabin, the magnitude of their mission weighed heavily on him. Rescuing Ava was one thing; taking a life was something entirely different.

Neil tossed and turned for several minutes, a kaleidoscope of memories and what-if scenarios bouncing through his head. Finally, resigned to sleeplessness, he threw off his holographic blanket and swung his feet onto the cold floor.

"Reggie, lights," he muttered, rubbing his tired eyes.

There was no response. The cabin remained dark.

"Reg—" Neil stopped mid-sentence, realizing his mistake. They were no longer onboard the Reaper. With a weary sigh, he corrected himself. "*Computer*, turn on the lights, please."

The lights flicked on, causing Neil to wince and turn away from the sudden brightness. He waited a moment until his eyes adjusted, then slowly stood.

"Computer, deactivate the bedding," he commanded, shuffling sleepily toward the food synthesizer. Behind him, the bunk, pillow, and blanket vanished.

"Computer, two Pop-Tarts … toasted."

"Unable to compute," the main computer responded evenly. "Please restate the command."

Neil dropped his shoulders in frustration. He would have to start from scratch and teach this new computer everything.

"Never mind," he grumbled.

As he made his way to the cockpit, Neil found Prince Kypa leaning forward in the clam-shaped pilot's chair, his attention locked on the HUD. Kypa's hands moved with practiced precision, making quick adjustments to the flight controls. Neil silently watched, mesmerized, as his friend manipulated the four control orbs, expertly threading the ship through hyperspace lanes. When the ship suddenly dropped out of hyperspace, the star-speckled emptiness of deep space replaced the swirling blue light outside the cockpit windows.

Kypa removed his hands and feet from the orbs and exhaled in frustration.

"What's wrong?" Neil asked, making Kypa flinch.

The Aiwan spun around sharply, fixing Neil with a stern gaze.

Neil offered a crooked smile. "Sorry, didn't mean to startle you."

Kypa took a deep breath, calming himself. "My apologies," he said, gesturing for Neil to come closer. "Please, come in."

"Any luck?" Neil asked.

Kypa waved dismissively at the HUD. "I keep losing the Reaper's tracking beacon," he explained with frustration. "The bounty hunters must be jumping in and out of hyperspace, making them difficult to track."

Neil arched an eyebrow. "To throw us off their trail?"

"Precisely," Kypa replied, begrudgingly impressed by the bounty hunters' cunning. "Every time they do, I have to reacquire their signal. It takes time … time Ava does not have."

An uneasy silence hung between them.

"But something else troubles me more," Kypa said with a sigh.

"What's that?" Neil asked.

"Based on the bounty hunters' last known trajectory, they are not returning to Ekator or Madreen. In fact, they are headed in the opposite direction."

Neil shook his head, confused. "I don't understand."

"Grawn Krunig runs his operations from Ekator, a spaceport hidden within the Mishi Nebula," Kypa explained. "I assumed the bounty hunters would go directly there to turn Ava and the Reaper over to Krunig. But that does not appear to be the case, unless they are planning to circle back, which is unlikely."

"And Madreen?" Neil asked. "You said Krunig was part of the Madreen Crime Syndicate."

"Correct," Kypa confirmed, impressed by his friend's memory. "The syndicate's headquarters is on Madreen, but I doubt Krunig would have the bounty hunters go there. He would not risk losing the blue crystal to the other grawns."

Neil's brow furrowed. "But you said you removed the blue crystal."

"I did," Kypa replied. "It is safe on Aiwa with my sister."

"So then, what value does Ava and the Reaper hold now?"

"Exactly," Kypa agreed, sharing Neil's confusion. "I have been asking myself that very question ever since the bounty hunters started jumping hyperspace lanes. Perhaps this is all just a precaution, a way to throw us off so they can collect their bounty from Krunig discreetly."

Reading Kypa's expression, Neil sensed his friend was contemplating a different scenario. "Or?" he prodded.

"Or," Kypa continued thoughtfully, "the bounty hunters are trying to double-cross Krunig and sell Ava and the Reaper to the highest bidder."

Taken aback, Neil remarked, "That doesn't make any sense."

"No, it does not. Without the blue crystal, the Reaper is just a ship. It is valuable, but it is not the formidable warship Krunig desires."

Neil pondered this, a thin smile forming. "Hold on. What if the bounty hunters don't know this?" he reasoned. "What if they're planning a big score without realizing they've lost their only bargaining chip?"

Neil's theory sounded plausible, although unsettling. "A fool's gambit if that is the case," Kypa agreed. "Either way, Ava is running out of time."

Nodding, Neil asked, "How can I help?"

Kypa tapped a command on the HUD to restart the search for the bounty hunters. "While I work on reacquiring their signal, you might want to continue your training on the forward gun."

Neil welcomed the suggestion. Practicing in the extractor's seat was both enjoyable and purposeful. He headed toward his seat, then paused. "By the way, I've been meaning to ask, you said before we left your lab that this prototype had a few modifications. What did you mean by that?"

Recalling the conversation, Kypa replied, "Technically, this ship is not a Reaper—at least not yet. I still need to install the terraforming components, so for now, the forward gun is just a standard turret. However, it does possess one piece of tech that my good friend, Luna, gifted me. But with all that has happened, I have not had a chance to properly field test it."

Neil's curiosity was piqued. "What kind of tech?"

"A cloaking device, for starters," Kypa replied matter-of-factly.

"A cloaking device?" Neil grinned. "Seriously?"

To him, a cloaking device was nothing more than the product of a science fiction writer's imagination back on Earth. But the more he considered it, the more he realized that stealth technology was not new. In fact, humans had been employing such tactics as far back as the Trojan horse. Kypa simply elevated the idea to a whole new level.

Kypa nodded. "You were not with us on Aiwa when we had an unfortunate run-in with a zemindar. A cloaking device would have come in handy."

"I heard it was pretty intense," Neil said, recalling Ava's description of their encounter with the energy-absorbing serpent. "She said you saved the day."

Kypa shrugged modestly. "Next to the syndicate, zemindars are our greatest threat. That is what prompted Luna to develop cloaking technology in the first place. The element of surprise will give us a distinct advantage."

Neil nodded approvingly. "Those bounty hunters won't know what hit 'em."

"Mm," Kypa murmured. "But it will not matter if we cannot find them before Krunig does."

With that, Kypa turned his attention to the HUD, eager to resume his search for the bounty hunters.

Neil took his cue and settled into the extractor's chair. He activated the conveyor system, which transported him to the forward cockpit at the ship's bow. Once his seat locked in place, Neil's HUD materialized, along with two orbs near his hands. He ignored them as the orbs controlled the exterior armatures for collecting crystals.

Instead, Neil issued a mental command to activate the targeting computer and charge the precision laser cannon. Normally employed to cut away crystals from ocean sediment, the laser could be combined with the ship's main disruptors to form a more formidable weapon system.

A sensor in the HUD scanned Neil's retinas, allowing the laser cannon to track his eye movements to lock onto targets. Then, with a simple mental command, he could fire at will.

Kypa had set up a simulation with holographic targets for training, reminiscent of the *TIE Fighter* computer game Neil had enjoyed so much as a kid.

While Neil focused on training, Kypa turned his attention to the cloaking device. His plan to rescue Ava relied on tracking the bounty hunters and landing nearby without detection. Beyond that, he had no idea how they would free her.

Kypa took a deep breath and reminded himself to take it one step at a time.

Just then, a sensor beeped, signaling an incoming transmission. Kypa's face brightened when he noticed the secure message was from Aiwa. With a quick tap on the HUD, he answered the hail. The sight of his mate, Maya, and their two daughters appearing on the screen filled him with a renewed sense of joy.

"Father!" Arya and Fraya erupted.

From the background, Kypa could tell they were seated on the couch in the living room of their residence at the royal palace. The girls nestled close to their mother, her arms wrapped protectively around them.

Kypa's face lit up with a broad smile. Seeing his family safe and sound was an immense relief. However, his smile faltered when he noticed Toma's absence. Reading his concern, Maya subtly shook her head, signaling him not to ask about their son.

Without missing a beat, Kypa greeted his daughters warmly. "It is good to see you! I miss you so much."

"We miss you," Maya replied, her voice warm but tinged with concern. "The girls wanted to see you before they went to sleep."

"When are you coming home, Father?" Arya, their middle child, asked.

"Soon, I promise," Kypa assured them. Not knowing how much Maya had shared about his absence, he added, "I have important business to handle first. Once it is done, I will come straight home."

"Are Neil and Ava with you?" Fraya asked, yawning heavily. "Can we talk to them?"

"Later. They are both busy at the moment," Kypa dodged. "But I will tell them you asked."

Fraya was too tired to protest; her blue eyes drooped with exhaustion.

"And Arya, how are you?" Kypa asked.

Arya was only two rotations older than Fraya, but she looked more and more like her mother each day. She shrugged with a sheepish grin and replied, "Good."

"Are you helping your mother?" Kypa followed up.

Arya nodded modestly, then nestled closer to Maya.

Kypa smiled proudly. "I knew you would. Now off to sleep you go. I need to speak with your mother."

Neither girl resisted; Arya gently led her little sister out of the room toward their sleeping quarters. The soft patter of their footsteps soon faded, leaving Maya alone by the comm unit. With a pained expression etched across her face, she leaned in closer, her eyes reflecting the strain of unspoken worry.

"Oh, Kypa, Toma is still gone," she said.

Kypa sighed, reflecting on the last time he saw his son. They parted in anger after he denied his son's request to help save Ava. While Toma's courage was admirable, he had no reason to be involved in the deal to exchange the Reaper for Ava. Toma's inexperience would have been a liability.

Kypa lamented the futility of it all. His plan to thwart the bounty hunters had failed, resulting in the abduction of Ava and Reggie.

"I regret the way we parted," he admitted somberly. "But I am sure Toma is fine. He just needs time to cool off. When I get home, I will make things right."

Maya accepted his answer with some reservation. Deciding to let it rest, she shifted the conversation to a different topic.

"How are things progressing with your search?" she asked.

"These bounty hunters are good at covering their tracks," Kypa replied, rubbing his eyes wearily. "It is taking longer than I thought, but I promise we will return as soon as Ava is safe."

Maya forced a supportive smile. "I know you will. Just be careful."

"Always," Kypa assured her. "Tell me, what is the mood in the capital?"

"Your sister and mother would know better than me," Maya admitted. "Boa has had us confined to the palace while he continues his investigation into your father's death."

Kypa nodded thoughtfully. "Any word from the High Court?"

"No, but I have heard there is growing discontent amongst the four wardens. Their constituents are demanding you return to Aiwa at once."

Kypa was not surprised by this. He anticipated that his decision to prioritize saving Ava—an off-worlder—over the needs of the Five Realms would provoke resentment. That is why he had chosen his sister, Princess Seva, to serve as Warden of Eos in his absence. He trusted her completely, and with his mother's guidance, he was confident that Seva could buy him time with the High Court.

"Please inform Seva and my mother that I will contact them soon," Kypa said. "With any luck, it will not be long. When Neil and I recover Ava and the Reaper, I will return to Aiwa and address my ascension."

"I will tell them," Maya promised him. "May Gwaru enlighten your path."

Kypa dipped his chin to accept the blessing. In the background, he could hear the girls' playful laughter.

Maya rolled her eyes. "I must go. *Your* daughters are not going to sleep like they should."

Kypa chuckled, then lifted his large hand to the display. Maya mirrored the gesture.

"I miss you," she said, smiling bravely.

"And I miss you. Soon, we will all be together again, I promise."

Maya ended the transmission with a nod. Kypa leaned back, releasing a slow, weighted breath. Ava was in grave danger, Aiwa was in turmoil, and Rose's unexpected activation of the Earth beacon added another layer of uncertainty. It felt like everything was piling up at once, testing his self-confidence. Doubts crept in—was he making the right choices? Was he doing enough? The magnitude of it all pressed down on him, threatening to crack the calm exterior he struggled to uphold.

3
UNDERCURRENT

Deep in the lowest level of the palace, the royal vault safeguarded Aiwa's most significant treasures: magnetarite crystals. These crystals, each a marvel born from the death throes of ancient magnetars, varied in hue and power. Most shimmered in shades of yellow to orange, their energy potential evident in their radiance. But among these gems, one crystal stood in a league of its own. Encased within a specially engineered containment field, the solitary blue crystal—known as maxixe magnetarite—was the rarest in the galaxy. Its deep azure glow pulsed with an energy far surpassing the others—a beacon of unparalleled beauty and immense power.

Princess Seva stood in the vast chamber in quiet solitude, her gaze fixed on the rare gem. Resting atop a sleek metal armature, the crystal twinkled under the carefully angled overhead lights, casting a mesmerizing sparkle that danced in the air. Seva was entranced by its beauty. The exquisite gem had a calming effect that eased the turmoil within her.

To her left, just beyond earshot, Commodore Boa engaged in a quiet conversation with Captain Nova, the Keeper of the Royal Vault and interim Commander of the Royal Guards. Nova, a middle-aged Aiwan male, stood the same height as Boa and had similar cranial markings. Wearing a maroon, sheer robe, he kept his hands clasped as they spoke. Yet, despite his composed demeanor, Nova's retractable energy pike hung within easy reach on his belt. His brow furrowed in concentration as he listened intently to Boa, though his eyes remained vigilant, ever alert to any threats even in this secure chamber.

While Boa and Nova conducted their business, Princess Seva contemplated her next move as acting Warden of Eos. In the wake of her father's death, a failed coup by Major Gora, and the sudden departure of her brother, Prince Kypa, Seva found herself thrust into a political quagmire. Her top priority was to calm the growing public fear in Eos. As the people mourned King Loka's death, they also faced the looming threat of a harvester invasion and the constant risk of civil war among the Five Realms. These were dangerous times, and the people longed for a protector—a leader who could restore order, unite Aiwa, and defeat their enemies. But whispers in the capital told a different story: the young, untested princess was not seen as a strong leader. Her father's rivals had become Seva's enemies, quickly moving to undermine her—and, by extension, Kypa—and claim the throne for themselves.

Seva rolled her shoulders back and took a calming breath. *Let them try.*

As she mulled over ways to combat these threats, Seva remained unaware that Commodore Boa's eyes were on her. Out of instinct, Aiwa's greatest military leader stole furtive glances in her direction every so often to ensure her safety. Haunted by his failure to protect her father, Boa silently vowed never to let such a tragedy happen again.

Seeing the princess standing straight-backed and deep in thought reminded him of Queen Qora, Seva's mother. Yet, Seva was undeniably her own person. He could only guess at her thoughts or how she was managing the stress of being so suddenly elevated to the role of Warden with no preparation. Boa sympathized with her plight and hoped she would be receptive to his counsel. Though untested, Seva was far from naïve. She showed wisdom beyond her years and had strong support from the younger generation, which now outnumbered his own.

Her passion for the Cirran refugees earned his most profound respect—especially since he was one of them. But despite his admiration, Boa's concern grew. They faced enemies on multiple fronts, and he worried about his ability to protect her and the royal vault. Hence his meeting with Captain Nova.

Like Seva, Captain Nova answered the call when the High Court appointed him interim Commander of the Royal Guards. Endorsed by Boa himself, Nova was a respected warrior with stellar military service and, more importantly, he was a trusted outsider. The assassination of King Loka by a few of his personal guards had cast suspicion over the entire order of Royal Guards. Boa needed someone he could trust unconditionally to rebuild the order, safeguard the royal family, and secure the blue crystal.

Confident that Captain Nova's security measures were solid, Boa shifted his focus to Seva.

"Princess—excuse me, *Lord* Seva," Boa corrected, dipping his chin in respect.

Unfazed by the verbal miscue, Seva turned to face Boa. "Yes, Commodore?"

"Captain Nova assured me all precautions are in place to secure the crystal. Extra sentries will be posted outside, and only you or I can deactivate the containment field."

Seva nodded thoughtfully, trusting his judgment. She gestured to the blue crystal. "We cannot allow the crystal to fall into enemy hands."

"Indeed," Boa agreed, tempted to ask if that included the humans, but held his tongue. If Prince Kypa returned with Captain Tan—a big "if" considering her current situation—it would be up to him to decide whether to return the crystal to Earth.

"When do you expect the court to rule on your father's successor?" Boa inquired.

Seva inhaled and released it slowly. "Soon," she replied, her tone carefully neutral. "We are still in a period of mourning."

"Of course," Boa agreed. "I meant no disrespect."

An uncomfortable silence settled between them. The question of who would ascend to the throne was less troubling to Seva than the mention of the High Court. In her brief dealings with the wardens from Fonn, Maeve, and Dohrm—each of whom was her senior by many rotations—she had sensed an undercurrent of shared loss that rendered their interactions distant and superficial at best. Seva's presence on the court was a stark reminder of the dark shroud hanging over Aiwa.

The court members did not regard Seva as a respected equal, either, a fact made glaringly apparent during the conclave. Lord Zefra and the others purposely withheld information from the young princess during their telepathic debate, perhaps because they viewed Seva as a temporary placeholder until Prince Kypa returned or a more suitable Warden of Eos was named. Nevertheless, Seva vowed to prove them wrong.

Shifting her focus to another pressing matter, she asked, "What news on your investigation?"

Boa cleared his throat. "We are pursuing every lead, my lord."

"Do you believe Krunig was behind my father's murder?"

"He did claim responsibility," Boa confirmed. "Prince Kypa also stated that Major Gora blamed your father for the fall of Cirros. Before his death, Gora swore that a new order was rising."

"What does that mean?" Seva asked.

Boa shrugged. "I knew Gora since he was a youngling, and I trusted him implicitly," he stated in a tone laced with admiration, regret, and confusion. "Gora's treachery is a strike at the very heart of our civilization. He and the others involved may have acted alone," Boa allowed, "but I fear this conspiracy runs much deeper. If Gora could be turned, then there could be others—sleeper cells of terrorists planning to attack you and the regime."

Seva raised her hand in warning. "Tread carefully, Commodore. I do not want the Cirran refugees unjustly persecuted for the seditious acts of a few zealots."

Once again, Boa held his tongue. He understood the princess had deep empathy for the refugees, so arguing the point before all the facts were known seemed pointless. Furthermore, as a Cirran himself, he had no desire to be associated with a group of terrorists. Nevertheless, the Cirran refugees remained his primary suspects, and that was where his investigation would focus next.

Seva sensed Boa's restraint and reined in her emotions. She needed his counsel more than ever, even if his views conflicted with hers.

"Forgive me, Commodore. My concern for the refugees tends to get the better of me at times. I appreciate your candor."

Boa waved dismissively. "No apologies necessary, my lord. I admire your stance. And, I support your efforts to restore Cirros to its former glory."

"I am pleased to hear you say that," Seva said, gesturing to the exit. "The court will be returning to conclave soon, and we can talk more along the way."

Boa fell in step beside the princess. As they passed Captain Nova, he bowed respectfully, which Seva acknowledged with a polite nod. Outside, her protection detail of four newly vetted royal guards formed a secure perimeter around them as they proceeded down the corridor.

"Speaking of the refugees," Boa continued, "I was hoping you might have connections within that community who would be willing to speak with my agents. Discreetly, of course."

"Informants?" Seva asked in a suspicious tone.

"Not necessarily," Boa replied. "We would like to speak with community leaders and concerned citizens who share your fears of unjust persecution. We need to find out who was behind the attack and bring them to justice."

Seva nodded thoughtfully, her gaze steady as she considered Boa's proposal. Though she trusted his sincerity, she could not ignore that he was walking a slippery slope.

"I have one or two contacts in the camp who may be willing to assist," she said. "I will reach out to them on your behalf and see if they are interested."

Boa's expression softened with gratitude. "That would be immensely helpful. Thank you," he replied, his chin dipping in appreciation.

As they continued their walk, the conversation shifted to updates on the planetary defenses. Boa filled Seva in on details that would provide greater context to the daily briefing he gave the High Court.

When they arrived at the imposing doors of the High Court's chamber, the two sentries at the entrance opened them. Seva paused just short of the threshold and turned to Boa with a serious expression.

"I suspect challengers to my brother's claim to the throne will emerge soon," she confided. "We do not have much time."

Boa's brow creased with confusion. "Time for what, my lord?"

Seva lowered her voice. "We both know there are forces who wish to annex Cirros. If that happens, I fear for the future of the Cirran refugees. I do not condone violence of any kind, but I understand oppressed people will turn to such measures as a last resort. I must use this opportunity to convince the High Court to resume the reconstruction of Cirros. It could stop a civil war."

Boa considered her words, forming his reply carefully. Your brother shares your unwavering dedication, and I hold your commitment to my people in the highest esteem. Yet, I must urge caution, my lord. With Krunig behind the attacks, we must confront that threat before all else. We cannot allow him to gain a foothold in our society." He paused, hoping his next thought would not trigger heartache for Seva.

"Even if we could rebuild Cirros, the greater challenge remains: who can unite the refugees? Prince Morga is gone; he was the last living member of the Cirran royal family. Finding a leader to rally behind will be no easy task."

4

LAZARUS EFFECT

Planet Earth
Satipo, Peru

Luna gazed out the window of the ATR 42 cargo aircraft as it circled the smoldering remains of Edmund Mathias's Peruvian laboratory. The once high-tech, donut-shaped facility now appeared as if a colossal bite had been taken out of its eastern section, courtesy of the U.S. Navy's SEAL Team Four and the Army's 160th Special Operations Aviation Regiment, known as the "Night Stalkers." Despite the heavy damage inflicted on Mathias's compound, his forces put up a gallant fight, evidenced by the burnt remains of an Army helicopter strewn across the battlefield.

From the brief telepathic connection she had managed with Mathias, Luna learned that a team of soldiers had successfully extracted her friend, Dr. Rose Landry, along with a man she had yet to meet, Choi Min-jun.

Luna allowed herself a faint smile, relieved that Rose was safe. But losing contact with her only true friend on Earth left the Aiwan feeling a deep emptiness once more.

Turning back to the scene below, Luna pieced together how Rose's rescue had unfolded. From her bird's-eye view, she could tell that the attack came from the south, where the wreckage of the downed MH-60M Blackhawk helicopter lay on the lawn. A significant portion of the perimeter wall had been blasted to rubble, the surrounding concrete pockmarked with bullet holes. Inside the compound, the eastern side of the main building had been destroyed by what appeared to be a massive explosion.

A costly engagement, Luna surmised, which was affirmed by the string of colorful expletives Edmund continually muttered from the cockpit.

She shifted her gaze to Mathias, who sat in the co-pilot's seat with his face pressed against the window. He was seeing the devastation for the first time, and no one onboard the aircraft needed telepathy to know what he was thinking. There would be hell to pay for this outrage, and the target of his wrath was certain: President Roger Fitzgerald.

Edmund turned away from the window in a huff. "I've seen enough," he said to the pilot with disgust. "Set us down."

The pilot confirmed the order and contacted the tower controller at the nearby airfield. His request to land was granted immediately.

Luna tightened her grip on the armrests, still uneasy despite having flown halfway across the world in this aircraft. She could not fully trust the reliability of such a slow, archaic form of transportation. The aircraft paled in comparison to Aiwan transports; it could not even breach the sound barrier. Yet, for all its shortcomings, the plane had done its job, delivering them safely to their destination.

Glancing up, Luna caught Ms. Diaz stealing a worried look in her direction. Edmund's executive assistant, seated in a jump seat behind the pilot, quickly averted her eyes, but her concern was written all over her face.

Like everyone else onboard, Ms. Diaz did not share her boss's trust in Luna. Mathias's sudden shift in protocol regarding the Aiwan had everyone scratching their heads. The attack on the Peru facility had already put the crew on edge, but Edmund's decision to allow Luna to roam freely, unbound, only heightened the tension in the cabin. The atmosphere was thick with unease, and when the wheels finally touched down at the airport in Satipo, the sense of relief was palpable.

The aircraft taxied into Mathias's private hangar and came to a stop. Aware of the uneasiness directed towards her, Luna remained seated, allowing the others to deplane first. Once the last of them had gone, she unbuckled and followed, bringing up the rear. As she made her way forward, she found Edmund waiting for her outside the cockpit, his earlier frustration replaced with a broad and somewhat cheesy grin.

Edmund stepped aside, extending his arm in a sweeping gesture toward the exit. With an exaggerated, almost theatrical flourish, he raised his hand as if unveiling a grand prize.

"After you, partner," he said in a light, amused tone as if it were the most ordinary thing in the world.

Luna dipped her chin to acknowledge his invitation, but as soon as she exited the aircraft, she froze, her breath catching in her throat. At the base of the stairs, a group of armed soldiers stood waiting, their weapons trained on her.

"Freeze!" Renzo shouted from below, his commanding voice echoing throughout the hangar.

Luna raised her hands in surrender, an outward show of the panic rising within her. As she surveyed the hostile crowd below, she saw their eager expressions and realized that one false move on her part was all the justification they needed to open fire.

"Hold your fire! Hold your fire, you morons!" Edmund shouted as he burst through the doorway. Waving his arms frantically, he stepped around Luna, positioning himself as a human shield. "Lower your weapons for Pete's sake! She's one of us now!"

A tense moment of indecision followed as the guards kept their weapons raised, waiting for Renzo's response. Finally, despite his better judgment, the Chachapoyan obeyed his boss's command and lowered his gun.

"Stand down," he ordered the others, raising his fist.

The guards complied in unison, lowering their gun barrels. The air filled with audible clicks of selector switches set to safe mode.

Edmund turned to Luna. "Are you alright?" he asked, his smile tinged with embarrassment. "They can be a bit overzealous at times."

Still visibly shaken, Luna nodded. It was clear to her that earning everyone's trust would take longer than anticipated.

Relieved, Edmund turned his attention back to the guards, his voice rising to address them all. "And it won't happen again!" he said firmly.

With that, Luna followed Edmund down the stairs. At the bottom, Renzo stepped forward, bowing his head and greeting Mathias while keeping a wary eye on the Aiwan.

"What the hell was that?" Mathias rebuked.

"I'm sorry, sir," Renzo apologized. "It was just a precaution."

As Renzo spoke, Edmund regarded him with the cautious scrutiny of someone assessing a stranger for the first time. Renzo looked remarkably well, considering his brush with death. He looked almost rejuvenated. The purple-black bruises that once marred his face and neck had faded, his busted lip fully healed, and even the limp from his damaged knee was gone.

But it was not his physical recovery that concerned Edmund—it was his emotional state. While he did not doubt the Chachapoyan's unwavering loyalty, which still burned fiercely in Renzo's eyes, Edmund questioned his effectiveness as an operator. Renzo had never failed him before, and under different circumstances, anyone else would have been eliminated without hesitation, especially given the recent debacle under Renzo's watch. But finding another fixer with Renzo's unique skills would take time—something Edmund could ill afford.

Yet, the question lingered: could Renzo be trusted as he once was? The aura of mystery and fear that had always surrounded him seemed diminished. For the first time, Edmund saw Renzo not as the unshakable force he had always relied on but as a man—flawed and undeniably human.

Or was he? Edmund mused.

Knowing that Dr. Vlachos had used the force enhancement serum to revive Renzo, Edmund was acutely aware that it was only a matter of time before the side effects began to manifest. The unstable formula still had several flaws, the most concerning of which was its gradual effect on patients, causing them to devolve into a feral state. Renzo was less than seventy-two hours removed from his injection and, so far, exhibited no signs of rabidity. Typically, symptoms did not appear for a couple of weeks, but when they did, they progressed rapidly, making the individual increasingly dangerous and difficult to control. For now, Renzo benefited from the serum's accelerated healing properties, heightened senses, increased speed, and enhanced strength.

"So, Lazarus is back from the dead, eh?" Edmund remarked with a sharp edge. "I heard the North Korean escaped."

The disappointment in his mentor's words cut Renzo deeply, though he had expected as much. In the days following the attack, rumors circulated that his severe beating came at the hands of one man, yet Renzo's loyal guards tried to spin the story differently. It did not work. No one was buying the guards' unconvincing attempts at damage control. In fact, it only invited further scrutiny.

Then, there was the unspoken concern that loomed over everyone— American gunships had attacked the facility. Initially, most believed it to be an outrageous act of industrial espionage, but several workers witnessed Dr. Landry's extraction. This fact muddied the narrative that the assault was unprovoked. The explosions on the east side—far from the extraction site— were clearly a diversion, contributing to the belief that it was not an attack but a rescue mission.

"The prisoner did escape," Renzo replied in shame. "I beg your forgiveness."

"Save it," Edmund snapped, waving his hand dismissively. "My facility wasn't built to withstand a gunship assault. The Americans will pay for this. But you …" Edmund's gaze narrowed. "Word has it you were bested by a man who was already half-dead."

Renzo felt his face flush with embarrassment but could not deny the truth. Straightening, he rolled back his shoulders and met Mathias's gaze. "I underestimated him. It will not happen again."

Edmund chuckled. "I would hope not—for your sake." His tone shifted to one of intrigue. "So, tell me, how do you feel?"

Renzo hesitated, careful not to sound cliché. The serum's effects were undeniable, almost overwhelming, yet he welcomed them.

"Invincible," he admitted with a wry grin.

Edmund's greedy smile widened, not to mock Renzo's simple response, but because it confirmed that the force enhancement serum was meeting his expectations. It was a breakthrough that could change the world and make him billions—assuming Dr. Vlachos could iron out the remaining flaws. Edmund was fully confident that his top scientist would succeed.

Nodding with satisfaction, Edmund climbed into the lead SUV parked inside the hangar. Before Ms. Diaz joined him in the back seat, she gave Renzo a brief nod, signaling him to take his place in the lead vehicle. A rare flash of relief crossed Renzo's face but quickly vanished beneath its usual cold, rugged demeanor. His eyes flicked toward the Aiwan.

Ms. Diaz followed Renzo's gaze and gave a quick nod of agreement. Turning to Luna, she gestured toward the second SUV. "You'll ride in that one," she said curtly.

A burly guard standing beside the second SUV opened the back door. Luna showed no outward sign of disappointment or resentment at being separated from the others. She dipped her chin in acknowledgment and quietly took her place in the vehicle.

Renzo watched as she entered the SUV, questioning his boss's decision to bring Luna into the inner circle. However, this was not the time to voice his concerns.

As Ms. Diaz circled the back of the lead vehicle and climbed in, Renzo spoke into his lapel mic. "We're moving. Look sharp."

He closed her door and took his place in the front passenger seat. The two SUVs rolled out of the hangar, soon joined by two more vehicles. With all air traffic temporarily halted, the motorcade crossed the runway toward the airfield's control tower. They pulled up beside a bullet-riddled Land Cruiser, its windows shot out, and dried blood spattered across the driver's seat.

"That vehicle belonged to Eduardo Salazar," Renzo explained. "We believe he was providing overwatch for the Americans who extracted Dr. Landry. Once the helicopter was gone, he drove this vehicle to the south wall and helped extract Mr. Choi."

"Salazar did this?" Mathias asked, sounding surprised. He knew the man primarily by reputation. Their paths had crossed only a few times during the construction of Edmund's facility.

"Yes, sir," Renzo confirmed. "We found his body on the side of the road—I'll show you." He then pointed to the destroyed SUV. "That's his blood in the driver seat."

"Apparently, Salazar cut a deal with the CIA," Ms. Diaz added. "The plane used to fly Mr. Choi out of the country originated from Lima. We have camera footage showing Lima Station Chief, Paul Wiggins, was also onboard."

Mathias nodded thoughtfully.

"We also interrogated the pilot," Renzo said. "We found him passed out in a brothel in town. It seems he was left behind and had no idea about the American operation."

"So, Mr. Choi stayed behind to buy time for Rose to escape," Edmund summarized. "Salazar and Wiggins then see him exiting the building and risk their lives to save him, but Salazar is killed in the process. Correct, so far?"

"Yes, sir," Renzo confirmed.

"So, who flew the plane? Wiggins?"

"No, sir. We think others were involved." Renzo handed over a black and white photo of Hector and Marlana Nunez, with Min-jun visible in the background. "This couple was traveling with Mr. Choi. We pulled their photo from the airport security footage in Lima."

Edmund glanced at the photo with mild interest. "Who are they?" he asked. Nothing about the husband-and-wife duo suggested they were intelligence operatives.

"Hector and Marlana Nunez," Ms. Diaz answered. "The three of them arrived in Satipo the day before Mr. Choi was captured outside the compound. Hector is ex-Air Force—a pilot," she said, arching an eyebrow, "—and his wife is still on active duty."

Edmund's eyes narrowed on Marlana, then his mouth fell open in surprise. "Wait a second, I know her." It took him a moment to recognize her out of uniform, but it was unmistakable once he made the connection. "She works at Groom Lake, on General Dukes' staff," Edmund said, slowly nodding as he recalled his last encounter with Colonel Nunez. "She's the one who arrested Garza and Sizemore."

"The plot thickens," Ms. Diaz remarked with a sly grin.

"She knows everything about the Aiwans, the mission to North Korea, all of it," Edmund added.

"And Dr. Landry?"

"Absolutely," Edmund affirmed, his gaze lingering on Marlana's image. This woman had caused a significant disruption to his global operations, costing him millions. A part of him admired Colonel Nunez—she certainly had cojones. But admiration would not absolve the couple from their actions. There would be consequences, and now the Nunezes were on his radar.

"So, where did they fly to?" Edmund asked.

"Our sources say the USS *George Washington*."

Taken aback, Edmund laughed. "Seriously? Now I'm really impressed," he said, picturing a civilian airplane landing on a nuclear-powered aircraft carrier. He handed the photo back to Renzo. "Okay, I've seen enough. What about the labs?"

Renzo signaled the driver to get underway. They departed the airport and headed toward the private road leading to Mathias's facility.

"The subterranean labs are secure and undamaged," Renzo assured his boss. "Minutes before the American helicopters arrived, multiple explosions occurred in the east wing mechanical rooms. This diversion allowed a two-man team inside the facility to locate Dr. Landry and Mr. Choi and lead them to the extraction site."

Edmund looked incredulous. "How the hell did they get inside?"

Renzo held up the photo of Marlana showing her forged security badge. "Colonel Nunez assumed the identity of Camila Hernandez, one of the housekeepers who was sick the night of the raid. Her story checked out," he added. "She had COVID."

Edmund shook his head in disbelief.

"According to the logs," Renzo continued, "Colonel Nunez entered the facility at twenty-two-fifty-one with this man, Lalo Aguilar." Renzo showed Edmund a gruesome photo of Lalo's dead body. "He worked on the maintenance staff."

Edmund's nose wrinkled at the sight of Lalo's mangled face. Poisoned by a blow dart, the man had died before doing a face-plant on the concrete floor inside Renzo's dojo. His nose was split open, and his cheeks caked with dried blood; however, it was the silent scream on Lalo's dead face that sent a chill down Edmund's spine.

"I killed him myself," Renzo said coldly.

Returning the photo, Edmund asked, "What about damage to the facility?"

"The east wing is a complete loss, I'm afraid," he said somberly. "We'll have to rebuild that entire section, including the perimeter wall. Right now, the facility is running off solar power and backup generators, so day-to-day operations in the subterranean levels remain unaffected. We're working on restoring power to the topside buildings."

Edmund nodded agreeably. *Finally, some good news.*

"How many casualties?" Ms. Diaz inquired.

"Seven dead, all from the security team who engaged the Americans," Renzo answered. "Ten others sustained non-life-threatening injuries."

Edmund expected those numbers to be higher. "Anyone from the science team?"

"No, sir. The attack came when everyone was asleep. No one was working in the mechanical rooms at that time, either."

"How's morale?" Ms. Diaz asked, concerned about employee turnover. "Did this scare anyone off?"

"Not that I'm aware of," Renzo replied. "Naturally, they're confused, but so far, everyone has reported in for their shifts."

Edmund beamed with pride, a testament to his team's loyalty and devotion to the critical research they conducted here. "Call an all-hands meeting as soon as possible. I need to address the team."

Ms. Diaz nodded in affirmation and scribbled a note in her binder.

"I want everyone present, no exceptions," Edmund said firmly.

"You got it," Diaz replied, underlining the word 'everyone' twice in her notes.

Satisfied, Edmund peered out the window and noticed a kettle of Andean Condors circling in the air up ahead. He leaned up in his seat to get a closer look. Edmund, an amateur bird watcher, wondered what kind of trouble they might be stirring up.

He narrowed his eyes, hoping for a juicy look-see at whatever meal they were hovering over. Edmund spotted a wake of additional condors on the ground a few feet from the road as they passed, pecking away at a decaying carcass. Through a hole in the carrion's huddle, he glimpsed shredded clothing and a human corpse with the body cavity exposed.

Renzo glanced in the visor mirror and saw his boss grimace at the bird gathering. "That's what's left of Salazar," he offered.

A twisted grin creased Edmund's mouth. It brought a small measure of satisfaction to watch the birds defile the dead man's body.

"Serves him right," Edmund remarked sourly.

But Salazar was only the beginning. Other cogs in the machine were responsible for the attack on his facility. This attack not only targeted Edmund's Peruvian operations but also jeopardized everything he had worked so hard to build.

As the passing motorcade scattered the condors in angry hisses, Edmund turned to the two people in his innermost circle.

"This attack puts us in a dangerous position. If we're perceived as weak, it could embolden our enemies to act against us. Harsh words and smear campaigns are not enough, I want to make a bold statement to Fitzgerald, *and the rest of the world*, not to screw with me."

Renzo turned to face his boss. "What would you have me do, sir?"

Edmund's eyes turned deadly serious, locking onto Renzo with unflinching intensity. "You're my fixer, right?" he said with a raised eyebrow. "So, fix it."

5
POKE THE BEAR

Planet Earth
Arlington National Cemetery, Arlington, VA

President Roger Fitzgerald sat stone-faced while six pallbearers representing each of the military branches positioned themselves around a flag-draped casket. With impeccable precision, the honor guard unit lifted the Stars & Stripes in unison and began folding the flag thirteen times into a crisp triangle.

To the president's left, the widow of Chief Warrant Officer Greg Bellamy cradled the couple's newborn baby, swaddled tightly to her chest. Despite the tears streaming down her cheeks, the grieving mom maintained a brave face. With courage and quiet dignity, she honored the life and service of her husband—the father their daughter would never know but through the memories of others.

This sorrowful scene tore at Fitzgerald's heart. Although Ernie Gutierrez, his chief of staff, had offered to send a representative from the White House in his place, Roger Evan Fitzgerald—a veteran himself—adamantly refused. He viewed taking time from his busy schedule to honor Chief Bellamy and his family as a privilege, not a burden. When he took the oath of office, Fitzgerald swore that America's fallen heroes would never be forgotten under his watch, especially those who perished on covert missions in far-off lands, where the truth of their deaths would remain forever hidden from their families and the public.

Operation Bold Fortress fit that bill. The mission to rescue two American assets from a Mathias Industries' research facility in Peru had succeeded—Dr. Landry and Mr. Choi were home safe—but the victory came at a steep price: three American soldiers lost in the line of duty. Today's funeral was the first to honor the service of those brave men shot down by a surface-to-air missile during the rescue operation.

As the funeral continued, the president's mind wandered to the satellite images of the crash site outside Mathias's facility, and his blood began to boil.

Who the hell builds a research facility with air defenses?

President Fitzgerald and his advisors had grossly underestimated Edmund Mathias. The eccentric billionaire was far from a mere businessman, despite what lobbyists and members of Congress—whose pockets were lined with his money—might argue. To the president, Mathias was now an enemy of the state. Groom Lake and Peru had made one thing abundantly clear: Mathias would pursue his interests at any cost and defend them without restraint.

As his gaze fixed on the empty casket, Fitzgerald reflected on how governments worldwide—including his own—waged war against criminal enterprises. From drug cartels and smuggling rings to the post-Soviet mafia and the Japanese Yakuza, organized crime posed a significant threat to global security.

Why should Mathias Industries be viewed any differently? he mused.

A juggernaut in biotech and pharmaceuticals, the company branded itself as a global leader in the fight to treat and even cure humanity's most debilitating diseases. In reality, the company only deepened consumer suffering. Backed by an influential Washington lobby, Mathias Industries kept drug prices high while using Federal grants to fund its research. Profits soared by draining consumer wallets, making the company's founder and largest stockholder, Edmund Mathias, one of the world's wealthiest and most influential people.

But you're not untouchable, the president vowed.

Thanks to the misdeeds of General Garza, Director Sizemore, and the late Susan Drake, Mathias's secret research lab at Groom Lake was exposed. And with his illegal human cloning and force enhancement experiments now public knowledge, Mathias Industries faced a decline in stock prices, at least temporarily. That was a minor consolation, but a roster of terror-sponsoring nations—many of which topped the State Department's list—remained Mathias's loyal customers.

Still, President Fitzgerald was steadfast in his resolve to take down Mathias, even with his path to a second term looking cloudier. Before Bold Fortress, his approval rating hovered at a respectable sixty-three percent, but recently, those numbers had dipped significantly. Any chance of establishing a future military base in South America was dashed—the Peruvian president made that clear. Meanwhile, fearmongering media pundits dominated the airways, stoking public discord about an alien invasion. Despite no new developments regarding the Aiwans or so-called harvesters, no news was not good news, which made President Fitzgerald easy fodder.

What Fitzgerald needed was to re-establish contact with Captain Tan and Prince Kypa. Getting them on the air to quell public fears was crucial. But until that happened, Fitzgerald's only recourse was to channel his energy toward a home-grown threat: Edmund Mathias. Nothing would please the president more than bringing the murderer to face justice. Even if it ended his political career, seeing Mathias in an orange jumpsuit would be worth it.

The president brushed that image aside as the honor guard finished folding the flag. Realizing the ceremony was nearing its end, Fitzgerald turned to the grieving widow.

"May I?" he asked with a warm smile, extending his arms to hold the baby.

"Of course," she whispered, gently passing the baby to the president. The grieving widow quickly wiped her face, a hint of embarrassment in her gesture.

After settling the baby in his arms, Fitzgerald was surprised to find her awake and content to be held by a stranger. He naturally started to sway, a muscle memory of holding his daughters at this age.

Captivated by the innocence in the baby's big blue eyes, Fitzgerald made a silly noise to elicit a smile. Inwardly, he promised her, *"Your father's sacrifice will not be in vain, I swear."*

The ceremony concluded shortly after. As the president and first lady prepared to leave, they shared heartfelt condolences with Mrs. Bellamy one last time. No words could genuinely comfort her, and the awkwardness of farewell only reinforced the harsh reality that life goes on despite the loss of loved ones.

Gently squeezing his wife's hand as they departed, the president led Candace away. Flanked by their ever-vigilant Secret Service detail, they made their way in silence through countless rows of white headstones marking the graves of America's fallen heroes.

The presidential state car awaited—a formidable limousine known as "The Beast," one of ten in the presidential fleet. The limo stretched eighteen feet long and was essentially a tank on wheels, equipped with weapons, armor, and a suite of Bond-style gadgets. From an oil slick and smoke screen to door handles rigged to deliver an electric shock, the Beast could withstand almost any attack.

With a reported price tag nearing two million USD per vehicle, the Beast also housed the most advanced and secure communication system. Operationally, it was a mobile mirror of the president's emergency operations center (PEOC) back at the White House. Within the Beast, Fitzgerald could maintain constant contact with his national security council while on the move—and even dispatch the codes to fire nuclear weapons if the situation demanded it.

Special Agent Andrew Hastings of the United States Secret Service stood patiently by the back door with his hands clasped in front of him. Dressed in a dark suit and sunglasses, he exuded the calm vigilance of his profession.

"Zephyr is on the move," a voice crackled in his earpiece.

"Copy that," Agent Hastings replied into his lapel mic. "Cadillac One, standing by."

Scanning the perimeter for potential threats, Agent Hastings quickly spotted the approaching detail. His gaze settled on the first couple walking hand-in-hand. It was a refreshing change to serve a presidential pair whose commitment to marriage and family surpassed mere political optics. Unlike Fitzgerald's controversial predecessor—a figure who had tarnished the esteemed Office of the President—these new occupants of the White House stood out for their genuine affection and integrity. Despite their solemn oath to protect the first family unconditionally, every agent's devotion was buoyed by the character of those they served. The Fitzgerald's genuine bond was a source of reassurance and motivation, reminding the agents why they endured their chosen profession's relentless hours and intense pressure.

As the first couple drew nearer, Hastings' hand subtly moved to the door handle behind his back and opened it. Candace Bethany Fitzgerald flashed the agent an appreciative smile as she gracefully entered the vehicle first. Her husband paused briefly at the door.

"Thanks, Andy," the president said before ducking inside.

Hastings noticed the heaviness in the president's expression, though he remained silent as he closed the door behind him. He quickly moved toward the front of the vehicle, casting a wary glance around the area.

"Cadillac One is ready to move," he announced on the radio before taking his seat.

Within moments, the presidential motorcade began moving. Ten sleek, black vehicles exited the cemetery onto Memorial Avenue, where the Washington D.C. Metropolitan Police Motorcycle Unit met them. The Metro Police seamlessly took the lead and guided the procession back to the

White House.

Sensing the weight of the day pressing upon her husband, the first lady gently placed her hand on his thigh. Roger did not react at first, his mind elsewhere, but as her hand slowly slid higher, it was enough to snap him out of his reverie.

He turned to his wife, one eyebrow arched in mild surprise. Candy, however, kept her eyes forward, her expression a picture of feigned innocence, as if to say, "Oh, don't mind me."

A mischievous grin creased the president's lips.

Before he could speak, Candy said entirely out of the blue, "Wallmont Senior High."

Roger gave her a curious look as he placed his hand in a similar location on her thigh. "What about it?"

"Our junior year," she replied as if conjuring an old memory. "I seem to recall how you managed to combine drivers ed and sex ed into my parent's old Subaru."

Roger burst into laughter, a sound that Candy had not heard nearly enough in recent weeks. She turned to him, grinning from ear to ear, her chuckle joining his. Hearing her husband laugh was something she deeply cherished, especially given the recent pressures they had both endured.

"Ah yes," the president nodded, his eyes alight with fond memories. "They don't make 'em like they used to."

Candy placed her hand over his and gave it a gentle squeeze. She had known Roger Evan Fitzgerald for most of her life. They had grown up together, dating through high school and college and marrying just before his commission with the Air Force. Now, her husband was the most powerful man on Earth. Yet despite this, there were moments when she looked into Roger's eyes and still saw the awkward seventeen-year-old boy struggling with self-confidence.

Like many leaders, Roger occasionally grappled with imposter syndrome. He was acutely aware of his fallibility and had no trouble swallowing his pride if it meant better serving the country. But as the weight of the world's problems pressed down on him, Candy could not bear to watch him shoulder that burden alone.

"How are you?" she asked with a worried look.

Roger was inclined to crack a joke, hoping to ease his wife's concerns, but he knew better—she had a keen talent for seeing through his façades. Instead, the president frowned and let out a heavy sigh. Candy smiled warmly, giving him space to gather his thoughts.

Shaking his head, the President of the United States reluctantly admitted, "I'm afraid."

Candy squeezed his hand again, offering reassurance. "What are you afraid of?"

Roger took a deep breath, releasing it slowly. "I'm afraid it's all going to come crumbling down," he confessed, his voice tinged with doubt. "Our country ... the world." He huffed in frustration. "We're one spark away from igniting a wildfire that could consume the entire planet. Society as we know it could be wiped from existence, and it's my responsibility to make sure that doesn't happen."

"You're not in this alone," she reminded him.

Roger suppressed the urge to scoff. He knew his wife was right and that her intentions were sincere, but it did not change the fact that humanity looked to him for answers. Rather than burden her, Roger smiled wanly, lifted his wife's hand to his lips, and kissed it gently.

Just as he opened his mouth to thank her, Roger glanced out the window. The motorcade was crossing the Potomac River, and at the end of the Arlington Memorial Bridge, he spotted a billboard with an image of Prince Kypa on it. The Aiwan leader's face was circled in red, and a line ran through it. The anti-alien message blared, "*E. T. Go Home!*"

Usually, the president dismissed something like this with the same indifference he showed to the zealots who picketed outside the White House. But a genuine hatred behind the words on that billboard—a misguided fear directed at Prince Kypa—troubled him deeply. Roger had met the prince personally at Groom Lake and once harbored similar worries. But now, he knew better. He still believed that humanity stood on the brink of a new era, one where an alliance between Earth and Aiwa could yield unimaginable benefits. But before reaching that future, they had to overcome the enemies standing in the way of peace.

Despite the defaced image of Prince Kypa, seeing the Aiwan stirred something in President Fitzgerald, reminding him why he sought this job in the first place—to make a difference.

It's on you, he thought, but the words did not feel daunting or burdensome. Instead, they fueled a renewed determination.

Candy looked at him curiously, sensing her husband's shift in attitude. "What?" she asked, a playful grin tugging at her lips.

Roger met her gaze, and the sparkle in her hazel eyes rekindled the depth of his love for this woman. Without a word, he cupped her face gently in his hand and kissed her with a quiet but profound affection.

When they separated, Candy blinked up at him, pleasantly surprised. "Wow."

"Right? Who needs a Subaru?" he replied, a sly grin spreading across his face.

Straightening in his seat, President Fitzgerald turned his attention to the brightening sky. The sun finally broke through the thick clouds, casting a warm light over the Capitol. Up ahead, the White House emerged—a powerful reminder of the work ahead. It was time to get back to it.

The White House, Washington, D.C.

Ernie Gutierrez leaned back in his chair, reading the CIA's daily security update. With a highlighter pen clutched between his teeth, he read each page methodically, marking key points—each annotation signaling either a potential crisis or an ambiguity requiring further explanation.

The beep of his desk phone interrupted his focus. The calm voice of the president's secretary, Sheri, said over the intercom. "Sir, the president just pulled up."

Ernie tossed the pen on the desk and leaned forward. "Thanks, Sheri. I'm going to need ten minutes with him first thing."

"You got it," came the reply.

Precisely ten minutes later, President Fitzgerald strode into the Oval Office, his presence commanding the room as usual. Standing by the *Resolute* desk, Ernie read the president's body language, noting purpose in his step.

"How'd it go?" Ernie asked as the president took his seat.

"It sucked, as always," Fitzgerald replied flatly, wasting no time to open his side drawer and retrieve his stash of jelly beans.

"Have you read Haley's brief?" Ernie inquired, diving right into today's business.

"I did," the president replied. "Honestly, I'm siding with the security council on this one. We cannot allow ... *non-humans* to defend our home. I think this Earth Defense Force idea has merit."

"Me, too," Ernie agreed, watching the president pop a handful of black candies into his mouth. Knowing there were worse vices, he wisely withheld judgment. "But I'm sure they'll expect us to foot the bill," he added warily.

Still chewing a mouthful, the president asked, "Does that surprise you?"

"No," Ernie admitted, "but in light of recent events, that's the kind of stuff that makes our base pucker."

The president could not argue with Ernie's assessment. First contact with an alien race aside, this administration had taken enormous risks lately. First, by sending Captain Tan into North Korea to steal the Reaper—killing its Supreme Leader in the process—then by picking a fight with Edmund Mathias. Neither decision to authorize covert actions on foreign soil was made lightly. Still, after staring at an empty casket this morning, even Fitzgerald had to admit they were gambling with house money. Things had yet to blow up in their faces, at least on a global scale, but if he kept tempting fate, it was only a matter of time before their luck ran out.

"*This is what separates the fools from the damn fools,*" echoed his grandfather's sage-like wisdom.

Heeding Ernie's advice, Fitzgerald decided it was time to rein in their approach and rethink their strategy.

"Schedule some time with Haley and Bill," he directed. "I want their thoughts on how we might get the rest of the Security Council to help shoulder the burden of this Earth Defense Force."

Ernie noted in his planner to contact Ambassador Nichols and Secretary of State Bill Nguyen when he returned to his office. As he scribbled, he heard the president toss the bag of candy back inside the drawer, pause, and then sigh in frustration before closing it again.

Ernie glanced over the top of his glasses. "Something on your mind, Mr. President?"

Fitzgerald rolled his eyes. If he did not know any better, Ernie could be half-Aiwan with his uncanny ability to read the president's emotions.

"Yeah, actually," Fitzgerald replied, sighing heavily. "On the way in from Arlington this morning, I saw a billboard with Prince Kypa's image on it. The sign read, *E.T. Go Home.*"

Ernie's face remained unreadable as he resisted the urge to comment on the creative yet inappropriate message. He was interested in the president's perspective. Having known Roger Fitzgerald for years, Ernie could tell when something was bothering him—and this was one of those times.

Setting down his pen, Ernie waited for the president to continue.

After a brief pause, Fitzgerald asked, "What about this other Aiwan?"

"Luna?" Ernie replied, puzzled. "What about her?"

"Will she help us?" the president inquired.

Ernie scratched the back of his neck. "We have to meet her first, but honestly, there's a better chance of monkeys flying out of my butt before

Mathias lets that happen."

The president chuckled. "Thank you for that image," he said dryly.

"Anytime, Mr. President." Ernie smirked. "Speaking of which, I talked to Ratliff while you were gone. Satellites located Luna this morning at Mathias's facility in Peru. It seems he cut short his trip to Challenger Deep."

A thin smile creased the president's face as he pictured the number of new screen doors Mathias's compound would need due to Operation Bold Fortress. It had been a week since the mission to extract Dr. Landry and Mr. Choi, and nearly every politician and lobbyist in Washington had been demanding an apology on Mathias's behalf. The president ignored their calls.

"So, Luna actually built him a cloaking device?" Fitzgerald asked, contemplating the idea as he began clicking his pen incessantly.

"That's what Dr. Landry said," Ernie confirmed.

The president shook his head in disbelief. "Hiding crystals is one thing, but this level of stealth technology could negate all our early warning systems."

"Tell me about it," Ernie agreed somberly. "Donnelly has DEVGRU assembling a deep-sea operation to investigate the site at Challenger Deep but she's not making any promises. There's a reason only a handful of people on Earth have ever worked at that depth."

"Dr. Landry's debrief stated she was able to communicate with Luna and establish rapport," Fitzgerald noted.

"Verbally," Ernie clarified. "No mention of telepathy like Garza and Sizemore claimed."

"But this is what I'm talking about, Ernie. Dr. Garrett and Dr. Landry were able to connect with the Aiwans despite interference from Garza, Sizemore, and Mathias. Kypa and Luna have seen the dark side of humanity but chose to build relationships anyway. They've opened the door for peaceful relations between our worlds but we're squandering the opportunity." The president pointed out the window toward the crowd gathered on Pennsylvania Avenue. "Fearmongers like the yokels outside are the ones who put up that hateful billboard I saw. They're trying to incite public hysteria."

"We anticipated this," Ernie said calmly. "We've planned for it. If the crowds get out of hand, we'll deal with them."

"This could spiral out of control if we don't stay in front of it," Fitzgerald warned. "I support the U.N. initiative, but only if the goal is to defend Earth from aggression, not to initiate a galactic war."

"Then we need to get you back in front of the cameras," Ernie stated emphatically. "The best way to combat public fear is with constant, clear communication. We need you to reassure the world that the Aiwans are our allies."

"That's gonna be hard without Kypa present," the president countered. "And when word gets out that Luna is helping Mathias harvest crystals—a venture funded by the Russians, Chinese, and North Koreans—you know what's going to hit the fan."

Ernie sighed heavily. It was rare for him to be at a loss, but there were no easy answers to these problems.

Fitzgerald leaned forward and spoke into the intercom. "Sheri, clear my schedule today and Ernie's as well."

"Yes, Mr. President," came the dutiful reply.

He added, "Also, summon my national security team. Have them meet us in the PEOC."

"Right away, sir," she acknowledged.

Fitzgerald ended the call. He turned to Ernie, who nodded in agreement. The harvester issue was a top priority; they needed all hands on deck.

Before standing, the president opened his side drawer and grabbed another handful of jelly beans.

"Ahem," Ernie coughed.

Fitzgerald looked up to find Ernie holding out his hand expectantly. The president grinned and asked, "A day of firsts?"

Ernie shrugged as the president handed him a small handful of candies. Even as the jelly beans tumbled into his palm, his mind was already working on the daunting task ahead. They had their work cut out for them, and as he popped the sweets into his mouth, the former Navy SEAL silently recited the motto that carried him through similar challenges: *The only easy day was yesterday.*

6
RECOVERY

Jessica Aguri felt the weight of guilt grow heavier as she entered the base hospital. The newly promoted Deputy Director of the CIA's National Clandestine Service knew it was her fault that her friend and longtime operative, Choi Min-jun, was here. Min-jun was recovering from complications after two deadly encounters in Peru—one with a hungry green anaconda and another with Edmund Mathias's henchman, Mr. Renzo. A blood clot had formed in Min-jun's left leg during the flight home, forcing an emergency diversion to Nellis Air Force Base.

That was all Jessica knew. Fortunately, she had been at Groom Lake when news of Min-jun's condition reached her, so it was a relatively quick drive from the Nevada Test and Training Range to Las Vegas proper.

Upon entering the lobby, Jessica headed straight for the reception desk, where an older woman greeted her with a warm smile from behind the counter.

"How can I help you?" the woman asked.

Jessica flashed her CIA credentials. "I'm looking for a Mr. Wang. He was brought in about an hour ago."

The greeter's eyebrows raised at the sight of Jessica's VIP status. "Oh, I see," she replied, her smile faltering as she returned the ID. "Just a moment, please. Let me see if I can locate Mr.—"

"—Wang," Jessica repeated. "Pei Wang."

The woman nodded and began typing on her computer. It was a slow process—she was not particularly adept with the system. After several minutes of searching, she finally located Min-jun on the third floor of the Critical Care Unit. His file had a high-security designation, indicating restricted access for authorized personnel only.

The greeter signaled to an airman stationed at the nearby security checkpoint. Clad in camouflage fatigues and a dark blue beret, the airman carried an M-18 Sig Sauer pistol securely strapped to his leg.

Jessica noticed the rank insignia on the guard's uniform. He was a technical sergeant, likely in his late twenties, which signified a solid career progression. She volunteered her ID without hesitation.

"Can you please escort our guest to the CCU, Room 12?" the greeter asked.

Assessing Jessica's credentials, his eyes flicked between the badge and her face, making a quick visual comparison. After a brief nod of approval, he returned the badge to her.

"Thank you, ma'am. This way, please," he gestured with a polite smile toward the checkpoint.

Jessica trailed behind the sergeant, bypassing the metal detectors and standard security scan. They headed to the "B" elevators, where two nurses stood waiting.

While they paused, Jessica read an interesting factoid on the wall. She learned that, besides being a Level III trauma center, the Mike O'Callaghan Military Medical Center was also the first Air Force medical facility to treat civilian and military critical care and trauma patients—a vital resource for local residents and one ex-North Korean special operative.

The elevator arrived seconds later, and they silently rode to the third floor, where Jessica parted ways with her escort. Due to restrictions in the Critical Care Unit, she signed in at the nurse's station, received a face mask, and washed her hands in a nearby scrub room. A nurse then buzzed her through the automated doors into the CCU.

"Straight ahead," the nurse instructed. "Last room on the right."

Jessica smiled behind her mask and replied, "Thank you."

Making her way through the sterile corridor, she passed several single-bed recovery rooms partitioned by glass walls. The steady beeping of heart rate monitors and ventilators echoed from each patient's room, but Jessica kept her eyes forward, respecting their privacy.

At the end of the ward, Jessica approached two law enforcement officers sitting outside Room 12. Each wore a black windbreaker emblazoned with the United States Marshal Service logo and stood as Jessica approached, no doubt given advance notice of her visit.

Jessica volunteered her ID.

"Good morning," the ranking deputy greeted. He gave Jessica's badge a quick once-over and handed it back. "Thank you, ma'am. I'm Deputy Grubbs. This is Deputy Sumpter," he said, gesturing to his partner. "The patient's inside."

"Has his condition changed?" she asked, glancing worriedly inside the room, but a drawn curtain blocked Min-jun from view.

Marshall Grubbs shook his head. "No, ma'am. All's quiet. I think he's asleep."

"Jessica?" came a female voice from inside the room, the Hispanic accent unmistakable.

Jessica turned to see Colonel Marlana Nunez emerge from behind the curtain, eagerly tiptoeing toward her.

Stepping out into the hall, Nunez briefly lowered her mask, revealing a wide smile before extending her arms for a heartfelt embrace. They held each other tightly for a long moment.

"I'm so sorry I got you into all this," Jessica whispered with remorse.

Marlana squeezed her tighter and patted Jessica's back. "No apologies. It's not your fault. Min and Rose needed our help, and we did what we had to do. End of discussion."

Jessica pulled back. "But you and Hector—"

"Hector? Please." Marlana waved away the notion like a foul smell. "He can't stop talking about landing on that stupid aircraft carrier."

Jessica sobered. "Uh oh."

"Don't worry," Marlana whispered. "I told him to put a lid on it, but santa mierda, he acts like he landed on the moon or something."

Jessica burst into laughter—a genuine, much-needed release.

Marlana wagged her finger playfully. "You created a monster, you know?"

"Me?" Jessica feigned innocence. "The plan was to take pictures, not reenact *Top Gun*."

Marlana chuckled and pulled Jessica into another hug. "I'm just teasing. It's really good to see you."

"It's good to see you, too." As they parted, Jessica's expression grew serious. She glanced over Marlana's shoulder at Min-jun. "So, how is he?"

"Much better," Marlana assured her. "The doc said he developed deep vein thrombosis, probably came on during that long flight from Peru. That was brutal," she remarked, rolling her eyes. "Anyway, they've got him on blood thinners. Min should be back on his feet in a few days."

Jessica bit her lip, struggling to suppress the guilt of putting her friends in danger. Noting her distress, Marlana offered a comforting smile and gently rubbed Jessica's arm in reassurance.

"He's been drifting in and out—you should go in," Marlana said, bobbing her toward Min's room, prodding Jessica inside.

Jessica shook her head with reluctance. "I don't want to disturb him."

"You won't," Marlana assured her. "Just be present. Go sit at his side. I'm going down to the morgue to see how many people Hector's bored to death with his airplane story—kidding," she joked.

Jessica shook her head, smiling as Marlana walked away. Taking a deep breath, she exhaled sharply, then quietly entered the room, careful not to disturb her friend.

Min-jun lay in bed with his leg elevated for circulation, but it was his swollen face, black eyes, and bandaged nose that tore at Jessica's heart. None of this should have happened. Min's mission into the bush was meant to be a straightforward surveillance operation—in and out, with Mathias being none the wiser. But a stupid snake changed everything.

Min-jun was lucky enough to survive the anaconda attack. Then, after enduring a brutal interrogation by Mathias's men, he risked everything to help Rose and Marlana escape. If not for the heroics of Hector and CIA Station Chief Paul Wiggins, Min-jun would likely have been recaptured or left to die alone in the jungle.

Standing at the foot of the bed, Jessica watched her old friend sleep peacefully despite the IVs and sensors attached to his battered body. She had not seen him look this bad since their first meeting ten years earlier—the night she pulled him from the icy waters of the Tumen River.

Jessica's eyes glazed over as she recalled the events of that fateful evening. She was the new station chief in Sanhe, China, leading a CIA-funded humanitarian organization called the Global Children's Relief Mission. Her mandate: secretly gather intel on Chinese and North Korean activities while helping impoverished children in the region.

Jessica was surveilling military movements along the Sino-Korean border the night she met Min-jun. Even now, she could vividly recall the tranquil stillness of the woods and the soothing murmur of the river that marked the border between the two countries. It had been a slow night with no activity to report on either side. But just as she was about to call it quits, all hell broke loose.

Out of nowhere, a woman yelped from downstream, shattering the calmness, followed immediately by the screeching cries of an infant. Jessica's breath hitched. Suddenly, a large searchlight on the North Korean side of the border lit up the area. She froze, her heart pounding. Every instinct told her to crawl out of there as fast as she could, but then she spotted two silhouettes in the middle of the river, struggling to cross.

Defectors!

Min-jun and his wife, Binna, were less than twenty yards away from Jessica this whole time, and she had no idea they were even there—a testament to Min-jun's stealth abilities. But the baby had blown their cover after Binna slipped on a rock and accidentally dunked their newborn son, Seo-jun, under the ice-cold water. Now, the child was awake and inconsolable.

Jessica watched helplessly as Min-jun aided his wife in fighting the current and slippery rocks. Once Binna regained her footing, the couple forged ahead.

Meanwhile, the border erupted with activity. A whirring alarm cranked up as a North Korean soldier barked through a bullhorn, ordering the defectors back to shore. Min-jun ignored the command, urging his family forward. They had come too far to surrender, and if they returned to the DPRK, both would be arrested and sent to labor camps, never to see each other or their son again.

Warning shots followed, kicking up water on either side of the defectors like supersonic stones skipping across the river. Jessica's eyes darted upstream. Bright orange and yellow muzzle flashes erupted along the bridge overlooking the river. The recoil of the soldier's AK-47s was unmistakable to her trained ear.

Seeing their warning had no effect, the North Koreans employed deadly force. The following shots found their mark. Binna went down first. The 7.62mm rounds impacted her petite frame with such force that it threw her sideways, killing her instantly.

"Binna!" Min-jun screamed as his wife and son were ripped violently from his grasp.

He watched in horror as Binna's lifeless body drifted face-first downstream. But his son's cries spurred Min-jun into action. Frantically searching the darkness, he located Seo-jun being swept away by the current. The infant was still bundled in a tightly wrapped blanket, bobbing up and down atop the mild rapids.

Suddenly, Min-jun felt a searing pain in his abdomen. His eyes widened in shock as he looked down and noticed the hole in his coat. Clutching his gut, Min-jun winced—the bullet had passed through. Ignoring the wound, he pressed on, determined to save his helpless son. But a second bullet tore into his shoulder, propelling him forward and plunging him beneath the water. When he broke the surface again, Min-jun struggled to stay afloat, his left arm limp and useless. He sank once more, and just before the darkness claimed him, he caught one final, heartbreaking glimpse of little Seo-jun vanishing under the water.

At this point, Jessica had no choice but to move downstream. Judging by the sound of military vehicles starting up, both sides of the border were mobilizing. Returning to GCRM was too risky now, as the Chinese soldiers might discover her. Instead, Jessica low-crawled through high grass to the river and slipped head-first into the water.

Riding the current downstream, Jessica found Min-jun moments later, hung up on a rock in the middle of the river with his head barely above water. She made it to him and rolled him over on his back with a Herculean effort. He was alive, for now.

Checking their six, Jessica scanned the area. As the large searchlight moved back and forth from one side of the river to the other, she noticed bouncing beams of white light moving fast through the woods on her left. The Chinese soldiers' flashlights betrayed their positions, and Jessica realized she had less than a minute before they would arrive.

Wrapping her arm around Min-jun's chest, Jessica swam to the Chinese side of the river, struggling to keep Min-jun's head above water. They hid under the exposed root system of a tall tree where the shoreline had eroded.

Holding Min-jun tight, Jessica caught her breath. Her lungs burned, and her heart pounded as she waited and listened, fearing the soldiers would discover them at any moment.

That moment never came. The soldiers passed them by.

Jessica waited nearly an hour until the searchlight abruptly cut off. She then hauled Min-jun through the woods back to GCRM before sunrise and treated his wounds. He woke up two days later to discover his wife and son were dead. His only solace was that Jessica had gone back for his family. She found both bodies on the Sanhe side of the river, apparently recovered by the Chinese soldiers and dragged to shore. Neither corpse had papers on them, making identification impossible. Binna and Seo-jun were left to be scavenged by animals, but Jessica got to them first. She buried them properly in the woods, digging their graves under a full moon, which, ironically, was the Chinese symbol of peace and family reunion.

In the following weeks, Min-jun observed the generous work being done by GCRM as he healed. Once physically ready, Jessica led him into the woods to say his goodbyes. She always remembered that night. Min-jun knelt beside the graves of his wife and son, rubbing his hands together and asking for their forgiveness. They must have spoken to him because Min-jun finished with a clear mind and purpose. He shared his history with Jessica, including his military service and reason for defecting.

Afterward, he asked her the most obvious question: "Why were you down by the river in the middle of the night?"

Jessica could have lied, but Min-jun was too perceptive. He would have seen right through her. Instead, Jessica told him the truth and her reason for being in Sanhe.

Min-jun's response was instantaneous. "I want in."

And just like that, Jessica had recruited her first operative. From then on, the two became an unstoppable team. Min-jun put his military skills to use extracting North Korean assets for the CIA while humbly serving as GCRM's property superintendent, supporting impoverished children the world cared nothing about. Both roles proved to be unexpectedly therapeutic.

When Jessica blinked back to the present, her eyes settled on Min-jun lying in the hospital bed. To her surprise, he was awake and had been watching her for some time during her quiet reflection. He smiled wanly, still groggy from the sedatives.

"Hey," Jessica spoke softly. She rounded the bed to his side and placed her hand gently on Min-jun's.

"Miss Jessica," he replied hoarsely, glad to see her.

"I'm here," she soothed.

"Water …"

Looking about, Jessica located a small sink and faucet with a plastic cup dispenser mounted on the wall. She filled a cup and returned to Min-jun's side. Gently lifting the drink to his mouth, she said softly, "Here you go."

Min-jun drank it all, then licked his pasty lips.

"Do you want more?"

Min-jun shook his head; then his eyes narrowed with purpose. "Rose and Marlana?"

"They're fine," Jessica assured him, patting his hand softly. "They both made it out safely because of you. In fact, Marlana and Hector are here. They're outside."

Min-jun relaxed, a thin smile of satisfaction creasing his face.

Jessica sighed heavily, fighting back tears. "Min, I'm so sorry," she pleaded. "This was all my fault. I should've never asked you to go. You didn't deserve this."

Min-jun turned to his friend. Seeing the tears welling in Jessica's eyes only confirmed what he already knew: Jessica's heart was in the right place. Their relationship transcended friendship. It was more akin to the "band of brothers" bond shared between soldiers. They had fought together, spilled blood, and would always be bound to one another for as long as they lived.

Min-jun coughed, then announced with a wry grin, "I retire now."

Jessica guffawed, then wiped her eyes. "You think?"

"No more snakes. I'm done," he said firmly. "It almost squeeze me to death."

Smiling behind her mask, Jessica shook her head, grateful Min could joke about the encounter. "I heard about it. Man, I can't imagine what that must've been like," she said. "I'm just glad you're safe. The doctors say you'll make a full recovery and should be back on your feet in no time."

Min-jun nodded, then asked, "How's Ji-eun?"

"She's fine," Jessica replied with a warm smile. "I checked in with Agent McDonnell earlier. Ji-eun is feeling very pregnant, but she asked about you."

Min-jun's brow furrowed. "Does she know about this?"

Jessica shook her head emphatically. "Nope."

Min-jun nodded understanding and changed the subject. "How long I stay here?"

Jessica frowned. "A few days. The doctors don't want you to travel because of the blood clot in your leg. Once that's resolved, we'll move you back to Missoula, I promise."

This was not the news Min-jun was hoping for. He missed rocking on the porch with Ji-eun, sipping hot tea, and watching the sunset. Funny how just a couple of weeks ago, he yearned for his old life in covert ops and eagerly volunteered to go to Peru. Now, all he wanted was to put his past behind him and live out his days in peace and quiet.

Sensing his melancholy, Jessica suggested, "Maybe you can Facetime each other?"

Min-jun had no idea what that meant. As Jessica explained, Min's eyes grew heavy, and he sank into his pillow. He was fast asleep moments later.

Taking her cue, Jessica patted his hand softly and whispered, "We'll talk more later."

She stood and smiled down at her friend once more. With Min-jun safe,

Jessica felt a sense of closure, knowing he could now pursue the retirement he deserved.

Perhaps with Ji-eun? she wondered—or rather, hoped.

Crazier things had happened, and the more she thought about it, the more it made sense. Despite their age difference, Min-jun and Ji-eun were a good match, in her opinion.

Just then, Jessica's phone vibrated in her pocket. She quickly left the room, fearful of waking Min. Out in the hall, Jessica retrieved her encrypted phone and checked the ID. It was her boss, Brett Brenham, Director of the CIA's National Clandestine Service.

"Yes, sir. This is Jessica."

"How's Mr. Choi?" he asked.

Jessica detected no judgment or lingering discord in Brenham's voice. Her boss had already ripped her a new one for involving Min-jun in an unsanctioned op. Lucky for her, both assets were safely recovered from Mathias's facility. Brenham gave her a mulligan for her bad judgment, and all seemed forgiven, but it was far from forgotten.

"He'll make a full recovery," Jessica answered. "They want to keep him here at Nellis for observation, and then we can move him back to Missoula."

"Good. And the Nunezes?"

Brenham's interest in Marlana and Hector sounded genuine, but she sensed her boss was leading to something.

"They're fine. Actually, they're here at the hospital."

"Perfect, because I've got an errand for you," Brenham replied, sounding opportunistic. "This comes straight from the top and I've already cleared it with General Dukes."

Jessica's chest tightened. Higher than Brenham meant Director Ratliff, maybe even the president. "Hold on, sir, while I find a place to talk."

She located a nearby supply closet and stepped inside. "Sorry about that," she continued. "What do you have in mind?"

"You and Colonel Nunez will fly to Atlanta to meet with Dr. Landry," Brenham explained. "She's our only link to the second Aiwan—Luna—and I figured the two of you could help prep her."

Jessica's brow furrowed, still unclear on her objective. "Prep her for what, exactly?"

"At some point, we're going to have to dance with the devil," Brenham answered with a sigh. "The devil being Edmund Mathias. After what happened at Groom Lake, the whole world knows he's dabbling in human cloning. But he hasn't perfected it yet. The two girls we recovered from that semi are proof of that. I just learned they both died within minutes of each other."

Jessica's heart sank.

"Mathias is also peddling some kind of force enhancement serum," Brenham continued. "But it has serious side effects, as well. Garza and Sizemore confirmed as much, but we don't think Mathias's buyers know he's selling them a defective product."

"Sounds like Mathias," Jessica remarked dryly.

Brenham agreed. "Working with the Russians, Chinese, and North Koreans is a gamble, but Mathias needs those revenue streams to fund a more ambitious venture."

"Crystals," Jessica speculated.

"Exactly," Brenham affirmed. "During Dr. Landry's debrief, she mentioned Luna had built some kind of cloaking device to hide the crystals in Challenger Deep. If that's true, this could have major national defense implications," he stated. "We need to know more about this tech and verify it actually works. That's where you come in. The president wants options, and right now, Dr. Landry's connection to Luna is our best shot."

Jessica was taken aback. "I doubt Rose or Mathias would agree to any kind of reunion, don't you think?"

"Mathias has no choice. He can't go it alone, and he knows it," Brenham said firmly. "The time may come soon when we have to force his hand. If there's ever an opportunity to reunite Dr. Landry with Luna, she needs to be ready."

Sensing the conversation had come full circle, Jessica repeated her question. "Ready for what, sir?"

With utmost seriousness, Brenham replied, "To help save the world from an alien invasion."

7

OVERDUE

Planet Mars
Approximately 140 million miles from Earth

Mars, known as the Red Planet, is orbited by two moons, both discovered in 1877 by American astronomer Asaph Hall. The larger of these moons, Phobos—meaning fear—boasts a heavily cratered surface covered with dust and loose rock, much like Earth's moon. Its most prominent feature, Stickney Crater, is a vast depression that defines much of its rugged terrain.

Perched along the crater's outer rim was an Aiwan deep-space probe, its long-range sensors fixed on a distant target: Earth. The autonomous craft, one of many dispatched by Prince Kypa to scour the galaxy for magnetarite crystals, had entered Earth's solar system six months earlier through a nearby hyperspace lane.

From this vantage point, the probe gathered endless data about Earth and its neighbors and fed it back to Kypa's secret lab on Pria-12. These findings prompted Kypa's exploratory mission to Earth, where his crash landing in North Korea set off a geopolitical firestorm. All the while, the Aiwan probe remained undetected on Phobos, quietly relaying a continuous stream of information.

The probe's initial scans of Earth were off the chart, indicating high amounts of magnetarite crystals buried deep within the planet's core. But something changed recently that could not be readily explained from this distance. The crystal readings had dipped sharply—not to the point of non-existence, but enough to warrant closer inspection.

The Aiwan probe, programmed to investigate such anomalies, retracted its sensor array into its beetle-like fuselage and ignited its rear-mounted thruster. Lifting off the Martian moon's surface, the probe kicked up a cloud of chalky gray dust and quickly launched into space on an intercept course with Earth.

Headquarters, Space Operations Command
Peterson Space Force Base, Colorado

A time-honored tradition in the United States military is congratulating a newly promoted enlisted member by having them "walk the gauntlet." Squad members line up in two opposing columns, and as the freshly promoted person walks down and back through the middle, they punch the new stripes on their arms.

Technical Sergeant Keegan savored this moment. Clenching his fist, he anticipated the pain he was about to deliver to his subordinate, Specialist Miller. With a dark grin, he said, "Okay, Miller, stand up. It's time to pay the piper."

Newly reassigned to the United States Space Force, Specialist Miller swiveled around his chair and looked to his supervisor, Sergeant Alvarez, for help. Alvarez shrugged, offering no sympathy.

"Sorry, dude," she said. "Everyone has to walk the gauntlet."

Fortunately for Specialist Miller, the gauntlet consisted of only two people. In bigger units, two trips through the gauntlet could be excruciating. Miller was getting off easy, but judging by the sinister expression on Keegan's face, he intended to make both of his punches count.

"Alright," Miller said, unenthused as he stood. "Let's get this over with."

Alvarez and Keegan took up positions on either side of Miller. Keegan went first and held nothing back. He punched Miller in the arm as hard as he could.

"Boo-yah!" Keegan said, watching Miller wince as pain shot down to his fingertips.

It was Alvarez's turn next, and instead of reeling back, she gently tapped Miller on the opposite arm.

Keegan rolled his eyes in disgust. "Come on. You grew up with brothers. I know you can hit harder than that."

Alvarez ignored him as they switched sides and repeated the process. Keegan delivered another bone-crushing blow that Miller shook off with a pained laugh. Then, it was Alvarez's turn. She reared her fist back, pretending she would get in one good lick, but instead, she lightly double-tapped Miller's other arm.

"Congratulations," she said, extending her hand. "You earned it."

Miller accepted, wincing as he lifted his hand, the sting of Keegan's punches still fresh in his aching muscles.

"Ditto from me, my young padawan," Keegan seconded, shaking Miller's hand vigorously and taking pleasure in his prolonged torture.

"Thank you, both … I think." Miller quipped, rubbing his sore arms.

"C'mon, there's ice cream cake in the breakroom," Alvarez announced.

"What?" Keegan protested. "You never got me a cake."

A sudden beeping from the nearby GEODSS terminal interrupted their fun. Keegan and the others exchanged tense glances. Alvarez, the closest, quickly dropped into her seat and grabbed her headset.

"Inbound NEO," she called out, her voice cutting through the tension. She referred to a near-earth object, but the term held new weight these days.

Keegan and Miller snapped into action, immediately taking their seats and throwing on their headsets. They initiated calls to satellite tracking stations worldwide, seeking confirmation of the object's trajectory and intent.

Was it just space debris or something more? they wondered.

Alvarez shook her head. How quickly things changed. Not long ago, her first instinct would have been to brace for a possible Russian or Chinese missile strike. But now, with the threat of harvesters, her thoughts jumped straight to the possibility of an alien invasion. The old threats felt almost quaint by comparison.

Miller was on the landline with NASA. "Houston confirmed the NEO. It originated near Mars, and they said they're detecting a strong heat signature."

"Then it's not an asteroid," Major Lannigan determined. "Where is it now?"

Miller looked over his shoulder to find his commanding officer standing over him. Major Lannigan had an unnerving habit of appearing out of thin air at the worst possible times.

"Moving fast, sir. It just passed the moon. Wait …" Miller held up his finger as the NASA contact provided more information. "Copy that," he said. Covering the mouthpiece, Miller reported to Lannigan. "Sir, the NEO has stopped. It's taken up orbit."

Keegan anticipated Lannigan's next order before it was given—he needed a visual. Quickly, Keegan switched the large wall-mounted monitor to NASA's video feed.

The images were fuzzy and granular, but the object's silhouette left no doubt. It was an alien spacecraft. After reaching Low Earth orbit, it powered down and drifted effortlessly, circling the globe at 17,000 miles per hour.

Alvarez and the others watched the probe in tense silence, holding their breaths as they waited for something to go wrong. Meanwhile, data poured in from the Combined Space Operations Center at Vandenberg Space Force Base in California. The initial analysis showed the probe to be considerably smaller than both the Aiwan mothership that crashed in North Korea and the battlecruiser that destroyed the International Space Station.

Nevertheless, a single, chilling question echoed in all their minds: *Is it friend or foe?*

Ekator

Silence filled Grawn Krunig's private chamber as the crime lord sat in his chair, staring at the red-orange clouds of the Mishi Nebula through the viewport. Outside, robotic cargo handlers whizzed by, efficiently transferring containers of contraband between transport ships. Krunig scarcely noticed them; his mind was elsewhere.

His hand clenched into a tight fist, and anger roiled within him, on the brink of eruption. The coup he had meticulously orchestrated on Aiwa had collapsed. Though King Loka was dead, his heir, Prince Kypa, had survived. Even worse, his sources on Aiwa had confirmed that the blue crystal—responsible for powering the tiny ship that decimated his fleet was now secured in the palace vault in Supra. This setback went beyond mere failure; it was a crushing blow to his ambitions and a dire threat to his very survival.

Kypa outwitted the bounty hunters, Smythe and Gort, and if Krunig had been in the same situation, sacrificing one human female and her ship to protect the most powerful crystal in the universe would have been a no-brainer. His only regret was not being there to call Kypa's bluff personally. He had trusted the bounty hunters to execute the exchange and deliver his prize, but that, too, seemed to be a mistake. They were overdue, and Krunig was yet to take possession of the Reaper.

With each passing moment, it became increasingly clear that something had gone terribly wrong—or that Smythe and Gort had betrayed him.

While their deaths were within the realm of possibility—they had undoubtedly amassed their share of enemies in the bounty-hunting profession—Krunig doubted it. Smythe and Gort were too cunning to walk into a trap. And they would have called for help if attacked.

That left the unsettling possibility that the bounty hunters were defying the syndicate and attempting to sell the Reaper to the highest bidder. If that were the case, it would be a reckless move; one Krunig had not expected from them. Yet, everyone had a price. Smythe and Gort had built their reputations on being consummate professionals—a rare quality in their line of work. For them to go rogue was troubling and disappointing.

No one is perfect, he reflected with a growing sense of calm.

Krunig relaxed his clenched fist, reassured that all was not lost—merely delayed. Soon, his network of spies would track down the bounty hunters, and then he would have the ship and exact his revenge. But therein lay the irony. Whether Smythe and Gort realized it or not, the Reaper was nothing without the blue crystal—they had no leverage.

Or did they? Krunig corrected himself.

His thoughts turned to Kypa—the engineer, not the prince. Transferring the blue crystal to the Reaper had been an unprecedented achievement, a true engineering marvel. Few had the expertise to replicate such a feat, making the integration of the blue crystal with any other vessel potentially catastrophic.

Krunig felt his temper rising again. He needed the Reaper and its captain as a contingency, and Smythe and Gort were needlessly delaying his plans.

"Fools," he muttered with disgust.

The bounty hunters' betrayal was costing Krunig precious time. He had promised Grawn Supreme that he would deliver the Reaper—a weapon capable of defeating any threat the Madreen Crime Syndicate ever faced, with one exception.

Me, Krunig mused behind his faceless mask, a wicked grin tugging at his lips.

A familiar bell chimed, breaking his concentration. Hoping it was news on Smythe and Gort, Krunig pressed a button on his chair's armrest, causing a side door to open. In the doorway stood Vekka, his most trusted aide.

"Enter," Krunig commanded.

Treading lightly around his boss was second nature for Vekka. Krunig's infamous temper rarely spared the bearer of bad news—it often resulted in a one-way trip out of the nearest airlock. Vekka moved cautiously across the room, his albino skin and tightly braided, long gray hair contrasting against the deep crimson of his customary tunic. Just as Vekka opened his mouth to speak, Krunig cut him off.

"Any news?" the crime lord asked, keeping his back to his aide.

Vekka cleared his throat and replied, "Still no word from the bounty hunters, my lord."

"Could they have run into trouble?"

"Perhaps," Vekka granted. "Prince Kypa is in pursuit, but our source on Aiwa has not received any updates to suggest he's been successful."

Krung tightened his fist once more. If the bounty hunters had held up their end of the bargain, they could have led Prince Kypa right to him. Then, he could have taken his time and killed Kypa slowly with his bare hands.

"What about Grawn Supreme and the other factions?"

Vekka shifted uneasily. "I've heard nothing from our usual contacts, not even a whisper."

Krunig knew the blue crystal and its whereabouts would not remain a secret much longer. Sooner or later, word would spread, and everyone—from his fellow grawns to every cutthroat in the galaxy—would be after it. That made Smythe and Gort's disappearance all the more troubling.

"What about known associates?" Krunig inquired.

"Smythe and Gort are very selective with whom they do business," Vekka replied, a tinge of admiration in his voice. "I know of a few contractors they work with occasionally. I'm having them followed."

"Good, I want to know where they go and who they speak with," Krunig demanded.

Vekka dipped his chin. "As you wish, my lord. We'll find them," he said with confidence. "There is more, sir. Good news, in fact. We just received the coordinates for the human homeworld."

Krunig swiveled his chair to face Vekka. "Show me."

Anticipating the request, Vekka extended a palm projector. A hologram flickered to life, revealing a stunning blue-green planet.

"Earth, my lord."

"Mm," Krunig grunted, his gaze fixed on the image, drawing comparisons to Aiwa.

"This footage is from one of Prince Kypa's probes," Vekka explained. "Once again, your connection on Aiwa has proven quite resourceful."

"Indeed." Krunig kept the identity of his agent in place a secret—for now. Shifting his focus to the data streams flanking the 3D projection of Earth, he scrutinized the readings, noting the planet's poor air quality. "A bountiful world," he observed, "yet these humans seem intent on poisoning it."

"Yes, my lord," Vekka agreed. "Overcrowding and famine have reached epidemic levels."

Krunig did not care about the surface dwellers. His focus was on Earth's oceans—and the untapped potential they held beneath the waters.

"Show me the crystals."

Bracing himself, Vekka tapped the display. The hologram shifted to reveal sporadic crystal deposits scattered across the globe. Krunig's eyes widened in surprise. The deposits were significant but hardly impressive.

Sneering behind his armor, Krunig pointed his upper right hand at the display. "Kypa risked everything for this?"

"No, my lord." Vekka cleared his throat. "This is what he came for."

Vekka adjusted the display, comparing today's findings to the extraordinary readings recorded before Prince Kypa's doomed ship crashed on Earth. The difference was stark—like night and day.

"Something has changed recently, my lord," Vekka stated. "We know the blue crystal is now on Aiwa, but the high concentration of remaining crystals, particularly in this region, have disappeared." Vekka pointed to Challenger Deep.

"Harvested?" Krunig speculated.

"That is a possibility, my lord. Our rivals may already be on site. Or perhaps—"

"—Perhaps what?" Krunig snapped, growing impatient.

"Perhaps the humans are more advanced than we think," Vekka suggested calmly. "Surely, by now, they realize the potential wealth they are sitting on. It stands to reason they would attempt to capitalize on this opportunity."

Krunig studied the readouts intently, furrowing his brow as he processed the data. "I see no signs of advanced technology."

"True, but the Aiwans have been to Earth twice. It's possible that humans have acquired their technology."

Krunig remained silent, acknowledging Vekka's logic and calculating his next move. Despite their perceived inferiority, humans had repeatedly demonstrated resourcefulness, posing an unexpected challenge.

Krunig turned his attention back to the planetary scans of Earth. The probe indicated that water covered about seventy percent of Earth's surface. One distinctive feature stood out—the polar ice caps. Unlike Aiwa, which lacked such formations due to its twin suns, Earth showcased these dome-shaped ice sheets at its poles.

"Hmm," Krunig muttered as the seed of an idea began to take root. But before executing any plans, he needed to appease Grawn Supreme and buy himself more time to locate the bounty hunters.

With renewed determination, Krunig rose from his seat. "Prepare my ship, Vekka, and send word to the supreme leader that I request a parlay with my fellow grawns."

8
ROGANTU

Planet Rogantu
The outer rim of the Milky Way

Smythe and Gort's freighter emerged from hyperspace in a brilliant flash of white light, decelerating smoothly as it entered normal space. Sitting in the cockpit, the two bounty hunters deftly operated the flight controls, slowing the ship from lightspeed.

Looming beyond the forward viewport was a bleak, desolate world as forbidding from orbit as it was on the surface. Shrouded with volcanic ash and streaked with rivers of molten lava, the primordial landscape of Rogantu was the ideal location to disappear and lay low.

"Nothing on long-range sensors," Gort reported, relief evident in his voice.

"Relax," Smythe tried to reassure his partner. "Nobody ever comes out this way anymore."

Gort rolled his eyes. "I can see why," he muttered.

Rogantu lay outside commercial traffic lanes for good reason. Once a hub for mining precious metals, corporations eventually abandoned it due to electromagnetic emissions from the planet's core. Already a harsh work environment, the interference disrupted operations, wreaked havoc on equipment, and made Rogantu too expensive to exploit.

"We'll be fine," Smythe said with cautious optimism. "Once Hiromi gets here, I'll line up a buyer and we'll unload the cargo once and for all."

"And then what?" Gort snapped, his frustration slipping out before he could catch himself. Still, it felt good to finally voice his discontent with Smythe's risky scheme. "Where can we go that the syndicate won't find us?"

"Calm yourself," Smythe warned, his voice edged with the icy detachment he usually reserved for those they hunted.

Gort swallowed hard, the tension tightening his throat.

"I know a place," Smythe explained, calmly walking back his annoyance. "When this job is over and we've made our last score, there's an uncharted world in the outer rim—an oasis—where we can both retire in peace and comfort."

Gort scoffed. Paradise sounded nice for ordinary people, but he and his partner were far from that.

"No offense but is that really what you want?" he dared to ask. "I don't see either one of us getting out of the game."

Smythe turned to his long-time partner, the closest being he had to a friend. "You would give up our biggest score?"

Gort shrugged. "I like this life," he admitted, gesturing to the cramped cockpit and dated flight instruments. "Chasing bounties is who we are, it keeps us sharp. Paradise sounds nice and all, but we'll be looking over our shoulders the rest of our lives."

Smythe had already considered this and calculated the risks and rewards. His only mistake was incorrectly assuming Gort would blindly follow him into retirement. That point of contention could prove unfortunate if push came to shove later. For now, Smythe knew he had to keep his options open.

After briefly reflecting, he replied, "We still have time to walk away. When Hiromi gets here, we'll hear what she has to say and then decide how to proceed. Who knows, maybe you'll warm up to the idea of retirement. Fair enough?"

Gort nodded submissively, although a sinking feeling in the pit of his stomach told him to be on his guard. If Smythe had his mind set on a big score, then nothing would stand in his way. Everything hinged on Hiromi's ability to hack into the Reaper and uncover its secrets.

Gort cleared his throat, his gaze momentarily shifting away. "It, uh, looks pretty rough down there," he remarked, steering the conversation in a different direction.

Smythe's gaze lingered on his partner. Satisfied that the matter was settled, he turned his attention to the task at hand.

"Divert power to the shields," he replied with a business-like tone. "I'm starting our approach."

The twin-engine freighter entered Rogantu's upper atmosphere and surged through the volcanic planet's roiling skies. Buffeted by violent crosswinds that threatened to tear the ship apart, Smythe wrestled with the controls, fighting to keep the ship steady. Crimson lightning cracked across the churning clouds, causing his flight instruments to flicker. Each shudder and jolt echoed the planet's fury as the freighter fought to maintain course amidst the turbulence.

The forward viewport cleared when the ship finally emerged, revealing a harsh and unforgiving landscape. Jagged mountains loomed ominously, their sharp peaks piercing the sky, while rivers of molten lava snaked through the terrain below, glowing with fiery intensity.

"The refinery should be dead ahead," Smythe said, relying on his eyes for navigation as the displays kept flickering.

"Can we not say it like that?" Gort said nervously.

Smythe ignored the remark as he piloted the freighter over the desolate wasteland. He spotted a large facility on the horizon, its four towering smokestacks standing silent, long since dormant.

"There it is." Smythe pointed.

Gort's bulbous eyes narrowed on the abandoned refinery. A sigh of relief escaped him before he asked, "So how did you come across this place?"

Smythe hesitated, his grip tightening on the controls. "I used to work in these mines," he finally said. "Back then, the company was desperate for labor, so they resorted to convicts. I was doing time at the Vellorum Penal Colony when they transferred me here. This place … it's brutal, and I'm not just talking about the conditions. There are things beneath the surface—creatures we didn't know existed until it was too late. So, whatever you do, don't go wandering off."

Gort made a face. "You don't have to tell me twice." After a brief pause, he asked, "So, what happened?"

"Workers were dying right and left, and quotas were missed despite the constant influx of prison labor," Smythe explained, the memories still fresh in his mind. "The company was bleeding credits on defenses, but it wasn't enough to keep the creatures out. By the time they decided to shut it all down, it was too late—the refinery was overrun. That's when I made my move. Me and a few others commandeered this freighter and escaped off-world."

Gort nodded thoughtfully. Despite all his years working with the insectoid, this was the first time he had heard this story or much else about Smythe's past. Their first encounter came after a bounty hunting job went sideways for Smythe, and he hired Gort to repair the damaged freighter. Over time, Smythe kept returning for more refits, and Gort's skills proved invaluable, so much so that Smythe eventually brought him on as a full-time partner.

Despite their shared history, Smythe remained private, keeping his past to himself. Even so, Gort came to trust his partner implicitly—not just because the insectoid had saved his neck countless times, but because Smythe had always been true to his word, offering Gort only one promise: wealth.

The freighter approached the abandoned refinery from the southwest and slowed to a hover. In the fading daylight, Smythe activated the ship's exterior lights to get a clearer view.

"Doesn't look like much has changed," he remarked, no love lost in his tone.

The refinery, abandoned for years, was a picture of neglect and decay. A three-story structure with rounded, bullnose corners, its once-white walls were now stained a permanent gray, half-buried beneath drifts of black soot. At the north end, four towering smokestacks teetered on the brink of collapse, just one storm away from toppling over. Shattered or missing windows lined the walls and roof, while part of the east side had already given way to time and ruin.

Smythe had seen enough. He steered the freighter over the refinery toward a massive borehole on the east side, plunging deep into the planet's core. An extensive conveyor belt system, now rusting and in disrepair, once ferried raw ores from the underground mines into the refinery for processing.

Smythe sneered at the memory of his days of toiling underground. The company had driven them mercilessly, dangling promises of reduced sentences in exchange for their labor. In truth, no one was ever released early. If the quotas did not kill them, the harsh conditions or deadly indigenous lifeforms would. No convict was meant to survive this forsaken place—but Smythe had proved them wrong.

Seeing the facility at a standstill brought some measure of satisfaction. During his darkest days, that conveyor had been his torment, a symbol of the company's insatiable greed and relentless exploitation. Now, its stillness marked the company's downfall—at least on this world.

Next to Smythe, Gort peered out the viewport and noted shield emitters lining the compound's perimeter. "So, they used ray shields to fence you in?"

"Actually, those were meant to keep the predators out," Smythe replied matter-of-factly, "but little good they did."

He pointed to a gap in the line where one of the cone-shaped pillars was missing. In its place, a crater appeared as if the shield emitter had been swallowed from below.

"Did something eat it?" Gort asked, not sure he wanted to hear the answer.

"Gracylai," Smythe replied, the mere mention of the name sending a shiver up his spine. "They're nasty carnivores with dozens of legs and rows of sharp teeth. They're very fast and very dangerous, including the larvae."

Gort arched his eyebrow and joked nervously, "I'm beginning to see why you were so anxious to leave this place."

Smythe hmphed. "Only a fool would try to escape this place on foot. No matter which direction you run, getting caught out in the open, especially at night, is a death sentence … and it's even worse underground. We found their boreholes everywhere."

Gort swallowed the lump in his throat in the uneasy silence that followed.

Smythe steered the ship to the south. "Over here's the landing bay … at least what's left of it."

The freighter banked to the right, approaching a circular structure connected to the refinery. The landing bay's ceiling door remained open.

Gort leaned forward in his seat and peered inside. "Looks empty."

"Looks can be deceiving," Smythe warned. "Hold onto something. I'm starting the landing cycle."

The freighter's landing struts extended beneath the fuselage as maneuvering thrusters fired. With a steady hand, Smythe carefully guided the ship through the open roof, kicking up a swirling cloud of dust as he eased the freighter inside the hangar.

Gort sighed in relief as his partner started shutting down non-essential systems. "What next?"

"First, we set up motion sensors along the perimeter, then we can have a little chat with our guest."

By that, Gort knew their hostage was in for an uncomfortable evening if she refused to cooperate.

"Speaking of which …" Gort retrieved Ava's nano-ring from his pocket. "I figured this thing out. I disabled everything but the translator. We should be able to communicate with her now."

"Perfect," Smythe replied. "Maybe we won't need Hiromi after all."

The insectoid stood and exited the cockpit, with Gort close behind. They moved aft through the central passageway. As they passed the storage closet where Ava was confined, Smythe and Gort ignored the sounds of her frantic kicks and shouts behind the door.

Passing through the cargo hold where the Reaper was held, they arrived at the freighter's exit ramp. Smythe opened a wall cabinet and retrieved two rebreathers, handing one to his partner. Both devices had been pre-fitted, so a tight seal formed when the bounty hunters pulled them over their heads. They could breathe comfortably in the harsh environment while the clear face shields protected their eyes.

Gort gave Smythe a webbed thumbs up, signaling he was ready. Smythe responded by unshouldering his short-barrel, fast-repeating blaster rifle. Gort followed suit, unholstering his blaster.

"Shoot anything that moves," Smythe warned, his voice crackling over the rebreather's built-in comm unit. "And remember, the gracylai move fast, so lead your target."

"Swell," Gort muttered grimly.

Smythe pulled the hood of his cloak over his head, readied his weapon, and opened the outer hatch. As the ramp lowered, a rush of warm, ash-laden air swept inside, thick with the acrid scent of scorched earth. Distant winds howled, echoing throughout the abandoned facility.

The bounty hunters stood at the top of the ramp as it extended, their eyes scanning the hangar's shadowy interior. They exchanged a glance—a silent agreement to proceed cautiously.

Descending slowly, they stepped onto the ground, and their boots sank into soft ash, leaving perfect imprints of studded soles. The hangar was as empty and desolate as it had appeared from above, steeped in the oppressive silence of a place long forgotten.

Gort went right, sweeping his half of the hangar. He noted a toppled stack of cargo containers near the eastside exit, leading outside to the massive borehole. Guessing the containers were empty, he made a mental note to check them later, just in case. If the company had departed in a hurry, there was no telling what treasures they might have left behind.

Meanwhile, Smythe ventured left. Tightening his grip on his weapon, he made his way around the underside of the freighter, darting his eyes from shadow to shadow, searching for any sign of movement.

Finishing their sweep, they met near the bow of the ship.

"All clear," Smythe reported, noting the relief on his partner's face. "Go grab the tripods," he instructed. "We'll start securing the perimeter."

"Sure thing," Gort replied and ducked inside the ship. He reappeared moments later with four cylinders cradled in his arms.

Smythe met him at the bottom of the ramp, still keeping a watchful eye for hostiles. Without a word, he took two devices from Gort and set out to place his first unit in the southwest corner of the bay. Gort did the same, taking responsibility for the southeast corner before moving to the north end.

They worked methodically, aligning the cylinders in their designated locations. When the system was activated, three legs extended from the base of each unit for stability. The sensors then synced together, forming a quadrangulated perimeter. A faint hum filled the air, signaling the network was active and ready to detect unwelcome visitors.

With the perimeter established, Smythe and Gort returned to the ramp. Despite fortifying their position as best they could, neither felt completely safe.

Gort glanced upward, frowning at the exposed ceiling. "Remind me to build a sensor that hovers," he said warily. "Something to give us overhead protection."

"Remember to build a sensor that hovers," Smythe replied sarcastically.

Gort gave him a look. "Funny."

"But you've got a point," Smythe said seriously. "With all this interference, I doubt we'll pick up any approaching ships, so stay sharp."

Sensing his partner was about to leave, Gort asked, "Where are you going?"

"Inspect the hull," Smythe answered. "Those Aiwan shoretroopers that got the jump on me might have caused some damage. I'll be in shortly. See if you can reach Hiromi and get her ETA. We don't have much time and the sooner we can leave, the better."

"You got that right," Gort seconded.

As he made his way up the ramp, Gort was unaware of the tiny larvae attached to the back of his boot.

9
ABOMINATIONS

Two guards, both former American military personnel, sat inside a small security control room filled with closed-circuit television cameras and alarm equipment. Their duty was to monitor Mathias's entire compound, but they were currently focused on the rooftop pool above the employee quarters. The only occupant was Luna.

"That's twenty minutes," the controller operating the surveillance system muttered, shaking his head in disbelief. "How long can she stay down there?"

"As long as she wants. She's a freakin' alien," his supervisor replied, not bothering to glance up from his comic book, his feet casually propped on the desk.

The controller zoomed in on the pool's deep end, where Luna sat cross-legged at the bottom. "But what's she doing down there?" he persisted.

"Underwater basket weaving," his supervisor quipped, yawning.

The controller shot an unamused look over his shoulder before returning to the screen. "I'm serious. I think she's up to something."

With an exasperated sigh, the supervisor slapped his comic shut and put his feet on the floor. "Will you relax already? She's a fish, that's what they do.

Now, fuhgeddaboudit," he said with a New York mafia accent.

Unsatisfied, the controller tried to increase the camera's optical zoom again, but he already had it set to maximum. Even with the water still and clear, this was the best image he could hope for.

The controller huffed in frustration. "I'm going to log it."

"Why?" his supervisor scoffed. "She's not doing anything." He tucked his comic inside his nearby backpack and came to his feet. "Speaking of logs, I need to take a dump. Don't do anything stupid while I'm gone … I mean it."

As the supervisor reached for the door handle, things got interesting.

"Hey, Supe, check this out!"

The supervisor stopped short of the door and rounded. "Now what?"

He did a double-take at seeing Deanna Crowder, Edmund Mathias's girlfriend, as she strode across the pool deck. The buxom blonde always made for good eye candy, so he eagerly returned to his seat with his eyes glued to the screen.

The two guards watched silently as Deanna selected an empty lounge chair and meticulously spread out her towel. She placed her vibrant designer handbag beside the chair, removed her sunglasses, and set them on the glass-top table. With a graceful motion, she slipped off her crocheted cover-up, revealing a sleek, all-black sling-style micro-bikini beneath.

The supervisor leaned closer to the screen and grinned. "Man, I've got dental floss that can cover more area than that."

The guards kept their eyes on Deanna as she casually slipped off her sandals. Bending over to retrieve a hair tie from her bag, she left little to the imagination, prompting the guards to shift uncomfortably in their seats.

Straightening, Deanna adjusted her swimsuit and strolled toward the pool's shallow end. As she passed the camera, she flashed a playful smile and blew a kiss, fully aware of the guards' attention. Her gaze then shifted to the pool's deep end, where the Aiwan remained motionless underwater.

Since returning from Challenger Deep, Luna had established a daily ritual of visiting the pool before every meal. Though confined, the private pool offered her a precious opportunity to exercise and occasionally meditate undisturbed.

Deanna cautiously tested the water with her painted toenails, unsure how Luna would react. To her relief, the Aiwan did not respond immediately. But Deanna was smart enough to realize that stillness did not equate to inaction; Luna could strike at any moment.

Deanna's goddess-like presence captivated the guards as she descended the steps. Only when the boss's girlfriend slid into the water did the guards think to check on Luna. Their expressions transformed from heavenly bliss to sheer panic as the Aiwan effortlessly kicked her way to the surface.

"No, no, no," the supervisor muttered as he fumbled for his radio. "Mike-1 to the pool! Repeat, Mike-1 to the pool! Code Red!"

Luna's head breached the surface just enough to reveal her mesmerizing, bulbous blue eyes. At the opposite end of the pool, Deanna stood waist-high in the water with a serene smile as she met Luna's gaze. Her hands gently skimmed the water back and forth, creating mild ripples.

"I knew I'd find you here," Deanna said, calm but confident. "I was hoping we could finally meet."

Luna lifted herself a few inches higher above the water, revealing her mouth and jutted chin. She knew who Deanna was and her connection to Edmund, though they had never formally met.

"I am Luna," she replied, her curiosity piqued by Deanna's intentions.

"Yes, I know," Deanna responded with amusement. She had spent countless hours watching video footage from the hidden cameras Edmund had placed in Luna's bedroom. "I'm Deanna, Edmund's girlfriend."

Luna arched her eyebrow. "Girlfriend? You are his mate?"

"Something like that," Deanna replied dryly, wading closer. "But I'm not his wife, if that's what you want to know."

Luna's brow scrunched slightly as she considered the foreign concept.

"What?" Deanna asked, reading her puzzled expression. "You don't have girlfriends on Aiwa?"

"No," Luna replied matter-of-factly. "On Aiwa, a female will choose her mate and remain together for life."

Deanna chuckled. "Til death do you part, huh?" Luna nodded. "It must be nice," Deanna continued. "Marital bliss is put on a pedestal here on Earth, but most newlyweds don't make it. Maybe humans can learn a thing or two from Aiwans in this area."

Picking up on Deanna's underlying sarcasm, Luna chose not to pursue the topic, at least for now. Instead, she asked, "Are you not afraid of me?"

Deanna smiled. "Should I be?"

Luna shrugged as she continued treading water effortlessly. "Most humans are either suspicious of me or want to study me in a lab. You are the first one to actually engage me in conversation."

Touched, Deanna smiled empathetically. "What about Rose?"

"You mean, Dr. Landry?" Luna corrected. "She was brought here for a purpose and now she is gone."

The Aiwan's response sounded harsher than Deanna expected. "Hm," she muttered. "Edmund seemed to think you two were getting along rather well. So, you don't miss her?"

"I miss our conversations," Luna admitted. "I also miss my home, but I cannot do anything about either at the moment."

Deanna started to form a reply when the side door burst open. Startled, both swimmers turned to find two armed guards entering the pool area and rushing toward them.

The men slowed at the pool's edge, chests heaving, only to realize it was a false alarm. Deanna and Luna floated calmly, showing no signs of a struggle or distress. Both were casually treading water, staring back at the guards, puzzled by the sudden interruption.

"Can't a girl swim in peace?" Deanna snapped irritably.

Catching his breath, the senior guard replied, "Sorry, ma'am. Is everything okay?"

"Do we look okay?"

The guards' eyes darted to Luna, who casually waved and smiled.

"Apologies, ma'am. We just wanted to make sure you're okay," the guard explained, fighting the urge not to steal a glance at Deanna's chest.

"I'm fine … *we're* fine," Deanna corrected, much to Luna's approval. "Now go back to your camera room, you pervs."

"You heard her," came a familiar voice.

Both guards rounded sharply to find Edmund Mathias approaching. He looked as if he had just stepped off his yacht, wearing a "smart casual" combination of white slacks, a dark blue button-down shirt, and a light gray blazer. With the alligator leather belt and matching tan loafers, the outfit cost more than both guards' monthly salaries combined.

The senior guard bowed submissively. "Very sorry, sir. We—"

"—Just do as she says and get lost," Edmund said flippantly, shooing them away like pesky gnats. The guards did not say another word and quickly made for the door. Over his shoulder, Edmund called to them, "And I'll be having words with Mr. Renzo about you when he gets back!"

Silence fell over the group as Edmund kept his head cocked sideways, listening patiently until he heard the door close. Alone at last, he turned to Deanna and Luna. His face brightened as if the ugliness of the last few seconds had never happened.

"Ah, much better," he said, straightening the cuffs of his shirt sleeves.

"Now, where were we?"

Deanna smiled at Luna. "We were just getting acquainted."

Edmund's eyes bounced from Deanna to Luna. Considering that Aiwans rarely wore clothes and his scantily clad girlfriend's attire barely qualified as such, he looked down at his outfit and quipped, "I feel so overdressed."

"There's room for one more," Deanna invited in a sultry tone.

Edmund grinned, although this was not the kind of threesome he had ever imagined. Clearing his throat, he steered the conversation elsewhere.

"Actually, I hate to spoil the mood but I'm afraid duty calls," Edmund said. To Luna, he added, "I need your help with something urgent."

"Is everything alright?" Luna asked, still treading water.

Edmund turned serious. "NORAD detected an object in space. It's not man made. They said it originated near Mars."

Luna's eyes widened with excitement, and she hurried toward the side ladder. Edmund grabbed Deanna's towel from the lounge chair and was there to meet Luna as she exited the water.

"Thank you," Luna said as Edmund wrapped the towel around her. As she began to dry off, she added, "There is a hyperspace lane near Mars. We used it to get here. Perhaps it is a rescue ship."

"Perhaps," Edmund considered, noting the hope in Luna's voice. "But it's much smaller than any of the other Aiwan ships we've encountered."

"Do you have visuals?" Luna asked.

Her choice of words initially threw Edmund off, but he quickly caught on. "Yes, hang on." He fumbled for his phone, pulled up the photos, and traded his device for Luna's towel.

Luna recognized the spacecraft immediately and furrowed her brow. "This is an Aiwan deep space probe," she explained, somewhat confused but still relieved that it was not a harvester vessel. "Kypa used similar probes to search the galaxy for magnetarite."

"It entered Earth's orbit a few hours ago," Edmund added, watching Luna closely for her reaction.

Luna's gaze drifted downward as she considered this unexpected news. It did not make any sense. Why would Kypa move the probe into Earth's orbit instead of sending a rescue ship or diplomatic envoy? If Earth and Aiwa were indeed on friendly terms, it seemed unlikely King Loka would brazenly dispatch a remote probe to scan the human's homeworld without their consent.

Then, it dawned on her: the cloaking device. As soon as the device in Challenger Deep went active, hiding the crystals, the probe would have detected the anomaly and moved closer to investigate. Luna considered this possibility. Although the probe's presence was not exactly ideal for diplomatic relations, there was a strong chance it had alerted Kypa, potentially expediting a response and a possible rescue mission.

Luna handed back the phone. "Thank you," she said. "Please keep me posted if there are any new developments. I will be in the lab."

Edmund stepped aside as the Aiwan made her way past him and crossed the concrete deck to the exit. He turned to Deanna, who was now resting against the side of the pool with her arms crossed under her chin. She winked as she lazily flutter-kicked in the water, playfully inviting him to join her.

"Not now," he muttered in a huff, tossing Luna's wet towel toward her as he hurried away.

Moments later, Edmund caught up with Luna as she waited for the elevator. She was pacing in a tight circle, deep in thought.

"Is it the cloaking device?" he deduced.

"I believe so," Luna admitted. "The probe would automatically investigate the sudden drop in its readings, which got me thinking about Earth's other crystal deposits. There might be more out there."

Edmund liked the sound of that, but a warning bell went off in his head. If Luna was right and more crystals existed, then they needed to cloak more than just Challenger Deep to keep off-world harvesters from eyeing his claim.

The elevator bell chimed, and the doors opened to reveal Dr. Vlachos. He blinked in surprise, not expecting to find Mathias and Luna standing in his path.

"Ah, Señor Mathias, I was just coming to see you."

Edmund stepped into the elevator first. "You got two minutes, Doc," he said, pressing the L2 button. "We're in a hurry."

Vlachos backpedaled, stepping into the back corner as Luna ducked inside. She made eye contact with the scientist and smiled politely, though her thoughts were still preoccupied with the probe.

As the elevator doors closed, Edmund asked, "So, what's on your mind?"

Dr. Vlachos hesitated, wondering if he could or should disclose sensitive information in front of the Aiwan.

"It's okay," Edmund assured him. "Like I said in the staff meeting, Luna's with us now. Whatever you have to tell me, you can say to her."

Vlachos nodded, clearing his throat. "Very well, it's about the serum. I'm afraid we're going to need more time."

Mathias blew out an exhaustive breath. "We don't have more time. Our buyers are hounding me for their first shipment. I can't stall them much longer."

"But the side effects—"

"Screw the side effects," Edmund said bluntly. "Without their money, our harvesting venture is dead in the water … pun intended. Everything we do at Challenger Deep has to be off the books, meaning I can't divert funds from the company without drawing attention."

Even as he said it, Edmund knew he was fooling himself. By now, every government in the world probably knew about his activities at Challenger Deep and was undoubtedly maneuvering to get a piece of the action—especially the Americans. Still, Mathias Industries had the upper hand and the necessary resources to pull it off, including his ace-in-the-hole, Luna. But the risk of political intervention, or worse, another military strike, could set him back indefinitely.

"Perhaps I can be of assistance," Luna offered. "If I knew the problem, I might be able to shed new light on the subject."

Mathias and Vlachos exchanged glances. Both were thinking the same thing—what harm could it do? Edmund nodded curtly, prodding the doctor to elaborate.

"Well," Vlachos began, "we have developed what we call a force enhancement serum. Its purpose is to boost human performance and allow soldiers on the battlefield to experience increased strength, agility, and speed with a quicker recovery time. Our test subjects exceeded all expectations, but within the first month of their initial dosage, they began to experience side effects."

"What kind of side effects?" Luna inquired.

"It starts with tremors in the hands." Vlachos explained, holding out his hand to demonstrate. "The symptoms progress to restless leg syndrome, insomnia, and increased aggression."

"They also stop responding to orders," Edmund added with dismay. "You see, we tried building upon MK-ULTRA, but our subjects tend to go rabid and die of cardiac arrest within three months."

Startled, Luna connected to Edmund's mind, swiftly searching for insight into MK-ULTRA. What she learned was appalling. MK-ULTRA was a covert, CIA-led project involving illegal human experimentation. They used hallucinogenic drugs to break down test subjects during interrogations, forcing confessions through brainwashing and psychological torture.

"Our serum works in two phases," Dr. Vlachos explained. "First, it makes a person susceptible to commands, then—"

"—It strips away their morals," Edmund finished, smiling with satisfaction.

"And that, above all else, is what our clients are buying. They want soldiers who will obey without question, kill without conscience, and march to their death without a second thought."

"I see," Luna said thoughtfully, masking her disdain. The serum violated every principle she held dear, but this was not the time or place to debate ethics. "I would like to observe your test subjects."

"Certainly," Vlachos replied, welcoming her involvement.

When the elevator arrived at Sub-Level 2, Edmund stepped out into the hallway first. Luna and Dr. Vlachos followed in an awkward exchange that ended with the doctor politely insisting Luna go next.

In the hallway, Luna naturally gravitated to the left toward her lab, where the dismantled Aiwan Seeker resided. However, Edmund turned right out of the elevator and led them down the corridor in the opposite direction. They passed several technicians along the way, some smiling cordially at Luna and even offering a hesitant wave, while others kept their heads down without making eye contact. It left Luna wondering what made them more nervous, Edmund's presence or hers.

Edmund remained oblivious to these subtleties. With his eyes fixed on his phone as he walked, he only occasionally glanced up to avoid colliding with a wall. Luna and Dr. Vlachos followed behind in silence, the sound of their footfalls echoing in the sterile corridor.

Luna could sense the tension in both men. Understanding the serum's critical role in Mathias's harvesting plans, she realized why they had detoured to Vlachos's lab. There could be no further setbacks with the serum; the orbiting probe would have to wait.

As they neared the doctor's lab, Luna detected faint cries in the distance. The muffled voices grew louder and more distinct with each step. Then, it dawned on her that these were not the cries of needy infants but rather the unmistakable screams of tortured souls.

"Criminy, can't you get them to shut up?" Edmund said irritably over his shoulder. "It sounds like a kennel down here."

"I'll take care of it," Vlachos replied, hoping to appease his boss. Inwardly, he knew he could do nothing about the noise aside from heavily sedating all of the test subjects, which was what they were already doing in the worst cases.

Vlachos was not the only one who caught Edmund's complaint. With enhanced hearing, the nearest test subject overheard the brief exchange between Mathias and the doctor, triggering a surge of desperation. The patient's frantic pleas to be freed echoed through the hall, sparking a chain reaction. One by one, the occupants joined in until the entire hallway erupted into chaos.

"This is what we're dealing with," Edmund said with frustration, raising his voice to be heard.

As he approached one of the random doors, Edmund put away his phone and opened the sliding peephole. He was greeted by the foul odor of feces and recoiled, wincing from the stench. A female test subject appeared suddenly on the opposite side. Staring wide-eyed through the opening, she foamed at the mouth, gnashing her teeth.

Mathias backpedaled sharply. "For crying out loud," he spat, straightening his jacket. "Freakin' animal."

Vlachos nodded with disappointment. "When they reach this state," he explained to Luna, "there's nothing we can do but wait for the serum to kill them."

Edmund turned to Luna, keen on hearing her insights. "What's your take?" he asked, gesturing toward the door, inviting her to see for herself.

Appalled at his callousness, Luna refrained from commenting and stepped in front of the door. Not wanting to startle the patient, she kept her distance, allowing the test subject a moment to observe her first. Surprisingly, the pounding and screaming suddenly ceased.

Luna remained still for a few seconds longer before approaching. Maintaining her composure, she calmly approached the peephole and peered inside. The concrete-walled cell was brightly lit and furnished with a metal toilet and a concrete slab to sleep on. However, the test subject was nowhere in sight.

Assuming the woman was crouched low against the door, Luna turned her head and pressed her ear to the cold metal. Blocking out the noise around her, she could hear the test subject's strained breathing—short, raspy breaths interspersed with deep-wheezing inhales—clear signs of congestive heart failure.

Closing the peephole, Luna turned to Dr. Vlachos. "This one is dying?"

"Sí," Vlachos replied. "Two … maybe three days tops."

Luna frowned. "Unfortunately, my expertise is not in human biology. Perhaps later, I could look at the patient's blood work and offer some insight, but for now, I would like to study the probe."

"Of course," Edmund agreed, hands clasped in front. He then gestured in the direction of Luna's lab. "Shall we leave Dr. Vlachos and his team to their work? I'm sure they'll resolve this little hiccup *sooner* rather than later," he said in a not-so-subtle, veiled threat. "By the way, you might try dialing back the Scopolamine. That might help."

Vlachos's eyes flashed with surprise. He had not expected Edmund to know of the compound commonly referred to as Devil's Breath, but the idea had merit. "That's an intriguing suggestion," he said thoughtfully. "I'll certainly look into it."

"You do that," Edmund replied snidely. "C'mon, Luna, I'll walk you to the lab. Luna?"

Edmund and Vlachos turned to Luna and found her standing still, eyes down in deep thought. She had closely observed the two men's brief exchange and found Dr. Vlachos's reaction to Mathais's unsolicited advice both curious and unsettling, though for reasons she could not quite explain.

Edmund eyed her curiously. "Luna?"

Blinking back to the moment, she replied innocently, "Yes?"

Edmund chuckled. "You zoned out on us there. Everything okay?"

Luna nodded with embarrassment. "Forgive me, my mind went elsewhere. You were saying?"

"Nothing, really," Edmund said, his tone deceptively casual. "Just that it's time we leave Dr. Vlachos to his important work." He tapped his Jaeger-LeCoultre watch. "Time is money after all, and we wouldn't want to waste either."

Setting aside her concerns, Luna bid farewell to Vlachos and quickly switched her focus to the Aiwan probe orbiting Earth. Edmund fell in step beside her, and they began discussing options on their way down the corridor.

Dr. Vlachos watched them leave, his thoughts still preoccupied with Mathias's suggestion to tweak the serum. Once the hallway cleared, he turned and strode in the opposite direction. Reaching a pair of double doors, Vlachos swiped his badge against the card reader. The doors swung open automatically, and he stepped into the research department just as Dr. Martin emerged from a side room with Zoe, his most promising patient. The faint, distant cries echoing in the corridor abruptly cut off as the double doors closed behind him.

Noticing Zoe's unsettled expression, Vlachos offered a warm smile as he approached. He bent slightly to meet her gaze, his tone gentle and reassuring.

"I'm sorry for all that dreadful noise," Vlachos said softly. "Soon, you'll be able to go home to your family, a wealthy woman."

But his words did little to comfort Zoe. The attack had planted seeds of doubt about her safety here, and for the first time, she yearned for the quiet simplicity of her village—far from the violent patients locked away in this facility. Yet, it was not the abominations confined behind those doors that truly terrified her. What chilled her to the core was the fear that they might turn her into one of them.

10
PAYBACK

Planet Earth
Embassy of the United States of America, Lima, Peru

The U.S. Embassy in Lima is the third largest embassy in the Americas and serves as the official diplomatic mission of the United States to the Republic of Peru. Situated on twenty-one acres in the Monterrico residential area of Santiago de Surco, the embassy was meticulously crafted in 1995 by Peruvian architect Bernardo Fort-Brescia. This five-story, rectangular structure seamlessly integrates ancient Incan motifs with modern elements that honor Peru's vibrant textile history. Yet, its architectural genius transcends mere aesthetics.

The embassy was purposely built in response to targeted attacks against Americans by the terrorist group Shining Path. Its façade, featuring a blend of pastel colors with bright surfaces, was cleverly designed to create the illusion of dimension. In reality, the building's exterior is entirely flat to prevent protestors and terrorists from scaling the walls—assuming they could even get that far. A reinforced concrete wall encircled the property, its imposing structure complemented by massive, ornate barriers at the entrance—designed to keep explosive-laden vehicles away from the building.

Lima Station Chief Paul Wiggins was grateful for the foresight of these security measures. Seated by the window, sipping his strong Arabica coffee, he peered outside his top-floor office, observing a group of protestors outside the main entrance. He noted that the crowd was larger than yesterday, and the day had just started.

Wiggins cocked his head sideways to listen to the group's faint chants.

"¡Abajo Estados Unidos!" *Down with the United States!*

Their anger, of course, was indirectly aimed at him for the overt attack against Edmund Mathias's lab in Satipo. However, Wiggins's involvement in Operation Bold Fortress and his identity as the CIA's chief intelligence officer in Peru remained a closely guarded secret—at least for now. Still, the protesters had chosen to vent their anger at the embassy instead, the quintessential symbol of American aggression in Peru. And since the attack became public knowledge, protests and bomb threats were daily occurrences at the embassy, creating an air of tension throughout the building.

Currently, the embassy was locked down, and visitors were not allowed. The United States Marine Corps Region 4 Embassy Security Group and every available special agent from the Diplomatic Security Service patrolled the perimeter. Meanwhile, State Department personnel stood ready to shred and burn classified documents at a moment's notice.

Wiggins hoped it did not come to that, but the repercussions of Operation Bold Fortress extended throughout the hemisphere. Edmund Mathias had seen to that. In the days following the costly rescue mission, the eccentric billionaire had spun the facts to turn public opinion against the United States. Now, every Peruvian politician on his payroll had taken to the streets, manning a bullhorn and screaming insults at President Fitzgerald in an effort to expel the Americans from South America. Meanwhile, Ambassador Tooley worked feverishly down the hall to find a diplomatic solution to clean up this mess.

A knock on the door startled Wiggins back to the present. He turned to find Deputy Station Chief Eileen Parker standing in the doorway. Wiggins chuckled at his own expense and waved her in.

Returning to the window, Wiggins gestured outside with his coffee mug. "Shades of Tehran in '79 out there," he said grimly, referring to the Iran Hostage Crisis when Iranian revolutionaries seized sixty-six Americans. The ordeal lasted 444 days before the hostages were eventually released, but the connection to today's situation did not escape Wiggins.

During the Iranian crisis, the U.S. conceived a bold rescue mission involving a retrofitted C-130 with reverse rocket engines mounted to the airframe. The plan was to make an unconventional, short landing inside the Shahid Shiroudi football stadium to extract the hostages. However, Operation Credible Sport never got off the ground. During a test flight, the retrofitted C-130 crashed when the reverse rockets fired too early. Fortunately, the test crew survived, but the mission was scrapped when the hostages were later freed. Ironically, that failed operation led to the creation of the 160th Special Operations Aviation Regiment—the same Night Stalkers who led Operation Bold Fortress against Mathias's compound.

Wiggins and his deputy, Eileen, were the only people in the building who could make this connection. While the ambassador was aware of Bold Fortress, she was not privy to the mission's details, which would stay a secret for everyone's safety.

Deputy Parker approached the window. Looking down at the crowd, she wondered how many of them actually knew what had happened in Satipo and why. It was more likely that Mathias was paying them a minuscule sum to stir up trouble.

She turned her attention skyward, where menacing clouds were approaching from the west. "Looks like we're in for some seriously bad weather," she grimaced.

Wiggins grinned behind his mug. "Yeah, Mother Nature's smiling on us," he replied, then took a sip. "If that storm's as bad as Cyclone Yuka, it should chase the crowds away for at least a few days. By then, maybe all this will blow over … pun intended."

Parker smiled and crossed her fingers, hoping that would make it so.

As if on cue, chubby raindrops began tapping against the window. "Speak of the devil," Wiggins said, raising his mug in mock salute.

Out of habit, he looked down at the flagpole outside to gauge the wind speed, only to find it bare. The ambassador had ordered "Old Glory" to be taken down to quell public outcry. Wiggins and many others disagreed, but it was not their call. Instead, he studied the trees and noted the wind had picked up as dark clouds moved over the capital.

As the rain intensified, Wiggins and Parker were relieved to see a growing number of people in the crowd lower their signs and disperse. Peru's government had been so unstable in recent years; the last thing they wanted was to be the catalyst for more upheaval.

Parker handed her boss several 8x10 photos. "For you," she offered.

Wiggins glimpsed the top photo. It was the Aiwan, Luna, in the pool at Mathias's compound to the north. Swiveling his chair away from the window, he situated himself at his desk. Parker crossed the room to close the door, then sat on the opposite side of her boss's desk.

The second photo made his eyes widen. "Whoa," Wiggins muttered.

"Yeah, I thought you'd like that one," Parker replied, which she too favored. "That's Mathias's girlfriend, Deanna."

"Does that even qualify as a swimsuit?"

Parker chuckled. "Exactly—that's the whole idea." She admired the photo a moment longer before shifting back to business. "Anyway, with round-the-clock drone support now, we can keep better tabs on the Aiwan and Mathias."

"I'm sure Mr. Choi will be thrilled to hear that," Wiggins quipped with a touch of sarcasm, flipping through the remaining surveillance photos. Mathias appeared in the later images before he departed with the Aiwan.

"Conclusions?" Wiggins asked.

"Mathias has a counter surveillance system generating white noise, so we weren't able to record any audio, but the video footage was interesting," Parker reported. "There's a couple minutes of Luna and the girlfriend talking one-on-one in the water before some overzealous guards interrupted. Then, Mathias showed up and sent them away. Maybe they perceived Luna as a threat," she speculated.

"Luna appears to be able to come and go as she pleases. That's interesting," Wiggins observed.

"I agree," Parker replied. "Mathias then said something to Luna, and she exited the pool immediately. In the last photo, you can see him showing her his phone, then Luna departed in a hurry."

"What do you think?" Wiggins asked.

"If I had to bet," Parker answered, "Mathias showed her that orbiting spacecraft. Maybe it has him spooked."

"Explain," Wiggins prodded, encouraging her analysis.

"My hunch is that this spacecraft is not here to land an invasion force. NASA says it's smaller than all three Aiwan ships we've seen before, including the Reaper. Maybe it's here to observe and gather intel."

"The fact it has not initiated contact makes me think it's not a diplomatic envoy," Wiggins speculated. "It may not be Aiwan at all. Could be one of those harvesters we heard about."

Parker frowned as she nodded in agreement.

Wiggins handed back the photos. "Send these to Langley and see what they think."

"Can do," Parker said as she stood up, a wry grin spreading across her face. "Need me to make any extra copies while I'm at it?"

Wiggins raised an eyebrow. "Very funny, but I'll pass," he said dryly.

With a casual shrug of indifference, Parker dropped the matter and saw herself out, closing the door behind her. As soon as she was gone, Wiggins rotated his chair back to the window and came to his feet. Looking outside, he was glad to see the crowds had dispersed entirely. The storm had intensified rapidly, unleashing a torrential downpour and fierce gusts of wind that whipped through the area, bending tree branches and scattering debris. To the west, jagged bolts of lightning tore across the darkened sky, followed by a deep, resonating rumble of thunder that seemed to shake the very air.

That was fast, Wiggins thought to himself, somewhat surprised.

While the storm had cleared out the protestors, it may have ruined his chances for a rendezvous with Elena, a local señorita he had been dating.

Comparing the current conditions outside to the trail of destruction inflicted by Cyclone Yuka, Wiggins remained hopeful. It was still early, and in a few hours, the storm might let up enough for him to sneak out.

He picked up his cell phone and texted a simple message to Elena: *Tonight?*

She responded immediately with two heart emojis.

Twelve hours later, it was past nightfall, and the storm showed no sign of letting up. The city was now cast in complete darkness; power was out in several areas, including a ten-block radius around the embassy. Backup generators kept the emergency lights on inside the building, as well as the exterior lights and security systems to protect the perimeter.

Wiggins eyed his watch, debating how much Elena's companionship meant to him this evening. The storm's severity certainly gave him pause, but he knew it had to be now if he was going to go. Most of the staff had retired to the basement, where a makeshift dormitory of foldout cots had been set up. Sneaking out unnoticed would be easy. Only the guards would be privy to his discreet exit.

"Screw it," he muttered, making the decision to go. *A man has needs.*

Picking up the phone, Wiggins hit the speed dial button for the security office on the ground floor.

A female Marine answered immediately. "Security Control, this is Corporal Dayley. How may I help you, sir?"

"Colonel Terry, please."

"Yes, sir. Standby one," she replied, then transferred the call.

After a brief pause, Colonel Terry, commanding officer of the Marine Corps embassy security detachment, came on the line. "This is Colonel Terry."

"Colonel, this is Wiggins. How we lookin' down there?"

"All's quiet, sir," Terry replied. "We've battened down the hatches and put everyone to bed. Fingers crossed it'll be an uneventful night."

"Well, I don't want to jinx it, but I need to go outside."

Terry hesitated, then replied tactfully, "Sir, I don't think that's a good—"

"—I understand your concern, Colonel," Wiggins interrupted. "Only a fool would go out in weather like this, I know, but duty calls," he lied.

Colonel Terry was well aware of Wiggins's role as Lima Station Chief, although the embassy directory listed him as a senior analyst in the office of the Intellectual Property Attaché. Yet, despite Terry's objections, his hands were tied. Wiggins outranked him.

"Then, can I at least send someone with you, sir?" he implored.

"That won't be necessary, Colonel. I'll be fine. Just let your team know I'm coming down the north stairwell and will be using the tunnel."

"Copy that."

"And Colonel," Wiggins added, "do me a favor and send a runner. I don't want this broadcast over the comms. Got it?"

"Yes, sir," Terry replied. "What time can we expect you back?"

Wiggins eyed the clock, imagining himself in a warm bed with Elena's slender naked body draped over him. He wrestled with how long he could tempt fate, considering the weather and commute time both ways.

After a brief pause, he replied, "I'll be back by zero four hundred."

"Copy that, zero four hundred," Terry confirmed, making a mental note.

"Thanks, I'm on my way down."

Wiggins ended the call and shut off his computer. He then stowed two classified folders inside his desk, tugging the drawer to ensure it was locked tight. Slipping into his black overcoat, Wiggins grabbed his umbrella and made for the door. Before leaving, he scanned his office once more, ensuring everything was locked down, and flicked off the lights.

After securing his office door, he headed swiftly for the north stairwell. The stairs were eerily quiet and dimly lit by emergency lights. Umbrella in hand, Wiggins gripped the handrail for guidance, descending eagerly toward the night ahead.

Arriving at the basement, he opened the exit door to find a darkened figure standing in his path. Wiggins froze, his breath catching in his throat.

"Whoa, you startled me," Wiggins said nervously.

"Good evening, sir," came the voice of a lone Marine silhouetted by the emergency lights running along the floor. "Your badge, please."

The Marine turned on his tactical flashlight as Wiggins handed over his security badge. Through the glow of the red light, Wiggins could see the Marine dressed in camouflage fatigues with an M-18 pistol holstered to his leg.

"Helluva night, huh?" Wiggins said, squinting in the light.

"It is," the Marine replied, comparing the photo on the badge to Wiggins's face. Satisfied, he switched off the light and returned the credentials. "Thank you, sir." After a slight hesitation, the Marine asked, "With all due respect, sir, would you reconsider going out in this weather?"

Wiggins chuckled. "Did your commander put you up to that?" Before the Marine could reply, he added, "Never mind, don't answer that. Rain or shine, we can agree that when duty calls, we answer, right?"

"Oorah," the Marine acknowledged and stepped aside. "Can I walk you out?" he offered.

"No, that won't be necessary, but thanks anyway," Wiggins replied. "See you soon."

The Marine nodded and continued his patrol. Wiggins watched him disappear down the hallway and then turned to an unmarked door on his left. He typed in his six-digit access code on the cipher lock's keypad. A soft click signaled the door's release, and he stepped into a pitch-black, underground tunnel.

Running his hand along the wall, Wiggins located the light switch and flipped it on. The ceiling lights blinked on in sequence, illuminating a long, narrow path to the exit at the far end.

After securing the door behind him, Wiggins began his three-block trek beneath the city. This excursion was the first time he had used the underground passage, built as an emergency exit to evacuate the embassy staff in case of a riot. As he moved through, his footsteps echoed in the concrete corridor, and a sly grin spread across his face. Wiggins could not help but wonder if any of his predecessors had ever used the tunnel for similar nocturnal activities.

By the time he reached the end, his demeanor turned serious. Putting on his game face, Wiggins knew that once he stepped outside, he would be vulnerable. Despite the storm and cover of darkness, he could not dismiss the possibility that unseen eyes might be watching the exit.

"Time for some dry cleaning," he muttered to himself.

"Dry cleaning" was slang for counter-surveillance techniques used by operatives to avoid detection or shake a tail. For Wiggins, this was Espionage 101. Every intelligence organization drilled these skills into their field operatives—and he would know. Ten years ago, Wiggins had trained cadets in these very techniques at The Farm, the CIA's secret domestic training base at Camp Peary in Williamsburg, Virginia. Tonight, he would put those skills to the test.

At the exit, Wiggins closed his eyes and took a calming breath to focus. He pictured his route to Elena's apartment four blocks away. Wiggins knew the area like the back of his hand and reminded himself always to have an out in case someone tried to stop him.

"Face down, eyes up," he reminded himself, planning to use his umbrella to shield his face from any possible surveillance.

He would be at Elena's in less than ten minutes if everything went according to plan. An image of her answering the door wearing nothing but a smile popped into his head, eliciting a grin before he quickly pushed the distraction aside.

He entered his access code on the wall-mounted keypad, and the exit door unlocked. Wiggins eased the door open, bracing for the possibility of someone waiting on the other side to force their way in. But the sally port—a small chamber with two steel doors on either end to control entry—was empty.

Relieved, Wiggins exited the tunnel and secured the door behind him. Now standing inside the dimly lit sally port, which was no bigger than a walk-in kitchen pantry, he entered his code at the second door. When it unlocked, Wiggins slowly pushed the panic bar open.

Again, he readied himself for unwanted company on the other side of the door—but found nothing but a steep flight of stairs. Wiggins ascended the stairwell, mindful of his noise discipline. At the top, he came to what appeared to be a solid, cinder-block wall.

Catching his breath, Wiggins tapped the tablet-sized monitor mounted on the wall to his right. The screen came to life, displaying a live video feed of the law office of Rodrigo y Herrera, a bogus legal firm used as a front by the CIA.

The night vision display confirmed the office on the other side of the faux wall was vacant, its large windows offering a stark view of the deserted street in the background. Satisfied, Wiggins entered his code for the third time. The hidden door unlocked, and he pushed it open, revealing the law office's administrative area, complete with three metal desks and a modest reception area.

Stepping inside the office, Wiggins found it shrouded in darkness and an unsettling stillness, broken only by the howling winds and steady patter of rain against the windows. He rounded on the open door behind him, where a bookcase was cleverly mounted on the opposite side. Among the neatly arranged books, only one stood out—*Constitución Política del Perú*. The book was slightly askew, but it slid seamlessly back into alignment as he closed the door.

Suddenly, a flash of lightning flooded the room with stark white light, casting sharp, fleeting shadows across the walls. Wiggins froze and waited for darkness to return. Crossing the room, he moved carefully, mindful not to disturb anything. At the front door, he could feel his heartbeat quicken—once outside, he would be out in the open, fully exposed to the elements and potential enemies.

Ignoring a last-ditch plea by his inner voice of reason to return to the embassy, Wiggins pressed forward. Flipping his coat collar up to shield his face, he braced himself for the storm.

As he opened the door, torrential rain and high-gusting winds took him by surprise. Muttering an expletive, Wiggins stepped outside and secured the front door behind him. Struggling to raise his umbrella, he quickly abandoned the effort, knowing it would be useless in these conditions anyway.

Pulling his coat up to cover his head, Wiggins squinted through the horizontal, blowing rain to scan up and down the street. Not surprisingly, he was the only person foolish enough to be outside on a night like this.

Wiggins set off for Elena's, keeping to the sidewalk. An ankle-high stream of rainwater steadily flowed along the gutter as the city's drainage system failed to keep up with the heavy downpour. He continued at a steady pace, using every overhang along the way as a brief reprieve from the elements and a chance to check his six for a tail.

Ten minutes later, Wiggins arrived safely at his girlfriend's residence. As expected, the five-story apartment building was blacked out like every other building in the area. Its sleek and minimalist design, a combination of glass and concrete façades, reflected the city's contemporary architectural style. Elena's apartment—partially funded by Wiggins—was on the top floor, and on clear days, its rooftop terrace offered spectacular views of the Pacific Ocean.

Wiggins ascended the building's front steps, opened the entrance door, and stepped inside the vestibule. Grateful to finally be out of the rain, he was soaked to the bone and shook himself off.

Crossing the hall to a wall directory, he buzzed Elena's apartment.

She replied immediately over the intercom. "¿Sí?"

The sound of her sultry, Hispanic voice warmed him. "It's me," Wiggins replied in Spanish.

The inner door buzzed and unlocked. Wiggins slipped inside and headed straight for the stairwell. As he climbed the five flights, his mind was on Elena, longing to touch her silky-smooth skin.

Arriving at the top floor, Wiggins stopped on the landing to catch his breath. As soon as he collected himself, he slicked back his wet hair, removed his jacket, and gave it a good shake.

Quietly opening the exit door, he poked his head out into the darkened hallway and found it quiet and deserted. Stepping onto the carpet, Wiggins carefully eased the door shut behind him and made for Elena's apartment.

Letting himself in, he locked the deadbolt behind him. Wiggins rounded, expecting to find the soft glow of candles—Elena loved candles—but the apartment was cast in darkness. The storm's fireworks illuminated the living room through the large, open windows. As lightning cracked, he caught a glimpse of Elena's silhouette by the far window.

Wiggins smiled. "It's horrible outside," he said in Spanish as he set aside his umbrella and hung up his coat.

Elena did not reply. She remained motionless by the window.

Wiggins furrowed his brow. "Elena?"

Lightning flashed outside the window once again, illuminating his girlfriend. Elena was naked from head to toe, using her hands to cover her breasts and nether region. A soft cry escaped her trembling lips, barely audible amidst the pelting rain.

Wiggins realized he was in serious trouble by the sheer terror on her face. Before he could react, he glimpsed movement to his right; a figure in the shadows raised a long, cylindrical device to his mouth. Wiggins's breath hitched. Then, he heard a short "whoosh" sound, followed by a sharp pain in his neck. Grimacing, Wiggins reached instinctively to his neck and found a dart embedded in his skin. He yanked it free, but the damage was done; the sedative had been delivered.

As the fast-acting drug took effect, Wiggins tried to escape. Fumbling with the door locks, he felt his legs weaken as the room began to spin. He staggered backward, then collapsed to the floor.

Laying on his side, on the edge of blacking out, Wiggins noticed a third figure. He watched helplessly as this person approached Elena from the left, raised a silencer-mounted handgun to her head, and fired. Elena crumpled to the ground.

Tears formed in the station chief's eyes as Mr. Renzo approached. Lowering his big bore blowgun, the Chachapoyan knelt beside Wiggins, his face devoid of emotion.

Renzo set aside his weapon and pried the dart free from Wiggins's hand. He then searched his victim's clothing until he found the man's cell phone. Renzo removed the SIM card, pocketed it, and then discarded the device.

The second intruder speed-dialed their driver, who was waiting in the building's garage. "We're on our way down," he said in Spanish.

Renzo stood and dismantled his blowgun with expert precision. Returning it and the used dart to its case, he slung the case over his head.

Wiggins was now completely unconscious. The duo turned him over on his back and zip-tied his hands and feet. Then Renzo stuffed a rag in his mouth for good measure. Without a word, the two men picked their prisoner up by his feet and shoulders and departed Elena's apartment. They made for the stairwell and proceeded down to the parking garage without incident, where a black SUV awaited.

The driver activated the automatic liftgate, and the two men loaded Wiggins in the back.

"I've got it," Renzo said, gesturing with a head bob for his accomplice to take his seat.

The stern-looking Peruvian man nodded dutifully, leaving his boss alone with their prisoner. Renzo pressed two fingers against Wiggins's neck, checking for a pulse. It was weak, and his breathing shallow, but he was alive, for now.

A sinister smile crept across the Chachapoyan's face; revenge would be sweet. He was anxious to start interrogating Wiggins, but as he reached up to press the tailgate button, he noticed his hand tremble. At first, it felt like a minor annoyance, a fleeting muscle twitch, but then the spasms intensified, and his fingers started to jerk erratically.

Renzo snatched his hand out of the air. Turning his back to the vehicle to hide it from his men, a wave of panic washed over him as he clutched his hand close to his body. Renzo tried to regain control, but it twitched and trembled as if it had a will of its own—an unsettling sensation unlike anything he had ever experienced.

Rubbing his hand vigorously, Renzo even tried wringing it in a futile attempt to make it stop. After a few tense moments, the spasms subsided.

"Everything okay?" the driver called to him.

Renzo cocked his head sideways, still cradling his hand.

"Sí," he replied without explanation.

Renzo opened and closed his fist several times to test his hand. The tremors had stopped, but his concern lingered as he realized this could be the first sign of side effects from the serum.

Vowing to keep the incident to himself, Renzo closed the liftgate and climbed into the front passenger seat.

With a dangerous look on his face, he said impatiently to the driver, "¡Vamos!"

It was time for some payback.

11
STOWAWAY

Planet Aiwa
Supra, Realm of Eos

High on the upper floors of the royal palace, Commodore Boa leaned back in his crescent-shaped holographic chair and rubbed his tired eyes. Before him, a head-up display projected surveillance footage showing Major Gora, the traitor, and his accomplices before the assassination of King Loka.

Boa had been at it for hours, attempting to trace their movements before the attack. He knew precious little about the assassins, aside from the fact they were all Cirran refugees living in the camps outside the city. According to Prince Kypa, Gora had claimed allegiance to Grawn Krunig. Why, he could not fathom. Yet, despite Boa's exhaustive efforts to root out more accomplices, one crucial piece of information eluded him—how did the assassins get onboard the yacht undetected?

The chime of an incoming transmission gave Boa a start. Annoyed, he replied curtly, "Yes, what is it?"

"Forgive the intrusion, sir, but I have an urgent message from Princess Maya," the female watch officer replied. "She demands to speak with you."

Boa's shoulders sagged as he let out a weary sigh. He knew how anxiously Maya awaited any word on Kypa and his mission to rescue Captain Tan. But

Boa had nothing new to share, and the hour grew late. Sleep beckoned as the weight of the investigation took its toll. Still, his sense of duty compelled him to accept the transmission.

"Very well," Boa relented, straightening in his chair. "Patch her through."

Seconds later, Maya flickered onto Boa's HUD. Her typically composed expression was now one of deep concern. Boa picked up on it instantly.

"Greetings, princess," he said. "How may I be of assistance?"

"I apologize for calling on you so late, but I had nowhere else to turn," she replied, her voice shaking. "Toma is missing."

"Missing?" Boa's body tensed. "How long?"

"Three days," Maya answered. "He and Kypa had an argument. Toma wanted to help Captain Tan, but Kypa insisted he stay behind. That was the last time I saw Toma, after he stormed out of our quarters. No one has seen him since."

"Not even his friends … classmates?"

Maya shook her head, her eyes watering.

Asking if the family had any enemies felt pointless. "What about ransom demands?" he pressed. "Have you received any?"

"No, nothing," Maya whispered in reply.

Boa dropped his gaze as he considered the situation. Given recent events, Prince Toma was a high-value target for their enemies. Even if he had not been kidnapped and simply ran away in defiance of his father, Toma was still at great risk.

Brow furrowed, Boa asked, "Who else knows of this?"

"No one, not even Captain Nova," Maya replied. "I came straight to you."

A wave of relief washed over Boa. Given recent events, he was not sure who to trust.

"You did the right thing coming to me," Boa assured her. "I—"

Boa paused mid-sentence. His eyes narrowed as he moved closer to the screen, focusing intently on Maya's neck.

Feeling self-conscious, Maya looked down at herself and asked, "What?"

Forgetting himself, Boa sat back in his chair. "Forgive me, Princess," he said, somewhat embarrassed, "but the necklace you are wearing. That looks familiar."

Taken aback, Maya instinctively raised her hand to the thin chain hanging loosely around her neck. She ran the tips of her long fingers over the necklace's smooth scales. It was so soft to the touch that Maya forgot she was even wearing it.

Then it dawned on her—the necklace was not a piece of jewelry but a nano-ring capable of tracking her whereabouts.

"Of course, how could I be so stupid," she scolded herself, wiping away her tears. "Kypa gave these to me and the children so he could track our whereabouts."

Boa breathed a sigh of relief. "I thought it looked familiar," he replied with a smile. "Do not beat yourself up. The important thing is now we can locate Toma. Stand by while I run a search."

Boa moved Maya's image to the side panel of his HUD. He then sent a neural command to his computer, initiating a search for the young prince's homing beacon. The results came back immediately.

Reading Boa's expression, Maya's hope evaporated. "What is wrong?"

"This is odd … the search came back negative," he explained, stroking his jutted chin. "Toma is not in the city."

"Not in the city?" Maya echoed, alarmed.

A sinking feeling came over Boa, but he did not want to jump to conclusions. Keeping calm, he was mindful not to feed Maya's fears.

"Let me expand the search," he suggested.

Using his personal access code, Boa tapped into Aiwa's more extensive security network, which integrated the undersea realms and surface-level sensors.

Boa frowned at the results. "Still no sign of him," he reported. His usual stern gaze returned as his brain jumped to crisis management mode.

Maya covered her mouth in horror. "Is he …"

Dead? Boa hated to think so. He felt his chest tighten. Losing the king and his grandson in the same week would plunge Aiwa into chaos—and shatter Maya's heart.

If there was no signal, that meant Toma was either dead or his nano-ring had been deactivated or destroyed. If he ran off in a huff, it stood to reason he would not want his father tracking him. Rumor had it Toma was every bit as sharp as Kypa—maybe even sharper—so perhaps he tampered with the device to spite his parents.

Then, another possibility crossed his mind. Boa straightened. "You said the last time you saw Toma, he wanted to go with Kypa to rescue Captain Tan …"

Maya nodded, brushing another tear from her cheek.

Acting on a hunch, Boa commanded, "Computer, show me the surveillance footage of the palace hangar."

A live feed of the hangar bay appeared before him.

"Show me three days ago—the moment when Prince Kypa boarded the

Reaper," he instructed.

The image jumped to when Kypa said goodbye to Boa and his mother, Queen Qora. He and Princess Seva then entered the spacecraft.

"Stop," Boa interjected. "Play it backwards, slowly."

The footage began rewinding. Kypa and Seva reappeared. This time, they climbed down the Reaper's boarding ladder and walked backward to rejoin Boa and Qora like before. Their group then walked in reverse, exiting the hangar bay. Dr. Neil Garrett appeared moments later. Walking alone, he had boarded the Reaper.

"Show yourself," Boa muttered as his eyes darted about the screen, searching for signs of Toma.

There!

Boa's eyes widened as Toma appeared on the display. He watched with bated breath as the young prince stealthily approached the Reaper. Then, to Boa's surprise, the ship's boarding ladder descended, allowing Toma to climb aboard.

Why would the ship grant him access and not me? Boa wondered. Though he was not offended, there had to be a reason. Most likely, Captain Tan's security protocols only permitted certain visitors.

Boa tabled that thought for later and turned to Maya. "I found him."

Maya's eyes widened, her hands flying to her mouth. "Thank Gwaru," she whispered, visibly relieved. "Where is he? Is he safe?"

The look of deep concern on Boa's face betrayed him despite his best effort to break the bad news to Maya gently. "My princess, Toma is not on Aiwa. He stowed away onboard Captain Tan's ship."

Maya's elation faded as the gravity of the situation sunk in. "But that would mean …"

"The bounty hunters have him," Boa confirmed.

Prototype II

Waves of blue and white lines streaked past the cockpit windows as Kypa pored over data on his HUD. Staring intently at the readouts, he analyzed the data streams, measuring the second prototype's performance in this initial test flight.

So far, so good, he thought, nodding with satisfaction. All the ship's systems were operating well within parameters.

Neil quietly watched his Aiwan friend from afar. Standing in the cockpit entry, Dr. Garrett ate a Pop-Tart, marveling at Kypa's tenacity while taking in the spectacular light show displayed by the hyperspace tunnel. Now and again, he caught Kypa mumbling something to himself in frustration, but Neil kept silent, not wanting to disrupt his focus.

After swallowing his last bite, Neil quipped, "You know if you keep that up, you'll go blind."

Kypa did not flinch. Instead, he closed his eyes, relaxed his shoulders, and exhaled deeply. He had been acutely aware of Neil's presence, even without using his telepathy and sonar-like senses. Despite Neil's attempt to remain unobtrusive, Kypa found it impossible to ignore the constant chewing and occasional gasps of wonder, which only fueled his frustration.

Still, Neil had a point. The weight of everything happening on Aiwa, along with Ava's abduction—both of which Kypa blamed on himself—left his mind tangled. He just needed a moment to concentrate, to find the clarity to steer them through the storm.

As his stress mounted, even the smallest distractions seemed to fan the flames of his irritation. But Neil's light-hearted comment broke through, offering a grounding presence that shifted Kypa's perspective. Recognizing the need to clear his mind and ease the tension in his aching muscles, Kypa leaned back, granting himself a moment of reprieve.

"You are right, of course," he admitted, rubbing his eyes. "I need a break."

Empathizing, Neil suggested, "Why don't you try eating something and catching some Z's?"

"Z's?" Kypa asked, unfamiliar with the phrase. With a practiced mental command, he effortlessly swiveled his chair to face Neil.

"Yeah, you know?" Neil replied with a grin. "Saw some logs, hit the hay, take a snooze. What I'm saying is that you look like you could use some sleep."

"Ah," Kypa said, nodding thoughtfully. The mention of food made his stomach growl loud enough for them both to hear.

"I have been craving some speckled surgefish," Kypa remarked, picturing the Aiwan delicacy. "Thank you for the suggestions."

Neil shrugged modestly. "Hey, it's what I do."

Kypa put his feet on the floor and stood. Stretching his long arms, he touched the ceiling. As he passed Neil to exit the cockpit, Neil activated the holographic table and chairs in the main hold using his own mental command.

"Thank you," Kypa said over his shoulder, making his way to the food synthesizer.

"Sure thing," Neil replied, happy to contribute in a small way. "Any updates on Ava's whereabouts?"

"As a matter of fact, yes," Kypa answered as his food materialized. He lifted the plate to his nose to savor the aroma, then joined Neil at the cozy table. "It appears the bounty hunters have finally stopped in the Rogantu system."

"Rogantu?" Neil repeated, picturing a beautiful world with pristine beaches and clear blue oceans. "It sounds exotic."

"To the contrary, it is a desolate wasteland," Kypa replied. "My interstellar charts are somewhat limited, so I contacted a trader I know. The data he provided paints a bleak picture of the planet. Rogantu's surface conditions are quite inhospitable. Volcanoes, lava fields, and an unstable core will make our task of rescuing Ava and Reggie that much more difficult."

"Swell," Neil remarked with a crooked frown.

"There is something else that troubles me," Kypa offered. "Actually, 'troubles' is not the right word—'puzzles' is more accurate. It is about Reggie. I believe it, or rather, *she* has achieved sentience."

"You're kidding?" Neil stammered. "How is that even possible?"

"I do not know," Kypa admitted with a look of deep concern. "It may have occurred when I integrated the blue crystal with the Reaper."

"But this is a good thing, right? I mean, you've created a new life form. That's awesome."

"Mm," Kypa muttered, not ready to celebrate this accidental achievement.

Kypa's brow furrowed, his gaze growing distant as he pondered Neil's remark. In truth, he felt conflicted about the unintended result of his actions. He never meant for Reggie to become self-aware, yet if that was indeed the case, the engineer-scientist within him could not help but find it extraordinary. The idea of Reggie's sentience fascinated him—he wanted to study it, understand it, and explore whether the phenomenon could be replicated.

But he reeled back those selfish desires. Ava's life was at stake, and Reggie's newfound consciousness added an unknown variable to an already dangerous situation. How might Reggie react to the threats they were up against?

Fight or flight—literally? Kypa considered, picturing Reggie abandoning Ava to protect herself in the face of danger.

Across the table, Neil watched his friend closely, patiently waiting as Kypa stewed on these thoughts in silence. Just then, an alarm beeping in the cockpit drew their attention.

Neil glanced over his shoulder to see what it could be. "Are we nearing—"

"—Rogantu," Kypa finished as he came to his feet. "No, this is something else," he said, concern evident in his voice. "We are being hailed."

Kypa returned his half-eaten dish of food to the synthesizer. It vanished in thin air before he made his way to the cockpit. Neil was right behind. Kypa took his seat in the pilot's chair and silenced the beeping notification before answering the hail. Commodore Boa appeared on his HUD.

"Commodore Boa?" Kypa greeted, sounding surprised to hear from his top military commander.

Boa dipped his chin in greeting and got straight to the point. "My king, I bring difficult news."

Kypa stiffened, his mind jumping to something horrible. "What is it?"

Before Boa could answer, Maya stepped in front of him. "Kypa, Toma is in trouble," she said frantically.

"Maya!" Kypa leaned closer to the HUD, resisting the urge to reach out and touch his mate's projection to comfort her. "Tell me what is wrong."

Maya wiped her teary eyes. "Toma is gone."

Kypa's chest tightened. His last encounter with Toma had not ended well. They had argued, and then his son had stormed off, giving his father a rude finger gesture on the way out.

"Toma is angry with me," Kypa replied with a heavy heart. "I do not blame him for wanting to help Ava but keeping him safe was the right decision. He just needs time to cool down."

Maya shook her head. "No, that is not it," she explained, her mouth trembling. "Toma is gone. He is off world ... aboard the Reaper."

"What!?" Kypa exclaimed, trying to fathom how this was even possible.

"It is true," Boa interjected with a calming voice of reason. "We confirmed it through our security footage. Toma was last seen boarding Captain Tan's ship before you departed the palace to make the exchange with the bounty hunters. He stowed away."

Kypa's shoulders dropped. He fell back in his seat, mouth ajar and speechless. A moment of silence bridged the interstellar gap between both parties. As Boa comforted Maya, he watched Kypa's response, waiting respectfully for his sovereign to process this unfortunate turn of events.

Maya spoke first. With a determined look, she challenged her mate, "Kypa, you must bring him home."

Kypa blinked back to reality. Composing himself, he cleared his throat. "Of course, I will, *we* will," he corrected, gesturing to Neil. "We will find Ava and Toma and bring them both back alive."

"You got that right," Neil seconded, joining Kypa's side. He leaned closer to the HUD. "Don't worry, Maya. We won't let anything happen to your son."

Maya mustered an appreciative smile, but the human's zeal offered little comfort considering his lack of experience. This responsibility fell on Kypa, whom she trusted implicitly.

"I have tracked the bounty hunters' location," Kypa reported. "They have stopped on the planet, Rogantu. We will be arriving shortly."

"I will dispatch a garrison," Boa stated.

Kypa raised his hand, signaling Boa to slow down. "Not yet, Commodore, but thank you. I want to get on site first and assess the situation without alerting the bounty hunters."

The question on everyone's mind was how, exactly, Kypa planned to accomplish that, but no one voiced it.

Sensing their unease, Kypa added, "Do not worry. I have a plan. If we need reinforcements, I will call for help. I promise."

Boa looked to Maya for her reaction. After a moment of hesitation, she nodded curtly.

"Very well, I will await your signal," Boa replied. "As for the rest of your family, be assured that they are safe here in the palace."

"And the crystal?" Kypa inquired.

"It is locked away in the royal vault, protected by Captain Nova and his guards," Boa reported.

"Good. Keep it that way," Kypa replied, his tone sharp and insistent. "Krunig is not the only threat Aiwa faces. Any updates in your investigation?"

Boa shook his head. "Nothing conclusive, but we are running down every lead. We will get to the bottom of Gora's treachery."

"I know you will," Kypa said confidently. To Maya, he added, "I must go now but do not lose hope. Remain steadfast. Arya and Fraya need you."

Maya put on a brave face as she grappled with the haunting thought of never seeing Kypa or Toma again.

"We will be fine," Boa assured Kypa. Then, fixing his gaze on Neil, he addressed the human for the first time. "Dr. Garrett, I am trusting you to protect our future king."

Neil felt his throat tighten as he swallowed nervously. "You can count on me, sir," he replied, though a flicker of doubt lingered in his mind.

"We will be silencing communications from this point," Kypa said. "Do not attempt to contact us. I will report back as soon as I have an update."

"Very well," Boa acknowledged. Again, he dipped his chin.

Kypa mirrored the gesture, his eyes tracking Boa as he respectfully stepped away. Then, Kypa and Maya gazed at one another, exchanging a quiet moment of understanding. With a reassuring nod, Kypa signaled that everything would be okay and then ended the transmission.

After a brief silence, Neil felt compelled to ask, "So, what's the plan?"

As if on cue, the navigation computer's alarm began beeping, signaling their arrival at Rogantu. Kypa silenced the alarm as they emerged from hyperspace in a flash of white light. The sleek spacecraft appeared momentarily in normal space, headed toward Rogantu, only to vanish as suddenly as it had arrived.

"There, now we are cloaked," Kypa said with a measure of satisfaction. "We should be hidden from any sensors that might track our approach."

Neil nodded approval. "That was easy enough."

"Luna deserves the credit," Kypa replied with a hint of sadness for the void she left behind in his life.

Neil, too, was stirred by the mention of Luna. He recalled Princess Seva describing Kypa's childhood friend during their tour of the royal palace. Kypa rarely mentioned her name, probably because the memory of losing Luna aboard the mothership that crashed in North Korea was too painful to confront.

"When all of this is over, let's raise a glass to Luna," Neil suggested, hoping to brighten the mood.

Kypa smiled wanly, appreciating the thought. He then turned his attention to the dark and menacing world now looming large outside the cockpit window.

Neil grimaced. "So that's Rogantu, huh? Looks like the backdrop for every nightmare I had as a child."

Kypa shared the sentiment. It appeared every bit as hostile as he imagined.

"Rogantu's atmosphere is breathable but due to all of the volcanic ash in the air, I recommend we keep our helmets on as much as possible."

"Good idea," Neil said. "Is it inhabited?"

"It would appear so. I am picking up life signs but there are no major cities or organized clusters of inhabitants." Kypa pointed to a location highlighted on the HUD and enhanced the image on the display. "The bounty hunters landed here at this abandoned refinery. As you can see, it is out in the open. Despite our ship's cloaking ability, we will not be completely invisible to the naked eye and can still be heard. We should land in this mountainous area to the west and approach the facility on foot."

Narrowing his eyes, Neil leaned closer to the screen and pointed to a speck at the base of the mountain ridge. "What's this?"

Kypa enhanced the image to reveal a tiny structure in the middle of nowhere. "It looks to be an outpost of some kind," he surmised.

"Might be a good idea to check it out," Neil suggested. "Maybe we can find a layout of the refinery where Ava and Toma are being held."

Kypa sighed, not because of Neil's reasoning—it made sense—but because the stakes were so high.

Neil sensed Kypa's inner turmoil and could only imagine what he was feeling. For what good it would do, he placed his hand on Kypa's shoulder and said earnestly, "I know it may not be too reassuring, but I meant what I said. You can count on me. We're going to get them back—all of 'em, including Reggie."

Kypa, deeply moved by Neil's unwavering support, patted his friend's hand with quiet gratitude.

"Besides," Neil added, "Toma's in good hands. Ava's the most dialed person I've ever met. She would charge into Hell carrying a bucket of ice water to help a friend," he attested. "Trust me, I'm sure she's got this all under control."

12
BLACK DOG

Planet Rogantu

Ava finally broke.

Confronted with the reality of her abduction, with no chance of escape and an uncertain fate ahead, Ava surrendered to despair. Curled on the floor, her hands bound tightly behind her, she sobbed uncontrollably.

Consumed by an overwhelming sense of failure, Ava cried so hard it made her head hurt. Tears streamed down her face, pooling on the metal surface under her cheek. All the while, her inner warrior pleaded with her not to feed the dreaded black dog—Ava's metaphorical demon for self-sabotage. Wallowing in defeatism was counterproductive, but she indulged herself anyway.

Her thoughts drifted to her ex-fiancé, Mark Jordan—her rock. His absence, especially now, deepened her isolation and triggered another wave of self-pity. Ava let the tears flow a little longer until an unexpected fluttering sensation with her nanosuit jolted her from her misery.

Blinking back her tears, Ava lifted her head and glanced sharply at her chest. To her surprise, a wave of the tiny nanites that held her suit together rolled down her body. The material separated slightly along the way, exposing the skin underneath, then snapped back into place. The wave continued down her left leg and stopped at her toes.

"That's weird," she muttered, examining her leg from different angles.

Ava felt a similar sensation on her right foot and rolled her ankle over for a look-see. Her eyes widened in horror at seeing a three-inch insect perched on her foot. The pale-yellow centipede had pupil-less black eyes and two pincher-like mandibles around its mouth. Its arched tail culminated with a stinger, poised for a swift and venomous strike.

Ava let out an ear-splitting screech and began kicking and flailing her legs, feverishly trying to dislodge the creature, but to no avail. The hungry insect sensed the body heat of her exposed head and neck and began crawling up Ava's leg.

Terror surged through her as the insect skittered up her torso. Unable to fend it off, Ava's heart pounded wildly, gripped by a paralyzing fear as the creature neared her face.

Suddenly, the closet door hissed open. Appearing in the archway, Smythe reached in, swiftly snatched the insect by the tail with his thumb and forefinger, and peeled it off.

Startled by her unexpected savior, Ava looked up at the bounty hunter as he inspected the tiny creature pinched between his fingers, writhing to free itself.

Relieved to be rid of at least one alien insect, Ava mutely stared at Smythe and tried to calm her breathing. She watched as the bounty hunter then used his free hand to pinch the insect's head and yanked off its tail. Dropping the tail to the floor, Smythe crushed it under his boot and ate the rest of the insect alive.

Ava made a face while listening to the bounty hunter chew his nasty snack. She fought back the bile rising in her throat and willed herself not to hurl. All the while, Smythe stared at her with cold eyes, ignoring her discomfort. In the unpleasant silence that followed, Ava wondered where this was leading.

Smythe reached into the pocket of his cowl and retrieved her nano-ring. Ava's pulse quickened at the sight of it, but she suppressed her excitement. That ring held the hope of freedom. With it, she could restore her suit's defensive capabilities and have a fighting chance to escape.

Eyeing the nano-ring draped over Smythe's bony fingers, Ava could not believe he was offering it to her freely.

Is this a test? she wondered, suddenly suspicious of the bounty hunter's angle. But nothing about Smythe told her he was a fool.

Balling the nano-ring in his fist, Smythe stepped inside the closet, reaching for Ava. She instinctively curled into a defensive ball.

"No!" she protested.

Smythe ignored her plea. He rolled Ava over and grabbed her under the armpits, then effortlessly lifted her off the floor. Held in mid-air, Ava feebly kicked and screamed, so Smythe released her. Ava dropped, managing to land on her feet just in time, surprising herself. She straightened and immediately retreated, wedging her back in the corner. With fear and loathing etched on her face, Ava eyed her captor warily.

Smythe stared back in silence, his creepy gaze unreadable. He opened his hand and dangled the nano-ring in front of Ava once again. Chest heaving, Ava darted her eyes between Smythe and the necklace, then she nodded curtly, signaling she would behave.

Stepping forward, Smythe held the nano-ring out. Ava cringed as he placed it over her head. They were so close that she could smell his stench. He reeked of death.

Once the nano-ring was in close proximity to the top of Ava's collar, it joined automatically to her nanosuit. She welcomed it back with a confident grin, and as Smythe stepped back, Ava activated her holographic helmet. A refreshing breeze hit her face as the suit began regulating her body temperature. She then balled her hands into tight fists behind her back and readied for a fight.

Picturing the nanites slicing through her bonds, Ava firmly commanded her suit, "Release!"

But nothing happened.

Ava felt a wave of panic. She wriggled her unforgiving bonds, trying to free her hands, and repeated, "Release! Release!"

Still nothing.

Ava's frustration quickly turned to anger as she shifted her gaze to a narrow gap in the doorway, left unguarded by the bounty hunter. Acting on impulse, she charged toward the opening, ready to fight her way through.

But Smythe read Ava's thoughts like an insecure datapad. He seized her by the throat and lifted her off her feet with ease.

"You tried this on Aiwa," Smythe reminded her, recalling when he finally caught Ava in the cave behind the waterfall. "You can't fly away this time."

Ava's eyes bulged with fear and desperation. Suspended mid-air, she squirmed helplessly, struggling to free herself of the bounty hunter's vice-like grip. Then, it dawned on her: *He speaks English!*

Ava's eyes widened in shock as she stared into Smythe's cold, yellow eyes. But as her face began to change color, Ava's will to fight waned. Consciousness started to slip away, and in her final moments, she realized the bounty hunter did not speak English at all; it was her helmet translating the alien dialect into her native tongue.

Sensing Ava had had enough, Smythe tossed her backward like a discarded ragdoll. Ava hit the wall and collapsed to the floor, coughing and gasping for air. The bounty hunter patiently waited for her to recover. When Ava could breathe again, she picked herself up off the floor to face her captor.

"Who are you?" she demanded.

Smythe ignored her question. Instead, he gestured to the severed tail on the floor. "You see that?" he asked in his raspy voice. "That is a gracylai. If it had been a few days older, its poison sac would have developed, and you'd be dead."

Ava cast a quick glance at the creature's discarded remains.

"So, am I supposed to thank you?" she asked snidely.

Smythe smirked. He knew Ava had been despondent earlier, crying and pleading to be released, but her defiance had returned. That was good—she was more predictable this way. But rather than engage in pointless banter, the bounty hunter cut to the chase.

"Why is your ship so valuable?"

Taken aback, Ava shot him a look. *Isn't it obvious?*

Her mind raced, and then it struck her—the blue crystal was no longer on board. Something that significant would be impossible to miss, even for a novice spacefarer like her. Kypa must have switched crystals before handing over the Reaper.

Ava grinned inwardly. The more she thought about it, the more it made sense. Kypa would never willingly hand over such power to an enemy of Aiwa, even if it meant sacrificing her. If their roles were reversed, she would have done the same.

However, this revelation did create a more immediate problem. If the blue crystal were back on Aiwa, the moment the bounty hunters figured it out, she and Reggie would become expendable.

Reggie!

Ava's heart fluttered. The bounty hunters may have deactivated her suit's defenses, but did that include her comms, too?

Ava subtly attempted to contact her ship by mentally activating the commlink in her helmet.

"*Reggie, can you hear me?*" she hissed in her mind. "*Reggie, come in!*"

No reply.

"Don't bother trying to contact your ship," Smythe informed her with a knowing tone. "We've disabled everything in your suit except the translator and life support, but even those can be deactivated if you choose not to cooperate."

Ava frowned, sighing in defeat.

"I'll ask again," Smythe repeated, emphasizing his point by resting his hand on his blaster. "Why *exactly* does Grawn Krunig want your ship?"

Thinking fast, Ava cocked her eyebrow and replied, "What makes you think he wants my ship?"

"I know what happened at Aiwa," Smythe replied. "You decimated Krunig's fleet, but our scans showed your ship doesn't possess such firepower."

Ava smiled modestly. "So, maybe it's me he wants. Have you considered that?"

Smythe's eyes, sharp and unwavering, never left Ava's face as he searched for any sign that she might be hiding something. Ava responded by maintaining steady eye contact with the insectoid.

"You're good, but not that good," Smythe granted. "How did you defeat his fleet?"

"Ancient Chinese secret," Ava replied with a smug grin.

The reference to the 1970s detergent commercial meant nothing to Smythe, but judging by Ava's arrogant tone, he knew she was toying with him.

Smythe tapped a button on the control pad attached to his forearm. Suddenly, the oxygen flow inside Ava's hologram helmet ceased, leaving her in a suffocating silence. She had no control over her suit to deactivate her helmet.

The bounty hunter stepped forward and pressed his hand firmly against Ava's chest, pinning her to the back wall. He stared into her panic-filled eyes as she desperately gulped at the thinning air.

"I'm in no mood for games," he seethed. "Now, tell me what I want to know."

Ava defiantly stood her ground. She had no intention of telling Smythe anything, even if it meant her death. On the brink of unconsciousness, stars began to dance before her eyes.

Smythe's commlink chirped, interrupting his interrogation.

"Yes?" he spat angrily.

Sensing his partner's tension, Gort replied tentatively, "Hiromi's on final approach."

"About time," Smythe said impatiently. "Meet me aft. And Gort?"

"Yeah, Boss?"

"We need to sweep the ship for other lifeforms. I found a gracylai on board, and where there's one, there's going to be a lot more."

"Swell," Gort replied, none-too-happy to have one more thing to worry about.

Smythe ended the transmission and turned to Ava. Regarding her with a callous expression, he let her suffer a bit longer, then stepped back and released control of her suit. Ava collapsed to her knees, sucking oxygen.

"We'll discuss this later," he promised. "In the meantime, I suggest you rethink your position."

With that, Smythe closed the door. As he started aft, he indulged in a small, satisfied smile at the sound of Ava coughing and gasping through the locked door.

Alone in her closet, Ava carefully repositioned herself, leaning back against the wall as she settled into a seated position. Her thoughts quickly turned to Hiromi, whoever that might be. The bounty hunters were bringing in a third person, but for what purpose, she had no clue. She stewed on this for several moments until a familiar voice unexpectedly broke her concentration.

"*Ava?*"

Ava sat bolt upright, uncertain if the voice she heard in her head was real or a figment of her imagination.

Focusing her mind, she replied telepathically in a skeptical tone, "*Toma?*"

"*Yes, it is me,*" Toma answered excitedly.

Ava's heart leaped. "*What are you doing here? Where's your father?*"

"*I am onboard the Reaper. I—*"

"*—What!?*" Ava blurted, sounding confused. "*How?*"

"*I snuck aboard before my father went to rescue you,*" Toma replied. "*My nanosuit has kept me hidden. Are you mad at me?*"

Ava let out an exasperated sigh, her hope meter dropping rapidly. Still, despite her disapproval, she was glad to hear a friendly voice.

"*I'm not mad, but your parents are going to kill us if we don't find a way out of here,*" Ava said, her tone suddenly urgent. She could imagine Kypa and Maya worrying themselves sick right now. Putting on her game face, Ava set to work on their escape plan. "*Where are you now?*"

Tiptoeing through the Reaper, Toma whispered in his mind, "*I am in the main hold. Where are you?*"

"*Handcuffed inside a closet aboard the bounty hunter's ship,*" Ava replied, testing her bonds once again, but they would not budge. Giving up in frustration, she said, "*Look outside the cockpit window … tell me what you see.*"

Toma stopped at the cockpit threshold. As with the rest of the ship, all systems were offline, leaving the cockpit dark and deathly quiet. Even the holographic furniture was gone, adding to the ship's eerie emptiness.

Entering cautiously, Toma kept to the shadows. As he peered out the cockpit windows, he described the scene to Ava.

"The Reaper is being kept inside a cargo bay of some kind. I can see mechanical arms holding the ship in place."

Ava recalled the freighter capturing her ship on the Aiwan beach. *"We're facing at least two bad guys, both armed, and a third one named Hiromi on the way,"* she explained. *"Are we still on Aiwa?"*

"I do not think so," Toma replied. *"I felt us take off and I am confident we made several hyperspace jumps."*

We could be anywhere, Ava thought grimly to herself. *"What else can you see? Any movement?"*

Toma changed positions several times to get looks from different angles. *"Nothing, just the inside of the freighter."*

"Good. They probably went to greet Hiromi," Ava surmised, hoping that would buy them some time. *"Does that name mean anything to you?"*

Toma paused to think, then shook his head. *"No, my father has never mentioned anyone named Hiromi."*

"I'm guessing it's a hacker."

Puzzled, Toma asked, *"What is a hacker?"*

"Sorry, that's an Earth term for someone who illegally accesses other people's computer systems to steal their data," Ava explained with no love lost for such scum. She had had her identity stolen once and remembered what a pain in the butt it was to get sorted out.

"Ah, my father told me about off-worlders who do this kind of work ... they are called slicers," Toma shared.

"Well, I'm guessing this slicer, Hiromi, *was brought here to disable Reggie's self-destruct protocol."*

"Self-destruct ...?" Toma repeated.

Ava sensed his unease and elaborated, *"Don't worry. We're not going to blow up. I invented the protocol to fool Boa and prevent any would-be thieves from trying to steal my ship. Reggie must've shut down when the bounty hunters seized her. Perhaps we can use that to our advantage."*

"Should I bring Reggie back online?" Toma suggested, eager to prove his worth. *"She knows me. I could call for help?"*

Ava knew Toma meant well. In his mind, the idea sounded as simple as pressing a button by the Reaper's cockpit entry and sending a distress signal to his father. However, nothing about their situation was that easy.

"No, don't touch anything," Ava replied firmly, her tone sharper than intended. *"They'd be all over you in a heartbeat and we can't risk you getting*

caught. Besides, as long as we're locked inside this freighter, I don't think we're going anywhere. Have you been down below yet?"

"Yes, why?"

"Did you see the blue crystal in the engine core?"

Toma searched his memory. *"Come to think of it, no. The crystal was orange,"* he replied, picturing the soft glow of the magnetarite.

Ava nodded. *"I figured as much. Your father was wise to remove it. But that's what the bounty hunter's really want, and when they figure that out, we're in trouble."*

"What can I do?"

"Just stay calm and keep out of sight for now, okay?" Ava instructed. *"We need to work together and be smart about this to stay alive. Someone will come for us,"* she assured him, then muttered grimly to herself, *"I hope."*

13
ALL THAT GLITTERS

Planet Rogantu

Orbiting the volcanic world of Rogantu, the second Reaper prototype remained safely hidden from enemy sensors thanks to its revolutionary cloaking device. Though, for how long remained uncertain. Interference from the surface wreaked havoc on the ship's systems, forcing Kypa to delay their approach until he could make adjustments.

Yet, the urgency pressed heavily on him. Every minute wasted up here only increased the danger for Ava and Toma.

A proximity alarm sounded on Kypa's HUD. He quickly silenced the warning and turned his attention to a small, single-engine transport entering the system. Through the static-filled display, Kypa watched as the unmarked vessel disappeared into the planet's upper atmosphere.

"Who's that?" Neil asked, looking over Kypa's shoulder.

Pinching his brow, Kypa replied warily, "I am not sure. The transport did not appear to be a syndicate vessel."

"Well, whoever it is, they certainly picked a remote spot to meet," Neil remarked.

Kypa nodded in agreement. "I was thinking the same thing. Perhaps this new arrival is here on Krunig's behalf, but if they are after the blue crystal, surely the bounty hunters know by now it is not on the Reaper."

"Maybe they do know and just want to cut their losses?" Neil suggested. "They could sell the Reaper to a third party."

Following Neil's reasoning, Kypa countered, "The Reaper has its own worth, even without the blue crystal. But Toma? He is an even greater asset. Krunig would not ignore the leverage of a political hostage."

"Good point," Neil conceded, grimly noting to himself that Ava held little value—if any—to her captors.

"On the other hand," Kypa continued, "if this newcomer does not represent Krunig, then it stands to reason the bounty hunters are unaware that Toma is onboard."

"Well, only one way to find out," Neil replied with a sigh, his tone carrying the weight of the ominous task before them. They were about to enter the unknown, where danger was a given and survival far from assured.

Kypa's HUD beeped.

"Uh-oh, more company?" Neil assumed, leaning in for a closer look at the display.

Kypa's eyes widened with joy. "No," he answered excitedly. "It is Toma! His suit's locator just activated." Kypa went to work, tapping the display to pinpoint his son's exact location. "The interference is making it difficult to stay locked onto his position, but Toma is definitely at the refinery with the Reaper."

"And he's alive, thank goodness," Neil said, patting Kypa's shoulder. "Can you contact him?"

Kypa was already on it. Mindful that enemies could be surrounding Toma, he hailed his son using a discreet, non-audible signal, one used while they hunted back on Aiwa. Kypa anxiously waited, desperate for his son's response, but none came.

Kypa tapped several commands on the screen in response.

"What is it?" Neil asked, sensing something was wrong.

Kypa leaned back in his seat, exhaling in frustration. "I lost the signal."

After reflection, Neil said optimistically, "Well, that could mean anything, right? Like you said, there's lots of interference, or maybe Toma's playing it smart and keeping himself hidden. Lord knows that suit saved my neck a couple of times back on Aiwa," he recalled, picturing the ferocious krakadon that nearly ate him for lunch.

Kypa nodded, grateful for Neil's positivity. However, it did not dispel his fears. Determined not to lose hope, Kypa straightened in his seat.

"Take your seat," he said. "We are going to the surface."

Neil grinned. "Now you're talking."

As Neil took his seat, Kypa powered up the twin nacelles and broke orbit. Despite being invisible to sensors, Prototype II was not intangible—it could still be seen when burning through the atmosphere or disrupting the air in dense clouds. To avoid detection, Kypa approached Rogantu on the planet's dark side, where a violent storm awaited.

Howling winds buffeted the hull as forks of lightning pierced the darkness. After several tense moments of jarring turbulence, the clouds gave way, revealing a barren wasteland scarred by jagged rock formations and plumes of black smoke billowing from active volcanoes.

Passing over an especially deep chasm, the ship's flight controls flickered erratically. A moment later, all systems abruptly deactivated—including the holographic furniture. Kypa and Neil thudded to the floor as an alarm sounded, and the soft red glow of emergency lights filled the cockpit.

As Prototype II began spiraling out of control, Kypa and Neil slid helplessly toward the front of the cockpit, overpowered by the centrifugal force of the spin.

Thinking fast, Kypa called out, "Computer, initiate autopilot!"

The ship's computer took control, leveling the spacecraft and restoring a fragile calm. Neil and Kypa lay side by side, their breaths heavy as they exchanged wary glances, each silently hoping the harrowing ordeal was finally over.

Resting on his elbows, Kypa looked up to the ceiling. "Computer, silence the alarm," he commanded. The cockpit fell silent, and the emergency lights extinguished.

"What was that?" Neil asked.

Kypa rolled onto all fours and stood. He then offered his hand to Neil, helping him to his feet.

"The electromagnetic interference is worse than I imagined," Kypa replied. Feeling a tickle in his nanosuit, he looked down at his arm and noticed the nanite material separating, then reforming. "This could be a problem."

Neil examined his own suit. "Should we switch to aquasuits?"

Kypa thought for a moment, then shook his head. "No, a slight adjustment to our nano-rings should suffice." To the ship's computer, he said, "Boost power to the shields and cloaking device to compensate for the increased interference."

"Transfer complete," the ship's computer replied immediately. It had the same voice as Reggie but delivered the information in a cold, robotic monotone.

"And reactivate the duty stations," Kypa added.

Both chairs materialized again to their previous configurations.

Kypa turned to Neil with a wry grin. "Perhaps it is time to rethink holographic furniture," he quipped, eliciting a chuckle. Kypa then removed his nano-ring and gestured to Neil. "May I?"

"By all means," Neil replied, lifting his chin to expose his neck.

Kypa deactivated Neil's nano-ring, detaching the flimsy necklace from his friend's suit and lifting it over Neil's head.

"Thank you," Kypa said, balling both devices into his large hand. "I will be right back." On his way out of the cockpit, he said, "Computer, hold position."

The ship's computer acknowledged the command and slowed the spacecraft to a hover at ten thousand feet.

With Kypa gone and calm restored, Neil stepped closer to the cockpit window. He clasped his hands behind his back and gazed out, his eyes fixed on the tumultuous landscape of the alien world below. For a moment, the exoplanet scientist's academic assessment was overwhelmed by childlike wonder, as though he was witnessing the mysteries of the universe unfold.

On the planet's surface, Hiromi's transport descended into the refinery's landing bay. Landing struts extended from the spacecraft's underbelly amidst a swirling cloud of dust and soot. The transport settled onto the deck beside Smythe and Gort's freighter, where both bounty hunters waited, blasters in hand, ready to welcome their guest.

Moments later, the boarding ramp lowered. Hiromi, a female cyborg and exceptionally gifted slicer, appeared at the top. With a petite, humanoid frame—two arms, two legs, and a proportionate head—her five-foot stature might have seemed non-threatening.

Hiromi resembled a porcelain doll. Her opalescent outer shell gleamed with a delicate, glossy white finish, and every inch of her was adorned with intricate, hand-carved patterns. Underneath this shell, Hiromi's metal endoskeleton was constructed of Nexium, a golden alloy that was very rare, very expensive, and even more difficult to destroy. Together, this combination blended the elegance of antique artistry with advanced robotic technology, creating a breathtaking and almost surreal fusion of beauty and power.

The slicer-for-hire descended the ramp and approached the bounty hunters, raising her tiny hands to show she was unarmed. Hiromi's pristine facial mask gave her an eerily serene façade that concealed any emotions her mechanically enhanced, organic brain generated.

"Smythe ... Gort," she greeted each in turn. Hiromi's mouth did not move, but her soft-spoken, synthetic voice resonated like a gentle caress.

Out of respect, Smythe kept the muzzle of his blaster aimed at the floor. Still, if she made one false move, he was prepared to decommission the cyborg—regardless of how skilled she was at hacking encrypted systems.

"Were you followed?" Smythe asked.

Hiromi found the question laughable. "Of course not. My upgrades may be new, but I was not born yesterday."

Smythe did not challenge her claim, but he was not taking any chances. He signaled Gort with a head bob to scan her anyway. His partner produced a handheld device and pointed it at Hiromi, scanning her up and down. Satisfied, he walked around her ship and scanned the hull for homing beacons.

"They're clean," Gort reported as he finished.

"See, nothing to worry about," Hiromi remarked, noting the bounty hunter seemed a bit edgier than normal.

Smythe made no apologies for the added precautions. In this line of work, one could never be too careful. He holstered his blaster and replied, "Welcome to Rogantu. Thanks for coming so quickly."

Hiromi surveyed the hangar, noting its state of disrepair. "I cannot say I'm impressed with your choice of locations," she remarked, gazing down at the black soot staining her opalescent feet. "I'll make this quick, Smythe. Word on the street is that Grawn Krunig is looking for you two."

Gort shifted uneasily.

"Is that so?" Smythe responded, unfazed. The absence of concern in his tone, coupled with his refusal to confirm or deny the rumor, spoke volumes about the secretive nature of their meeting. "If you want out, now's your chance to walk away."

"I'm here, aren't I?" Hiromi stated, affirming her commitment.

"Fair enough. Your cut will be triple your usual fee," Smythe baited. Knowing Hiromi's preoccupation with her appearance, a fee this large was too big to pass up. It could buy her a lot of upgrades.

Hiromi was thinking the same thing, although her unmoving faceplate hid her excitement. She replied evenly, "Triple, huh? Tell me more."

"We've captured an Aiwan vessel that holds significant value to the syndicate," Smythe explained. "I want to know why. The ship is locked down, and we're holding its captain, but we cannot risk triggering the ship's self-destruct protocol. That's where you come in. We need you to bypass the ship's security, so we can unlock its secrets."

"Aiwan?" Hiromi remarked, her interest doubly piqued. Access to such advanced tech was a rarity and presented an irresistible challenge. Still, the cyborg was no fool. Going against the syndicate, particularly Grawn Krunig, carried a death sentence if they were caught. "You're playing a dangerous game, Smythe. What if we don't find anything?"

"If I'm wrong, we hand the ship over to Krunig and you get paid regardless," Smythe replied. "But something tells me this ship is worth a whole lot more than he's offering."

"Half," Hiromi said bluntly. "I want half of whatever we find."

A thin smile tugged at the corners of Smythe's lipless mouth. Despite Hiromi's delicate appearance, he knew she was a shrewd negotiator, fully aware of her worth and capable of commanding a premium for her unique skill set. To Smythe, they were credits well spent.

"Deal," Smythe agreed.

"Then it's settled," Hiromi responded. "Now, since time is of the essence and I don't particularly enjoy standing out here collecting dust, I suggest we move inside so I can get started." She gestured toward the freighter. "Shall we?"

Smythe preceded Hiromi up the ramp while Gort followed. No words were exchanged, but both bounty hunters thought the same thing: it was time to find out if their gambit was truly worth it.

Kypa returned to the cockpit carrying Neil's nano-ring, his own device already reattached to his suit. He found his friend gazing out the window, lost in thought. Joining Neil, Kypa stood beside him in silence, taking in the harsh landscape before them.

Neil noted Kypa's presence, then turned back to the ominous view. "All that glitters isn't gold," he said with a sigh.

Kypa cocked his head slightly, intrigued by the remark. "I am not familiar with that phrase. What does it mean?"

Neil chuckled. "It's something my mom used to say," Neil recalled fondly. "It means things aren't always as glamorous as they appear, especially people."

Kypa nodded agreeably. "Wise counsel."

"Smartest woman I ever knew," Neil attested. "Her words have been running through my head ever since we left Earth. It's been one misadventure after another," he said, thinking back to all they had experienced and the dangers that lay ahead. "It's not what I expected."

"Few things ever are," Kypa replied, understanding all too well. Who could have predicted the events that had unfolded since his crash on Earth? Yet, despite the hardships and losses, one bright spot remained: their friendship.

"Here," he offered, handing Neil his nano-ring. "I made some adjustments to help stabilize your suit, but it may need further tweaks after we reach the surface."

"Thanks," Neil said, slipping the ring over his head so it could merge with his suit—the integration was instantaneous. With a mental command, he activated the holographic helmet. Neil's personal HUD flickered to life, and after rolling his head about to test the helmet's range of motion, he gave Kypa an approving thumbs-up.

"So, what's the plan?" he asked next.

Kypa shrugged and said casually, "Simple, we go rescue Ava and Toma without getting ourselves killed."

Neil blinked, momentarily thrown off by his Aiwan friend's nonchalance. Cracking a smile, he replied with a chuckle, "Can you be a little more specific, especially the part about not dying?"

"Not really, no," Kypa responded with unabashed honesty, deflating the mood somewhat. "As you say on Earth, we will have to play it by ear and roll with the punches."

Neil rolled his eyes. "Swell," he muttered, then gestured at their nanosuits. "Well, at least we're not wearing red shirts," he joked.

Judging by Kypa's blank response, Neil's attempt at *Star Trek* humor fell flat.

"Never mind," Neil said with a dismissive wave.

Kypa clapped Neil's shoulder. "Everything will be alright, I promise. Now, take your seat. It is time to land."

Resuming his place in the pilot's chair, Kypa engaged the four orbs and took manual control of the spacecraft. He then throttled up the nacelles, and the tiny ship surged forward, leaving two contrails in its wake as it descended toward the surface.

Hugging the ground, Kypa skimmed low over the sprawling lava fields to avoid visual detection. As they approached their destination, the landscape transformed into a rocky, mountainous formation, forcing him to weave through a maze of jagged outcroppings. Minutes later, he throttled back and brought the ship to hover above a small alcove carved high atop a mountain, providing a clear view of the nearby outpost and the refinery in the distance. With practiced precision, Kypa deployed the landing struts and set the ship down smoothly.

"This is as close as we can get," Kypa explained as he powered down. "We will have to walk from here."

Neil stood and followed Kypa to the main hold. There, he used the HUD in his helmet to locate the outpost. "A three-mile hike ain't so bad."

Kypa appreciated Neil's resourcefulness but did not share his optimism. "It is not the distance that worries me," he admitted. "The terrain will be treacherous. We must be cautious."

Heeding Kypa's warning, Neil subconsciously placed his hand on his blaster, seeking a sense of security in its presence.

Kypa retrieved his gun belt from the storage closet and secured it around his waist. He then drew his blaster and checked that it was fully charged.

"Do you remember how to use this?" he asked. Neil nodded. "Good. Let us hope we do not need it."

Returning his weapon to its holster, Kypa led Neil down to the engineering section. There, they made their way to the outer hatch on the floor.

Kypa crouched beside it, but before opening the hatch, he looked up at Neil and said, "There are three hours of daylight remaining, and we do not want to get caught out in the open after dark. If we get separated, meet at the outpost."

"Got it," Neil replied with a curt nod, shaking his arms and legs to limber up. "Don't worry about me."

Kypa regarded him with a faint grin but said nothing. "The atmosphere is breathable," he added, "but keep your helmet on."

"Got it," Neil replied, letting out a steady breath to calm his nerves.

With that, Kypa opened the hatch, automatically triggering the down ladder to extend to the ground. As Kypa descended, Neil followed close behind, scaling the hatch on his way out.

The ladder automatically retracted when Neil stepped off onto the volcanic surface. Moving away from the ship toward a nearby precipice, they stood for a moment and looked out at the daunting landscape. At the base of the mountain, a barren field cracked by a web of volcanic fissures stood between them and the outpost. Rogantu was the polar opposite of Aiwa, whose lush jungles teemed with life. Everything about this desolate wasteland was a stark reminder of impending death.

Neil cautiously leaned forward and peered over the edge. The steep descent sent a shiver down his spine, and he quickly backpedaled.

Kypa turned to him with a look of concern. "Are you afraid of heights?"

"Not really, it's the long fall and sudden stop that doesn't agree with me," Neil nervously quipped. "This is my first attempt at free climbing."

Kypa empathized. It was his first time, too. "We will take it slow and make up time when we *safely* reach the bottom."

"Sounds good," Neil agreed, taking the lead. "Here goes nothing."

Neil dropped to his knees and stretched out flat on his stomach, inches from the cliff's edge. The wind whipped around him as he took a calming breath, then carefully swung his left leg over the side. Kypa knelt close beside him, ready to assist.

Straddling the edge, Neil brought his other leg around and glanced up with a nervous grin. "Now I know why Rose decided to stay behind," he joked.

Kypa chuckled, a hint of reassurance in his expression as he watched Neil disappear gradually over the edge and begin his descent. The treacherous slope was covered with ash-colored scree—loose sheets of rock that would challenge even the most experienced climbers—but Neil handled himself well.

Kypa mirrored Neil's movements, preparing to swing his long legs over the side. Yet, thoughts of Dr. Landry lingered. Her silence struck him as unusual; it seemed odd that she had not used the beacon again to contact him.

Perhaps it was just a false alarm, he told himself, hoping that was true.

Whatever the reason, Rose would have to wait. For now, he and Neil had a more urgent mission, and he could only hope that she was safe.

14

THE FARM

Planet Earth
Arbor Ridge, Georgia

Dr. Rose Landry nearly jumped out of her skin at the sudden sound of the doorbell. Even though she was expecting guests, the bell jarred her nerves. The memory of her rescue in Peru still haunted her.

Frustrated and embarrassed, Rose closed her eyes and took a breath to steady herself. But instead of feeling calmer, flashes of that chaotic scene replayed in her mind. She was running across an open field in her nightclothes, muscles straining and lungs burning. Swirls of smoke and dust filled the air as explosions roared and rapid bursts of gunfire echoed around her. Directly ahead through the murky haze, she locked eyes on the Navy SEAL team leader, urgently waving her toward the waiting helicopter.

"*Run!*" he shouted.

Rose had no recollection of boarding the chopper or taking off. It was not until she was safely onboard the USS *George Washington* that the fog had lifted. Yet, the trauma lingered as the doorbell rang a second time and sent her heart racing.

Jolted back to the present, Rose opened her eyes and reached for a nearby glass of Chardonnay. She drained the wine in one swift gulp, removed her apron, and tossed it on the kitchen counter.

Crossing the living room, she heard several knocks at the door. "I'm coming, I'm coming," she said irritably.

Before answering, Rose hesitated with her hand on the doorknob. She paused to straighten her blouse and put on her best face, hoping her guests would not see right through her façade. Finally, she opened the door and found Marlana Nunez standing on her porch.

"Hey, Chica!" Nunez greeted her with open arms.

Rose brightened and unlatched the screen door. She and Nunez embraced in a warm, tight hug, which lasted long enough for Marlana to sense Rose needed it more than she did. When they separated, Rose turned her attention to her other guest, Deputy Director Jessica Aguri of the CIA's National Clandestine Service.

Though they had spoken once on the phone, this was their first face-to-face meeting. As Rose and Jessica locked eyes, an unspoken understanding passed between them, sparking a warm and instant connection. After all, Jessica had gone out on a limb to arrange the rescue mission for her and Min-jun in Peru.

"Hi Rose, it's nice to finally meet you," Jessica said with a kind smile. She held up a bottle of red wine in one hand and a box of chocolates in the other. "We come bearing gifts."

The emotions Rose had tried to suppress a moment ago breached her tear ducts. She wiped her watery eyes and insisted on a hug. As they embraced, she whispered in Jessica's ear with heartfelt gratitude, "Thank you so much."

Those simple words offered Jessica much-needed solace. She was still grappling with the loss of three American soldiers during the rescue. Having read the SEAL team's after-action report, she knew how the chaotic scene had unfolded, none of which Jessica could have predicted. It was a miracle any of them made it out alive.

Jessica tenderly rubbed Rose's back, offering what comfort and reassurance she could. Rose chuckled softly as she pulled away, a bit embarrassed, and wiped her eyes again. Then, she opened the door and waved them inside.

"Please, come in. Dinner's almost ready."

Marlana and Jessica filed into the foyer. Before following them inside, Rose glanced at the black SUV in front of her house. Seeing the protection detail gave her a reassuring sense of security, but it also served as a constant reminder that the bubble of safety she had once lived in no longer existed. And while she was happy to see her friends, Rose knew the purpose of tonight's dinner was more than just a girls' night in.

"Mm, smells good," Jessica remarked, inhaling the aroma wafting from the kitchen.

"I hope you like Italian," Rose replied as she joined them. Jessica handed her the wine and candy.

"Oh, we *love* Italian. Right, girls?" Nunez said, elbowing Jessica mischievously.

Jessica reacted with a mix of shock and amusement at Marlana's candor. "I think Rose meant the dinner," she said, chuckling.

Marlana gave a nonchalant shrug. "You say so," she replied with an impish grin.

"You can hang your coats there," Rose gestured to a tall wooden coat rack by the door. "Go ahead and make yourselves at home. I need to check on the *lasagna*," she said, making air quotes and winking playfully at Nunez.

As her guests kicked off their heels and stowed their coats and purses, Rose made her way to the kitchen. She peeked inside the oven, savored the aroma, and checked to see if the top layer of cheese had browned evenly.

Marlana and Jessica joined her in the kitchen, taking their seats at the counter on barstools. Nunez noticed the open bottle of Chardonnay and three large wine glasses, one of which showed signs of recent use.

Feigning offense, she said, "How dare you start without us?"

Rose turned to find Nunez holding up her used wine glass. She smiled and shrugged unapologetically. "Chef's prerogative," Rose replied. "Next time, get here early."

"Amen to that," Jessica chimed in, nudging a glass toward Nunez to have her pour.

Marlana jumped at the chance and began pouring generous amounts into each glass. Meanwhile, Rose carefully pulled the lasagna out of the oven and placed the hot pan on the stovetop.

Closing her eyes, Nunez inhaled deeply and savored the aroma. "Mm-mm. Girl, that smells delicious," she said before taking a sip.

"That's not even the best part," Rose replied. Next, she removed a sheet of homemade garlic knots from the oven's bottom rack.

"Oh-ho, you've outdone yourself," Jessica remarked. "That smells so good."

Since returning from China, she had lived mostly on cafeteria food at Groom Lake. She could not remember the last time she had an honest-to-goodness, home-cooked meal.

Rose removed her oven mitts. "Thank my daughter," she said. "My family was here when I got back from Peru, and they stocked my freezer. There's no way I can eat all this alone."

Jessica held her glass close to her lips and asked, "Grandkids?"

Though she already knew the answer from reviewing Rose's file, Jessica posed the question anyway, hoping to spark a more personal connection.

"Two rambunctious little boys," Rose replied, smiling as she used tongs to transfer the bread into a basket. Glancing over her shoulder, she asked, "What about you? Any family?"

"Not yet," Jessica responded, a fleeting sadness crossing her face as she thought of the GCRM children back in Sanhe. "Work keeps me pretty busy. I don't have much of a social life."

"I'm going to fix that," Nunez swore as if Jessica had no say. "I know just the workaholic for you … that is if you go for the tall, handsome, and smart type."

"Oh yeah?" Jessica grinned behind her glass.

An attractive woman, Jessica Aguri had never had problems finding dates. However, her travel schedule and all-consuming career had killed every relationship that held the possibility of becoming remotely serious.

"You know who I have in mind?" Marlana asked, raising her glass with a playful glint in her eyes. Rose, caught off guard, shrugged, utterly clueless. Nunez exchanged a knowing look with her host as if it should have been obvious. "NASA boy," she said finally.

Taken aback, Rose replied, "Neil?" She chuckled. "Now, it could be the wine talking, but last I recall, you were predicting he'd hook up with an alien and make—quote-unquote—Yoda babies."

Jessica guffawed, nearly spraying her wine across the kitchen.

Next to her, Nunez laughed heartily at the memory. "I did say that," she admitted. "Wouldn't that be his dream come true?"

"I'm not sure I could compete with that," Jessica chuckled. "Nor would I want to."

Nunez waved flippantly, then raised her glass. "Hey, when in Rome …"

"Okay, okay," Rose interjected. "Before this conversation gets completely out of hand, let's eat while it's hot."

Marlana and Jessica each grabbed a plate, serving themselves generous portions of lasagna and Caesar salad, while Rose placed the breadbasket in the center of the dining room table. Moments later, they settled into their seats, paused to appreciate the feast on the table, and then dug in.

"I will say one more thing about Neil," Nunez punctuated her words by pointing at Jessica with the piece of bread in her hand, "If he hasn't eloped with an alien queen, I promise to set you two up when he returns." She popped the last bite into her mouth as if to bind the deal.

"I appreciate the whole intergalactic matchmaker idea," Jessica said with a grin, gesturing with her fork mid-chew, "but I'll find my own dates, thank you." She washed down her food with a sip of wine before turning to Rose. "Speaking of Dr. Garrett, have you heard from him or Captain Tan lately?"

Rose felt her cheeks flush, though it was not from the wine. "Me? No," she replied with a nervous smile. "I'm not sure my cell phone has that kind of range."

Jessica chuckled.

"They've been gone a while now," Nunez remarked as she started on her lasagna. "I'm starting to worry."

Rose opted not to respond, focusing instead on her meal.

"I would've thought they'd be back by now—or at least send word," Jessica mused. "How did Luna react when you told her Kypa went home?"

Rose's chest tightened. The mention of Luna's name evoked a wave of regret for abandoning her Aiwan friend. Not that it was Rose's fault; Luna had left for Challenger Deep with Edmund before the rescue happened. If Luna had been there, the SEALs would have extracted her, as well.

Rose pushed food around the plate with her fork as she pondered Luna's situation. She had worried through many sleepless nights, hoping Luna did not resent her for leaving when she had the chance. Ironically, Rose missed their telepathic exchanges of past memories and future hopes.

Before Rose could answer Jessica's question, Nunez chimed in, "I wonder how Kypa would react if he knew Luna survived the crash."

Unable to keep her secret any longer, Rose dropped her fork onto her plate with a loud clatter that startled her guests. "Okay, I contacted Kypa, alright!" she confessed.

Jessica and Marlana froze, their eyes widening in shock as the room fell into a heavy silence. They exchanged glances, the gravity of Rose's admission settling in.

Finally, Jessica turned to Rose and asked, "How?"

Rose reached for her glass, trying to appear calm despite the slight tremor in her hand. She downed the rest of her wine while Jessica and Marlana watched her intently, waiting for what she would say next. Setting the empty glass back on the table, Rose paused, carefully choosing her words. The last thing she wanted was to invite another search of her home or, worse, be dragged back to Groom Lake.

Clearing her throat, Rose asked Marlana, "Remember the night we said goodbye to Kypa, Neil, and Ava?" Nunez nodded curtly, the memory still vivid. "Kypa gave me something," Rose continued, "… a gift."

Marlana's gaze dropped as she searched her memory for any sign of Kypa passing an object to Rose that night. Nothing came to mind. Curiosity and suspicion rising, she asked sharply, "What gift?"

Rose's eyes darted between her guests, knowing there was no turning back now. She stood, placed her napkin on the table, and excused herself, saying, "Wait here."

Jessica and Nunez watched Rose disappear down the hall, then exchanged knowing looks—both fully aware of the national security risk at play.

Moments later, Rose returned with something clutched in her hands. Standing beside the table, she took a deep breath and placed a metal bracelet on the oak surface.

Jessica and Marlana leaned closer, scrutinizing the object with the same befuddled expression.

"Is it jewelry?" Nunez asked.

Rose shook her head. "No, it's a beacon," she explained. "You press the jewel in the center, and it sends a signal. Kypa told me to use it if ever I needed him, and he would come."

"So, you used it," Jessica said, not to pass judgment but to clarify the facts.

Rose nodded. "Yes. It was the first thing I did when I got home from Peru. I was afraid for Luna, so I contacted Kypa hoping he would return to help."

"Did he respond?" Jessica followed up.

"Not yet," Rose replied, sounding deflated. "I pressed the button, and it flashed briefly, but nothing else happened."

"Can you speak to each other with it?" Nunez asked, eyeing the device from different angles, unwilling to touch it.

"I don't think so," Rose answered. Fretting, she added, "I'm sorry, I know I should've reported this, but Kypa made me promise not to tell anyone."

A torrent of concerns swirled in Jessica's mind. She had an obligation to report this incident to her superiors, and when she did, it was going to spark an uproar. However, noticing the panic on Rose's face gave her pause. Dr. Landry had been through so much already, and she was clearly torn between loyalty to her friends and family versus doing the right thing for her country.

Jessica decided to move forward with this new information rather than belabor the wisdom or rationale of Rose's choices. She extended her hand to Rose with a warm smile. "It's okay, Rose. You're not in trouble. You did the right thing."

Rose accepted Jessica's hand, tears welling in her eyes. "Thank you," she whispered.

Nunez stood and rounded the table to give Rose a big hug.

When they finished, Jessica got back to business. "Did Kypa leave anything else behind?"

Rose wiped her eyes and shook her head. "Not with me," she answered honestly, then pushed the beacon toward Jessica. "Here, you take it," she insisted. "You could get in a lot of trouble if you don't report it, and I won't have you sticking your neck out for me again."

Jessica nodded in agreement and placed the beacon in the chest pocket of her blouse.

With that settled, Rose visibly relaxed. She gestured to the nearly empty bottle. "More wine?"

The trio burst into laughter, only to be followed by an uneasy silence. They sat quietly, each in their own thoughts, their food and drinks untouched.

Rose noticed Marlana subtly nudge Jessica with a head bob and asked, "What is it?"

Jessica turned to Rose and sighed with a frown. "I hate to bring this up, but I need to talk to you about your time in Peru."

"About Mathias?"

Jessica nodded. "And Luna, of course."

The thought of Edmund Mathias revolted Rose. "When it comes to him, there are bad words in my head that I don't want to say."

"Oh, I've got plenty of words I'd love to say about him," Nunez volunteered. "I met him once at Groom Lake … Mathias is a creepy little spud. And those goons he surrounds himself with, they certainly grew up on a steady diet of glue sticks."

Marlana's blunt humor helped lighten the atmosphere, so much so that Rose lifted her fork and began eating again. Jessica and Marlana joined her.

After finishing a bite, Jessica continued. "We know that Mathias is conducting illegal cloning experiments in Peru and developing some sort of force enhancement serum that splices human and animal DNA."

"And he wants to do the same with Aiwan DNA," Rose attested. "He has blood and tissue samples from Kypa and Luna."

"Mathias wants to create some kind of super soldier," Nunez added. "That's why he was in cahoots with Garza and Sizemore."

"That's right," Jessica affirmed. "Speaking of which, we know that Kypa used some sort of telepathy on those two," she recounted from Nunez's official report and Rose's testimony. "Does Luna have those same abilities?"

Rose swallowed the lump in her throat. "I'd assume so. Why?"

"That's a very powerful tool for coercion," Jessica stated the obvious. Her brow furrowed slightly. "So, Luna never attempted to control you in any way?"

"Control me? No," Rose answered truthfully, shaking her head emphatically. "My role was strictly as a go-between, someone to bridge the communication gap the way Neil and I did for Kypa."

Jessica studied Rose intently, searching for any hint of deception in her eyes and body language, but decided not to press further. Instead, she shifted her focus back to Rose's former protégé.

"Is Luna controlling Mathias?" Jessica asked, probing the potential implications.

"It's possible, but from what Kypa said, to control another being's mind can be dangerous for both parties," Rose spoke earnestly. "Edmund knew the risk, so he implemented strict protocols to restrict Luna's access to employees."

"Mathias is a very powerful man and a threat to our country," Jessica pointed out. "If he were to be compromised by Luna, who knows where that could lead."

Nunez leaned back in her seat, tracing the rim of her wine glass with her fingertip as she imagined Luna taking control of Edmund's mind. "What if Luna made him believe he was a little girl?" she said with a naughty grin.

Jessica chuckled, but Rose was not amused. Her expression turned serious.

"Luna isn't the threat," she clarified. "The only reason she agreed to help Edmund cloak the crystals was because he promised her half. All Luna wants is to get home and help restore Cirros."

Jessica's brow furrowed. "What's Cirros?"

Rose took a moment to organize her thoughts. "Cirros is one of Aiwa's five realms," she explained. "It was destroyed by earthquakes caused by over-harvesting crystals. Thousands of her people perished," she added somberly. "Luna, like so many others, is a refugee."

Resisting the temptation to say more about how Luna had telepathically shared life-like memories of Cirros, Rose sipped her wine instead. She genuinely liked Jessica and felt indebted to her for what went down in Peru, but as Deputy Director Aguri, she knew Jessica had a job to do. With the treasonous actions of Garza and Sizemore still fresh in everyone's memory, Rose was not sure who she could trust.

After briefly reflecting, Jessica said, "I can only imagine how alone Luna must feel. Before all this business with Kypa and Luna, I worked in China helping impoverished children. Some of the kids are orphans, but most are abandoned by their family—either because their parents had too many mouths to feed, or they simply didn't want them anymore."

"That's so sad," Nunez remarked, shaking her head.

"After all that Luna's been through," Jessica continued, "I'm sure she appreciated having someone like you to talk to … someone who would listen."

Rose shrugged meekly. "I was kidnapped, remember? But yes, we became friends, at least for my part."

Jessica nodded. "You know Mathias retracted his money, right?"

Rose hmphed. "Not surprising," she said dryly. "Actually, I'm glad he did. I was never comfortable with our arrangement, especially the money. All I really wanted was for Joe to get credit for the Chron's research Edmund stole. That's why he offered me twenty million, to let bygones be bygones."

"It's a lot of money," Nunez pondered aloud.

"I know," Rose agreed, "but it wasn't as if I had a choice in the matter. I seriously thought Edmund would have me and my family killed if I didn't cooperate. And then there was Luna. I didn't want her only human connection to be with someone like Mathias."

Jessica patted Rose's arm reassuringly. "You made a tough choice, and now you may be the only human on this planet that Luna trusts."

"I wouldn't be so sure about that," Rose countered. "Look at me. I'm home now, safe and sound, while she's still stuck in Peru with Edmund. God only knows what she thinks of me."

"Do you want to find out?" Jessica proposed, gauging Rose's interest.

Rose paused and set down her half-raised wine glass. "What do you mean?"

Jessica leaned closer and confided, "Well, we know Mathias wants the crystals in Challenger Deep—"

"—Yeah." Rose scoffed. "He wants to take Mathais Industries intergalactic."

"Exactly, and to do that, he's getting in bed with Russia, China, and North Korea. They're all lining up to place orders for his force enhancement serum, which we think Mathias is using to fund his harvesting venture."

"So, how does that involve me?" Rose asked, trying to figure out where this was leading.

With a determined look in her eyes, Jessica replied, "To put it bluntly, Rose, you might be the key to stopping them. For all of Mathias's grandiose ambitions, he knows he can't go anywhere without Luna, especially with the prospect of off-world harvesters moving in on his claim. Someone has to get to

Luna and turn her away from the dark side, so to speak."

"Oh yeah, Neil would definitely dig you," Marlana nodded as if it was a done deal.

Rose ignored the remark, turning her thoughts to Jessica's offer. In her heart, she knew Jessica was right—Luna was in danger, and someone had to warn her, someone Luna trusted. But to do so meant getting involved again.

Rose exhaled heavily. "I'm almost afraid to ask, but what do you want from me?"

Jessica glanced between Marlana and Rose before responding, "Nothing now. You've already done so much, and I know you're anxious to get your life back. So, for now, just sit tight. But if an opportunity presents itself, would you be willing to meet with Luna again?"

Without hesitation, Rose nodded. "Of course."

Jessica expressed her gratitude by reaching out again and gently squeezing Rose's hand. "Thank you," she said warmly.

Rose smiled and returned the squeeze. "By the way, can you do anything about my chaperones?" she said, thumbing in the direction of the protection detail parked outside. "I appreciate the effort, but their presence somehow adds to the stress."

Understanding her concern, Jessica considered her request. "I'll talk to my boss and see what I can do."

Camp Peary
Williamsburg, Virginia

Six hundred miles north of Dr. Landry's home, right off Interstate 64, sits Camp Peary. Nestled on a 9,000-acre military reservation in York County, the heavily wooded property has a long history of supporting America's defense, yet its true mission remains shrouded in mystery.

Dating back to 1942, Camp Peary primarily trained Navy Seabees and even held Italian and German POWs during World War II. Over the years, the installation's mission changed. Its official designation was AFETA—Armed Forces Experimental Training Activity—but the United States government has never publicly acknowledged it as "The Farm," the Central Intelligence Agency's secret domestic proving grounds.

Jokingly referred to as spy school, The Farm serves as one of two off-site locations used by the CIA and DIA to train covert operatives. Its sister site, The Point, was in Hertford, North Carolina, but young agents learned their craft here at Camp Peary. Agents attend either a six-week or a three-month course, learning everything from dead drops to surveillance tactics, such as trailing someone without being spotted—aka "rabbiting." The Farm even has a defensive driving course to teach escape and evasion techniques and an airfield for parachute training should an agent ever need to jump out of a perfectly good aircraft.

President Fitzgerald was making a rare appearance at Camp Peary this evening. At the request of CIA Director Maxine Ratliff, the president came to show his support and share a meal with the recruits. In difficult times like these, he believed it was important to remind those serving on the front lines how important they were to the country's defense.

Marine One, the presidential helicopter, along with two matching decoy helicopters, made the trip from Washington in under an hour. The trio of Sikorsky VH-60N "White Tops"—because of their white-painted roofs— touched down at Camp Peary's small airfield just after sundown.

Brett Brenham, CIA Director of the National Clandestine Service, awaited President Fitzgerald's arrival, flanked by the president's Secret Service detail. As Marine One's rotors wound down, Brenham stepped forward to greet his boss, Director Ratliff, and the commander-in-chief.

"Welcome to The Farm, Mr. President," Brenham offered a firm handshake after they disembarked the helicopter.

"Hello, Brett. Thanks for having me," Fitzgerald replied, fully aware of the enormous logistical effort behind a presidential visit. The president had long since stopped apologizing for the inconvenience, especially since this was Ratliff's idea.

Brenham welcomed Ratliff, then gestured toward Cadillac One. "The recruits know you're coming, sir, and they're really excited to meet you," he said enthusiastically.

"It's always a pleasure to break bread with America's heroes," Fitzgerald replied, starting toward his motorcade.

In truth, the president welcomed the distraction. With the fallout from Operation Bold Fortress and the increasing public tension surrounding the possibility of alien invasion, he needed an evening away from Washington.

A Secret Service agent, hidden behind a pair of dark sunglasses, opened the back door to The Beast as the president approached. Fitzgerald signaled Ratliff to enter first, followed by Brenham, who climbed in and sat in one of three rear-facing seats. Fitzgerald entered last, taking his place beside Ratliff.

Within moments, the motorcade was moving. They drove along a narrow, paved road surrounded by dense forestry. Along the way, Brenham provided a brief overview of the activities and courses taught at The Farm. This trip was the president's first visit to Camp Peary—which he found quite impressive. A self-proclaimed James Bond geek, Fitzgerald marveled at the tradecraft of today's covert operatives.

A few miles along Niagara Road, the motorcade pulled up to Shooter's Mess Hall, a nondescript, single-story building with an off-white exterior and dark metal roof. Surrounded by barracks and several gun ranges, the dining hall stood out as noticeably newer than the other structures. A tornado had destroyed its 100-year-old predecessor, and it was only recently rebuilt.

By the time Cadillac One arrived, the president's advance security detail had already locked down the perimeter. Despite Camp Peary's rigid security protocols, the unit treated the site the same as if the president were visiting an elementary school or a foreign nation.

As soon as Cadillac One came to a halt, an agent stepped out of the front passenger seat. One hand touched his ear mic, while the other rested on the sidearm concealed under his dark suit coat. His sharp eyes scanned the surrounding area for threats.

"All units, stand by. Zephyr is on the move," he said into his mic as he opened the car door.

The trio, led by Director Ratliff, stepped out of the vehicle and made their way up the sidewalk to a set of double doors. There, a second agent awaited and opened the door for the VIPs.

Inside Shooter's Mess, the lead instructor called the room to attention. Two dozen hungry recruits, seated around rectangular folding tables, came to their feet. Each spy cadet, dressed in camouflage fatigues to blend in with the Army personnel stationed at Camp Peary, was drenched in sweat and muck from a grueling day of physical training. Their instructor kept them in the position of attention as the president entered the room.

The mess hall immediately fell silent, as if the very air had paused in respect. Fitzgerald surveyed the recruits, beaming with admiration. They reminded him of himself—thirty years earlier—a young man in the best condition of his life, proudly serving his country and making lifelong friends along the way.

"As you were," the president said with a raised voice.

The recruits dropped their shoulders in unison, relaxing slightly but remaining in place, their full attention focused on the president.

"Ladies and gentlemen, I'm honored to be here with you tonight," Fitzgerald said, his eyes moving about the room. With a grin, he added, "Judging by your appearance, I can tell you've had another easy day of training." His remark elicited several good-natured grumblings, which the president responded by raising his hands in defense. "I'm only kidding, of course. On behalf of myself, Directors Ratliff and Brenham, and a grateful nation, I personally want to thank each of you for your service to our great country. Now, let's eat!"

En masse, the hungry recruits began shuffling towards the serving line. Fitzgerald used this opportunity to move amongst them, mingling, asking questions, and shaking hands. The recruits quickly warmed up to him and relaxed. It was not every day that they got to meet the president.

Ratliff joined in. She, too, was welcomed wholeheartedly by the recruits. For Maxine, this was her first trip back to The Farm since being appointed Director by the president. Forty-some-odd years ago, she had been a raw recruit just like them, proving what was possible with hard work and dedication.

Brenham felt his phone vibrate in his pocket while Ratliff and Fitzgerald made their way around the room. One glance at the caller ID told him it was urgent, so he excused himself and stepped outside to take the call.

The male voice on the other end was direct but carried a note of empathy. Brenham listened intently, his face tightening with shock as the devastating news sunk in. The conversation was brief, lasting no more than sixty seconds.

When the caller finished, Brenham steeled himself and responded somberly, "Thank you."

He hung up and lowered his phone, his grip tightening around it as he stared blankly into the distance. Alone outside the mess hall, his mind swirled with anger and sorrow. He felt a visceral urge to lash out, to scream into the void, but he forced himself to maintain control.

Taking a deep breath, Brenham re-entered the building. He locked eyes with Ratliff, and she could immediately tell something was wrong. Excusing herself, she made her way across the room and followed him out the door.

As soon as they were out of earshot, Brenham turned sharply to face his boss, his expression dark with restrained fury.

"What is it?" Ratliff asked, concern etched on her face.

Seething, Brenham delivered the grim news. "Paul Wiggins is dead."

15
BOTTOM OF THE FUNNEL

Planet Earth
Satipo, Peru

Luna lay asleep on the floor of her darkened bedroom. She had spent the night restless, caught in a storm of dreams that offered no peace. With a sharp gasp, Luna jolted upright in a disorienting rush of consciousness. Chest heaving, she propped herself on one elbow, blinking several times to clear her vision. Gradually, the familiar outlines of her room began to emerge from the shadows, grounding her in reality once more.

As her breathing steadied, Luna's nightmare lingered. She could still see the two figures from her dream: Renzo and Mathias. The scene had unfolded one floor down, inside the Chachapoyan's private dojo. Renzo stood at a sink, meticulously removing blood from under his fingernails, while Mathias leaned against the door frame. Edmund watched in silence, a satisfied grin playing on his lips as he listened to the gory details of the capture, torture, and murder of CIA Station Chief Paul Wiggins.

Panicked and confused, Luna asked herself, *How can this be?*

Wiggins's gruesome demise notwithstanding, she was deeply troubled by the realization that this was no dream. Evidence of Renzo's heinous crime came to her by chance, an accidental telepathic connection to Mathias while she slept.

Alarmed by the possibility of an unrestrained mutual link, Luna clutched her chest, pondering the unthinkable—*What did I show him?*

She had never experienced this phenomenon or heard of it happening to other Aiwans. Stress seemed the most likely culprit. The unexpected appearance of the Aiwan deep space probe had everyone at the compound, especially Mathias, on edge. Pressure was mounting to find a permanent solution to hiding the crystals as the threat of a harvester invasion appeared imminent.

Closing her eyes, Luna inhaled deeply to calm her unsettled mind. As she did, she searched for any lingering traces of a mental connection to Mathias. To her relief, Luna found none.

She opened her eyes slowly, her gaze drifting upward to the return vent above the window. Luna knew Mathias kept a hidden camera there to observe her, only discovering it after their initial connection aboard Edmund's ship, *Billy Bones*. She chose not to confront him about it. But now, in her moment of vulnerability, the thought resurfaced, gnawing at her unease.

Averting her gaze, Luna wondered if Mathias was watching her now and, if so, what thoughts were running through his mind. Since establishing their telepathic connection, Luna had sporadically tapped into Mathias's brain to gather intelligence. Only once had she planted the seed of an idea into his subconscious, and that was merely to allow her to roam free without a tracking device attached to her ankle. In hindsight, all her probing occurred while they were both awake. But an unsettling thought crept in—if they had connected while asleep, without Luna exercising self-restraint, the information exchange might have gone both ways.

As troubling as that thought may be, Luna hid her misgivings well. Ignoring the camera, she glanced at the clock on the dresser. Seeing it was almost time to get up anyway, Luna came to her feet and crossed the room in the darkness, searching her mind for any hint that she may have compromised herself.

Luna departed her bedroom and went to the rooftop pool for some much-needed exercise. As expected, the pool was empty. She swam alone, grateful Edmund's girlfriend, Deanna, had not invited herself. Luna was in no mood to make small talk. If stress had been a factor in her telepathy miscue, then rigorous exercise could be the solution.

Luna attacked the pool for the next hour, lapping back and forth at high speed without a break. While this routine did not compare to swimming in the open ocean, it achieved the desired effect. By the time Luna finished, she was exhausted and hungry, though no closer to a solution.

After toweling off, she exited the pool area and took the stairs down to the cafeteria on the first floor. Several workers greeted Luna with genial smiles and friendly waves as she walked the corridors unhindered. Despite having Mathias's no-touching-the-alien-mandate lifted, many staffers remained hesitant to approach her, which was understandable—Luna took no offense. Even so, many staffers enamored by the Aiwan could not resist a chance to meet her. And while selfies were out of the question—cell phones were prohibited inside the facility—Luna seized every opportunity to "connect" with staffers and grow her network through handshakes and fist bumps.

Luna grabbed a food tray inside the cafeteria and went through the serving line like everyone else. One of the workers behind the counter saw Luna and retreated to a nearby refrigerator, retrieving one of many specialty seafood plates created just for the Aiwan. With a warm smile, the server presented Luna with her favorite dish: raw octopus on a bed of fresh seaweed.

Luna accepted the plate, dipping her chin appreciatively. "Gracias Juanita. Se ve delicioso."

Juanita, a middle-aged woman from Satipo, beamed. "De nada, señorita Luna," she replied. She smiled cheerfully and returned to her station to serve the other patrons scrambled eggs and bacon.

After grabbing a bottle of water, Luna scanned the bustling cafeteria for a seat. Her eyes settled on a nearby table where a few familiar staffers sat. She joined them, sliding into a seat at the end of the table before digging into her meal. In between bites, Luna entertained the group's questions about Aiwa and intergalactic space travel. The staffers listened with rapt attention, hanging onto Luna's every word. Each sentence she spoke seemed to cast a spell, drawing them deeper into her world.

"Quite a captive audience," came a familiar voice.

Luna glanced over her shoulder to find Mathias standing behind her. Shadowed by his personal assistant, Ms. Diaz, Edmund's appearance swiftly extinguished the positive mood around the table, causing an immediate shift from a spirited conversation to an uncomfortable silence.

Edmund looked about the table. "I hope I'm not interrupting anything important," he said with a disingenuous smile.

His dark undertone sent a clear message: breakfast was over.

Collecting their trays, the staffers vacated the table and hurried away, many without touching their meals.

Feigning confusion, Edmund turned to Diaz with a playful, almost mischievous smile. "Was it something I said?"

Diaz shrugged with a suppressed smile.

Edmund swiftly shifted gears. He was brimming with excitement, itching to speak with Luna.

"May I join you?" he asked.

His singular reference was Diaz's cue to excuse herself. Taking no offense, Diaz dutifully gave them privacy and walked away to wait by the cafeteria exit.

Luna's gaze narrowed subtly on Edmund. With last night still fresh in her mind, she sensed something different about Mathias and eyed him with wary curiosity.

"Of course," Luna replied without hesitation. She gestured to the many seats now available. "Please."

"Wonderful," Edmund replied, taking a seat across from her. He leaned across the table and spoke in a hushed tone. "I had an epiphany last night … something I wanted to run past you."

Luna swallowed the lump in her throat. "Is that so?"

"Yes, it's about cloaking the crystals," Edmund explained eagerly. "You got me thinking when you said there could be more crystals on Earth. It makes perfect sense, right?" he asked rhetorically.

Luna opened her mouth to respond, but Edmund kept talking.

"The question is, how do we find them?" he posed. "Since we cannibalized that Seeker to build our first cloaking device, that won't be of much use." He frowned. "We know Captain Tan shot down a few others but locating them on the ocean floor would be like spotting a speck of dust on a sunbeam—impossible."

Edmund slumped his shoulders in a defeated pose for effect. Then, a sly grin creased the corners of his mouth as he straightened again.

"But what about the Aiwan probe orbiting Earth?" he asked, pointing to the ceiling. "At first, I wanted to capture the probe or maybe shoot it down somehow, but that was ridiculous," he said, laughing at himself for such an absurd notion. "Then, it dawned on me that we don't need that probe. We have the next best thing right here on Earth—Kypa's escape pod!"

Edmund leaned back, crossing his arms in a gangsta pose, expecting Luna to gush with praise at his brilliance.

Instead, she reacted with a measured expression. Luna's brow furrowed as she carefully considered the intriguing prospect, paying no mind to Edmund's eager gaze from across the table.

After contemplating, she began to nod slowly as the idea gained merit.

"The equipment on board the pod could be used to boost the signal of our device," she responded thoughtfully, "but—"

"—But not enough to cloak all of the crystals on the planet, I know," Edmund blurted as he leaned closer.

Luna was taken aback by Mathias's enthusiasm, especially how effortlessly he completed her thought. The incident triggered her fears from the previous night.

Edmund misinterpreted her reaction, accepting her surprise as validation that he was onto something significant.

"So, how do we use Kypa's pod to cloak the entire planet, you ask? Simple," Edmund explained. "We'll connect it to military satellites and broadcast a global scrambling signal into space—one powerful enough to disrupt the long-range sensors of approaching ships." He punctuated his idea with a confident mic drop.

Leaning back in his seat, Mathias watched Luna with a hopeful gleam in his eyes as she weighed his proposal carefully. All the while, Luna probed her own mind to see if he had somehow gotten into her head.

"Your thinking is sound," Luna said, musing. "In theory, networking satellites to the escape pod could effectively boost the cloaking signal and hide the crystals from enemy sensors. However, re-tasking your satellites would take a monumental effort, not to mention the unprecedented cooperation of many rival nations. Is that possible?"

"Let me handle that," Mathias said with self-assured hubris. "I've already identified which countries have the satellites we'll need. All I have to do is convince one man—my nemesis in the White House," he said, rolling his eyes. "As President Fitzgerald leans, so does the rest of the G7. Normally, that might concern me, but the elections are right around the corner and the president can't afford to miss the boat on this … no matter how much he hates me," Edmund said with a sly grin.

As Mathias spoke, Luna could not help but notice how he radiated even more confidence than usual—if that was possible. The sparkle in his eyes and resolute smile hinted at a more profound conviction, as if he knew he was on the brink of genius.

Feeling the weight of Luna's gaze, Edmund gave her a curious look. "What?" he asked, suddenly feeling self-conscious. "Do I have something in my teeth?"

Luna shook her head, chuckling softly. "No, it is not that. It is something more. I noticed a change in you this morning—a vibrancy and confidence that was not there before."

Edmund raised an eyebrow, a smirk forming as he rolled his shoulders back.

"Oh yeah?" he asked, his voice carrying a note of casual intrigue. "You know, I never let myself get too high or too low when it comes to business. Things can change in a heartbeat. Take this week for instance, the attack on the facility was certainly a downer, but then I had this epiphany about tweaking the serum. Vlachos said that was exactly the fix we needed to stabilize the formula."

A shiver ran down Luna's spine—this could not be a coincidence.

Luna maintained a façade of admiration, her smile a practiced mask of warmth and approval.

"Congratulations," Luna said, slightly dipping her chin. "That is very impressive. I am sure your investors will be quite pleased."

Still utterly oblivious to the cause of his newfound cognitive awakening, Edmund scoffed. "They better be," he replied. "I'm meeting with some of them today to share the good news."

"And your idea to network satellites against the harvesters is ingenious," Luna praised.

Edmund nodded with self-satisfaction. "I know, right? My thinking has just been so clear these past few days. It's like I've unlocked my brain somehow and all the neurons are firing. I've got all these new ideas just swirling about," he said, laughing with a semi-crazed look in his eyes. "It's like an avalanche of access!"

Luna nodded politely, masking her thoughts. Inwardly, she vowed to sever their involuntary connections before Mathias unlocked any more of his mind. The idea of him potentially developing his own telepathic abilities made her shudder.

Edmund glanced at Ms. Diaz, who was standing by the exit. She tapped her wrist, indicating it was time for his meeting with the North Koreans. Edmund responded with a nod and an okay sign.

"Tell you what," he said to Luna, rubbing his hands together like a greedy banker, "I think we're onto something here. How about after my meeting, I'll join you in the lab and we can tackle this scrambling signal idea together?"

"Very well," Luna agreed. "I have a good idea what Kypa's escape pod is capable of … assuming it is still in working order. If you can obtain the specs on the satellites in question, we can begin to construct a model to test your hypothesis."

Edmund grinned. "Spoken like a true scientist," he said, sliding his chair back and standing. "You get started and I'll see you in a few."

Before Luna could respond, Mathias was gone. She twisted in her chair and watched him walk away. As he departed, Edmund snatched an uneaten chocolate donut off the plate of a staffer who had just sat down to begin her breakfast.

"Don't mind if I do," Luna heard Edmund say cheerily as he walked on, leaving the woman speechless.

At the exit, Mathias joined Diaz, patiently waiting with a black leather portfolio tucked against her chest. Edmund said something indiscernible before taking a bite out of the donut. He then tossed the remainder into a nearby trash receptacle.

While her boss was preoccupied, Diaz cast a subtle glance at Luna across the room. Her eyes narrowed slightly, her expression inscrutable. With no love lost between them, at least on Diaz's part, her lingering gaze left Luna wondering what might be going through Diaz's mind.

Oblivious to the silent exchange, Mathias grabbed a napkin from a nearby wall dispenser and wiped his mouth. After tossing it in the trash, he continued out of the cafeteria, followed close behind by Diaz, who quickly adjusted her pace to catch up.

As Luna returned to her meal, she noticed the staffer whose donut Mathias had stolen. They exchanged a brief, knowing look, both feeling violated by Edmund to some degree. It was strange how he had that effect on people.

Ten minutes later, Edmund entered his office with Diaz in tow. She closed the door behind them as Mathias took a seat behind his stylish desk. Positioned in front of a large window overlooking the Amazon rainforest, the desk was a striking piece of craftsmanship. Valued at over one hundred thousand euros, it was custom-made in Italy, featuring an arched-glass top and a hardwood base. The front was adorned with a dark red leather panel, providing a stylish barrier that concealed Edmund from the waist down.

Seated in a high-back leather chair, Mathias placed his thumb on a biometric reader embedded in the desktop. Once authenticated, the desk came to life, and a fifty-seven-inch curved monitor rose from within its base. The glass top illuminated with a laser projection of a virtual keyboard, touchpad, and IoT control panel, allowing access to everything from the lights in the room to the numerous cameras hidden throughout the compound.

Edmund loved his new toy. With a grin, he tapped the control panel to dim the glass behind him so his investors would not be distracted by the lush jungle backdrop. As Diaz settled into a seat across from him, Edmund woke up his computer and started the video conference a few moments ahead of schedule.

The North Korean investors were already in the queue waiting to be admitted into the meeting—an encouraging sign. Edmund straightened his posture and cleared his throat. Diaz flashed him a reassuring thumbs-up for good luck.

In sales terms, Edmund's North Korean prospects were at the bottom of the funnel. After all his schmoozing and promises, Mathias had them poised to become paying customers. It was time to close the deal on his first official sale of the force enhancement serum.

Turning on his game face, Edmund flashed a wide grin as the stern-faced North Koreans appeared on the screen. The first to catch his eye was acting Supreme Leader Kim Sol-ju. The younger sister of the late Kim Sung-il bore a striking resemblance to her heavyset brother, including the trademark unibrow. Her black hair was cut in a state-approved, classic bob, and she wore the same style of charcoal Mao suit favored by her predecessors.

The Supreme Leader was seated at the head of a long conference table. Flanking Sol-ju on either side were four middle-aged men wearing DPRK Army uniforms decorated with medals. Among them, one stood out to Edmund: General Kang.

Kang was seated directly to Sol-ju's right. Edmund had personally recruited the general to be his inside man—a calculated move that promised Kang significant wealth once they finalized today's deal.

Smiling inwardly, Edmund bowed respectfully to his esteemed guests. "Greetings, Supreme Leader," he said, maintaining eye contact. "We meet at last. My name is Edmund—"

Before he could finish, Sol-ju cut him off, her voice snapping in rapid Korean to General Kang. The words flew by too quickly for Edmund to catch, but her tone indicated she had no patience for pleasantries.

So much the better, Edmund thought to himself.

"The Supreme Leader demands to know why the shipment you promised has been repeatedly delayed," Kang said firmly, not wanting to show weakness.

The remaining officers at the table mirrored the Supreme Leader's scowl, glaring sternly at Edmund in a unified show of support.

"My apologies for the delay, Supreme Leader," Edmund answered with feigned sincerity. "As you know, the Americans attacked my facility here in Peru—a blatant attempt to steal industrial secrets. Naturally, they failed, thanks largely to the missile launchers you so generously provided," he said, gesturing to Sol-ju with a grateful smile.

But his words met a wall of stony silence; the Supreme Leader and her entourage remained impassive. Edmund quickly recovered and cleared his throat. "However, I am pleased to report that production is back on schedule and your order is ready for delivery."

Sol-ju spoke again, keeping to her native tongue.

When she finished, Kang asked, "What about the aliens you are harboring?"

Edmund shifted in his seat. With a forced smile, he answered, "There is only one Aiwan here. Her name is Luna and—"

Again, the Supreme Leader interrupted. This time, she leaned forward and pounded her fist angrily on the table to drive home her point.

Kang relayed Sol-ju's demand as she spoke. "The Supreme Leader says this alien is responsible for her brother's death and conspired with the Americans to attack our country. She wants Luna's head."

Edmund never thought he would catch himself missing Sol-ju's late brother. But that was the case. Not intimidated by her antics—which were better saved for North Korea's state media—Edmund paused to allow the tension to subside. Maintaining his composure, he carefully chose his next words. The fate of their deal hinged on his response.

"Dear Leader, I am deeply sorry for your loss," he said with empathy. "Please accept my sincere condolences." Edmund paused so Kang could translate, then continued. "I, too, share your disdain for the American president. His arrogance is appalling, and his actions … criminal. You have my solemn pledge that I will help you exact your revenge, but with all due respect, I cannot hand over the Aiwan in my care. Luna was not part of the attack on your country, nor did she play a role in your brother's unfortunate passing." Kang translated, and before Sol-ju could rebut, Edmund added. "Instead, as a gesture of good faith, I offer you something even better … the heads of your betrayers: Vong Ji-eun and Choi Min-jun. Ji-eun is the daughter of General Vong Yong-hae, the man who conspired with the Americans and masterminded the sinister plot that resulted in the Aiwan ship exploding in North Hamgyong Province," Edmund explained.

He darted his eyes toward Diaz, who gestured for him to tone it down a bit. He was laying it on a bit thick, even for his taste.

"Furthermore," Edmund continued, "The traitor, Choi Min-jun, helped General Vong's daughter defect to the United States. They have both been granted asylum by the Americans. With your permission, I have the means to capture them and deliver them to you … alive."

Judging by how Sol-ju's eyes lit up at the mention of capturing General Vong's daughter, Edmund knew she had taken the bait.

Sol-ju nodded to Kang, who covered the microphone with his hand so they could converse in private. The other generals leaned in close as they spoke in hushed tones, each nodding in affirmation.

When they finished, Sol-ju and the others sat back. Kang removed his hand from the mic and spoke calmly, "The Supreme Leader agrees to your terms on one condition. She insists on sending a team of our people to help capture the traitors."

"Yes, of course," Edmund allowed. "I've already dispatched my best man. If it is alright with you, once we conclude our business, General Kang and I can coordinate the logistics."

Kang relayed the message to the Supreme Leader, who nodded in agreement. Turning back to Mathias, Kang said, "The serum funds will be released today. We expect delivery by the end of the month."

Edmund quickly assessed the feasibility of their expectations. The U.S. blockade of North Korea made illegal imports challenging but not impossible.

"Agreed," he replied with a contented smile. "On behalf of Mathias Industries, I want to thank you for your business, Dear Leader. I promise you won't regret it."

Sol-ju bowed, a rare display of respect that relieved the generals around her. The meeting then ended. As soon as the screen went blank, Edmund sat back in his chair and pumped his fists in the air.

"Yes!" he exclaimed, envisioning the influx of cash heading his way. "That's how you do things in the big league!"

"Congratulations," Diaz said, clapping excitedly. "Well played!"

Edmund exhaled heavily, savoring his victory and glad to have that first order under his belt.

"Let me know as soon as the funds arrive," he instructed. "When Polokov and the others hear of this, they'll be crawling all over themselves to be next in line."

Diaz allowed Edmund a moment to bask in the glory of his achievement before abruptly changing subjects. "So, when did Renzo leave?" she asked.

Still caught up in the afterglow of his success, Edmund responded with a slightly irritated, "Huh?"

"Renzo," Diaz repeated. "You said earlier that he left for America. I didn't realize he was gone."

Frowning at his assistant for interrupting his self-praise, Edmund sighed, "He left last night and hopped a container ship to Mexico."

Surprised by Renzo's transportation choice, Diaz gave her boss a curious look. "So, he doesn't like flying anymore?"

"Renzo's off-grid on this one," Edmund explained. "There's too much riding on this North Korean deal, so I asked our smuggler friends in the Sinaloa Cartel to arrange discreet passage for him."

"In exchange for what?" Diaz replied, knowing the cartel did nothing for free.

"They get control of Salazar's old territory," Edmund replied. "Plus, my support with the federales."

Still skeptical, Diaz remarked, "Dangerous bedfellows, boss."

Edmund waved dismissively. "I'm not concerned. El Maestro agreed to keep his operations out of Satipo, so we can proceed with the town's development."

Sensing it was a moot point, Diaz dropped the subject. Then, a troubling thought crossed her mind. "What about Renzo?"

"What about him? He can handle himself," Edmund insisted.

"It's not his abilities I question, it's his … condition," Diaz implied.

"Ah, well, bad timing that," Edmund replied flippantly. "The train's already left the station, and I can't risk sending Renzo a vial of the new serum. The last thing we need is some nosy customs agent stumbling upon our formula. Renzo will just have to complete his errand before the side effects kick in. When he gets home, we'll administer a new dose."

Diaz reluctantly nodded, accepting the harsh truth that Renzo was a ticking time bomb, and they could do nothing about it.

"So, what's next?" she asked dutifully.

"I need you to call our Sinaloan contact in Culiacán," Edmund replied. "Tell him Renzo is en route and find out where and when they'll be dropping him off at the Texas border. Then, I need you to call General Kang back and arrange for his people to meet up with Renzo."

"Got it," Diaz said, jotting down a few notes.

Edmund stood and walked around the desk. "I'll be downstairs with Luna. I think we found a way to prevent harvesters from detecting all the crystals on Earth," he said excitedly.

Diaz stood as well. "That sounds promising."

"It is." Edmund grinned. "And if it works, that means pack your bags."

"Oh yeah," Diaz responded with a sparkle of intrigue in her eyes. "Where are we heading?"

"Sin City, baby. We're going home!"

16
PARLAY

Syndicate Gunship, *Minerva*
Enroute to Madreen

Inside the gunship's cockpit, the two-member flight crew sat tensely at the controls as the navicomputer's display ticked down the final seconds before exiting hyperspace. The pilots exchanged uneasy glances, wondering what kind of reception awaited them on the syndicate's homeworld.

In their opinion, coming to Madreen was the mother of all bad ideas, especially without an escort. After Krunig's epic defeat at Aiwa, it was no secret that their leader had a target on his back. Grawn Krunig's days as an underboss in the Madreen Crime Syndicate were numbered, and his rivals no doubt smelled blood in the water. Krunig's move to face his brethren in person was either brazenly bold or incredibly foolish—both pilots leaned toward the latter—but one thing was certain: their necks were on the line, the same as his.

Summoning his resolve, *Minerva's* pilot eased back the engine control lever. The shuttle re-entered normal space in a flash of white light near a dark and gloomy planet. Shrouded in a perpetual, dim grayness, Madreen loomed large in the forward viewport as the shuttle approached.

A proximity alarm sounded the moment the gunship entered the system. The pilot instinctively silenced the alarm as he checked his scopes. It was as he feared—a pair of short-range fighters were on an intercept course and closing fast.

"We're being hailed," the co-pilot announced, tension evident in his voice.

"At least they didn't shoot first and ask questions later," the pilot quipped. "Okay, let's hear it."

The co-pilot opened a channel on the comms. As he started to answer, one of the interceptor pilots abruptly cut him off.

"You are in restricted space," a stern voice said over the comm. "Identify yourself."

Clearing his throat, the shuttle pilot responded, "This is special envoy, *Minerva*, requesting permission to land."

Seemingly unimpressed, the interceptor pilot replied, "Lower your shields immediately and transmit your security code clearance. You have ten seconds to comply."

Minerva's flight crew complied. When the co-pilot dropped their shields, the pilot sent the code.

"Transmission commencing," the pilot relayed. Muting the comms, he turned to the co-pilot and said with a hint of sarcasm, "For what it's worth."

A tenuous silence followed as the pilots waited. Neither had an affinity for sleeping with the stars, so they kept their hands steady on the flight controls, ready to jump to lightspeed at the first sign of trouble.

The hailing frequency sounded again.

"Code confirmed, *Minerva*," the interceptor pilot stated. "You may proceed. Follow the designated flight path and do not deviate from the controller's instructions," he warned, insinuating they would be fired upon for any variance.

Minvera's pilot dropped his shoulders, exhaling in relief. "Understood," he acknowledged. "Thank you."

Wiping his sweaty palms on his pants, the pilot glanced at his display and noticed an incoming transmission from ground control with their landing coordinates. He transferred the data to the shuttle's navicomputer with the touch of a button.

The pilot then gave his co-pilot a head bob, cueing him to restore the shields. Once they were ready, the pilot pushed the throttle forward, and the gunship approached the surface.

In the passenger compartment, Grawn Krunig and his trusted aide, Vekka, sat opposite one another, patiently awaiting their fates. Sensing the ship was moving again, Krunig recognized they had cleared the first hurdle, but safe passage was far from assured. Even though the syndicate's governing body— "The Table"—granted him a parlay, he was still vulnerable. The protections afforded to him per the Brethren's Codex only went so far, and Krunig had many enemies on Madreen. He would not breathe easy until they concluded their business here and were safely back on Ekator.

Entering Madreen's upper atmosphere, *Minerva* descended toward the dreary, bog-covered planet below. The gunship passed through turbulent layers of dense clouds, which soon dissipated, revealing the outlines of towering skyscrapers in the distance. Obscured in a thick blanket of fog, the sprawling metropolis gave off a hazy glow as pulsating neon streetlights reflected off the mist.

As *Minerva* entered the city, the gunship steered clear of the bustling commercial traffic lanes, opting instead for a flight path designated exclusively for the grawns. Its running lights pierced the thick, gloomy haze, illuminating the way as the spacecraft proceeded steadily toward the city's core.

Madreen's capital stood as a testament to engineering brilliance. The planet was covered with murky waters and sprawling marshlands, offering no solid ground for traditional construction. Instead, every building seemed to float above the surface, sustained by advanced magnetic levitation technology. With their sleek contours and glimmering facades, these gravity-defying structures mirrored the lush hanging gardens, creating a stunning and otherworldly landscape.

Ahead, the mist shifted, and the pilots caught sight of the syndicate's headquarters, a building that embodied the infamous symbol of the galaxy's most feared criminal organization. The towering structure featured a downward-pointing hexagon—symbolizing magnetarite—with two circles carved into its center. The inner circle radiated lines representing the rays of a star, while the outer circle depicted a planet brimming with crystal deposits.

Minerva completed its approach, gracefully settling onto a private landing pad perched near the top floor of the syndicate's headquarters. The ship's engines hummed to a stop as the boarding ramp slowly descended with a mechanical hiss.

Grawn Krunig rose from his seat and turned to Vekka, who stood with respect.

"You know what to do," Krunig stated, his voice firm. It was not a question but a declaration of unwavering confidence.

Vekka gave a slight nod, a thin, calculating smile forming on his lips in response to the silent trust placed in him. "Consider it done, my lord," he replied dutifully.

Without further exchange, Grawn Krunig departed, descending the ramp with quiet purpose. At the base, two grenadiers awaited him, each clad in light armor and carrying energy pikes and shields. They bowed in unison before falling in step behind Krunig as he moved toward a nearby side door.

As they crossed the landing platform, the roar of *Minerva's* engines filled the air. Krunig did not turn as the gunship lifted off, leaving him alone in the eerie stillness of the looming metropolis. Now, he faced the moment of truth—when his meticulously crafted plan would either unravel or succeed.

Both grenadiers peeled off at the building's entrance and assumed their assigned posts on either side of the door. Krunig stepped forward and placed his lower-right gloved hand on the wall-mounted control panel. A molecular recognition system scanned the composition of Krunig's personalized armor and verified the exosuit belonged to the true Grawn Krunig, while the wearer's identity remained a mystery.

The panel beneath Krunig's hand turned from red to green, and the door slid open.

"Welcome, Grawn Krunig," an automated, feminine voice announced.

Krunig entered the building with measured caution, stepping into a well-lit and spacious boardroom. His gaze quickly swept across the room, counting the fifteen metal busts perched atop pillars—each depicting a current member of the organization's governing body. Krunig's eyes settled on the bust with his likeness, a silent affirmation of his good standing within the group, at least for now.

Krunig turned his attention to the hexagon-shaped table in the center of the room. After taking a quick headcount, he noted that all the members were present.

Excellent, Krunig thought to himself, taking this as a good omen.

His emergence abruptly ended the group's discussion. The room fell silent, and all eyes turned to Krunig. He stepped forward, his footsteps echoing on the glossy marble floor. Krunig's confident stride belied the tension in the air. Facing the scrutinizing gazes of his peers, he felt the weight of their judgment. His fate would be determined before this unprecedented gathering concluded.

Grawn Supreme sat at the far end of the table, hidden behind golden armor, signifying his status as leader of the group. The remaining underbosses, including Krunig, wore distinct crimson armor that concealed their features, erasing any trace of gender or race. Like Krunig, each grawn had adopted a nom de guerre—the assumed identity of their predecessor—to preserve the syndicate's carefully crafted shroud of secrecy. None of the figures seated around the table knew the true identities of their peers. This long-standing tradition, passed down through generations, reflected the syndicate's emphasis on immortal personas. As individuals, they were all expendable, but their armor symbolized unbroken continuity and strength.

Krunig approached the table and raised his clenched fist to his chest, saluting his brethren. Grawn Supreme returned the gesture, as did his fellow grawns—some less enthusiastically than others. This display helped Krunig gauge the atmosphere in the room.

"Welcome, Grawn Krunig. We were just talking about you," the supreme leader remarked. He settled his loaded comment with a calculated pause before gesturing to Krunig's open seat. "Please, join us."

Silence hung heavy in the room as Krunig took his place at the table. The grawns then collectively shifted their focus to their leader, anticipating Grawn Supreme's judgment regarding Krunig's fate.

"You requested this parlay, Grawn Krunig," their leader began. "State your business."

"Thank you, sir, and to my brethren," Krunig responded. "I know my standing before the group is in question following the setback at Aiwa. I share your frustration, and I will not waste your time making excuses. You are no doubt aware of the vessel that turned the tide of the battle. It is known as the Reaper."

Krunig touched his gloved hand to a scanner on the armrest of his chair, activating the holoprojector in the middle of the table. He transferred footage of the Reaper captured during the Aiwan conflict and displayed it for all to see.

The grawns watched in silence as the Reaper decisively ripped through their fleet with impressive power and precision. The battle was over in moments; the relative ease of the tiny vessel's victory elicited several grumblings around the table.

"Enough," Grawn Supreme ordered. As the hologram disappeared, he stated, "We are well aware of your failure at Aiwa, Grawn Krunig. Your task was to bring us this Reaper. Have you succeeded?"

"I have not, my lord," Krunig answered with no hint of shame or regret despite the expected disapproval of his peers. "The Reaper is no longer a threat to us."

Noticing the grawns shift in their seats to rebut, Grawn Supreme raised his hand to quell their arguments. "You are on a short leash," their leader said with measured patience. "Explain."

"At the time of the battle, the Reaper was powered by a rare piece of maxixe magnetarite," Krunig replied, surveying the group as he spoke. Judging by their lack of reaction, this bit of news came as no surprise.

"That blue crystal no longer resides inside the Reaper," Krunig continued. "It was removed by Prince Kypa and is being stored inside the royal vault on Supra … that is the capital of Eos, one of Aiwa's five realms," he clarified. "I am in the process of obtaining the blue crystal as we speak. My agents were successful in killing King Loka, and it is just a matter of time before we take possession of the crystal."

"How can you be so sure?" Grawn Tyrus asked skeptically, casting doubt on Krunig's competence.

"Aiwa is in a state of turmoil," Krunig retorted. "Our attack did not achieve ultimate victory, but the Aiwans still suffered significant losses. With the death of their king and their crystal stores depleting, the Aiwans are vulnerable, and they know it. Prince Kypa abandoned his people to rescue his friend—the Reaper's captain—whom I have also captured. Kypa left his young and inexperienced sister to lead. Now, the Five Realms are at each other's throats. My agents are orchestrating more chaos to facilitate a civil war," Krunig declared. "Once we have the blue crystal, we can harness its destructive power to bring Aiwa to its knees once and for all, that I promise."

"And if you fail?" Grawn Draven posed, daring Krunig to sentence himself.

Krunig straightened in his seat and replied with cold resolve. "Then I will save you the trouble and take my own life."

Draven scoffed. "That is no recompense for our losses," he countered snidely. Feeling emboldened, Draven leaned forward to address the group. "If Grawn Krunig should fail us again, I submit that his seat at this table be forfeited, and his operations divided amongst us," he argued with unwavering conviction.

Several grawns seconded the motion by pounding their fists on the solid table in unison.

Noncommittal, Grawn Supreme allowed their dissent, then raised his hand to restore order. Once the echo of their thundering display dissipated and the room returned to silence, he spoke with an even tone.

"Since the inception of this organization, there have always been fifteen members at this table. That will not change," their leader made clear. "However, Grawn Draven has a point. You promised to indemnify us, Grawn Krunig. Your debt has come due."

"You are right, of course," Krunig admitted humbly. "I appreciate the group's patience in these matters. As a recompense, I offer you one hundred percent of the revenue generated from my operations on Gomaiyus for the next year. That is double what I owe each of you."

Knowing Gomaiyus was a cash cow, the majority of the group reacted favorably to Krunig's offer, nodding with approval. Not even Grawn Draven could argue with a twofold return on investment.

For a brief moment, it seemed Krunig had placated his doubters, and then Grawn Supreme pulled the rug out from under him.

"Those are generous terms, Grawn Krunig," he began, his fingers drumming a slow rhythm on the table. "But I believe you can offer us an even more lucrative option. Perhaps you could share the details of your recent harvesting efforts on the planet called Earth."

Krunig responded without skipping a beat. "Of course. I was just about to get to that," he lied with practiced ease.

All eyes turned to the center of the table where Krunig changed the holoprojector display to show the Aiwan probe's findings at Earth.

"As you recall," Krunig explained, "Prince Kypa led a mission to this planet, known as Earth, in hopes of resupplying Aiwa's crystal stores. That mission failed because of the attack I orchestrated on his ship while in hyperspace, forcing it to crash on Earth. However, Kypa was right about the crystals … at least one, that is. A single piece of maxixe magnetarite was recovered and used by the Reaper against us in the battle at Aiwa. But as you can see," Krunig gestured to the probe's readouts, "aside from that one blue crystal, it appears Kypa's initial assessment of Earth's crystal deposits was vastly overestimated. There are trace amounts of crystals present, mind you, but not the windfall he had hoped for."

Sensing deception, Draven countered sharply, "How can we trust this data?"

"Draven has a point," Grawn Tyrus interjected. "The data could have been manipulated to make it appear unprofitable."

Krunig replied calmly, "I found no evidence of corruption, and I give you my word I haven't falsified the data in any way."

Draven refrained from openly accusing Krunig of lying. To do so without proof or without seeking Grawn Supreme's permission beforehand could get him killed. Instead, Draven leaned forward on his elbow and spoke directly to Krunig, "Have you been to Earth to confirm these results?"

"Not personally, no," Krunig answered, "but I trust my source on Aiwa who provided this data."

Expecting as much, Draven leaned back and replied, "Then I motion we send a scout ship to Earth to confirm the results firsthand. Krunig said himself that this Earth has crystals, so why not harvest what crystals we can and split the profits evenly?"

Draven's motion was seconded immediately, and the majority pounded their fists on the table in support. Even Krunig, who had anticipated the group's "trust but verify" response, reluctantly joined in to give the impression he had nothing to hide. However, he had manipulated the probe's data, as Draven had accused him. Earth was as lucrative as Kypa predicted, if not more so. Krunig pivoted to his alternate plan.

"The motion is passed," Grawn Supreme affirmed. "Grawn Draven, you and Grawn Krunig will go to Earth to survey the planet and verify its harvesting potential."

Draven dipped his chin respectfully. "As you command, Supreme Leader," he said with a hint of gloating that did not escape Krunig.

Krunig interjected with a raised hand. "Supreme Leader, I have urgent matters to tend to on Ekator. If it pleases the group, my trusted advisor, Vekka, will accompany Grawn Draven in my stead."

Vekka was well-known among those present for his competence and unwavering loyalty to the organization, prompting unanimous agreement around the table.

"Very well," Grawn Supreme responded. "Draven will report his findings as soon as Earth has been properly surveyed. Based on those results, we will revisit Grawn Krunig's proposal and decide a fitting amount to compensate us for our losses."

With this matter settled, at least for the time being, the group shifted their focus to other matters. As Grawn Supreme continued speaking, Krunig's mind wandered to Vekka. The stakes were even higher now on the success of his clandestine meeting with a potential ally.

17

SUB ROSA

Planet Madreen
Headquarters, Madreen Crime Syndicate

One benefit of Madreen's perpetual fog was that it served as a natural cloak to hide the movements of those who preferred working in the shadows. Vekka fit that bill, at least for this covert task. After dropping off Krunig, he disembarked *Minerva* once it set down on the opposite side of the building.

Making his way past a line of shuttles, Vekka entered the headquarters and immediately started toward the ground level. Pressed for time, he moved as fast as he could without drawing attention. He knew Krunig's parlay would not last long, especially if things did not go according to his boss's plan.

The building's interior was a masterpiece of modern architecture, meticulously crafted to reflect corporate elegance. Its sleek, floor-to-ceiling glass walls on clear days provided an uninterrupted, awe-inspiring view of the sprawling metropolis. Wide and pristine corridors were accented with luxurious furnishings, while contemporary art pieces hung on the walls, creating a minimalistic yet sophisticated aura.

As usual, the corridors were bustling with the activity of the galaxy's sharpest minds and diverse species. Each being was dressed immaculately in the finest attire credits could buy—tailored outfits, polished shoes, and designer accessories that spoke of wealth and power. They moved with the calm efficiency of leaders accustomed to wielding influence, seamlessly operating the largest and most feared criminal empire in the cosmos. Yet, they wore their power with deceptive ease, their clean-cut appearance more suited to boardrooms and luxury penthouses than the ruthless underworld they governed.

As Vekka strode through these gleaming halls, a profound sense of alienation crept over him. This atmosphere differed from the gritty, cutthroat environment he worked in. With their impeccable grooming and calculated charm, these white-collar criminals were a world apart from the brutal, battle-scarred Madreen fighters he usually dealt with.

Despite his best efforts to maintain a low profile, Vekka's shabby cloak elicited curious stares from passersby. Many recognized him as Grawn Krunig's second-in-command and paid no heed to his clothing. If Vekka had pulled the cowl over his head to hide his features, he could have blended in better, but that would have raised more suspicion. The syndicate could track his every movement inside the building, but outside, where the elements worked in his favor, he could disappear from prying eyes.

Vekka used a nearby lift that took him to the ground floor. Exiting the lobby, he stepped outside, and a swirling gust of damp, chilly air greeted him. At this level, the fog was so dense that he could barely see in front of his albino-skinned face.

So much the better, he thought.

Vekka pulled the cowl over his head and began his journey into Madreen's underworld. As he distanced himself from the headquarters, it felt as if he had entered a ghostly realm where carbon-based and robotic pedestrians materialized unexpectedly. Forms emerged mysteriously from the mist and vanished into the fog as soon as they passed. These conditions made navigating street traffic a bit tedious, but Vekka used it to his advantage. He began an intricate dance of weaving his way through the pedestrians to ward off any would-be followers.

After crossing an open sky bridge, he crossed the street quickly, narrowly avoiding several commuter transports. Vekka then disappeared into a dark alley. With his back pressed against the wall, his hand resting on the grip of his blaster, he watched and waited for signs of a tail. The pause also gave him a moment to center his mind on his impending meeting with the reclusive scientist, Baroness Shae. Her radical theories had alienated her from the scientific mainstream, yet she held the key to Krunig's ultimate victory.

Feeling confident he was not followed, Vekka made his way to Baroness Shae's quarters nearby. She resided in the harbor district, a gritty, rundown part of the city teeming with all manner of criminal scum. It was a haven for rogues, mercenaries, and outlaws—those seeking work on the loading docks or discreet passage off-world.

Reaching the harbor, Vekka moved past a series of long, flat-deck vessels moored along the docks. Each ship hovered effortlessly in place, held aloft by magnetic levitation technology similar to that used in the city's towering structures. Massive robotic cranes loomed overhead, methodically loading and unloading cargo. Once the cross-docking was complete, a fully loaded vessel would shuttle its freight to an awaiting starship, ready to transport the containers of contraband across the galaxy.

Vekka kept his head down, threading seamlessly through the bustling docks and arriving at Shae's quarters. He pressed a call button mounted on the wall beside the door. After a few moments without a response, Vekka rang again, pressing the button repeatedly.

"Yes, yes, it's not a toy!" a female voice crackled over the intercom. "State your business or be off."

Vekka cleared his throat. "Baroness Shae?"

"Who wants to know?" the woman retorted testily.

"We spoke earlier," Vekka replied evenly. "You're expecting me."

"Who's me?"

Vekka resisted the urge to roll his eyes, knowing the cantankerous scientist was probably watching him on a hidden camera. After a quick glance around, Vekka leaned close to the comm unit and spoke in a hushed tone, "Vekka."

A moment of silence hung on the line as he waited patiently for Shae's decision; then, with an audible click, the door unlocked and slid open.

"Get inside and be quick about it," Shae said impatiently.

Vekka slipped inside, stepping into a narrow foyer as the door sealed behind him with a soft hiss. Directly in front of him, a set of metal stairs led upward to the second floor. He ascended the steps cautiously, his senses on high alert for any signs of a trap.

Vekka found an open door at the top of the landing. He stopped short of entering and gazed inside at a cluttered room stacked from floor to ceiling with disorganized heaps of spare parts and random debris. But there was no sign of the scientist.

"Baroness Shae?" Vekka said tentatively.

"Come in, come in!" she prodded impatiently, her voice distant. "And close the door behind you!"

Crossing the threshold, Vekka stepped into a cramped space and closed the door. He navigated a winding path, leading deeper into the chaotic maze of Shae's scattered belongings. Eyeing the precariously stacked clutter, he moved with care—one misstep could set off an avalanche.

As he pressed on, a light steadily brightened ahead. Near the end of the stacks, he had to shuffle sideways to slip through a narrow gap, which opened into a modest workspace. There, hunched over a table, sat Baroness Shae, repairing the circuit board of a broken droid.

Shae did not bother looking up from her work and continued welding.

"Make it quick," she snapped. "I haven't got all day."

Unfazed by her bluntness, Vekka replied evenly, "Very well, as I stated in my transmission, I am interested in a weapon you once designed for the syndicate. To my knowledge, it was never field tested, but in theory it could deliver a thermonuclear blast with zero radioactive fallout. Do you recall this weapon?"

"My Blazecaster? Of course, I remember it," she glowered. "I remember all of my children."

Shae deactivated her welding torch and set it aside. Removing her goggles, she turned to Vekka with a scrutinizing gaze.

"Tell me," Shae continued, her voice edged with curiosity, "what does the all-powerful Grawn Krunig want with such a weapon?"

"I cannot share specifics," Vekka responded firmly, "but I will say he admires your work and will put your Blazecaster to good use. Now, shall we discuss payment?"

"I don't care about credits or accumulating wealth," Shae remarked, although her hoarder tendencies said otherwise. "I'll waive my fee if you let me watch my creation at work."

Vekka scoffed. Allowing the reclusive scientist to tag along was not part of his boss's plans. "I understand your attachment, Baroness, but—"

Shae interrupted with a dismissive wave. "—You'll need my help," she insisted. "Someone has to keep you from blowing yourselves up. That's bad for my reputation and bad for business."

Shae had a point, especially the part about blowing themselves up. They had no idea what her weapon was capable of, and being pressed for time, Vekka reluctantly agreed.

"Very well," he replied. "How many of these Blazecasters do you have available?"

Shae searched her scattered brain. When it came to mentally cataloging her inventory, Shae's mind was as sharp as a tack. She could recall every minute detail instantly and with complete clarity. But in personal matters involving people, places, and events, Shae had selective amnesia—like the facts surrounding the unfortunate demise of her spouse, Baron Liepold, who was "accidentally" incinerated by one of her contraptions.

"I don't have any warheads in stock, but it wouldn't take me long to assemble a unit," Shae explained. "How many do you need?"

"Enough to melt the polar ice caps on an Alpha-class planet."

The delicate lines of crow's feet around Shae's eyes expanded with excitement as she envisioned unleashing her weapon on a global scale. Shae tossed her goggles over her shoulder with the rest of the junk and asked with a mischievous grin, "When do we leave?"

The syndicate's governing body concluded their business, Grawn Krunig's parlay being the focal point. Pending Grawn Draven's personal inspection of Earth, Krunig's immediate fate appeared secure, temporarily.

Grawn Supreme adjourned the group, and each of the grawns stood from the table to salute their leader as he departed. Once he was gone, the sidebars began. The group fractured into clusters around the room, huddling together to debrief and strike deals away from the main gathering.

Alone momentarily, Krunig touched a button on his forearm, discreetly summoning Vekka. He received an immediate reply: a coded message that the meeting was successful and Baroness Shae would be joining them.

Trusting Vekka's judgment, Krunig grinned with satisfaction behind his mask, then turned his attention to his fellow grawns. He imagined the many hushed conversations were about him—conspiracies forming, alliances shifting—as they maneuvered to exploit the outcome of Draven's investigation. If Draven proved him a liar and the syndicate learned of Earth's vast wealth of crystals, Krunig would face swift justice. He would either be killed and replaced, or worse, the persona of Grawn Krunig permanently removed from the table, and his territory divided among the other grawns.

On the other hand, if his ruse worked, Krunig would accumulate immeasurable wealth. He would be richer than all his peers combined, and using the Reaper as his instrument, he could destroy anyone who stood in his way.

That is a battle for another day, Krunig thought to himself as he ventured to the front of the room where a tall statue of his likeness resided. As he awaited Vekka, Krunig eyed the faceless bust, reflecting on his legacy. Since stepping into this armor, he had built his faction into one of the syndicate's most powerful arms. Now, all his hard work and planning were about to pay off.

"A bold move, Grawn Krunig," came a familiar voice from behind. "For your sake, I hope you know what you're doing."

Krunig did not bother turning around. His armor had alerted him to Grawn Draven's approach before his rival uttered a syllable. Keeping his gaze on the statue, Krunig replied calmly, "In this business, survival belongs to the audacious. Wouldn't you agree?"

Draven chuckled in assent as he circled around Krunig, stopping beside the statue to face his counterpart. Draven's voice took on a dangerous edge as he said, "Unfortunately, the line between audacity and recklessness is perilously thin."

Krunig understood the veiled threat perfectly. He was about to challenge Draven's remark when he caught sight of his gunship descending onto the landing platform outside. A quick glance around the room revealed that the hushed side conversations had stopped; all eyes focused on the silent standoff between him and Draven.

Krunig turned his attention back to Draven. Gesturing outside, he calmly said, "Perhaps we can continue this discussion later … after you have returned from Earth to vindicate me, of course."

Draven rounded to find Vekka descending the gunship's boarding ramp. Despite Krunig's confident façade, Draven remained unconvinced. With a skeptical huff, he muttered, "We shall find out soon enough."

In spite of their differences, Krunig raised his fist to his chest, saluting his brethren. Draven reciprocated, though more for appearances than out of respect.

As Krunig left, Draven stayed behind, joining his fellow grawns as they watched Krunig stride across the landing pad to meet Vekka. No words passed between the group, yet their silence was telling—each of them quietly conveying a shared suspicion that Krunig was up to something.

Meanwhile, Krunig met Vekka outside. They stopped in the middle of the platform, where Vekka pulled back his cowl and bowed, causing his long, silver-braided hair to fall over his shoulder.

Knowing their exchange was not private, Krunig informed Vekka that he would accompany Grawn Draven to Earth. Vekka acknowledged, appearing as if this was an unexpected development.

"It will be done, my lord," he assured his boss.

"Very good," Krunig responded. "Send word as soon as your task is complete. I want to hear all about it."

A faint grin creased Vekka's lips. Nothing more needed to be said. He dipped his chin respectfully and proceeded indoors. Meanwhile, Krunig boarded the gunship. As the hatch closed behind him, he made his way aft to the passenger compartment, where he found Baroness Shae strapped into a jump seat.

"Greetings, Baroness," Krunig said as he took his place across from her. "Thank you for accepting my offer."

Shae beamed with excitement; her entire body quivered with anticipation. "How could I possibly resist?"

As the shuttle lifted off, Krunig regarded the elderly scientist. Despite her frailty, Shae's eyes flickered with a hint of crazed intensity, suggesting an undeniable zeal for her work.

"We have much to do and precious little time," Krunig explained, purposely vague. "I trust you gave Vekka a list of everything you require."

Shae nodded fervently.

"Good. Then by the time we return to Ekator, your lab should be up and running, and you can get to work right away."

"Yes, yes," Shae agreed, rubbing her hands together. "And which planet will be the recipient of your wrath?"

Krunig leaned back in his seat and replied coldly, "A primitive world known as Earth."

18
NEEDFUL SANCTION

Planet Aiwa
Supra, Realm of Eos

Inside the Grand Hall of the High Court, Commodore Boa stood with unwavering composure before the governing council. Remaining at the periphery of the pavilion, the military commander inclined his head in deference to Lords Wahla and Cara seated to his right and repeated the gesture towards Lord Zefra and Princess Seva on his left.

"Report," Lord Zefra of Fonn commanded.

As he gathered his thoughts, Boa's eyes were drawn to the empty throne, a stark reminder of the void left by King Loka. The late sovereign was a beacon of leadership, guiding the Five Realms through tumultuous storms with unshakeable resolve. More than that, he had been a balancing force on the court, representing the interests of Eos and Cirros while maintaining select powers in the democratic monarchy. Now, the court was evenly divided among the four remaining wardens, and Boa felt the weight of impartiality pressing down on him. With each warden championing the best interests of their respective realms, he was acutely aware that his influence could tip the scales and shape the future of all Aiwa. He had to remain above the political fray, just as King Loka would have, guiding with fairness and restraint.

"Members of the High Court," Boa began, his tone steady. "My investigation into the assassination of King Loka is ongoing. Grawn Krunig has claimed responsibility, but we are actively following every lead to root out his conspirators and bring them to justice. At present, the evidence points toward the Cirran refugees … or at least an extremist cell within their ranks."

"Their ranks?" Princess Seva interrupted with a derisive scoff. "You speak as if they are an army, Commodore. Need I remind you that these refugees are citizens of Aiwa. They have lost everything."

"Of course, Princess," Boa replied evenly. "I do not wish to appear callous to their plight. I am merely following the evidence."

"I understand Major Gora's treachery," Seva countered, "and we know the attackers aboard my father's yacht were also Cirran. But their actions do not represent the majority—that much I am certain. The refugees only want to live in peace and rebuild their kingdom, and it is the court's responsibility to protect them until Cirros is restored."

Boa moved his mouth in readiness to speak when Lord Zefra raised her hand to interject. "The princess raises a valid point, Commodore. Anti-Cirran tensions in Supra have worsened since the king's assassination."

"With all due respect, I am Cirran, and I am well-aware of the atmosphere in the capital. I have no wish to exacerbate the situation nor bring unjust scrutiny to my people," Boa stated as tactfully as he could muster. "However, a threat still exists that puts all of Aiwa in danger. I realize that sending in soldiers to sweep the refugee camps for these traitors would send the wrong message. That is why I am being transparent and seeking your approval to use less intrusive means to hunt down Gora's accomplices."

"And if we were to sanction your request," Lord Cara of Maeve posed, "what exactly are you hoping to find?"

Boa carefully retrieved a small, circular device from a pouch on his belt. He held the charred disc between his thumb and forefinger for all to see. "This is what we seek, Lord Cara. It was discovered aboard the king's yacht, and we believe it belonged to the assassins. It is our only lead."

Squinting, Lord Zefra beckoned Boa to bring it closer. "What is it?"

"A portable teleportation unit," Boa replied, "at least what is left of it." He held the puck in his hand for Zefra and Seva to examine. "This particular device can only transport one person at a time, and judging by its condition, we believe the assassins set it to self-destruct."

"Did the attackers teleport onto my father's yacht?" Seva asked, deeply concerned.

Boa nodded. "It appears that way. The five assassins who died in the attack were all Cirran. They were not on the ship's manifest, nor were they seen boarding the king's yacht before departure. We believe Major Gora planted the device onboard and supplied them with Royal Guard uniforms."

Stepping away, Boa crossed to the other side of the pavilion to give Lords Wahla and Cara an opportunity to examine the puck.

As Lord Cara eyed the device in Boa's palm, she pictured the assassins materializing aboard the king's yacht before launching their attack. Her brow furrowed, and she asked, "If five assassins died aboard the yacht, and Major Gora died in the cave, who does that leave?"

"That is the question I seek to answer, Lord Cara," Boa replied, curling his long fingers over the device as he returned to the center of the pavilion. "Perhaps all of the assassins perished in the attack or maybe some survived. We do not know. Major Gora's involvement suggests this was a suicide mission, and if his accomplices knew they were being sent to their deaths, they may have destroyed the teleporter the moment they reached the yacht."

He paused, letting his audience process that statement, then added, "Or perhaps the teleporter was destroyed to cover the tracks of those who escaped."

Lord Zefra's eyes grew wide, filled with a dawning realization that sent a shiver down her spine. "You believe someone stayed behind?"

"It is a distinct possibility," Boa attested, his voice low and grave. "I cannot be certain because of its current state, but we believe the device had to be destroyed manually. There is also the fact that the Royal Guards have been compromised, so it stands to reason there could be more traitors in our midst. What we know for certain is that the insurgents not only came for the royal family, but also for the human, Captain Tan. However, thanks to Princess Seva's quick thinking, the humans managed to escape to the surface."

"Yet Captain Tan and her ship were later captured by a bounty hunter," Lord Wahla pointed out.

"That is correct," Boa admitted with a sigh. "The bounty hunters must have jumped past our orbital defenses and emerged from lightspeed before crashing onto the surface. A bold move for a skilled pilot—one which we have no defense against."

Lord Zefra had heard enough. Leaning forward, elbows on the table, she said, "Two breaches on the same day, Commodore Boa. That is inexcusable. What do you plan to do about it?"

"We need to locate the other end of this," Boa responded, holding up the teleporter. "With your permission, we will focus our efforts on the Cirran refugee camps and follow the evidence wherever it leads us. That is why I am here—to ask for your cooperation. Should my investigation expand to the other realms, I want your assurance that my teams will not be hindered."

Zefra, Wahla, and Cara exchanged incredulous glances and scoffed at Boa's insinuation. Seva, on the other hand, welcomed the parity. While her counterparts talked over one another, vehemently dismissing any hint of impropriety, the young princess cleared her throat and cut through the noise.

"You have my support, Commodore Boa," she said authoritatively. "Eos welcomes any efforts to bring these assassins to justice as long as you do not infringe on the rights of innocent Cirrans."

Seva's statement silenced the other members, her words carrying an unexpected weight. Boa dipped his chin in appreciation, a flicker of approval crossing his features. He then turned his gaze to the remaining wardens, quietly urging their support. They voiced their approval one by one, replacing their previous dissent with a united front.

"Thank you," Boa said, bowing. "I will bring a swift end to this matter. You have my word."

With that, he excused himself and exited the Grand Hall. He was eager to pursue the investigation in the refugee camps outside the city without further delay.

Meanwhile, the High Court carried on in conclave. Their telepathic discussion regarding the king's successor ebbed and flowed, punctuated by moments of enthusiastic agreement and heated debate. When the session finally adjourned, Princess Seva left the hall mentally drained. Captain Nova was waiting for her outside, standing at attention with his energy pike in hand.

Their eyes met briefly, but neither spoke as Seva started toward the nearby lift. As her assigned bodyguard, Nova followed dutifully in silence. Foot traffic in the atrium was light, allowing them to cross the room unimpeded. Several passersby nodded politely at the princess, which she returned in kind. Still, none dared to approach her—whether out of deference to her status or, more likely, deterred by Nova's looming presence and piercing gaze.

Moments later, they boarded the lift, beginning their ascent to the royal family's private quarters on the upper floors. Riding in silence, Nova kept his bearing and made no attempt to elicit casual conversation. He could see exhaustion written plainly across her face. The weight of her new responsibilities had taken a visible toll. Instead of the sparkle of innocence that endeared her to so many, she shouldered the burden of leadership that was far beyond her years.

As they neared the top floor, Nova was caught off guard when Seva turned her head to him and spoke softly, "I am sorry for your loss, Captain." Nova's brief look of confusion prompted Seva to add, "Commander Rega and Lieutenant Nica were fine warriors."

Nova reflected on the harsh reality of her remark. Gora's betrayal had sent a shock wave through the Royal Guards, and he and his warriors were still grappling with its aftermath.

Seva sensed his quiet turmoil and felt a deep sense of understanding. "I know how you feel," she empathized. "Betrayal by those closest to you can be a bitter truth."

Before Nova could respond, the lift arrived at their destination with a soft chime. As the doors slid open, Seva turned away, stepping into the empty hallway that stretched toward the main living area. At the far end stood Queen Qora, regal as ever. A heartwarming smile creased Qora's thin lips at the sight of her daughter.

Seva immediately straightened, instinctively mirroring her mother's poise. She turned to Nova.

"Thank you, Captain. That will be all for tonight," Seva instructed, her tone shifting from warmth to formality. "I will see you first thing in the morning."

"As you wish, Princess," Captain Nova replied with a curt bow.

Nova watched Seva walk down the hall to join her mother as the lift's doors began to close. For a fleeting moment, he felt the urge to offer his condolences to her or at least wish her a good evening, but the sight of Queen Qora's stately presence made him pause. His hesitation lingered just long enough, and before he could act, the doors shut, and the opportunity slipped away.

19
SUPERCELL

Planet Rogantu

With each careful step, Neil gradually descended the steep slope. Loose rocks scattered beneath him, tumbling down the mountainside in a rhythmic cascade as he searched for stable footholds amidst the rugged terrain.

After what felt like an eternity, his arduous descent finally ended at the valley floor. Setting foot on solid ground, Neil took a deep breath, grateful to have that harrowing climb behind him.

The sharp sound of gravel shifting drew Neil's attention upward. He spotted Kypa sliding toward him on his stomach, struggling to halt his uncontrolled descent. Acting on instinct, Neil lunged forward, catching Kypa before he pitched face-first into the dust.

"Whoa, I got you," Neil said, awkwardly steadying Kypa in his grip and helping him to his feet. "You okay?"

"Yes, I believe so," Kypa responded as he straightened. Dusting himself off, he said, "Thank you, my friend."

Neil stepped back, taking a moment to survey their surroundings. His eyes lingered on the menacing slope above, and the thought of the return climb made his stomach tighten. "Any thoughts on how we get back to the ship?" he asked grimly.

Kypa's gaze followed Neil's, but no solutions came to mind. "Not at the moment," he admitted. "But we will find a way."

Before his words could settle, a low rumble reverberated through the air, distant yet unmistakable. Neil and Kypa rounded toward the sound. To the east, between them and the outpost, stretched a barren field riddled with fissures and slow-moving lava streams. Beyond those obstacles, a towering wall of swirling ash and debris loomed, blotting out the horizon. Thunderous cracks of lightning ripped through the roiling supercell, briefly illuminating the storm as it consumed everything in its path.

Neil eyeballed the distance between them and the nearby outpost. "That's a lot of ground to cover," he said with uncertainty. "Can we make it?"

Kypa did not hesitate.

"We are about to find out," he replied, hastening Neil forward. "Run!"

Tearing off into a sprint, they charged across the open field with Kypa leading the way. Zigzagging nimbly, they dodged erupting gas vents and leaped over glowing veins of magma as the encroaching storm grew stronger. As they progressed toward the outpost, a fierce headwind emerged, pelting their helmets and suits with biting grains of sand. The advancing wall of grit and wind slowly enveloped them, choking the light from the sky and reducing visibility to near zero.

Unable to keep pace with Kypa, Neil slowed and soon lost sight of him. Straining against the roaring winds, he shouted in a panic, "Kypa!"

But Kypa did not respond. Neil trudged forward, ever mindful that one false step could land him in hot lava. He pressed on, shielding his face with his hand, hoping he was still heading in the right direction. With interference from the storm and Rogantu's magnetic field causing his HUD to flicker in and out, Neil found himself walking blind.

Moments later, he reached a fissure blocking his path. Confident he could clear it, Neil backed up, then leaped over the six-foot gap. But a sudden gas vent erupted beneath him mid-air, lifting him higher than expected and nearly sweeping him away into the storm.

Kypa appeared just in time, snatching Neil one-handed by the ankle.

"Hold on!" he shouted to Neil, who was flailing in the wind like a battered kite in a hurricane.

Kypa wrapped both hands firmly around Neil's ankle and squatted, lowering his center of gravity. Neil dragged him a few feet before Kypa was able to plant his feet and stop himself. With one strong tug, Kypa pulled Neil down until gravity took over. Neil dropped to the ground, landing with a thud on his stomach.

With no time to relax, Kypa crawled to Neil's side. Rolling him over, Kypa leaned close and shouted over the roaring wind, "Are you alright?"

Neil coughed, then responded with a reassuring thumbs-up.

"We have to keep moving!" Kypa shouted, then he stood and helped Neil to his feet.

They set off once again, this time hand in hand. Struggling against the relentless wind, they pressed on until the outpost eventually emerged. The circular, single-story structure looked weathered and beaten, worn down by decades of neglect in the unforgiving landscape.

They took refuge within a narrow overhang outside the main entrance. With Neil huddled next to him, Kypa went to work, trying to pry open the rusted access cover to a control panel mounted on the wall. While he was busy with that, a loud banging sound caught Neil's attention. He turned to find an antenna array dangling precariously over the side of the building. It had broken loose and remained tethered by cables to the roof. With a sudden, ear-piercing screech of metal, the cables suddenly snapped. Neil flinched as the array violently tumbled away, disappearing in the raging storm.

Finally! Kypa growled inwardly after forcing the stubborn panel open. His effort was rewarded when he discovered the outpost still had power. With the touch of a button, the doors to his left slid open.

Neil and Kypa hurried inside, stepping into a darkened room with computer stations lining the perimeter. In the middle of the room, elevated on a dais, stood an oversized chair—once used by whoever was in charge. Layers of dust caked the equipment, and the outpost's dilapidated state suggested it had been abandoned for quite some time.

"Whew, we made it!" Neil sighed in relief as the doors began to close behind them.

But Kypa sensed danger. His eyes swept the room, and he suddenly extended a hand, pressing it firmly against Neil's chest to halt him in place.

Startled, Neil turned to Kypa in surprised confusion.

Kypa raised his long index finger to his mouth, urging silence. He then pointed to his right, where the remains of a decaying corpse lay on the floor.

Neil gasped just as the doors sealed shut behind him and the room went pitch black. Outside, the winds howled relentlessly, while inside, an eerie stillness settled inside the room.

"*Illuminate,*" Kypa instructed his suit using a neural command. The optics of his holographic helmet instantly changed to night vision mode, casting his surrounding in green infrared light.

Kypa kept his left hand pressed firmly on Neil's chest, a silent reminder to stay put. Slowly, he drew his blaster from its holster, searching for any sign of danger.

A few heart-pounding moments passed, yet nothing stirred. Kypa started to relax when he spotted a faint glimmer in an open storage room in the back corner. His breath caught as two glowing specks stared back—a pair of eyes reflecting the infrared light. Whatever lurked in the shadows had targeted them with a cold, unblinking stare.

Without moving, Kypa reached out to Neil telepathically. "*We are not alone,*" he warned, his voice steady in Neil's mind. "*Switch your helmet to night vision mode.*"

A chill ran down Neil's spine. He instinctively opened his mouth to respond but quickly realized Kypa's message required thought, not words. Silently willing his helmet's AI to switch optic modes, Neil blinked as the environment shifted to infrared.

"*Far corner,*" Kypa cautioned, never taking his eyes off the creature. "*Be ready.*"

Neil scanned the back of the room, frantically searching for whatever lay in wait, but he saw nothing. When Kypa removed his hand from Neil's chest, he turned to see the Aiwan creeping slowly along the perimeter of the room. That was when he noticed the blaster in Kypa's hand. Swallowing hard, Neil quietly drew his own weapon, struggling to resist the urge to panic.

Kypa moved with purpose; each step placed heel to toe to muffle any sound. With the open storage room now fully in view, he tightened his grip on the blaster, keeping it trained on the motionless figure inside. As he advanced, Kypa's heartbeat pounded in his ears, drowning out the silence.

When he was thirty feet from the door, Kypa paused. Sweat beaded on his brow, tickling his olive-colored skin in the most unnerving way. But he dared not break his focus. The creature's eyes remained locked on him, unblinking and unmoving in the dark.

Kypa slowly raised his weapon, taking careful aim. His finger hovered over the trigger, ready to fire.

"Show yourself," he commanded firmly in Basic.

But the creature remained silent, its unyielding gaze locked on the Aiwan.

Caught in indecision, a surge of compassion stayed Kypa's hand. He did not know what they were dealing with yet; killing the creature outright felt too hasty. Instead, Kypa resolved to draw it out.

Shifting his aim above the storage room door, Kypa fired a warning shot. The instant he pulled the trigger, he realized he had made a dreadful mistake. The blaster bolt erupted in a brilliant flash, and the explosion released a spark-shower of light. Still in night vision mode, both he and Neil turned away as a searing pain pierced their eyes.

Blinded and disoriented, Kypa waved his blaster about frantically in the direction of the storage room, anticipating an attack.

"Neil!" he called out.

"I can't see!" Neil responded, his voice laced with fear.

Kypa blinked repeatedly, trying to force his eyes to adjust faster. He kept sweeping his weapon back and forth, hoping to catch a glimpse of movement before the creature pounced. But no attack came. As his vision gradually returned, Kypa reacquired the storage room, steadying his aim. To his surprise, the creature had not budged despite the chaos.

With his heart racing, Kypa inched closer, his eyes wide as saucers, bracing for the creature to spring to life. Then a sudden realization hit him: he was chasing a ghost.

Dropping his shoulders in relief, Kypa lowered his weapon. A tiny droid sat dormant inside the storage room. The bi-pedal unit was offline, its twin optical receptors reflecting Kypa's infrared, creating the illusion of menacing eyes staring back at him.

Feeling foolish, Kypa said to Neil, "You can put your weapon away. It is just a droid."

"A droid?" Neil replied, his interest piqued.

Holstering his weapon, Neil made his way to the back of the room with growing curiosity. Considering all that had happened since his first contact with Kypa aboard the USS *Anchorage*, Neil had yet to meet an alien droid.

Joining Kypa at the storage room, Neil leaned in for a closer look. The squatting gray and white droid was perched on top of a container coated in a thick layer of dust. Armless, its two legs were oddly attached at the shoulders of its small torso, ending in matching, cup-shaped feet. Atop its neck sat a binocular-shaped head, complete with two photoreceptor eyes and a pair of disc-shaped audio sensors resembling Princess Leia's iconic hairstyle.

Neil grinned with delight. *Oh, I'm definitely keeping you!*

Meanwhile, Kypa made his way back to the alien corpse. Standing over the body, he examined the grisly remains. The decomposing worker stared wide-eyed at the ceiling, mouth agape, with his skeletal hands clutching a nasty gut wound.

Neil joined Kypa. His face twisted in disgust at the sight of the mummified corpse.

"Ugh ... he looks like a Proboscis Monkey," Neil remarked, referring to the worker's prominent long, pendulous nose and distended belly. "What happened to him?"

"Judging by the wound, it appears this person was shot at close range," Kypa remarked.

"Murdered?" Neil muttered with a pained expression.

"Perhaps," Kypa replied. Turning away, he began scanning the room, expecting to find more bodies or clues about what had happened. Nothing stood out.

Moving to the dais in the center of the room, Kypa noted, "The outpost must be running on reserve power. I will try to access the main computer."

"What can I do?" Neil offered.

"Keep a lookout ... and do not touch anything," Kypa warned, a bit firmer than he intended.

Neil raised his hands in mock surrender. "No arguments here." He glanced around and asked, "So, what is this place?"

"A control room, I think," Kypa replied, giving the dusty chair a cautious rock to test its stability. Satisfied, he settled into it and tapped the screen embedded in the armrest to wake it up.

While Kypa worked on accessing the main computer, Neil circled the room. Stopping at one terminal, he ran his fingertip along the counter, creating a considerable track in the thick layer of dust.

"Looks like this place has been abandoned for some time," he remarked.

"Nearly five rotations," Kypa responded, reading from the display on his chair. "That is the date of the last log entry."

"I can't imagine why they'd want to leave this paradise," Neil quipped.

"Disable your night vision and close your eyes," Kypa instructed. "I am going to turn the lights on now."

After doing so, Neil closed his eyes and said, "Go for it."

Seconds later, Neil could see the room illuminated through his eyelids. He slowly opened his eyes to slits, blinking repeatedly until his vision adapted. The first thing to catch his attention was a stack of containers on the back wall. Curious about what other high-tech gadgets he might discover, Neil crossed the room for a closer look. He examined the stack from different angles before carefully shifting position to peer behind the back row.

"Hey, Kypa, I found an exit back here," he called out. "The doors are welded shut."

Kypa looked up from his display and swiveled the chair in Neil's direction. His brow furrowed as he eyed the stack of containers, noting it was blocking the only door leading to the other sections of the outpost.

"Step away," he instructed. "Perhaps the log entries will explain what they were trying to keep out."

Neil backpedaled cautiously, suddenly alert to the possibility of danger lurking just beyond. He flinched as Kypa activated a hologram and whipped around to see it.

The image projected from Kypa's chair was the same worker now lying dead on the floor a few feet away.

"This is Eilon Vahr, second shift supervisor," the worker began, speaking in Basic with desperation etched on his face and in his voice. "The gracylai have breached the tunnel but the shield barricades are holding, at least for now. We're making our stand here in the control room. If we make it until morning, the storm is expected to clear, and the company will send a shuttle." With a sigh of defeat, the worker added, "As far as I know, we are the only survivors."

Just before the recording flickered and ended abruptly, Kypa spotted a person passing behind Eilon Vahr. His breath hitched. In a panic, he rewound the recording and played it again.

"As far as I know, we are the only survivors," the message repeated.

Kypa froze the recording. His eyes widened in disbelief. The figure in the background was the same insectoid bounty hunter he fought on the Aiwan beach.

"Him!" Kypa said, pointing to Smythe. "That is the bounty hunter I fought on Aiwa. He has Ava and Toma."

Incredulous, Neil leaned in closer, taking in the insectoid's creepy yellow eyes. "You're kidding?"

"No," Kypa responded. "I will never forget that face." He sat back in the chair, processing this turn of events. "At least now we know why he chose this planet."

Neil scoffed. "Yeah, this place is a death trap. What the hell is a gracylai?"

Kypa shrugged. "Animals of some kind," he speculated. "Whatever they are, they forced the company to abandon this facility. If I could access the main computer, perhaps we could learn more about what happened."

"Maybe we should head back to the ship," Neil suggested, resting his hand on his blaster. "You know, pivot to Plan B?"

Kypa dismissed the idea with a raised eyebrow. Given the deadly storm raging outside, returning to the ship was not an option.

Neil chuckled nervously. "That's the same look my high school guidance counselor gave me when I told her I wanted to be a ventriloquist."

Kypa remained silent, his thoughts drifting to Ava and Toma. Not only did they have to contend with the bounty hunters, but an unknown darkness reigned in the depths of this planet—creatures of such ferocity that they wiped out all the workers and forced the company to shut down its operations. Kypa sighed heavily. They had their work cut out for them.

After a brief pause, he said, "The hologram mentioned a tunnel with barricades. I am guessing it is on the other side of that door and probably leads to the refinery."

"And who knows what else," Neil murmured.

"It is a risk," Kypa granted, "but Ava and Toma are running out of time. If we wait for the storm to pass, they could be moved again, or worse." He refrained from following that train of thought. "Besides, the outpost has been abandoned for some time. Perhaps these gracylai are gone."

Neil scoffed. "That's a big maybe." The more he thought about it, the crazier this idea sounded. "Listen, assuming you're right and there is an underground tunnel, the hologram said it had been breached by those gracylai things. We don't even know if it's passable."

"Correct," Kypa replied, "but I think I know someone who might."

20
ID10T

Planet Rogantu

Kypa returned to the open storage room with Neil close behind. Kneeling before the dormant droid, he gave it a quick once-over before reaching behind its torso.

"There should be a power switch here somewhere," Kypa thought aloud, his fingers fumbling across the droid.

Neil eyed the droid's dusty exterior. "Looks like it's seen better days," he commented.

"There you are," Kypa said, locating the power switch on the back of the droid's binocular-shaped head. With a quick press, the droid's photoreceptors flickered to life with a soft blue glow.

Neil brightened. "Hey, you did it!"

Kypa kept a watchful eye on the droid as it powered up. A low hum emanated from within its torso before it straightened its legs, rising to just over one foot tall. Once fully upright, the droid tilted its head, rotating it three hundred and sixty degrees.

"Whoa," Neil uttered, startled by the unsettling resemblance to *The Exorcist*.

A flush-mounted compartment on the droid's torso opened, revealing a pair of mechanical arms. Each arm ended in a three-pronged pincer, which the droid clicked together like salad prongs. After retracting the arms, the droid lifted off the ground with a soft whir, hovering in place using tiny repulsors mounted under its feet.

Kypa stood as the droid rose to eye level and spun in a tight circle like it was stretching its wings for the first time.

Neil chuckled. "Man, he's all full of surprises."

"Mm," Kypa muttered, less impressed than his counterpart. "Droid, identify yourself," he commanded, speaking in Basic.

The droid lowered itself back onto the container. Looking up at Neil and Kypa, it responded excitedly, repeating a series of chirps and beeps that both their helmets translated to "ID10T."

Neil chuckled, but the hidden meaning of the translation escaped Kypa.

"Quiet, Ten-Tee," Kypa ordered with a hint of annoyance. The droid immediately fell silent. Speaking slowly, Kypa asked, "Now tell us, what is your prime directive?"

Neil and Kypa watched and waited expectantly, but Ten-Tee remained silent.

Kypa rolled his eyes. "Ten-Tee, it is okay to answer," he clarified. "Tell us your prime directive?"

Still nothing.

Neil turned to Kypa. "Why is he not answering?"

"I am not sure," Kypa replied, thinking. "Perhaps it does not have one. I will run a diagnostic."

Ever the optimist, Neil was quick to point out, "Hey, if we take him with us, that could work in our favor, right?"

"Not necessarily," Kypa said warily. "Without a master program, the droid could be a liability where we are headed."

Neil shrugged, somewhat disappointed. "Seems harmless to me."

"Ten-Tee may know the way to the refinery," Kypa explained, "but without proper social parameters, every new experience could trigger an unpredictable reaction. It would be as if we were being led by a hyperactive toddler," he added bluntly. "The last thing we need is this droid compromising our position."

"Fair point," Neil agreed. Looking about, he asked, "What do you want me to do?"

"Search those containers," Kypa said, gesturing toward the barricaded door. "See if there is anything useful. And while you are at it, check the body, too."

Neil's shoulders sagged as he looked at the corpse. A frown crossed his face, but without a word, he steeled himself and set out to tackle the grisly task ahead.

Kypa picked up Ten-Tee and carried it to the central dais. Setting the droid down in the controller's chair, he said, "Ten-Tee, connect to the central computer. Run a full self-diagnostic and display the results."

Ten-Tee replied with a compliant beep and opened the compartment in its torso. A three-pronged armature extended outward. Ten-Tee opened its finger-like pincers, revealing a hexagon-shaped palm, which doubled as a data port. Pressing it against a reader on the chair's armrest, Ten-Tee successfully interfaced.

The chair's holographic display reappeared, now streaming data reflecting Ten-Tee's internal systems. Kypa changed positions for a better view. Narrowing his bulbous blue eyes, he scrutinized the data flowing across the display, rapidly absorbing every detail.

Meanwhile, Neil crouched beside the dead worker's lifeless body and began the unenviable task of searching its remains for anything of value. Cringing as he went through each pocket, Neil deliberately avoided eye contact with the deceased, whose vacant stare remained fixed on the ceiling.

"Ugh," Neil grumbled, forcing back the bile in his throat.

Just then, he discovered two objects in the worker's pant pocket. Neil retrieved the first item, an access card with a company logo imprinted on the front next to the worker's image and name.

"I found an access card," Neil called out, raising it in the air.

Kypa stepped away from Ten-Tee, and Neil handed him the card. Kypa examined the image, comparing it to the deceased's remains to make a positive ID.

"EDO Corporation," Kypa read aloud.

Looking up at his friend, Neil asked, "You know it?"

Kypa shook his head as he flipped the card over. "No, but this access card may come in handy."

Neil frowned, none-too-thrilled about Kypa's plan to use the outpost's underground tunnel to reach the refinery. He wanted no part of those gracylai creatures, but rather than argue, he turned his attention to the second item recovered from the deceased. It was a weathered, brown leather pouch closed by a drawstring. The small, weighty bag jingled when Neil shook it. He opened it and dumped a dozen pieces of rectangular coins into his palm.

"What are these?" he asked, holding up the stack of coins.

"Those are credits," Kypa responded, "the galactic currency."

A smile crept across Neil's face as he realized what he had stumbled upon.

Spreading the credits in his palm, he said, "Computer, count these credits. Display the highest value to the lowest."

His suit's AI responded instantly, displaying the numeric value for each credit on his personal HUD.

"Two thousand credits," Neil remarked. "Is that a lot?"

"Depends on what you are trying to buy," Kypa replied. "But it is a good start."

Neil's gaze lingered on the credits, his excitement fading as thoughts of this poor worker crept into his mind. Feeling a tinge of guilt, he wondered aloud, "You think this was his life savings?"

Kypa shrugged, watching Neil's conflicted expression in silence. He chose not to interfere, letting his friend wrestle with the dilemma of whether to keep the credits.

After a moment, Kypa broke the silence, "He will not be needing the credits any longer," he said gently. "You can put them to good use by sharing them with others back on Earth. I expect you will have many stories to tell when you return home."

Neil chuckled at the prospect. He had not thought about what he would do if and when he ever returned to Earth, but a book deal and lecture circuit sounded appealing.

Neil closed his fist around the credits and came to his feet.

"Did you find anything else?" Kypa asked.

"Not yet," Neil replied, dumping the credits into the pouch. "I was going to start on the containers next."

Ten-Tee beeped, indicating the diagnostic had finished. Kypa gave Neil an affirming nod and returned to the droid, eager to review the results.

Before heading to the stack of containers, Neil faced another dilemma—his nanosuit had no pockets, and neither did his gun belt. Briefly, he considered leaving the credits behind, but then inspiration struck.

"*Computer,*" he commanded, "*form a leg pocket in my suit big enough to hold this pouch.*"

The nanites responded instantly, forming a cargo pocket on his left leg. Neil slid the pouch inside, and the nanites seamlessly closed around it, snug enough to keep the credits from jingling as he moved.

"Nice," Neil said to himself, grinning at his resourcefulness.

Satisfied, he turned his attention to the storage containers. Crossing the control room, Neil opened them one at a time to inspect the contents. Much of what he found required assistance from his suit's AI to identify, such as personal protective equipment for the miners.

Neil discarded those items, confident their nanosuits would provide more than adequate protection. However, the contents of the last container caught his attention. Inside, he found a carton full of grenades.

"Hey, Kypa, I found a small arsenal over here," he called out. "Looks like toxin grenades and explosives."

Kypa, still occupied with Ten-Tee, glanced over his shoulder and replied, "Leave them for now. I will take a look as soon as I finish with the droid. In the meantime, start clearing a path to the doors."

Neil set to work, hauling each container off to the side and stacking them carefully to clear a narrow path. Muscles straining, he maneuvered the heavy crates as quietly as he could. Finally, with the last container in place, he stepped back, breathing hard as he surveyed the results with a small sense of approval.

Taking a seat, Neil deactivated his helmet and wiped the sweat from his brow. But the feeling of accomplishment was fleeting. A sudden chill prickled the skin on his neck. Slowly, he swiveled his chair toward the sealed doors behind him. Something felt off.

Neil stood and cautiously approached the doors with slow, deliberate steps. When he was inches from them, he stopped, holding his breath. His ears strained for the faintest sound—anything that would betray movement on the other side. But the silence was heavy and unnerving.

Neil hesitated, then mustered the courage to hold his ear against the doors' cold surface. Listening intently, the muffled echoes of distant noises reverberated through the metal, creating an eerie and hollow acoustic. Neil pressed his ear closer, determined to find out if the unsettling noise was real or just his imagination.

"Hear anything?" Kypa asked, breaking the tension in the air.

Neil almost jumped out of his skin, gasping with an awkward, nearly comical spasm. He rounded sharply to find Kypa standing behind him.

"Holy crap on a cracker!" Neil snapped, clutching his chest. "Don't sneak up on me like that. I almost pissed myself."

"My apologies," Kypa said with a slight grin, though genuinely contrite. "Do not be ashamed. If you were to lose bladder control, your suit is designed—"

Neil held up his hand to interject. "—I know how it works. Thank you," he responded warily. "I just don't need help putting it to the test." Regaining his composure, Neil quickly changed the subject. "What'd you learn from the droid?"

"Good news," Kypa replied. "Ten-Tee has a basic operating system, and while it did not have a prime directive, it was able to interface with the central computer and download a map of the entire facility. Just as we suspected, these doors lead to an underground tunnel that runs directly to the refinery," Kypa explained. "Ten-Tee will be our guide and alert us to any dangers."

Neil nodded in agreement. "Sounds good. Anything else?"

Kypa grimaced. "The tunnel is equipped with electronic barriers for protection, but they are offline."

"Bummer." Neil frowned. "Can they be repaired?"

"I will not know until we get down there, but there is more," Kypa added reluctantly. "The tunnel has been breached in at least one section—part of the ceiling has collapsed. Again, we will not know the full extent of the damage until we are inside, but it is likely we will need to venture outside the tunnel to find a way around. That means we will be exposed to potential attacks and ..." Kypa hesitated.

"And what?" Neil asked, almost afraid of the answer.

"Lava," Kypa answered. "This area is riddled with underground lava flows. Ironically, the company built the tunnel in response to the planet's unpredictable storms. They used a rail system to transfer workers to and from the refinery. But Rogantu's unstable core caused tectonic shifts, weakening the tunnel and leading to its collapse."

Neil absorbed the information, taking it in stride, yet felt his chest tighten.

Kypa sensed his unease and added, "I realize this is not ideal, but the tunnel is still our quickest and probably safest way to the refinery."

"I know," Neil agreed, running his hands through his hair. "We just need to be smart about this. And I'm not just talking about getting to the refinery," he clarified. "Even if we somehow manage to rescue Ava and Toma, those bounty hunters aren't going to let us just walk out of there."

Kypa paused, a wry grin creeping across his face. "No, I suspect we will have to run."

Neil gave him a flat look, then let out a chuckle. "Your sense of humor is really coming along, isn't it?" he said with a smirk.

Kypa shrugged modestly. "I find levity calms the nerves."

Neil grinned. "Yours or mine?"

"Honestly, I was referring to myself," Kypa confessed.

They shared a brief laugh, but as their eyes met, their joking faded. A silent understanding passed between them—whatever dangers lay ahead, they would face them together.

Kypa nodded and turned his attention to the container Neil had set apart.

Six explosive grenades and six toxin grenades lay inside. He frowned slightly, understanding why the workers kept such weapons on hand. Tucked inside were a pair of tactical vests. Kypa pulled one out and held it up.

"It's definitely you," Neil quipped.

"We may need the grenades where we are headed," Kypa said, passing the vest to Neil. "Load the grenades while I figure out how to open the door."

As Neil went about his task, Kypa approached the doors and studied the weld line that ran from top to bottom. He traced it with his long fingers before noticing a welding tank and torch off to the side. After a quick inspection, he let out a frustrated sigh.

"Empty," Kypa muttered.

"What about him?" Neil suggested, gesturing to Ten-Tee, who stood in the controller's chair. The tiny droid was looking away, curiously scanning the room with its photoreceptors, and utterly oblivious to Neil and Kypa's conversation.

With no other options in sight, Kypa agreed.

"Ten-Tee, come over here, please," Neil called.

At the sound of its identifier, Ten-Tee's head snapped toward Neil. Spotting the human waving it over, the droid beeped excitedly and hopped onto the floor. It scurried toward Neil, chirping a series of joyful noises that sounded like, "Ten-Tee! Ten-Tee!"

The droid stopped in front of Neil and looked up at him, eager to be of service.

Tickled, Neil pointed toward the door and asked, "Can you cut through the weld on these doors?"

Without moving the rest of its body, Ten-Tee swiveled his head and emitted two beams of blue light from its photoreceptors, scanning the doors' welded seam up and down. After Ten-Tee finished its scan, the droid turned to Neil and nodded confidently.

"Perfect," Neil replied, resisting the urge to pat the droid's head like a puppy. "Okay, get started … and try to be quiet about it," he added.

Neil and Kypa watched closely as Ten-Tee went to work. The droid approached the doors, opened the compartment in its belly again, and extended its other arm, this one equipped with a laser cutter in the palm instead of an interface port. Ten-Tee started at the base of the door, slicing through the weld with precision and showering the area with white-hot sparks.

As the task progressed, Ten-Tee activated its repulsors, hovering off the ground to continue cutting upwards toward the top of the doors. Cringing at the unavoidable crackling bursts of molten metal, Kypa and Neil stood ready with their blasters.

Ten-Tee finished soon enough and lowered itself gently to the floor.

"Good work," Neil whispered, motioning for the droid to move away. "Now, get behind me."

Ten-Tee scurried behind Neil as the room fell deathly quiet. Neil and Kypa collectively held their breaths, hoping Ten-Tee's racket had not rung the dinner bell for the gracylai.

With his ear to the door, Kypa listened intently for what seemed like an eternity, slowly convincing himself the coast was clear. Hearing no sounds to suggest danger, he relaxed and cautiously declared, "I think we are okay."

Neil exhaled heavily, knowing deep down that things would only get more intense from this point on. He handed Kypa a loaded vest and then buckled on his own.

Kypa fastened the straps tightly and double-checked that each grenade was securely in place. "Before we go any further," he said, "I am sending you Ten-Tee's map and a schematic of the refinery—just in case we get separated."

Neil's mouth fell open slightly. Dropping all pretenses, he protested, "There's no way in hell you're leaving me alone down there."

"That is not my preference, either," Kypa replied, keeping his voice steady to mask his own anxiety. "But if it comes to that, we will meet at the refinery. Agreed?"

Neil nodded vigorously. "And then what?" he asked. "I mean, how exactly are we going to mount a rescue?"

Kypa hesitated, caught off guard. His confident façade wavered for a moment as he scrambled for an answer. The truth was that he had no plan. Ever since leaving Aiwa, every decision was on the fly, driven by a singular focus: rescue Toma and Ava at any cost.

"I do not know, but like I said earlier, we will find a way," he said with a glimmer of determination in his eyes.

Realizing that was the best answer he could hope for, Neil forced a smile and cracked a nervous joke, "Let's try not die today, okay?"

"Agreed. Now we have a plan," Kypa said with a grin as he patted his friend's shoulder. "Now let us see if this access card still works."

Kypa stepped over to the control panel. Before inserting the dead worker's ID card into the slot, he turned to Neil. "Ready?"

Neil glanced down at his feet to ensure Ten-Tee was still with him. Taking a calming breath, he nodded and aimed his blaster where the doors met.

Kypa inserted the card. As soon as the light above the reader turned green, he pressed the open button and quickly raised his weapon as the doors slid open with a hiss. In unison, Neil and Kypa's breath hitched, anticipating an attack. But none came. The doorway was empty, shrouded in silence, leaving them both perplexed and relieved.

With their weapons still at the ready, Neil and Kypa watched as Ten-Tee moved forward, entering the adjacent corridor. The droid stopped and scanned the area using its photoreceptors but found no threats.

After exchanging anxious glances, Neil and Kypa slowly crept forward. They found the corridor untouched and in disrepair. Overhead, lights flickered, casting eerie shadows amidst a haunting stillness. It appeared the gracylai had not made it this far. Neil and Kypa had both expected to find blood-spattered walls and the mauled remains of dead workers, but there was no trace of a last stand.

"The barracks are that way," Kypa whispered to Neil, pointing to his right. "The tunnel is this way."

Neil followed Kypa down the corridor, taking careful, measured steps. Reaching the end, Kypa stopped in front of a single door on his right. A sign on the wall indicated this was the emergency exit leading down to the underground tunnel.

Kypa turned to face Neil. They exchanged looks of shared apprehension; then he glanced down at Ten-Tee.

"Switch to quiet mode, understood?" he instructed in a hushed tone. Ten-Tee nodded. To Neil, Kypa placed his finger to his mouth, beckoning silence, and reached out to him telepathically. *"No noise going forward. Neural communications only."*

Neil swallowed the lump in his throat and responded with an affirming nod.

Turning toward the door, Kypa took a calming breath before pressing the open button. It slid open with a hiss. He anxiously scanned the opening with his blaster—thankfully, no creatures were there to meet them.

They stepped through the door onto a landing that overlooked the underground tunnel. To their left was an empty stairwell leading down to the tubular passage. It was carved out of volcanic rock and lined with a beige, artificial material for stability—similar to what Kypa had used with the Reaper to reinforce the crystal mines in Cirros. Pipes and power conduits ran along the ceiling while soft-glowing white lights lined the side walls, providing a good measure of visibility.

Kypa pointed to the single rail line running the length of the tunnel. He noticed an old rail sled parked at the base of the stairs.

"*They must have used the sled to transport workers to the refinery,*" he said to Neil. "*Perhaps it still works.*"

"*That'll save us some time,*" Neil replied, sounding hopeful.

Kypa descended the stairs cautiously—his eyes constantly moving, ever vigilant. Neil followed, along with Ten-Tee. When they reached the bottom, Kypa inspected the sled. He only needed a second to realize it was out of commission.

"*There is no power to the rail line,*" he told Neil, disappointed. "*It looks like we will have to walk.*"

"Figures," Neil muttered sourly. He realized his mistake a second too late and instinctively snapped his hand to his mouth, inadvertently hitting his invisible helmet.

He and Kypa froze, straining to listen. For a few heart-pounding moments, they waited tensely for a stirring that never came.

"*Sorry,*" he apologized. "*Won't happen again.*"

Kypa remained silent, much to his credit. As he turned away, surveying their surroundings, Neil felt a nudge on his lower leg. Glancing down, he found Ten-Tee prodding him. Neil crouched, ready to ask the droid what was wrong, but before he could speak, Ten-Tee scrambled up his arm with the agility of a monkey, settling itself on his back shoulder.

Caught off guard, Neil thought, *Umm … okay.*

The tactical vest provided an ideal perch, allowing Ten-Tee to monitor their rear and the path ahead. Once comfortably positioned, the droid tapped Neil's shoulder, signaling it was ready to move out.

Watching their exchange with a hint of amusement, Kypa met Neil's gaze, receiving a nod to proceed. Silently, he turned and began leading them forward into the tunnel. Yet, a dark thought lingered—what if they arrived at the refinery too late to save Ava and his son?

21
SKULLDUGGERY

Planet Rogantu

Aboard the bounty hunter's freighter, Ava sat alone on the floor inside the cramped confines of her storage closet. With her eyes closed, an empathetic smile creased her lips as she and Toma used telepathy to discuss young love.

"*Take it from* The Supremes," she advised, "*you can't hurry love.*"

"*What is a supreme?*" Toma replied eagerly as if the answer would unlock the secrets of the universe.

"*They're a musical group back on Earth,*" Ava explained, "*but never mind that. All I'm saying is don't rush into things. Give this girl at the Citadel time to get to know you and let nature take its course.*"

"*Did you and Mark take it slow?*" Toma asked innocently.

Touché, Ava thought with a wry grin. "*Well, no, actually. At the risk of sounding cliché, it was love at first sight with us. We were inseparable from Day One,*" she recalled with a wistful smile tinged with melancholy. "*I guess the stars were aligned for us.*"

"*What do you mean?*"

Ava paused for a moment, gathering her thoughts. "*Well, in my humble opinion, the thing about love is that it's not just about finding the right person. It's about finding the right person at the right time; so to say 'the stars were aligned'*" *means the timing was right for both of us. We were ready to make that commitment to each other, and in the short time we were together, it was perfect."*

Silence followed. Lost in a brief moment of nostalgic reverie, Ava then added, *"Just be patient, Toma. When you get to the Citadel, show this girl you have interest in her and see where it leads. You are a prince after all,"* she reminded him. *"I'm sure you'll have flocks of girls swooning—"*

Toma cut her off sharply. *"—Someone is coming!"* he said in a panic.

Nearby, in the quiet stillness of the dormant Reaper, Toma jolted to his feet, his heart racing. He stood in the lower-level engineering section next to the open hatch. When he heard the faint sound of footfalls outside, he immediately jumped into his hiding place. Situating himself between the Reaper's bulkhead and the makeshift wet bath his father had constructed for Ava and Neil, Toma cocooned himself within his nanosuit.

Fighting to calm his breathing, Toma listened intently, hoping whoever was coming would continue on. But no such luck. The clanging of heavy boots on the freighter's metal-grated flooring outside grew louder. Then came the unmistakable sound of someone climbing the ladder to board the Reaper.

Toma's breath hitched.

"Stay calm," Ava urged. *"You got this."*

Toma closed his eyes, dreading they would discover him at any moment.

"I'll get started," came a muffled, feminine voice just inches from Toma's position.

With his heartbeat pounding in his ears, Toma listened as the new arrival passed his position and climbed the steps leading to the Reaper's main hold.

Silence followed.

Opening his eyes, Toma listened a few moments longer. Once he was sure he was alone, he reached out to Ava.

"I think they are gone," he whispered in his mind. *"They went upstairs to the cockpit."*

"Good job," Ava replied. *"Any idea who it was?"*

"No, but there was more than one. That, I am sure of," Toma answered. *"Should I have a look?"*

"No, no, stay put," Ava insisted. *"It's too risky. Can you hear what they're saying?"*

"Not from here," Toma said with disappointment. Then, an idea struck him. *"Wait, I have an idea."*

Embracing his covert assignment, Toma severed his telepathic connection with Ava and went to work, increasing the ambient noise his suit's audio sensors picked up. It helped somewhat, but he knew moving closer would be better, especially as the confines of this protective cocoon were growing claustrophobic.

Since revealing his presence to Ava, Toma had not dared to leave the Reaper. His only venture outside his cocoon came a day earlier when he quickly swept the Reaper, tiptoeing up to the cockpit, only to find it empty and Reggie offline. That brief recon was the extent of his efforts, and Ava made it clear—he was to stay put and not attempt to find her aboard the freighter. There was no sense risking his capture without a solid plan for escape.

In hindsight, that might have been their best chance of catching their captors off-guard. Since then, things had only gotten worse. They were now facing three bad guys instead of two, and with the Reaper trapped inside the bounty hunters' freighter, any hope of taking off was out of the question.

Activity around the Reaper had ramped up as well. Their captors came and went more frequently, forcing Toma to remain hidden in his cocoon. Fortunately, they spent most of their time in the Reaper's cockpit trying to bypass Reggie's security protocols. So far, their efforts had been in vain, but Toma knew it was only a matter of time before the bounty hunters succeeded. When that moment came, he would have no choice but to fight.

Toma imagined what he might do—how he would rescue Ava, vanquish their enemies with his adolescent claws, and return home a hero. But reality's gravity soon grounded his lofty daydreams. This was life or death; if recent events had taught him anything, it was the danger of acting rashly. Their only hope was to be patient, seize the right moment, and work together.

Resolved, Toma took a steadying breath and focused on eavesdropping on their captors' conversation, waiting for an opportunity to present itself.

Hiromi stood in the dark cockpit, quietly meditating while gently polishing her exquisite porcelain exoskeleton with a fine silk cloth. She found this practice soothing. It helped to clear her mind so the powerful microprocessors enhancing her organic brain could compute faster without the distraction of emotions, which, at the time, were inhibiting her progress.

To say Aiwan technology was challenging would be a gross understatement. Hiromi knew this when she accepted the job, but circumventing the Reaper's security systems had proven exceptionally difficult.

Slicing the ship's systems involved more than plugging into a port and running a decryption algorithm. Hiromi would have used the terminal below in the engineering section if that were the case. And it was not the neural and holographic interfaces preferred by Aiwans that had her stumped, either. She knew workarounds for both. Rather, it was the artificial intelligence that impeded her progress. All Aiwan ships were embedded with such technology, which Hiromi likened to a crew member with a life debt to the ship's captain. Whomever the ship recognized as its captain trumped everyone else, so any attempt to bypass the captain's security protocols would be detected by the AI and trigger its defenses. Hence Hiromi's conundrum.

"How's it coming?" Smythe asked, breaking Hiromi's concentration.

The cyborg slicer stopped her self-care and turned to face the bounty hunter.

"More difficult than expected," she admitted with reluctance. "Aiwan technology is unique. If I had more time, I might be able to test a few theories, but perhaps we should consider a more invasive approach?"

Smythe cocked his eyebrow. "Such as?"

"Rather than slicing into the ship's computer," Hiromi replied, "I suggest we remove Captain Tan's skull cap and hack into her brain instead."

The cyborg's deceptively delicate tone was icy calm, which surprised the heartless bounty hunter. Smythe was rendered momentarily speechless by the callousness of Hiromi's crude yet innovative solution.

Realizing she was serious, he said with indifference, "Do whatever it takes, but I need her alive … at least for the time being." Getting a nod of affirmation from Hiromi, Smythe then retrieved the commlink from his belt. "Gort?" he called.

"Here, boss," his partner answered dutifully.

"Get over here and help Hiromi with the prisoner," Smythe instructed. "I'm heading outside to check the perimeter."

"Sure thing," Gort replied. "Let me finish what I'm doing, and I'll be right over."

Smythe ended the transmission and returned the commlink. "Wait for Gort," he cautioned. "Our prisoner may be small, but she's got a lot of fight in her."

"That will not be a problem," Hiromi assured him. Despite her fixed expression of serenity, the cyborg's inanimate faceplate was unsettling.

"Suit yourself," Smythe allowed. "But I wouldn't underestimate her if I were you."

"I never do," Hiromi replied with unwavering confidence. As Smythe started to leave, the cyborg asked, "What do you plan to do with Captain Tan after you have her ship?"

Smythe paused, caught off-guard by the question. He turned to face

Hiromi, a puzzled expression crossing his insectoid face. "Sell her, most likely," he answered, trying to make sense of her unexpected inquiry. "The Pleasure District on Gomaiyus is always looking for fresh meat. Why?"

Shrugging, Hiromi replied coyly, "I could take her off your hands if you're willing to subtract her from my cut."

Wondering what the cyborg's interest in the human might be, Smythe responded, "Let's focus on getting control of the Reaper first. Then we'll talk."

Hiromi dipped her chin in agreement and silently followed the bounty hunter out of the cockpit.

"*Ava?*" Toma hissed, reaching out with telepathy. "*Ava, can you hear me?*"

"*I'm here,*" she answered. "*What did you find out?*"

"*They are coming for you,*" Toma said frantically.

"*It's okay, Toma,*" Ava soothed. "*Calm down and—*"

"*—No, Ava. Listen,*" Toma cut her off. "*They mean to access Reggie by cutting into your brain.*"

"What!?" Ava exclaimed, her voice sharp with fear, echoing inside the cramped closet.

Ava's heart rate rose as she sat cross-legged on the floor, her hands still bound behind her. She strained against her restraints, her gaze darting frantically around the dark space. Vulnerable and barely able to rise to her feet, Ava was trapped. Every breath grew shallower as the weight of her captors' plan pressed in on her. Desperate, she needed a way to fend them off.

"*Tell me exactly what you heard,*" she demanded.

"*Ava, they want to cut you open,*" Toma replied, his voice trembling. "*What are we going to do?*"

Ava's face blanched with terror. What could she do handcuffed? Her breath quickened, and she teetered on the edge of hyperventilation. Then, unexpectedly, a sound broke through her panic. A deep bass reverberated through the walls and floor. Bewildered, Ava looked up as the unmistakable beat of a 1980s classic song by Men Without Hats filled the air.

"S-s-s-s … A-a-a-a … F-f-f-f … E-e-e-e … T-t-t-t … Y-y-y-y … Safety Dance!"

Ava's eyes widened in startled confusion, and then, unable to hold it, she burst out laughing.

"*Ava!*" Toma called out urgently.

"*Toma?*" she replied, trying to block out the music to focus. "*What's happening?"*

"*I do not know!*" he winced, powerless to cover his ears inside the cocoon as the music blared.

Ava's gaze darted around, searching for an explanation. Then, it hit her. Tears welled in her eyes as she shouted with joyful realization, "Reggie!"

22
SIDE EFFECTS

Planet Earth
Mike O'Callaghan Military Medical Center, Nellis AFB, Nevada

Hector Nunez had a knack for standing out in a crowd. Usually, his colorful, flower-patterned camp shirts were enough to draw people's attention, but today he had upped the ante. The Air Force retiree stood beneath the shade of palm trees outside the medical center's main entrance, holding a plush, oversized stuffed bunny that attracted approving smiles from small children who passed by.

Behind Hector, a sleek black Cadillac Escalade with government plates idled in the roundabout reserved for patient drop-offs. Inside, a thirty-something-year-old deputy with the United States Marshals Service sat behind the wheel, waiting for his partner to return with their package.

Stifling a yawn, the deputy glanced at the dashboard clock, eager to wrap things up. Today marked the final day of their protection detail for Mr. Pei Wang, aka Choi Min-jun. The assignment had been a mind-numbing routine with little more to do than keep watch over the recovering patient. Their duty would end as soon as they delivered Min-jun and his companion, Hector, to the flight line at Nellis. An FBI team waited there to escort them to Missoula, Montana so that Min-jun could resume his new life in witness protection.

Hector's face brightened as the entrance doors slid open, and the man of the hour appeared. Min-jun was seated in a wheelchair, pushed by a cute nurse dressed in dark blue scrubs. A second deputy wearing dark sunglasses accompanied them.

Taking his first breath of fresh air in almost a week, Min-jun closed his eyes and savored the morning sun on his face despite the dry heat.

"Hey, hey, there he is!" Hector said boisterously.

Recognizing Hector's voice, Min-jun's eyes fluttered open. Shielding his face in the sunlight, he spotted the silhouette of a colossal bunny approaching, but no sign of Hector.

"Free at last! Free at last!" Hector chanted, bouncing the stuffed animal in front of him so its ears flopped wildly. He peeked around the bunny, flashing a playful grin that drew a giggle from the nurse, earning her an innocent wink. But Min-jun was lost for words, trying to decipher the cultural significance behind Hector's antics.

Hector's face softened as he read his friend's confused expression. "Sorry, buddy. Too much?"

That was an understatement. Barely two months removed from his old life exfiltrating North Korean defectors for the CIA, Min-jun was still grappling with the overwhelming rush of American culture. The vibrant, diverse, and fast-paced nature of everyday life in the United States was exhausting by comparison.

From navigating crowded department stores to enduring endless daytime television shows in his hospital room, the barrage of stimuli made Min-jun's head spin. He missed the simplicity of his life back in Sanhe, China—helping the GCRM staff with daily chores and playing with the children. In contrast, the constant noise of America put him on edge, ill-prepared for civilian life in the land of excess.

Though his unsanctioned operation in Peru had not gone as planned, at least it had given him a brief sense of purpose akin to his former career. However, the sight of the oversized bunny was a stark reminder of the uncertainty ahead; it left him feeling hollow and yearning for a home that no longer existed.

Hector and the nurse exchanged a glance of shared concern.

"Maybe we should give him some space?" the nurse suggested with a polite smile.

Nodding in agreement, Hector resituated the stuffed animal in his arms and took a step back.

"Sorry," he apologized, feeling embarrassed. "It's a gift for Ji- ...er, rather, Samantha and the baby," he corrected himself.

The mention of Samantha Ri, aka Vong Ji-eun, caught Min-jun's attention. He looked up sharply, brow furrowed with concern, and asked Hector, "Is she safe?"

Hector glanced at the deputy. His eyes shielded behind dark sunglasses, the deputy subtly shook his head, signaling Hector to drop the subject immediately.

Taking the hint, Hector responded casually, as though nothing was amiss. "Oh, sure, she's fine," he said. With a nod toward the SUV, he smoothly redirected the conversation. "Your chariot awaits, my friend. How about we get you out of this heat?"

Sensing Hector's evasion, Min-jun did not press him for more information. They proceeded in silence to the vehicle. Once there, Hector opened the rear passenger door and tossed the bunny over the back seat. All the while, the deputy kept a watchful eye on their surroundings.

At the curb, Min-jun gingerly rose from the wheelchair. Though his body still felt stiff from prolonged bed rest, he was grateful to stand under his own power. His doctors had assured him he would make a full recovery in the weeks ahead. The physical injuries from his encounter with the anaconda and his fight with Mr. Renzo were healing, and the blood clot in his leg had dissolved enough for him to fly.

Standing, Min-jun steadied himself and shared a triumphant smile with Hector.

"Look at you," Hector remarked, proud of his friend's progress. Seeing Min-jun brighten for the first time in days, he grinned and added, "You know, my mother always said a smile is like a new pair of underwear—it just lifts the cheeks."

The nurse shook her head, softly chuckling as she moved the wheelchair aside. She and Hector stood by, ready to assist Min-jun into the vehicle, but he managed on his own, easing himself into his seat and fastening the seat belt.

"Okay, Mr. Wang, you're all set," the nurse said cheerily. "You take good care of yourself now. You hear?"

Min-jun nodded. Clearing his dry throat, he said, "Thank you."

The nurse smiled warmly and closed the door as Hector circled the vehicle to sit beside Min-jun. The deputy quietly settled into the front passenger seat. As the SUV pulled away, the nurse waved goodbye, unsure if her former patient returned the gesture through the dark, tinted window.

She pushed the wheelchair back inside, where one of the Air Force security guards approached her.

"So, what do you make of that?" he asked, intrigued by the secrecy surrounding the high-security visit of the Asian man.

The nurse shrugged. Turning toward the exit, she caught a final glimpse of the SUV before it disappeared.

"They didn't tell us much," she replied honestly. Lowering her voice, she added, "We treated him for a wicked snake bite, but the rest of his injuries came from someone else."

The guard raised his eyebrows. "He looked like he'd been through a serious beatdown," he remarked, imagining the Asian man in a vicious brawl. Considering the extent of Min-jun's injuries, the guard grimaced. "Man, I'd hate to see what the other guy looks like."

Marine Logistics Ship, *Zaragoza*
150 Nautical Miles from the Port of Panama

Javier and Pedro, two mechanics working aboard the Panamax container ship *Zaragoza*, leaned on a metal railing overlooking the engine room, watching Renzo in amazement.

One hundred and ninety-eight ... one hundred and ninety-nine ... two hundred, Pedro counted off to himself.

Shaking his head in disbelief, he leaned in close to Javier. Speaking into his co-worker's ear, loud enough to be heard over running engines, he said in Spanish, "That's two hundred pushups!"

Javier raised his eyebrows, clearly impressed by the stranger's display of physical prowess. He and Pedro had been watching Renzo work out for the past ten minutes. Two hundred pushups were impressive enough, but it seemed he never tired after the same number of pullups.

Javier scoffed. "He looks strong, but he's lean. C'mon, let's get to it."

Renzo noticed the gawkers but paid them no mind as he pushed himself through another grueling workout. Since taking the force enhancement serum, he was surprised at the remarkable increase in his strength and stamina. Each day, Renzo tested his limits, consistently reaching new heights. His performance ceiling appeared unlimited.

No wonder the North Koreans and Russians are climbing over each other for Dr. Vlachos's formula, he thought, smiling inwardly with a measure of satisfaction.

Renzo wiped beads of sweat from his brow with a hand towel, tossed it aside, and then sat on the floor to begin crunches. The workouts not only helped him gauge his newfound abilities but also helped him pass the time. Today was

Day Three of an eight-day, monotonous voyage aboard the container ship. His boss, Edmund Mathias, had called in a favor to the CEO of Marine Logistics and arranged a last-minute passage for Renzo from the Port of Callao in Lima, Peru, to the Port of Progreso in Mexico. Once there, Renzo would rendezvous with members of the Sinaloa Cartel, who agreed to escort him to the U.S.-Mexico border and smuggle him into Texas. In the meantime, Renzo had to find creative ways to keep himself occupied, which was easier said than done.

Traveling under an assumed identity, his presence aboard the merchant ship remained shrouded in mystery. Despite being offered the captain's stateroom, Renzo opted to steer clear of the crew as much as possible and avoid drawing attention to himself. This meant remaining below deck during the day and only going topside when the sun was down and most of the crew was asleep. He ate alone and slept in an empty storage room buried deep in the ship's bowels. The cramped room was no bigger than a prison cell, but at least it had a foldout cot and a nearby bathroom, which was much more than he had growing up on the streets of Lima.

With so much downtime, Renzo kept himself sharp by working out and studying the dossiers on his two targets: Choi Min-jun and Vong Ji-eun. The woman, he learned, was the daughter of a high-ranking North Korean general who aided the Americans in their recent theft of an alien spacecraft known as The Reaper. Considering the treasonous act resulted in the death of the Supreme Leader, Kim Sung-il, it was no surprise the current regime in Pyongyang wanted Ji-eun to pay for her father's crimes against the state.

Choi Min-jun was another matter. He, too, was involved in the epic heist, and while the North Koreans also wanted his head on a platter, they would have to get in line. Renzo had a personal score to settle. It was the driving force behind his grueling workout, pushing him harder as he envisioned the moment he would exact his revenge—inflicting maximum pain on the man who bested him and left him for dead.

Finishing his workout fifteen minutes later, Renzo departed the engineering section and made his way back to his room. Passing a lone crew member along the way, Renzo kept his head down, avoiding eye contact. In a vessel this big, he was surprised by how small of a crew it took to operate the ship. The *Zaragoza* was one of the largest container ships allowed to pass through the Panama Canal. Measuring 950 feet in length, this Panamax vessel boasted a container-carrying capacity of 12,400 TEU (Twenty-foot-long container equivalent units), which made passing through the canal challenging.

In a brief discussion with the ship's captain, Renzo learned that the

Zaragoza would take at least eight hours to traverse the canal due to the water locks—the mechanisms that lift vessels onto the artificial lake between the Atlantic and Pacific Oceans. Renzo looked forward to watching the process, even though they would pass through the canal at night.

Arriving at his room, Renzo reached for the door handle and froze; it was slightly ajar. In a rush of anger, he threw the door open and found two crewmembers inside, both dressed in matching orange jumpsuits, rummaging through his belongings. Renzo recognized them immediately—they had watched him working out earlier. He quickly pegged them both as Venezuelan based on their dark complexion, high cheekbones, and charcoal-black hair.

Pedro, the would-be thief farthest from Renzo, was a scrawny-looking man with an unkempt mop of hair. Weighing a buck forty soaking wet, at most, Renzo did not see him as much of a threat. However, Pedro's partner in crime, Javier, was a mountain of a man. He stood six feet two inches tall with bulging biceps and the chiseled physique of a Greek god.

Pedro and Javier had their backs to the door when Renzo barged in. Startled, the crew members rounded sharply. A tense silence hung in the air, filled with unspoken accusations. But it was fleeting. Relieved not to be discovered by their captain, Pedro and Javier gave Renzo a once-over and smirked, clearly not deterred by being caught red-handed.

Renzo's heart rate spiked at the sight of Pedro holding his prized big-bore blowgun and Javier skimming through one of his private files. His eyes then darted to the empty carrying case lying open on the bed. Setting his jaw, he clenched his fists and demanded, "Put them back." His words were quiet and measured, at odds with the fire boiling in his blood.

Pedro scoffed at Renzo's audacity before erupting into laughter. Javier quickly joined in, but Renzo stood firm, showing no outward fear or intent to back down.

As the tension mounted, Pedro's laughter gradually died off. His lip curled into a sneer at Renzo's defiance. "Get him!" he ordered Javier.

On command, Javier tossed the folder on the bed and stepped toward Renzo. Wearing a confident, malicious grin, he cracked his knuckles as if relishing the task of inflicting pain. Inches from Renzo, he thrust both hands at Renzo's chest, expecting to push him backward out the door. But Renzo easily deflected the telegraphed move, slapping Javier's hands outward to expose his face and midsection. With lightning speed, Renzo followed up with a crushing blow to Javier's solar plexus, instantly knocking the wind out of him. Javier's knees buckled, and he collapsed to the floor, gasping like a fish out of water.

But Renzo was not finished with him. In one swift movement, he grabbed Javier by the hair and thrust his palm upward, breaking his nose. Javier keeled over as the metallic flavor of blood touched his lips.

Renzo turned toward Pedro. Fire blazed in his eyes, and his chest heaved in ragged breaths. He could feel the serum coursing through his veins, igniting every nerve with searing intensity. The Chachapoyan had to summon all his self-control to suppress the animalistic instinct clawing to the surface of his mind.

Pedro saw the killer lurking inside Renzo. He slowly placed the blowgun on the bed with shaky hands, then raised them in surrender.

"There, it's yours," he said, wanting no part of it now. "Just let me go."

Renzo's eyes flicked from Pedro to the bed, where his confidential files lay scattered. He knew these two imbeciles had seen too much and would likely talk. Fighting the influence of the serum, his rational self urged restraint; escalating now would only risk drawing unwanted attention.

Suddenly, two large hands clamped around his neck from behind. With a guttural growl, Javier lifted Renzo off the ground. Feet thrashing, Renzo fought Javier's iron grip, but the brute's hands were unyielding, bent on choking the life out of him.

Through the haze of his struggle, Renzo caught Pedro's smug grin; he clearly enjoyed watching him suffer.

"Not so tough now, huh?" Pedro taunted.

At that moment, something snapped inside Renzo, and the serum took hold, awakening a feral aggression. The cramped quarters offered him little space to maneuver, but Pedro was just the leverage he needed. Renzo drew his legs up and kicked off the scrawny man, slamming Pedro against the hull and propelling himself backward. Pushed off-balance, Javier's foot caught on the cot's leg, and he stumbled, crashing into the bulkhead with a force that reverberated through the metal walls.

As Renzo's feet touched the ground, he threw his elbow back in a quick thrust, connecting with Javier's ribs. The blow landed with brutal precision, weakening Javier enough for Renzo to free himself from the chokehold. He gasped, clutching his throat, but Javier was right back on him. Wrapping his thick arms around Renzo in a crushing bear hug, Javier pinned the Chachapoyan's arms to his sides and squeezed tighter than an anaconda. Javier then hauled Renzo outside, ramming the man's head against the door frame on the way out.

A sharp, searing pain shot through Renzo's skull, briefly disorienting him as Javier carried him into an open space and dumped him onto the cold, unforgiving floor. Renzo landed on his knees, sucking air. But Javier grabbed him by the collar and waistband before he could recover. In an instant, Renzo was airborne, his body colliding with a wall before collapsing onto his stomach.

Thinking Renzo would stay down, Javier relaxed. He had no intention of killing the man—just beating him within an inch of his life. But Renzo was just getting started. His pain was fleeting, and he recovered faster than expected. He picked himself up off the floor without a flicker of mercy in his eyes. Like a lion stalking its prey, driven by an innate thrill of the hunt, Renzo approached Javier, ready for more.

Javier shook his head in disbelief, then curled his lip in a snarling rage. In one swift motion, he shifted his body weight to his front foot and brought his right hand around in a lead cross to crush Renzo's jaw. But Renzo ducked and countered with a lightning-fast combination of punches into Javier's sides, holding each blow against his ribs long enough to complete the energy transfer.

Javier groaned as his ribcage collapsed with a bone-crunching pain. He staggered backward, staring at Renzo in shock, confused by his smaller opponent's uncanny strength. That look quickly morphed into horror as he locked eyes with Renzo and saw a wild animal staring back.

Renzo attacked, tackling Javier around the waist and taking him hard to the ground. Though outweighed by over eighty pounds, the Chachapoyan unleashed a ferocious barrage of punches to Javier's face. Overmatched and entirely on the defensive, Javier did his best to protect himself, but Renzo was unrelenting. He landed punch after punch, making mincemeat of the big guy's face. And with each strike, Renzo felt the serum burning hotter in his veins, heightening his senses and increasing his strength.

"Help!" Javier cried out in a desperate plea for assistance.

Renzo did not hear the man in this primal state; even if he had, no quarter would be given. He continued the onslaught without reservation or remorse—those were human emotions.

Javier went for Renzo's face to slow his attacker down but inadvertently grabbed a handful of hair. To his surprise, a large clump came free with relative ease, leaving a bald spot atop Renzo's head as if scalped.

Renzo instinctively pulled back, equally shocked. Seeing the black mass of hair in the crewman's hand, he exchanged a shared look of bewilderment with Javier. But the surreal moment was short-lived.

WHACK!

Something struck Renzo across the back of his head. The jolt registered a distracting pain in his mind, but Renzo shook it off. With a look of annoyance, he rounded to find Pedro standing behind him, holding the shattered remains of his prized blowgun.

Renzo slowly rose to his full height. Leaving Javier battered and bruised on the deck, the Chachapoyan redirected his simmering rage toward Pedro.

The scrawny crewman froze. Though his brain screamed for him to run, Pedro could not move, as if his feet were cemented to the floor. As Renzo neared, Pedro's expression filled with fear and regret. All he could bring himself to do was hold out the splintered half of the blowgun in his palms, conveying deep sorrow.

With a shaky voice, Pedro begged, "Forgive me."

Renzo remained silent, his gaze fixed on the shattered weapon. His chest rose and fell—not from fatigue but in a struggle to regain his composure. With steady hands, Renzo took the splintered half of the blowgun from Pedro's trembling grip and studied its remains. The damage was irreparable, but what truly made him pause was the subtle tug in the back of his mind. Somehow, his connection to the weapon anchored him, slowly pulling him back to his rational self.

Pedro said nothing at first, observing Renzo with a blend of fear, curiosity, and uncertainty. The Chachapoyan stood motionless as he stared blankly at the blowgun, lost in thought.

Sensing the weight of the moment, Pedro ventured softly, "¿Señor?"

The sound of his voice broke Renzo's concentration. Blinking back to the moment, he wrapped his fingers around the wooden shaft and struck without warning. Grabbing Pedro by the hair, Renzo rammed the jagged end of the blowgun into the man's neck, impaling him with such force it severed Pedro's spine.

Pedro's eyes widened in shock, mouth agape. An awful gurgling sound escaped his lips as he collapsed to the floor, paralyzed from the neck down. A steady stream of blood funneled out of his body through the blowgun's mouthpiece, draining his life.

Renzo stepped back, his face void of emotion as he regarded his victim. A heavy silence settled, giving him a moment to quell the chaos in his mind. He closed his eyes and slowed his breathing. Little by little, the primal fury that had consumed him ebbed away. When he finally opened his eyes, it was as though he had awakened from a nightmare—his mind clear, his focus sharp. Renzo felt in control once more.

With the Jekyll-Hyde episode seemingly behind him, Renzo's first thought was not damage control—it was hair loss. He touched the bald spot on his scalp. Feeling no tenderness or pain, he removed another clump. The hair came out with ease. Renzo shook it from his hand and continued pulling more free. With each handful, the realization set in: Dr. Vlachos's test subjects experienced the same side effects.

Eyeing the sweaty strands stuck to his palm, Renzo accepted the inevitable. *It's happening.*

Time was running out, and if he hoped to complete his mission before devolving into a rabid beast, he had to find a way to control his animalistic outbursts.

"El Diablo," came a raspy voice behind him.

Renzo turned to find Javier cowering in the corner. The man's bloodied face had turned pale, beaded with sweat.

Javier no longer posed a physical threat to Renzo, but he had seen the confidential files; no doubt he would talk if allowed to live. Without hesitation, Renzo disappeared into his room and returned moments later with a poison-tipped blow dart. Javier made a feeble attempt to push Renzo away, but he struck swiftly, plunging the dart into Javier's thigh, sealing his fate.

"Stop!" a voice bellowed.

Renzo looked up to find the ship's captain flanked by two other crew members, all armed with shotguns. Taking in the gruesome scene, their horror deepened as Javier began foaming at the mouth and convulsed before going still.

Renzo darted his eyes between the captain and his men, assessing each for strengths and weaknesses but taking particular note of their weapons. Serum or not, he could not outrun a bullet, although a part of him wanted to test how many shots it would take to put him down.

Captain Gallardo surveyed the carnage, stunned. Unable to reconcile the situation, he murmured, "What have you done?"

Renzo did not bother answering. He retrieved his dart, straightened, and then pressed his finger to his lips—a chilling warning that they would share the same fate if they spoke of this. Without another glance, Renzo turned and headed back toward the nearby bathroom, intent on cleaning up before taking a nap.

Watching the Chachapoyan walk away, seemingly unbothered, the captain ran his hand over his head, unsure what to do. "But señor, how am I supposed to explain this?"

"Throw them overboard," Renzo replied callously over his shoulder. He paused at the door and turned to the captain. "And one more thing," he added, "when we dock, there better be another blowgun waiting for me—same model. Understood?"

The captain swallowed the lump in his throat. He lowered his gaze to Pedro, the dead man's face soaked in his own blood as it pooled on the floor. Gallardo's eyes settled on the blowgun lodged in Pedro's throat, and the weight of Renzo's demand sank in. Nodding, the captain accepted the grim task without another question.

Satisfied, Renzo shut the door behind him and stood in front of the small mirror above the sink. He stared at his reflection for a long moment, barely recognizing the face that looked back. Redness rimmed his pupils, and dark circles shadowed his eyes, making him appear to have aged a decade.

Over the next few minutes, he calmly pulled out the remaining tufts of hair from his head. Now completely bald, he examined his new look in the mirror from different angles, reflecting on how easily he had dispatched both crewmembers without breaking a sweat. A faint, inward smile tugged at him. Renzo liked what he had become.

23
DEEP SIX

Planet Earth
Royal Fleet Auxiliary Ship, *Proteus*

Since the 1700s, humans have worked systematically to map the vast ocean floor, a practice known as hydrography. It began with Alexander Dalrymple of the British Admiralty, who conducted the first underwater soundings of coastal regions to support the growing maritime economy. In the 20th century, hydrography expanded as companies laid submarine pipelines to carry communications and fuel between continents.

Over time, hydrography evolved beyond commercial purposes to include military applications. The advent of undersea warfare, including minesweeping and defense against enemy submarines, drove rapid technological advances, vastly increasing the scale of the sea floor infrastructure. This growing access to the ocean's dark and dangerous depths gave rise to modern "seabed" warfare.

Cold War operations such as *Ivy Bells*—a joint mission between the United States Navy, CIA, and NSA to wiretap Soviet undersea communication links—initiated this new battleground. In the following decades, sea floor attacks became a real and present danger for modern navies. With increased reliance on transoceanic pipelines, fiber optics, and power cables to transfer data and energy worldwide, seabed security concerns were no longer theoretical—

as Russia's presumed attack on the Nord Stream pipelines showed. Given the difficulty of defending against seabed sabotage, nations have invested heavily to modernize their global seabed warfare capabilities.

The RFA *Proteus* represented one response to these growing undersea threats. A recent addition to the Royal Navy's Hydrographic squadron, this multi-role ocean surveillance ship monitors and protects British seabed communication cables and energy pipelines. However, on this particular day, *Proteus* ventured halfway across the globe to spy on one of Mathias Industries' so-called research vessels, the *Billy Bones*.

Holding position two hundred nautical miles southwest of Guam, the crew of *Proteus* was hard at work preparing to launch *Cetus*, the Royal Navy's first crewless submarine to enter service. Named after a mythological sea monster, *Cetus* represented the future of British underwater warfare.

Unlike other underwater autonomous vehicles used for minesweeping and delivering SpecOps teams, like the United States Navy's SEAL teams, *Cetus* was known as an ELAUV—Extra Large Autonomous Underwater Vehicle. The unmanned submersible measured twelve meters in length and had an estimated operating radius of one thousand nautical miles. Even more impressive, *Cetus* could fit inside a standard shipping container, making it easy to transport anywhere worldwide.

Regarding *Billy Bones*, the Royal Navy was not about to sit on the sidelines, entrusting its new baby to the Americans. As tensions between the United States, Russia, China, and North Korea escalated, the British Admiralty saw fit to take matters into its own hands to ensure Mathias's secretive activities in Challenger Deep did not go unchecked.

A large crane hoisted *Cetus* overboard from *Proteus's* deck and dropped the autonomous vehicle into the water on the port side. Within minutes, the crew aboard *Proteus* had *Cetus's* single screw churning. Releasing ballast, the unmanned sub descended below the water line and started its five-hour journey to reach *Billy Bones* and begin surveillance.

At the outset of its mission, the sub deployed active sonar arrays to gather intel on Mathias's ship, vigilantly monitoring for any signs of submersible activity. This routine continued over the next four days without yielding any notable findings. But soon, *Cetus* faced a critical constraint as it neared the limits of its operational endurance. With time quickly running out, the crew aboard *Proteus* decided to send *Cetus* to the depths of Challenger Deep to investigate the location of the energy crystals known as magnetarite.

It was widely known that Mathias's ultimate objective was to harvest these crystals, yet the full scope of his operation remained a mystery. The British admiralty held high hopes that *Cetus* would finally provide the answers they sought.

Cetus dove to thirty-five thousand feet, nearing the deepest point of the Marianas Trench. Operating in stealth mode, the ELAUV captured footage of its descent to the ocean floor, with the data to be analyzed later by British Intelligence aboard *Proteus*. At such depths, transmitting signals of any kind was impossible.

Upon reaching the coordinates provided by the Americans, a small door opened on the ELAUV's bow. Moments later, *Cetus* released a smaller autonomous underwater vehicle (AUV) to enter the mysterious cave of crystals.

This task was tedious and fraught with opportunities for failure. The Brits knew the location of the magnetarite deposits but not how to navigate within the cave, which meant the smaller AUV's course could not be programmed beforehand. It had to navigate the passage on its own using sonar pings to chart a path, thus announcing its presence to anyone listening.

With its external running lights illuminating the cave's pitch-black interior, the AUV methodically advanced toward its target. Enduring pressures of roughly 16,000 psi—one thousand times higher than at sea level—the AUV maneuvered through the passage until it emerged into a sprawling cavern.

But the space was empty; no crystals were in sight.

Had this been a live feed, the analysts aboard *Proteus* might have been scratching their heads, suspecting the Americans had misled them. However, the AUV was not programmed to make such assessments. It had one job: to capture images, not analyze them and form conclusions. The AUV continued its mission by pinging the interior and mapping the cavernous space while its cameras recorded every detail of the barren area.

In less than fifteen minutes, the image gathering was complete. The AUV exited the cave and successfully returned to *Cetus* before starting its journey back to *Proteus*.

Russian Navy Ballistic Missile Submarine, *Imperator Alexander III*
South Pacific Ocean

The crew of the *Porteus* was unaware they were being watched. Patrolling the waters around Challenger Deep was the Russian Navy's newest Borei-A class, nuclear-powered, ballistic missile submarine, *Imperator Alexander III* (K-554). After completing its sea trials the previous year, K-554 had entered active service in the Russian Pacific Fleet two months prior.

Engineered to replace the aging Typhoon-, Kalmer-, and Delfin-class ballistic missile submarines, the Borei-A class sub displaced 24,000 tons when submerged. With its streamlined hull and advanced pump-jet propulsion system, K-554 boasted stealth capabilities far surpassing its predecessors—operating at noise levels five times lower than the Akula-class attack subs. As a formidable second-strike option within Russia's nuclear triad, *Imperator Alexander III* loomed as a silent, powerful presence beneath the waves.

"Conn, Sonar!" called out the sonar operator. "Possible contact bearing three-five-zero, designated Sierra-1." Seconds later, his computer identified the contact, and he added, "Conn, Sonar, contact Sierra-1 classified as submerged autonomous vehicle—speed ten knots, estimated range 3,000 meters, bearing three-five-zero."

Seated in the middle of the control room, Captain First Rank Ivan Zaitsev came to his feet and straightened his uniform. After hours of patiently awaiting the British submersible's return from Challenger Deep, K-554's captain readied himself to engage the target.

"Da," Captain Zaitsev acknowledged. In Russian, he added, "Load tubes one and two. Prepare firing solution to target."

The command generated immediate tension in the room as the bridge crew realized this was not a drill. Captain Second Rank Sorokin, the starpom (first officer), acknowledged the captain's directive and relayed it to the weapons officer seated five feet away. The weapons officer confirmed the order and promptly contacted the weapons room to carry out his instructions.

In the submarine's bow, crew members inside the weapons room sprang into action, loading two RPK-2 Vyuga anti-submarine missiles into identical 533-millimeter torpedo tubes. The meticulous task took five minutes to complete.

Upon receiving confirmation, the weapons officer turned to Captain Zaitsev and relayed, "Tubes one and two loaded, Comrade Captain. Firing solution confirmed. Awaiting your orders."

Captain Zaitsev acknowledged with a nod, his demeanor calm despite the international incident he was about to create. "Flood tubes one and two," he commanded.

The weapons room carried out the order. Moments later, Captain Zaitsev received confirmation that *Imperator Alexander III* stood ready to execute its unfortunate but necessary strike.

"Fire tubes one and two," the captain ordered without hesitation.

Royal Fleet Auxiliary Ship, *Proteus*

The sonar officer aboard *Proteus* sat up at his station the moment *Cetus* breached the surface.

"Sir, I've reestablished contact with *Cetus*," he reported eagerly to the ship's captain. "All systems operational. Data transmission commencing."

Cetus initiated the upload of video footage and sonar maps gathered from Challenger Deep. The encrypted data was then bounced off a military satellite and transmitted directly to *Proteus* and Secret Intelligence Service headquarters in London. As the first images of the empty cave appeared, the crew exchanged identical looks of bewilderment.

Where are the crystals? they wondered.

The transmission then suddenly ended, leaving only the unmistakable echo of an underwater explosion as all contact with *Cetus* vanished.

24

DAMAGE CONTROL

Planet Earth
Satipo, Peru

Edmund Mathias's receptionist, Vera, was sitting at her computer scrolling through social media posts when she heard the distant click-clack of high heels echoing up the corridor. Recognizing the purposeful steps, she closed the screen with practiced precision and seamlessly transitioned to a façade of busy efficiency just as Ms. Diaz arrived.

She smiled politely as Diaz reached her desk.

"Is he busy?" Diaz asked, wasting no time with pleasantries.

That's an understatement, Vera almost let slip but held her tongue. Clearing her throat, she suppressed a knowing grin and replied, "Yes, Ms. Diaz. Mr. Mathias asked not to be disturbed."

Diaz huffed. She had a pressing matter to discuss that could not wait. "For how long?" she snapped.

"He said twenty or thirty minutes … give or take," Vera tactfully replied. "That was ten minutes ago."

Reading the subtle hint on the receptionist's face, Diaz drew her conclusion. "Deanna?"

Vera smiled sheepishly.

Diaz rolled her eyes. "Oh, please," she grumbled, then moved toward Edmund's office. She pressed her ear to the door but heard nothing, so she wrapped her knuckles twice on the door loudly.

"Ms. Diaz—" Vera protested, but Diaz waved her off sharply, shushing her.

Putting her ear to the door again, Diaz heard a hushed argument between Mathias and his lover, Deanna. A loud thud soon followed, accompanied by Edmund's hissed curse about stubbing his toe. Diaz shook her head, cringing at the thought of what kinkiness she interrupted.

Throwing caution to the wind, Diaz cracked the door open and announced, "Boss? It's me," she said cautiously, keeping her eyes down. "We need to talk. It's urgent."

"For crying out loud, Diaz, I'm busy," Edmund replied tersely. "Go away!"

"Sorry, but this can't wait," Diaz insisted.

A brief moment passed as Diaz could hear the couple fumbling about. Finally, Edmund said with annoyance, "Fine, what is it?"

Diaz glanced up, relieved to find Edmund standing behind the desk—wearing pants—and casually buttoning his designer shirt. By far, this was not the worst thing she had ever caught him doing, and thankfully, nothing was happening that she could not unsee.

She stepped inside and closed the door behind her. Before speaking, she scanned the room for Deanna and noticed the light under the bathroom door in the back corner.

"Trouble with Renzo," Diaz said absently, then shifted her focus to Edmund, her tone turning grave. "He killed two crewmen on that ship. The captain said he attacked his men like a wild animal, completely unhinged."

Edmund paused, intrigued by this news. He knew Renzo to be a methodical killer—clean and efficient. If what the captain said was true, the serum must have taken hold of him. A thin smile creased Edmund's lip as he imagined the carnage.

"So, what's the problem?" he asked, his voice calm and indifferent.

What's the problem? Diaz scoffed inwardly.

Maintaining her composure, she replied evenly, "Sir, word will spread. Even though the captain threw the dead men overboard, the rest of the crew is bound to talk … and the captain's worried there may be more incidents before they dock."

"Remind him he's being paid handsomely to look the other way … and by whom," Edmund added, referring to the cartel. He then waved dismissively. "Just make it go away, okay? I have a full day ahead."

Just then, the bathroom door opened, and Deanna appeared. Wearing a form-fitting red minidress that accentuated every curve, the boss's girlfriend strode past Diaz on her way out. Deanna threw her gorgeous blonde hair to one side as they exchanged glances and playfully winked at Diaz with a confident grin.

"Tootles," Deanna said, wiggling her fingers.

Diaz cringed inwardly. She had always maintained a semi-cordial demeanor with Deanna but harbored an unspoken discomfort because of instances like this. Diaz could not fault her boss for keeping Deanna around. She certainly had a role to play and was enjoying an extravagant lifestyle in exchange. Still, when pleasure interrupted business—especially during business hours—Diaz felt she had to work even harder for Edmund to see her from the neck up.

When Diaz turned her focus back to her boss, he was crossing the room to the bathroom. Edmund stepped inside, leaving the door wide open, lifted the toilet seat, and began urinating.

Repulsed, Diaz looked away. Moving toward the far window, she tried shutting out the echo of Edmund's continuous stream by pulling out her phone and opening an investment app. Checking the status of her sizable portfolio, she thought to herself, *Two more freakin' years, then it's off to Belize, sipping Mai Tais on the beach for the rest of your life.*

Hearing the toilet flush, Diaz snapped back to her current reality. She quickly closed the app and pocketed her phone as she rounded to face Edmund.

"Is that all?" he asked.

"Renzo damaged his blowgun in the fight," Diaz added. "Seems he impaled one of the crewmen with it." She grimaced, the gruesome image flashing briefly in her mind before she shook it off. "Anyway, he's asked for a replacement. I'll handle it."

Edmund nodded distractedly as his desk phone buzzed. Moving back behind his desk, he thumbed the intercom button. "Yes?"

"Sir, I have the Kremlin on Line 1 ... General Morosov's office," Vera answered.

Taken aback, Edmund exchanged a look of surprise with Diaz. A call from the Chief of the General Staff, the highest-ranking military officer in the Russian Armed Forces, was unprecedented. Mathias had only met the general a few times at state dinners in the Grand Kremlin Palace in Moscow. Intermediaries usually handled the nuts and bolts of his business dealings with the Russian Federation.

"This can't be good," Edmund muttered with a sense of dread.

Taking his seat, he snapped his fingers and pointed to the empty chair across from him, signaling Diaz to sit. She did so with haste, just as eager as her boss to learn the purpose of the call.

Edmund took a deep breath and pressed the intercom button. "Thanks, Vera," he replied. "I've got it."

Edmund brightened as if on cue just as he pressed the flashing button on his phone. He instantly adopted a façade of genuine excitement while his photographic memory flawlessly recalled minute details of past encounters with the Russian military leader.

"General Morosov!" he greeted enthusiastically. "What a pleasure—"

"—Stand by for General Morosov," a man with a heavy Russian accent interrupted.

Edmund looked at Diaz and rolled his eyes; then, the general joined the call. "Mr. Matias?" Morosov said in a no-nonsense tone.

"Yes," Edmund replied. "General Morosov, it's so nice to hear from you. To what do I owe this honor?"

"There has been an unfortunate development," the general said gravely. "Normally, I would have others deliver such news, but in light of recent events, this warranted my personal attention. There is too much at stake for both of us, yes?"

Edmund's brow furrowed, wondering where this was leading. "Of course, General," he said cautiously. "Thank you for personally coming to me. Has something happened?" he asked, not sure he wanted to know the answer.

"As agreed, we pulled our surface ships from the area of Challenger Deep, leaving one submarine on station to keep an eye on the Americans. As it turns out, the British are also involved. They surveilled the area with an unmanned submarine—one of their extra-large autonomous underwater vehicles," he clarified. "In response, we destroyed the sub as soon as it reached the surface."

Edmund nodded slowly, thinking. "I see. Can you tell me how deep the sub dove? Did it reach Challenger Deep?"

"Da," Morosov answered. "We lost track of it for approximately one hour and assumed it reached the sea floor. We reacquired the target shortly afterward as it attempted to return to *Proteus*, the British spy ship."

"And you say it reached the surface," Edmund repeated back. "The ELAUV would've had to reestablish contact with a satellite before any encrypted transmissions could be sent, and even then, the Brits might've waited to extract any recordings until after the ELAUV had been recovered. From the sounds of it, I'm not sure we have anything to worry about."

"Da, that was our assessment as well. However, there will be repercussions," Morosov warned. "NATO will not take kindly to this overt act."

"Let me handle NATO," Edmund offered with confidence. "For all they know, the ELAUV was simply lost at sea. It happens all the time. And if the Americans and Brits suspect it was torpedoed, there was no loss of life, so they can bill me. Call it retribution for their attack on my facility."

"And what of your facility?" Morosov inquired. "President Polokov has budgeted billions of rubles for your much-touted force enhancement serum, yet you keep stalling."

Edmund remained unfazed. "I have good news, General. The serum has passed human trials, and production is ramping up. Are you ready to proceed with your order?"

"Like the North Koreans?" Morosov remarked in an accusatory tone. The general did not pretend to hide his knowledge of Mathias's other customers nor his displeasure that Russia was not the first to acquire the serum.

"They are yet to take possession," Edmund clarified. "Would you like to place your order today?"

"Da. Make it happen," General Morosov instructed.

Edmund flashed Diaz a smile and gave her two enthusiastic thumbs up. "Perfect," he replied with a polished warmth. "Consider it done. Anything else?"

"You are harboring a female alien, yes?"

Mathias's smile faded, replaced by a steely tension in his jaw. Morosov's interest in Luna was no surprise—North Korea had shown similar intentions—but Mathias could not afford to appear weak. A moment of vulnerability might encourage the Russians to attempt a brazen move like the Americans had done. Yet, while Edmund lacked the military might to dissuade Morosov, he possessed something just as dangerous: unyielding audacity.

Edmund leaned back, fingers steepled. "Correct, General. Her name is Luna. We are business partners."

"Partners?" Morosov scoffed derisively. A discerning silence followed, prompting the general to turn serious. "I wish to meet her."

"And you will, sir, very soon," Edmund assured him with a vague promise. "I'm ironing out the final details but should have more information for you by the end of the week."

Morosov furrowed his thick eyebrows. "Explain," he insisted.

Edmund rolled his eyes, making a mock choking gesture as if throttling the man on the other end of the call. Diaz suppressed a laugh.

Regaining his composure, Edmund replied evenly, "General, let's just say that if everything goes according to plan, you'll be getting more than just access to my Aiwan partner, but NATO defenses as well."

A brief silence hung in the air before Morosov finally spoke.

"That is a bold claim, Mr. Matias. I'm not sure what game you're playing, but I hope for your sake, you can back it up."

The general's thinly veiled threat did not rattle Edmund. He glanced at Diaz, who wore a look of puzzlement. With a reassuring grin, he answered her confusion with a confident wink.

"Rest assured, General," Edmund continued. "It's all under control. Who knows, maybe when all is said and done, Polokov will award you your second Order of Saint George."

Morosov took this with a grain of salt. "I do not seek medals, Mr. Matias. I expect results. You will report back to me by this time tomorrow to finalize delivery of our order and clarify this NATO business. Is that understood?"

Edmund made a talking puppet with his hand, mocking the general with exaggerated movements. "Of course, sir," Edmund replied. "Twenty-four hours, if not sooner. You have my word."

The line went dead.

Edmund raised his eyebrows, staring incredulously at the phone. Normally, he was the one hanging up rudely on others. Dropping his shoulders, Edmund let out a heavy sigh, relieved to have that conversation behind him.

Diaz studied him with a look of uncertainty. "You sure about this, boss?"

Edmund rubbed his tired eyes. "It'll work," he replied. "Besides, what choice do I have? If it's not the Russians, North Koreans, or Americans breathing down my neck, it'll be the harvesters."

He opened his eyes and pressed the intercom button. "Vera, please find Luna and have her report to my office immediately."

"Right away, sir," the receptionist replied.

Edmund hung up and turned to Diaz, dread already creeping in as he anticipated the next call he had to make. He raised his hand with a wry smirk and a touch of biting sarcasm and quipped, "Alright, who's up for hugging a cactus?"

25
OLIVE BRANCH

Planet Earth
Joint Base Andrews, Prince George's County, Maryland

President Fitzgerald's motorcade glided onto the tarmac at Joint Base Andrews, making a beeline for Air Force One. The president's airborne command center stood ready, its sleek fuselage—painted in the iconic robin's egg blue—glistening under the late afternoon sun. Around the aircraft, Secret Service agents stood like vigilant sentinels, their eyes sweeping every corner of the airfield.

As the motorcade drove past the gleaming Boeing 747-200B series aircraft, the black armored limo carrying President Fitzgerald and his Chief of Staff, Ernie Gutierrez, smoothly peeled away from the procession. Cadillac One rolled to a stop precisely on its mark near the aircraft's nose.

A Secret Service agent waiting at the base of the mobile boarding stairs approached the vehicle and opened the rear door. The commander-in-chief stepped out first. With the low, guttural hum of the jet engines in the background, Fitzgerald quickly saluted the senior enlisted airman standing at the base of the stairs and ascended the steps leading to the aircraft's executive entrance.

Ernie remained inside the vehicle until the president was halfway up the stairs. With reporters gathered in the distance, he was not about to block a good photo op for the president. Once the moment passed, Ernie emerged from Cadillac One and headed to the secondary boarding ramp at the rear of the aircraft, reserved for everyone except the first family and special guests.

President Fitzgerald reached the top of the stairs, turned, and waved to no one in particular, but it was protocol. He then entered the aircraft and walked to the back of the plane reserved for the press. A dozen journalists were already seated there and would accompany the president on this trip to Iowa. Fitzgerald took a moment to greet them by name and exchange witty banter.

Ernie appeared again. Without saying a word, he passed through the press area, heading toward the front of the aircraft. Fitzgerald followed moments later as Air Force One readied for take-off. Returning to the front of the plane, the president ascended the steps to the communications room, where he greeted the flight crew before entering his private office, dubbed the "Oval Office in the Sky."

CIA Director Maxine Ratliff was there to meet him, along with Ernie. Fitzgerald's smile faded as he noted the metal briefcase handcuffed to her wrist. Usually, a military aide accompanied the president on trips carrying the "nuclear football"—a metal briefcase storing the launch codes for America's nuclear arsenal. Seeing Ratliff with a similar setup gave the president pause; this was a first.

Fitzgerald gestured to the elephant in the room. "Ernie said you had something pressing. Looks like he wasn't kidding."

Ratliff raised the briefcase and nodded. "You definitely want to see this, sir."

His interest piqued; the president gestured to an open seat and said lightly, "Well, Maxine, I hope you like Des Moines."

Fitzgerald assumed his place behind an L-shaped desk with Ratliff and Ernie seated across from him. Each buckled in as the aircraft began to taxi.

"Mr. President, we've had some new developments regarding the Aiwans," Ratliff said as she unlocked the case. Lifting the lid, the CIA Director retrieved the beacon Prince Kypa had gifted to Rose. She held it out for both men to see.

Fitzgerald eyed her quizzically. "What is it, a bracelet?"

A thin smile played across Ratliff's lips. "It's more than jewelry, Mr. President. This is an interstellar beacon. It was given to Dr. Rose Landry by Prince Kypa before he departed Earth."

The president's surprise seemed tame compared to Ratliff's reaction when she learned of the device from Brett Brenham and his deputy, Jessica Aguri.

"And she's had it all this time?" Ernie interjected, understandably miffed.

"Yes," Ratliff confirmed. "Kypa made her promise not to say anything about it. He gave her instructions to only use it in an emergency."

Incredulous, Ernie glanced from Ratliff to the president. "How do we know it's not a bomb?"

Ratliff glanced sideways at the White House Chief of Staff, silently conveying her annoyance that he would accuse her of being so reckless. "We did test it," Ratliff assured them. "Scans showed no signs of internal explosives, and we used robotics to press the activation button, here." She handed it to the president and pointed to the top of the beacon.

"And what happened?" Fitzgerald asked, eyeing the device from different angles.

Ratliff shrugged. "Nothing, sir. Just like Dr. Landry said when she pressed it. The device flashed for a few moments, then turned off."

"And when was this?" the president followed up.

"Right after she returned home from Mathias's compound in Peru. Dr. Landry said she was worried about Luna—the other Aiwan—and called Kypa for help."

"This might explain the arrival of the Aiwan probe," Ernie reasoned, "but it's just sitting in orbit and hasn't moved. Do you think it's been communicating with Dr. Landry?"

"She says no," Ratliff answered, "and I believe her. In fact, I'm not even sure Dr. Landry knows that probe is up there."

Trusting his gut, Ernie exchanged an uneasy glance with the president. "I don't know, something's not right about this."

"With respect, Dr. Landry is a sixty-five-year-old grandma who was kidnapped, dragged to the other side of the world, and then violently rescued by our special forces," Ratliff reminded them. "She was rattled and scared and naturally didn't trust anyone, Mr. President. Notifying Kypa that another Aiwan survived the crash in North Korea would certainly qualify as an emergency."

"I agree," Fitzgerald seconded. He paused as Air Force One took flight and scrutinized the beacon silently. Turning back to Ratliff, he asked, "So, why did Dr. Landry turn it over to us now?"

"Like I said, she's afraid for herself and her family. She wants to help Luna, but fears retribution from Mathias and, quite frankly, doesn't want us putting her in any more danger."

"There won't be any of that … not on my watch," the president affirmed. "Dr. Landry has served this country admirably, I want her looked after."

Ratliff nodded subtly in agreement. However, her body language hinted she was withholding something.

"What?" Fitzgerald prodded.

"Protecting our own, sir … it isn't easy," Ratliff said soberly. "FYSA," she added—meaning 'For Your Situational Awareness'—"my station chief in Lima, Paul Wiggins, was found murdered yesterday afternoon."

Fitzgerald instantly recognized the name from Operation Bold Fortress. Shock hit him first, quickly followed by a flush of heat rising to his cheeks. The memory of three soldiers killed in action still stung, and now, the news of Paul Wiggins's death churned up fresh waves of anger and guilt. But he tempered his emotions. Despite Maxine's brave face, the president could see the pain in her eyes and softened his tone.

"I'm sorry for your loss, Maxine," he said with genuine sincerity.

Ratliff responded with a curt, appreciative nod. After a brief pause, she said, "Thing of it is, Paul made a bad decision, and it cost him his life."

"How so?" the president asked.

"Well, needless to say tensions have been high in Lima this past week," Ratliff answered, pointing out the obvious. "The embassy was locked down due to protests, but apparently Paul decided to sneak out—alone. It was a rookie mistake. He went to see his girlfriend when he should've stayed hunkered down until it all blew over."

"Any idea who's responsible?" Ernie asked, although he could hazard a guess.

"We're still investigating, but this doesn't look like a random mugging. We found Ketamine in his system and judging by the excessive bruising and lacerations to his extremities, Paul was definitely tied up and tortured."

"Mathias?" Fitzgerald offered, nodding as Ratliff confirmed. "He's become a perpetual headache," the president continued, steepling his fingers under his chin. "I should've known he wouldn't stop at media attacks. Mathias wanted more blood and now he's gotten it."

Ernie shifted in his seat. "Rumor has it, he's behind a new super PAC that's funneling in millions from the Russians and Chinese. He definitely wants you out of the Oval Office."

"Well, I'm not going down without a fight," the president vowed. "And I'm for damn sure not allowing Edmund Mathias to carry out his own private war against this country." He looked to Ernie and Maxine for options. "Thoughts?"

Before they could answer, the intercom on the president's desk phone beeped.

Fitzgerald pressed the answer button and said, "Yes?"

An Air Force colonel replied. "Sir, I have Senator Hawthorne on Line 1.

She says it's urgent."

The president exchanged looks with his chief of staff. Senator Georgia-Berry Hawthorne (D-GA) was a three-term senator who currently chaired the Armed Services Committee. She was also rumored to be exploring a bid for the White House.

"Any idea what she wants?" he asked Ernie.

Clueless, his chief of staff shrugged.

Rolling his eyes, the president hovered his finger over the speaker button. "I thought you were supposed to know everything," he quipped.

Ernie straightened, a sly grin forming. "I'd agree with you on that, Mr. President, but then we'd both be wrong."

The witty remark drew a chuckle from both Ratliff and Fitzgerald before their expressions turned serious. With a polite veneer, the president pressed the speaker button and addressed his political rival. "Senator Hawthorne," he greeted. "This is an unexpected surprise."

"Thank you kindly for taking my call, Mr. President," Hawthorne replied with her southern charm. "I know you have a lot on your mind right now, so I'll get to the point. I have Edmund Mathias on the line. He wishes to speak with you about an urgent matter."

Fitzgerald's jaw tightened, anger rising within him like a storm. A torrent of biting words threatened to spill out, but he restrained himself, determined not to let Mathias or Hawthorne witness even a crack in his composure.

Looking from Ratliff to Ernie, whose mouth hung open in a "WTF" expression, Fitzgerald took a measured breath to collect himself.

"What do you want?" he asked sternly.

"Mr. President," Edmund chimed in, his tone resonating with his trademark cockiness. "Forgive the end around, but I knew you wouldn't take my call otherwise." He paused; the silence on the other end of the line told Edmund he had the president's attention. "Senator Hawthorne, thank you for your assistance. I will speak with Roger now, mano a mano."

"Of course," the senator replied shrewdly. With a parting shot, she added, "See you on the campaign trail, Mr. President."

Sensing the president's inner turmoil, Ernie rose from his seat and moved to stand beside the desk, ready to step in if necessary. But Fitzgerald knew the game all too well—so much so that a wooden plaque in his private office bore the carved words of William Clay:

"This is quite a game, politics. There are no permanent enemies, and no permanent friends, only permanent interests."

Taking those words to heart, Fitzgerald knew he needed Hawthorne's support to pass his defense spending bill, so he had to play nice. And in the delicate dance of power, Senator Hawthorne's posturing was her way of securing her place in the game. The logic even applied to mega-donors like Mathias. The eccentric billionaire had the clout to sway every paper bag senator in Washington who voted whichever way the wind blew. However, Mathias did not own the Office of the President of the United States of America, which made this phone call inevitable. Mathias needed the president more than he cared to admit, especially with the harvester threat looming.

"Say what you have to say," Fitzgerald said evenly.

"Very well, I'll get right to the point," Mathias replied. "Too bad this isn't a video conference, because I'd love for you to put a face with a name. Nevertheless, it is my distinct honor, Mr. President, to introduce you to Luna—Earth's newest visitor from the planet, Aiwa, and who just so happens to be my new business partner."

"Greetings, President Fitzgerald," Luna said cordially. "It is a pleasure to finally meet you."

Caught off-guard, Fitzgerald stammered a reply. "The, uh, pleasure is mine, Luna. Is there a formal title that you'd prefer I use?"

"Luna is fine, thank you," the Aiwan replied politely.

The president leaned close to the phone with concern etched in his voice. "Luna, I don't know what Mathias is promising you, but he does not represent the free nations of Earth."

"With all due respect, Mr. President," Edmund interjected, "neither do you. You're interfering in matters beyond your control."

Fitzgerald scoffed. "And you're not? I'm still the president of the most powerful nation on this planet," he said testily.

"For now," Edmund said snidely. "But you and your allies in the U.K. may have just put us all at risk."

Taken aback by the perplexing statement, he looked from Ernie to Ratliff. The CIA Director made a slicing hand signal across her throat, prompting the president to mute the call.

"Mr. President, there was an incident near Challenger Deep earlier today," Ratliff shared. "A British submarine was sunk. We believe the Russians are behind the attack."

"What?" Fitzgerald hissed. "How many casualties?"

"Zero casualties," Ratliff assured him. "It was an ELAUV, an extra-large autonomous—"

"—I know what an ELAUV is," the president interrupted. "You're sure it was the Russians?"

Ratliff nodded affirmatively.

Taking some consolation that no lives were lost, the incident signaled a definite escalation in Mathias's plans to harvest Challenger Deep.

Playing coy, Fitzgerald unmuted the line. "Would you care to elaborate?"

"Of course," Edmund played along. "It's no secret that I plan to harvest the crystals in Challenger Deep, but time is of the essence, Mr. President. Off-world harvesters are coming—Prince Kypa said as much and Luna knows it, too. When the harvesters do come, they will take everything and decimate our planet in the process … but not if we act first," Edmund added, dangling the carrot.

"What do you mean?" the president asked impatiently.

"Luna developed a cloaking device to help me hide the crystals from long-range sensors. That British sub interfered with my efforts, so the Russians dealt with it."

"At your request," Fitzgerald retorted. "They're one of your biggest customers, right?"

Edmund chuckled. "Like I said, Mr. President, I have invested a great deal in Challenger Deep, and the Russians are helping to fund those efforts. Now, granted, their actions were rash; you and I both know that dealing with Polokov is like walking a cat on a leash; he doesn't like to be controlled."

"The bottom line," Edmund continued, "is that I'm not backing down, and neither are my associates. You would be wise not to cross me on this, especially if you want to avoid further bloodshed."

Edmund's casual reference to the deaths of three American service members and one CIA station chief was the breaking point for Fitzgerald. His blood boiled, and a surge of rage took over before he could stop himself. He pounded his fist on the table with a resounding thud.

"I won't lay down for you, you sunuvabitch!"

The outburst sent a wave of tension through the room, the echo of his words lingering in the charged silence. After a long, agonizing moment, Fitzgerald straightened, smoothing his tie and taking a steadying breath.

An uncomfortable silence hung in the air like a thick, suffocating fog.

Finally, Edmund exhaled and said, "First off, you attacked my facility, remember? That blood is on your hands, Mr. President, not mine. Secondly, I have every right to defend my property *and* to profit from the crystals—at least the ones in international waters."

The president blinked in disbelief, momentarily stunned as he processed Mathias's statement. Unsure if he had heard correctly, Fitzgerald asked hesitantly, "What did you just say?"

Edmund chuckled at the president's expense. "Oh, that's right, you don't have the benefit of Aiwan know-how, do you?" he replied smugly. "Well, let me enlighten you, Mr. President. Challenger Deep is just the beginning. Earth is filled with crystals, too many to be ignored by off-world harvesters, and unless you want to risk the lives of billions, we need to put our differences aside and work together."

Ernie stepped in, hands raised in a calming gesture, urging the president to control his emotions and hear Mathias out.

Fitzgerald exhaled slowly, forcing himself to stay composed. He gave a reassuring nod to Ernie and replied in an even but guarded tone, "Go on."

"Gracias," Edmund replied, savoring the discomfort he caused the president. "Let me hand it over to Luna," he continued. "After all, this is her idea. Luna, would you mind?"

"Of course," she chimed in. "Mr. President, as Edmund eluded, we deployed a cloaking device in Challenger Deep to hide those crystals. However, knowing that other crystals exist elsewhere on Earth, it became evident that our device would be insufficient. We can cloak a small area, but not hide an entire planet," she explained. "So, what I am proposing is a global signal to confuse long-range sensors. Using the escape pod left behind by Prince Kypa, I want to network together a series of satellites around the world and project a scramble signal out into space. If it works as planned, any harvesters attempting to scan Earth from a distance would be fooled into thinking there are no crystals on the planet."

"What about the probe already in orbit?" Ernie whispered to the president.

Nodding, Fitzgerald repeated the question.

"Ah, yes, that is troubling," Luna replied with a note of concern. "That is an Aiwan probe, but who sent it and why is unclear. I find it hard to believe Prince Kypa would send another probe to Earth searching for crystals—he has already established that fact. This is something else."

"Harvesters?" the president posed.

"Possibly," Luna considered. "But one thing is certain, as long as the crystals remain out in the open, Earth is vulnerable to attack."

Fitzgerald leaned closer to the phone. "So, what I hear you saying is that you want access to the Aiwan escape pod and several satellites?"

"Military satellites," Luna clarified. "Edmund has provided a list of potential satellites that could be re-tasked for this project."

Edmund interjected, "We need your cooperation, Mr. President, and we need you to convince other nations to grant us full access."

Fitzgerald scoffed. "I assume you're talking about the G7. If that's the case, you're even more delusional than I thought. They'll never go along with this—neither will Russia, China, or Congress, for that matter."

"Senator Hawthorne will take care of that with your support," Edmund responded calmly. "And as for Russia and China, leave them to me. All we need from you is to sell it to Germany, Japan, and the U.K." He paused and asked, "Will you do that?"

The president weighed the proposal before answering. "I'll have to think about it. But before I do, I have a feeling there's one more big favor you're about to ask. Am I right?"

Edmund chuckled. "You're sharper than I give you credit, Mr. President," he said with a sly grin. "And yes, you're right. If Luna and I are to return to the U.S., I'll need full immunity from any past, present, or future criminal and civil charges—for myself and Mathias Industries."

"And in return," the president countered, "those nations who agree to grant you *limited* access to their top-secret military satellites, including the United States, will each have inspectors on-hand to count every crystal you harvest from Challenger Deep and elsewhere."

"Sounds reasonable," Edmund conceded.

"*And*, we get half of your share," Fitzgerald added, locking eyes with Ernie, who responded with an enthusiastic two thumbs up, prompting a grin. Hearing nothing but silence on the other end, the president quickly continued, "I know you've already promised half of everything to Luna, and I would not dream of asking for a share of her cut. Aiwa needs those crystals more than us. So, what do you say, Edmund? Do we have a deal?"

Before Mathias could respond with a counterproposal, Luna cut him off. "We have a deal, Mr. President," she said decisively.

"Luna," Mathias hissed between gritted teeth.

The line suddenly went quiet, leading the president to assume Mathias had muted the line to convince Luna to renegotiate. Fitzgerald followed suit, muting his end as well.

"What do you think?" he asked Ernie and Maxine.

"Well played, sir," Ratliff remarked with a nod of approval. "Of course, we'll need to dive much deeper into the details of their plan before agreeing to grant access to top secret equipment. But insisting on on-site inspectors and securing a cut of the share—that was brilliant."

"Agreed," Ernie added. "Lots of red flags, but Luna's proposal makes sense. It's actually quite ingenious."

Just then, Mathias rejoined the call. Judging by his subdued tone, it was clear he was not pleased about being overruled by Luna but had resigned himself to accepting the terms.

"You have a deal, Mr. President," he said. "My lawyers will draw up the paperwork for my immunity agreement. You'll have it by the time you land in Des Moines. Once I have pen to paper, Luna and I can meet with you and the leaders of the nations I mentioned to iron out the details," Edmund suggested. "If everything goes as planned, and everyone plays nicely, we'll meet at Groom Lake so Luna can begin working on Kypa's escape pod. Agreed?"

"Agreed," Fitzgerald replied. "I will make the arrangements."

"Good. And no funny business, Mr. President," Edmund warned. "Like I said, the Russians can be hard to corral, if you know what I mean."

The president hmphed just as Edmund hung up. The steady drone of the dial tone lingered over the intercom before Fitzgerald finally ended it. He leaned back in his chair, shaking his head in disbelief, and said with a sigh, "This is *definitely* not how I thought today would go."

26
SLOW BURN

Planet Aiwa
Supra, Realm of Eos

On the outskirts of Supra, an unmistakable tension permeated the Cirran refugee camps. Lieutenant Vylara noticed it as soon as she entered the area. The seawater seemed to hum with discord, reflecting the collective frustration of displaced survivors. Left behind by the devastation of the great quakes, they grappled with the harsh reality of an uncertain future.

The murder of King Loka made the situation worse. Since the assassins were Cirran, the finger of blame naturally pointed to the refugee camps. Every dweller in the makeshift communities was now a person of interest, pushing the simmering discontent closer to a tipping point.

The investigation into King Loka's murder had stalled, with no accomplices to Major Gora's treachery yet identified. Progress was slow, hindered by the locals' unwillingness to cooperate and Princess Seva's ban on door-to-door searches. The only lead so far was the teleportation device recovered from King Loka's yacht, but its elusive counterpart remained undiscovered.

Attempts to extract actionable intelligence from the camps had yielded little, but Vylara hoped to succeed where others had failed. Handpicked by Boa, Vylara's half-Cirran heritage and family connections within the camps made her the ideal operative for the mission.

As a half-breed, Vylara experienced bias all her life—a prejudice now mirrored in the treatment of the Cirran refugees in the camps. Like many of them, she had lost loved ones during the quakes, forging a bond of shared grief that played in her favor. If sleeper agents loyal to Grawn Krunig were hiding among the refugees, Vylara might be the one to expose them.

Her best option was a childhood friend named Hera. After losing her mate in Cirros, Hera moved with her young son, Koba, to the camps outside the capital. Regrettably, the demands of Vylara's military career had caused them to lose touch over the years. Even so, Hera welcomed a reunion despite Vylara serving a regime many in the camps blamed for their plight.

Swimming through the well-lit streets, Vylara made her way to Hera's homestead. With the rolling blackouts lifted, there was no sense trying to operate in the shadows. Sans her military uniform, Vylara swam freely amongst the locals, exchanging polite head bows with most while ignoring a few suspicious glares from others.

Arriving at Hera's dwelling, Vylara paused at the front door and pressed the call button. Hera's face soon appeared on the display, brightening at the sight of her friend.

"Vylara!" Hera exclaimed, raising a finger. "One moment. I will be right out!"

Vylara casually scanned the street as she waited, her calm demeanor masking a watchful vigilance. Pedestrian traffic was sparse, as expected for this time of day when most adults ventured beyond Supra's protective shield to hunt and forage. She remained unhurried, her focus steady, until the door finally slid open.

Vylara turned to find Hera hovering in the doorway, an infectious smile on her face. With a graceful flutter-kick, Hera glided toward her friend, arms outstretched in warm greeting. They softly touched foreheads, forming an instant telepathic connection.

"*It is so good to see you,*" Hera said as a wave of joyful relief washed over her.

Vylara shared in the excitement, but beneath Hera's composed exterior, she detected a faint tremor in her friend's embrace—a silent indication that something was wrong.

"*I missed you, too,*" Vylara replied in a soothing tone. "*It has been too long.*"

They held each other a moment longer before gently pulling away, their eyes meeting in shared understanding. Despite the time and distance, their bond remained strong. Vylara and Hera were more like sisters, their friendship effortlessly picking up where it had left off.

This unbreakable connection made pretense unnecessary. "*What is wrong?*" Vylara asked bluntly.

Hera rolled her eyes with embarrassment. Vylara had an uncanny—if not unnerving—ability to read people. Pretending everything was fine would be pointless. Vylara would persist until she got the truth.

"*I …*" Hera's thought trailed off as her brow furrowed, and she glanced distractedly over Vylara's shoulder.

Following her friend's eyes, Vylara turned and noticed two Aiwans across the street. One was an adult male, the other a lanky adolescent. They were engaged in a heated telepathic conversation as the adult male, whose imposing stature loomed over the younger Aiwan, exerted a measure of authority in his body language.

"*Koba!*" Hera yelled angrily, her unfocused thought allowing Vylara to hear her telepathic call.

The adolescent turned sharply to find himself looking down the barrel of his mother's stern glare. He started toward her, but the adult male took him by the arm to hold him up. Whatever the adult male said next to Koba left an impression. Koba hung his head briefly as if under a weight, then nodded solemnly.

"*Leave him!*" Hera demanded firmly as she swiftly kicked toward her son.

The adult male turned his attention to Hera. Seeing the fire in her eyes as she approached, the Aiwan male sneered, then released his grip on Koba and swam away.

Vylara lost sight of him as he disappeared into the crowd, but she watched as Hera slowed in the middle of the street and tried to engage her son. Avoiding eye contact, Koba brushed her off and swam past with a brooding face.

As Koba approached the house, he briefly glanced in Vylara's direction. Despite her inviting smile, he did not pause to acknowledge her.

Vylara frowned slightly as the door closed behind Koba. With the source of Hera's troubles now evident, Vylara turned to her friend. Hera lingered in the middle of the street, her face etched with pain and uncertainty.

"*Koba has grown,*" Vylara remarked with a gentle smile.

"*Too fast,*" Hera replied with an arched eyebrow. "*Actually, he is a good kid, very smart. His father would be proud of him, as am I,*" she said with a glint in her eyes. "*I never had to worry about Koba before, but this place is a bad influence.*"

"*What do you mean?*" Vylara asked innocently.

"*You saw who he was with,*" Hera replied, not hiding her disdain. "*That *was Manta, a local thug who has been trying to recruit Koba.*"

Taken aback, Vylara blinked. "*Recruit him for what?*"

"*The cause,*" Hera scoffed, her mental voice dripping with sarcasm.

She caught herself before saying more. Even with the privacy of telepathy, being seen out in the open with Vylara—an outsider—posed risks. And Hera's fierce protection of her son had not endeared her to Manta and his followers, either.

Anxiously, Hera scanned the crowd, her eyes darting up and down the street, searching for signs of eavesdroppers. Nothing stood out; passersby swam along, seemingly absorbed in their own lives. Yet, her instinct told her they were better off moving their conversation indoors.

Hera gestured toward her home. "*Come inside, we can talk.*"

Vylara followed as Hera activated the front door. It slid open, revealing a small anteroom designed for two full-grown Aiwans, at most. Ahead was an entryway into the dwelling, shielded by a translucent electronic barrier that kept the seawater out. Their skin instantly dried as they passed through the harmless barrier and into the dwelling's interior, which remained comfortably humid.

Hera's temporary housing unit was as minimalistic as possible. The front room held a simple, cushionless, L-shaped couch. During the rolling blackouts, the regime prohibited holographic amenities, so Hera pieced together their furnishings from salvaged materials left behind after the camp's construction.

Like many Aiwan dwellings, the space was practical and free of unnecessary clutter. No art or family pictures adorned the walls, but Vylara noticed a datapad on the couch displaying an image of Hera, Koba, and her late husband.

Two bedrooms branched off the front room—one door stood open while the other remained closed, no doubt occupied by Koba.

Dropping the telepathy, Hera said aloud, "Welcome to our humble abode. It is not much, but it is home." She gestured toward the kitchen. "Are you hungry?"

"No, thank you," Vylara replied with a gracious smile. "I ate earlier."

Just then, Koba reappeared.

Hera lit up at the sight of her son. "Koba," she said, reaching out, but he ignored her, still carrying a chip on his shoulder. Livid, Hera snapped, "Koba!"

"It is time for my shift," he muttered, his tone full of irritation.

Vylara, standing closest to the door, swiftly stepped into the adolescent's path, blocking his exit. Koba stopped, surprised by her audacity.

Locking eyes with him, Vylara spoke in a firm, no-nonsense tone, "You should listen to your mother."

Koba quickly sized up Vylara. Realizing she was not intimidated by him and was not about to back down, he relented.

Turning to face his mother, he asked in a huff, "What?"

Hera dropped her shoulders, exhaling with a heavy-hearted sigh. She stared at Koba for a long moment, her eyes filled with anguish and disbelief as she tried to figure out where she had failed.

"We will discuss what happened outside later," she promised, her tone calm but authoritative. "But in this home, you will welcome our guests properly. Now, apologize to Vylara."

Koba's expression softened at the sight of his mother's frustration. A wave of remorse washed over him. He turned toward Vylara and politely extended his palm. "My apologies," he said earnestly, though his inability to meet her gaze betrayed his discomfort. "Welcome to our home."

Vylara exchanged a brief glance with Hera before a thin smile tugged at the corners of her mouth. She extended her hand, pressing her palm against Koba's, allowing a connection to be made. "Apology accepted," she replied warmly. "Now, where are you off to in such a hurry?"

"I, uh, have an apprenticeship at the central core," he answered, retracting his hand.

Impressed, Vylara widened her eyes in approval. "That sounds exciting."

"It is," Koba replied, some of the angst from earlier melting away.

"He wants to follow in his father's footsteps," Hera added proudly.

Vylara's face lit up. "Is that so?"

"Yes," Koba answered with a spark of enthusiasm in his voice. "I want to devise alternative energy sources that do not rely on harvesting crystals."

"Gwaru knows we certainly need it," Vylara remarked with a hint of hope laced with subtle sarcasm. Not wanting to dampen the young Aiwan's spirit, Vylara patted Koba's shoulder and added cheerily. "If anyone can do it, it is you."

Koba beamed.

"Now, off you go," Vylara urged, stepping aside.

Koba flashed a quick smile in his mother's direction. Hera returned a curt nod, confirming all was good between them. Koba then passed through the electronic barrier and departed.

"Nice save," Vylara remarked, hoping to alleviate any lingering unease Hera might be feeling.

Hera rolled her eyes. "It is a daily challenge," she admitted, sounding weary. "Koba has a good heart, but there are forces at work trying to corrupt him. If only his father were still alive."

Vylara regarded her with a thoughtful look. "You mentioned that earlier. What do you mean?"

Hera shot her friend a skeptical look. "Do not play coy with me. We have known each other too long for that."

A tightness gripped Vylara's chest as her training nudged her to feign innocence and deny everything. Yet, Hera's deadpan expression made it clear that the charade would be pointless. Embarrassment washed over her, accompanied by a sheepish smile.

"Am I really that transparent?" she asked.

With a heavy sigh, Hera sank on the couch. "Before the king's death, you would never see patrols down here. Now, they are everywhere looking for more Cirran assassins … and then you contact me out of the blue …" She tried to keep her tone neutral, though concern seeped through.

Vylara settled beside her. "Please do not hate me," she implored. "You know how much I care about you and Koba."

Hera gently squeezed Vylara's hand. "No one hates you," she said earnestly.

"I wanted to contact you," Vylara replied, "I did, but—"

"—I could have just as easily reached out to you," Hera interjected, sharing the weight of the blame. "We both had our own lives to live and responsibilities to juggle. That is behind us now. Let us not speak of it anymore."

Vylara smiled, her agreement heartfelt. Just then, their conversation took an unexpected turn.

"But perhaps we can help each other?" Hera suggested, gauging her friend's reaction.

Intrigued, Vylara raised an eyebrow as a flicker of realization dawned—Hera accepted the invitation not merely to rekindle their friendship but with deeper motives of her own in mind.

"Does it have anything to do with what happened outside?" Vylara asked.

Hera nodded.

At that moment, a silent understanding passed between them, their eyes locking in a dangerous accord.

"Very well," Lieutenant Vylara replied, speaking in a tone that meant business. Realizing Hera might be the insider she needed for her investigation, Vylara asked, "Tell me about Manta and his cause."

27
BLAZECASTERS

Ekator

Grawn Krunig strode through the corridors of his hidden base in deep thought. With his two lower limbs clasped behind his back, Krunig's two upper limbs remained ready to grab the sickles mounted to his chest armor should the need arise. Mutiny remained a possibility, though the tension amongst his crew had eased considerably since his meeting with Grawn Supreme.

Many had not expected their boss to survive the trip to Madreen, so Krunig's return came as a surprise, if not a disappointment. But that only added credence to the crime lord's nom de guerre. If his fellow grawns had sanctioned a hit on him, Krunig's faction would never know the difference. A new occupant could be donning Krunig's crimson armor at this moment, and they would be none the wiser.

Fortunately for Krunig, that was not the case. However, this was a pirate horde; sooner or later, someone would be foolish enough to challenge his leadership—it came with the territory. On a typical day, he welcomed a spirited fight. It was a great stress release and served as a bloody reminder of who was in charge, but not today. Krunig did not need the distraction. The elements of his plot were now in motion, and the slightest misstep could unravel the crime lord's meticulously crafted plans. Of these moving pieces, only one was currently in his direct control: Baroness Shae.

Krunig enlisted the arguably "mad" scientist to develop a series of doomsday weapons known as Blazecasters. Although he found the name somewhat cliché, he had to concede it was apt. Once deployed, Shae's creations had the power to unleash catastrophic devastation on a planetary scale, all without polluting the environment. The galaxy had never encountered such a destructive yet "clean" weapon, and for good reason. The warheads harnessed a volatile chemical compound universally banned in most star systems. Upon activation, the compound ignited a rapid exothermic reaction, releasing a scorching heat bloom of unprecedented magnitude.

Krunig planned to deploy multiple Blazecasters against Earth's polar caps, melting the vast ice sheets and drastically altering the planet's geography. Most of the surface-dwelling population would simply vanish overnight, along with their polluted cities and toxic inventions that poisoned the lush world. With this destructive power, Krunig could seize control of the crystal-rich planet without an invasion force, reshaping it into a world of his design.

However, several pieces needed to fall into place before that could happen—hence Krunig's visit to check on the baroness. Shae's lab was located in a remote section of the base at the end of a long corridor. This precaution served a dual purpose: it safeguarded against potential experiments gone awry and kept her work hidden from the crew. Grawn Supreme and others had spies onboard, and Krunig could not risk showing his hand too soon.

Krunig was taking no chances; he had ordered the lab off-limits to everyone but him and assigned a security detail to guard it. On his way to check Shae's progress, the crime lord rounded the bend and found two of the four guards loitering by the lab entrance. Krunig's blood began to boil.

The detail leader, Skargg, spotted Krunig approaching and immediately tensed. He was a hulkish brute—broad-shouldered, barrel-chested, and laced with muscle from head to toe. His mahogany skin contrasted sharply with his fiery red eyes, pointed ears, and the white mohawk atop his bald head. Yet, despite his imposing appearance, the sight of Grawn Krunig filled him with dread.

The two guards, meant to be patrolling, quickly dispersed. As they passed Krunig, the guard in front lowered his gaze in submission, noticing his boss's fist clenched tightly in his lower arm. That fleeting moment of distraction proved to be the guard's undoing.

With lightning speed, Krunig struck with his upper right arm, seizing the unsuspecting guard by the throat and lifting him off the floor in one fluid motion. The guard's eyes bulged as he clawed futilely at Krunig's massive, armored grip. Unable to even gasp, the guard's eyes began to roll back in his head, and his face turned blue while his partner watched in horror.

"What part of roaming patrol did you not understand?" Krunig hissed behind his faceless armor.

Wisely, the second guard did not attempt a feeble excuse. "A thousand apologies, my lord," he said, voice shaking. "It won't happen again, I swear."

Krunig held his vice grip around the guard's throat a moment longer—one squeeze would snap the neck. Instead, the crime lord showed leniency and relaxed his hand, allowing the guard to fall to the floor in a crumpled heap, clutching his throat and gasping for air. The second guard, hesitant to offer assistance for fear of reprisal, waited until Krunig continued toward the lab before helping his partner.

As Krunig reached the lab entrance, Skargg and the other sentry snapped rigidly to attention on either side of the door. Krunig paused before entering and turned to face Skargg.

"Fail me again, Skargg, and it will be the last time," he said icily.

Skargg kept his gaze fixed on the wall ahead. "Yes, my lord," he responded, trying to keep his voice steady.

After a brief pause, Krunig turned to face the door. A scanner above the archway projected a beam of green light over his armor, authenticating his identity. The door slid open, revealing a spacious interior. Krunig entered and, as expected, found Shae hovering over a worktable on the far wall. She was flanked by three droids, each with their backs turned to her. Rather than assisting with her delicate procedure, the paranoid scientist used them as a shield to conceal her movements from prying eyes.

Krunig had picked up on this earlier. He had been monitoring the reclusive scientist since her arrival using a hidden video feed inside the lab. But Shae must have had a sixth sense for such things because she made it impossible for him to see her actions, and, as a result, she made herself indispensable. But Shae also worked at a frenetic pace. She rarely took breaks to eat or sleep, becoming so engrossed in her tasks that self-care became an afterthought.

Truth be told, Krunig had no intention of harming the baroness once she finished her deadly creations. Even the powerful Grawn Krunig had limitations, one being the resources needed to reverse engineer Shae's designs. If time was not the enemy, he would try, but under the circumstances, it was enough to leave the bomb-making to her and stay on schedule.

"Stop! That's far enough," Shae commanded without lifting her gaze.

Behind her thick goggles, Shae's eyes gleamed with a maniacal intensity as she poured a fluorescent green liquid into a large, cylindrical warhead. Krunig halted. Unaccustomed to being given orders, he held his tongue and waited in silence, allowing the baroness to finish her delicate task.

When the last drop trickled into the warhead, Shae gently handed off the empty vial to one of the droids. "Add this to the others," she instructed, "and dispose of them outside … carefully."

"Yes, Baroness," the droid replied in a mechanical monotone before disappearing into an adjacent room.

Shae screwed the cone-shaped cap onto the warhead, ensuring a tight seal. When finished, she placed her palms on the table and breathed a sigh of relief. The reprieve was short-lived, however.

"You," she said curtly, pointing to one of the other droids. "Open the storage unit."

The droid dutifully obeyed.

With utmost care, Shae cradled the warhead in both hands—one supporting the bottom and the other steadying the top—as she crossed the room. One false step could blow them all into cosmic dust.

By the time Shae arrived, the droid had already opened the nearby storage unit. A drawer slid out from within the wall, revealing thirteen identical warheads. Shae placed the explosive into an open slot and stepped back. Without prompting, the droid retracted the drawer and closed the unit.

Assuming they were past any danger, Krunig said, "I came to check on your progress."

Shae turned to the crime lord. "Your timing is impeccable, Grawn Krunig. I just finished the last warhead. All I need to do now is construct the delivery vehicles."

"Excellent," Krunig replied. "And you are confident in the blast yield?"

Before Shae could answer, a container filled with the discarded vials used earlier was ejected into the nebula, where a turret promptly targeted it and fired. The resulting detonation created a brilliant explosion in the distance, sending shockwaves rippling back, which rattled the entire station.

Shae cocked her eyebrow with a self-assured smirk. "You were saying?"

Krunig nodded with approval. If the residual of Shae's compound had that much destructive potential, he could imagine the havoc fourteen warheads would create.

Just then, his commlink chirped. "Yes?" Krunig answered the call from Draxx, his acting first officer, while Vekka was away with Grawn Draven.

"My lord, we found the bounty hunters," Draxx shared. "They are on Rogantu."

Finally, Krunig mused upon receiving this much-anticipated news. Uncertain of Rogantu's location, he accessed a star map on his internal HUD. Instantly, Krunig understood why Smythe and Gort had chosen such a remote world to lay low. Rogantu was a desolate wasteland long abandoned by miners due to its extremely harsh environment.

The display pinpointed their location, and Krunig smiled cruelly behind his faceless armor.

You can run, Smythe, but you cannot hide.

Krunig pushed aside thoughts of how he would exact slow and painful retribution on the bounty hunters for their betrayal and replied, "Good work, Draxx. Begin preparations for an immediate departure."

"Yes, my lord," Draxx responded.

Deactivating his commlink, Krunig turned to Shae. "Can you finish your work onboard my ship?"

Shae nodded thoughtfully. "The delicate tasks are complete. All I need is a workspace. If you can transfer the warheads and the remaining materials to your ship, I can resume my work."

"Excellent. I will see to it immediately," Krunig replied with satisfaction. "I hope you are up for a little trip, Baroness. It is time to test your weapons."

"I can hardly wait," she replied with a grin. "And the other matter?"

"Soon," Krunig replied as he made for the door. *Very soon.*

28
THIEVE'S REMORSE

Planet Rogantu

We can dance if we want to
We can leave your friends behind
'Cause if friends don't dance and if they don't dance
Well, they're no friends of mine

Hiromi finally reached her breaking point with the song *Safety Dance* by Men Without Hats. The tune had blasted continuously over the Reaper's intercom for hours. Initially a mere annoyance, the repeating melody became maddening, multiplied by her inability to hack into Reggie's operating system.

Seated on the floor inside the Reaper's cockpit, Hiromi threw up her arms in exasperation. "Quiet!" she erupted, her usual gentile voice piercing the loud noise.

To her surprise, the music cut off abruptly, leaving a stark silence. Hiromi scanned the cockpit in disbelief, unsure of what happened and why. Suspecting a trick, she hesitated to believe the silence would last. Hiromi waited, as still as a statue, half-expecting the irritating music to flare up again at any moment. After a long, tense pause, she cautiously allowed herself to relax. Mimicking the behavior of organic beings, Hiromi slumped her shoulders as a wave of relief washed over her.

Finally, she told herself.

If the cyborg's porcelain face cover could display emotion, it would be smiling with gratitude in the blissful vacuum of utter silence.

Refocusing, she felt a surge of determination to attack the Reaper again. In front of her lay an open conduit with a maze of fluorescent cables exposed inside. Hiromi leaned forward on all fours, ready to take another shot at what was quickly becoming the most challenging slice she had ever attempted.

Suddenly, the music blared back to life—this time at triple speed, the vocals sounding much like *Alvin and the Chipmunks*.

Hiromi let out a low, menacing growl. She was moments away from blowing up when the bounty hunter, Smythe, called out her name.

"Hiromi!" he yelled again over the music.

Caught in an awkward position, Hiromi crawled backward on her hands and knees so she could see him. She did not bother getting up.

"What?" she snapped, the sharpness in her voice starkly contrasting with the serene expression on her unmoving face.

Smythe's eyes flashed with annoyance. With an impatient thumb flick over his shoulder, he gestured for the cyborg to follow him. Hiromi stood and departed the cockpit without saying a word. They disembarked the Reaper, passing through the freighter's cargo hold into an adjacent corridor, seeking a quiet place to speak. Smythe closed the blast door behind them, muffling the obnoxious dance music.

Rounding to face Hiromi, the bounty hunter demanded, "Status?"

"The ship's AI is fighting me," Hiromi replied, stopping short of admitting defeat. "Its security protocols are formidable—the best I've ever seen."

"Coming from you, that says a lot," Smythe remarked. "But you can crack it, right?"

Hiromi shrugged. "Eventually, maybe," she admitted. "Worst case scenario, we wipe the operating system. But if we do that, we run the risk of losing whatever is making this artificial intelligence so unique."

Smythe considered the option carefully, struggling to reconcile how an advanced AI could defeat Krunig's forces so soundly. That victory was not due to strategy or advanced computations—it was raw firepower. Somehow, the Reaper possessed the destructive potential to annihilate an entire fleet, but how it generated such immense energy remained a mystery.

Taking a controlled breath, Smythe conceded, "We're running out of time. If we can't unlock the Reaper's secrets soon, I'll have no choice but to hand the ship over to Krunig. How much more time do you need?"

"I have no idea," Hiromi confessed. "You saw me back there, crawling on my hands and knees. I cannot find any vulnerabilities—nothing! And look at these scratches," she added, lifting her knee to show the scuffs. "I'll need a week at Starhaven to buff these out."

Smythe resisted the urge to roll his beady eyes. He had never encountered a cyborg so obsessed with her appearance in all his travels. Hiromi took vanity to a whole new level. He wondered if she had always been like this, even before her cybernetic implants.

Unwilling—and uninterested—in exploring the subject further, Smythe forced a crooked frown. It was the closest thing to empathy he could muster.

"Keep at it," he urged. "Crack this, and I'll throw in two weeks at Starhaven … on me."

While Smythe's offer sounded appealing, it offered Hiromi little comfort. The fact remained: she had no idea how to defeat the ship's sophisticated security protocols. Her mind raced through every trick and hack she knew, but none seemed sufficient to penetrate defenses of this caliber. The more she thought about it, the more impossible the challenge seemed—this AI was engineered to prevent the kind of infiltration she was attempting.

Just then, Smythe's commlink chirped. "Yeah?"

"We need to talk," Gort replied curtly. "Where are you?"

Smythe grimaced, anticipating more bad news. "Sub-level one, by the cargo hold."

"Stay there, I'm on my way."

Taking her cue, Hiromi headed back to the Reaper. Smythe tracked her departure, watching until she vanished from sight. Once she was out of earshot, he exhaled a deep breath, the weight of his regret settling in as he questioned the wisdom of this reckless pursuit.

Meanwhile, Hiromi re-entered the Reaper through the engineering section, ignoring the blaring music. Muting her audio receptors would have been simple enough—a trick she had tried once before—but she found she needed all her senses on high alert for this delicate job.

As she climbed the ladder up to the main hold, she welcomed her favorite part of the song: the end. The music faded out, leaving a brief void of silence before it looped again. In that fleeting moment, an audible thump sounded behind her. She froze mid-climb, tilting her head and listening closely.

Certain she had not imagined it, Hiromi remained motionless as the music resumed. This time, she adjusted her audio receptors, filtering out the tune. Sure enough, there was another thump, followed by a scratching noise. She was not alone—something or someone was onboard.

Cautiously, Hiromi backed down the ladder, each movement silent and deliberate. Retracing her steps through engineering, she followed the noise, creeping back toward the hatch leading outside. Calling for help briefly crossed her mind, but there was no time. Whatever it was, she did not intend to let it slip away.

Reaching the wet bath, Hiromi paused outside the door. Her receptors caught the low murmur of a voice inside—a welcome relief. Smythe had warned her about the gracylai, and she had no desire to encounter one.

Then who could it be? she wondered with anticipation.

Hiromi reached for the door handle with her left hand, poised to spring her trap. In one swift, decisive motion, she flung the door open, her right hand cocked and ready to deliver a lethal strike.

Her sudden entry startled poor Toma. No longer cocooned, he was absorbed in tinkering with his glitchy nano-ring and had not noticed the cyborg outside, thanks to the blaring music. His bulbous blue eyes widened in surprise as he let out a comical yelp, his adolescent voice cracking as he scrambled to react.

Initially shocked to find the young Aiwan, Hiromi said with a faint trace of satisfaction, "Greetings."

Without a moment's hesitation, she clenched her hand into a fist and delivered a brutal punch to Toma's face, knocking him out cold.

Back inside the freighter, Smythe turned at the sound of his partner's approach. He could hear Gort's lumbering footsteps echoing on the grated, metal floor halfway across the ship.

"What's wrong?" he asked when Gort appeared, somewhat out of breath.

"In two words: maxixe magnetarite."

Smythe furrowed his brow. "What do you mean?"

"We've been duped," Gort replied, his tone laced with frustration and embarrassment. "Word on the street is that the ship we captured was powered by a blue crystal when it took down Krunig, not the orange one we've got onboard the Reaper now. Prince Kypa must've swapped them out before making the exchange."

Smythe clenched his fists and growled in anger. *I should've known!*

Gort watched and waited as Smythe wrestled with his emotions. It was rare for Smythe to be outplayed, and it could not have come at a worse time.

"You're sure of this?" Smythe asked, though deep down, he already knew the answer.

Gort nodded with a frown.

Now it all made perfect sense, Smythe mused. Krunig did not want the Reaper; it was the blue crystal within. No wonder he had kept it a secret. After witnessing the crystal's destructive potential firsthand, Krunig would stop at nothing to get his hands on it before the rest of the galaxy learned of its existence. Such a gem could fetch an outrageous sum on the open market, but Krunig did not intend to sell it. He wanted power, and whoever possessed that blue crystal would be invincible.

Gort studied his partner curiously, trying to read Smythe's thoughts. But the insectoid's expression was impossible to decipher, prompting Gort to suggest, "Maybe we should quit while we're down?"

As the question hung in the air, Smythe lifted his gaze. The bounty hunter's eyes seemed to look straight through Gort, lost in thought as he weighed his options. After a long pause, he finally spoke.

"Does Krunig know the blue crystal is still on Aiwa?"

"Probably," Gort answered. "Word travels fast on the street, you know that."

"Then I doubt he'll be too upset about us delivering the ship a little late," Smythe reasoned, sighing with resignation. "Contact Krunig and let him know we're on our way. I'll go tell Hiromi."

Gort shook his head. "No can do. That storm just kicked up again—even nastier than before. I can't send or receive anything, and there's zero chance of taking off in this weather. We're stuck for now."

Smythe hmphed, frustrated at his streak of bad luck. "How long?"

"Search me." Gort shrugged. "The storms on this planet are impossible to predict. They show up out of nowhere and just when you think it's passed, another cell pops up right behind it. No wonder they abandoned this place."

"Very well. Go keep an eye on it and prep the ship for departure," Smythe instructed. "As soon as there's an opening, we're getting out of here."

"Sounds good," Gort said with relief. He hesitated mid-step as he started to leave, glancing curiously at the cargo hold.

Smythe noticed the shift and followed Gort's gaze. "What is it?"

"The music … it stopped," Gort responded.

Smythe cocked his head a moment to listen, then bolted aft, blaster in hand. He opened the door to the cargo hold only to find it eerily quiet. The

Reaper remained just as he left it, with the boarding ladder still down.

The bounty hunter scanned the area for threats and found none. Without a word, he glanced over his shoulder, gesturing for Gort to stay put and cover him. Gort nodded, gripping his blaster a bit tighter.

Moving cautiously, Smythe inched forward into the cargo hold, ready to shoot the first thing that moved. He reached the base of the Reaper and, leading with the barrel of his weapon, stole a peek into the Aiwan ship.

"Hiromi!" he hissed.

"Here!" the cyborg responded calmly. "It's fine. You can come up—I've captured a stowaway."

Smythe blinked in disbelief. *A stowaway!?*

Blaster still held at the ready, the bounty hunter climbed the ladder. Reaching the top rung, he peered inside. His eyes quickly landed on Hiromi, standing by the console where the orange crystal powering the ship hovered behind a protective containment field. In front of her, Toma lay unconscious on the floor.

"An Aiwan?" Smythe uttered in shock.

"Not just any Aiwan," Hiromi said, a hint of triumph in her voice. "This one's royalty."

29
THUNDER GOD

Planet Rogantu

Kypa, Neil, and their newest team member, Ten-Tee, continued their trek through the underground tunnel in silence. Dim lights flickered in the passage, casting eerie shadows along the single rail line to the refinery. Leading the way, Kypa moved deliberately while Neil followed close behind. Ten-Tee, perched on Neil's shoulder, scanned the tunnel ahead for any sign of danger. Since leaving the outpost, the small droid had remained glued to Neil, ever watchful.

So far, they had found the tunnel intact and were able to move swiftly through the circular passage with unexpected ease. Even more encouraging, there was still no sign of gracylai. With each measured step, however, the stress intensified, and their senses heightened to the slightest sounds and movements. Shadows played tricks on their eyes, and the silence amplified every breath and shuffle of their boots against the dirt floor.

As they ventured further into the tunnel, a more profound sense of dread settled upon them—they had passed the point of no return. Even with the aid of Ten-Tee's scanners and the occasional service ladder leading topside, retreat was no longer an option. If they encountered any hostile creatures, fleeing back to the outpost was out of the question—they would have to stand their ground and fight.

Ten-Tee tapped Neil's shoulder to get his attention—their first sign of trouble. Neil halted abruptly, instinctively raising his weapon. His pulse quickened as he silently reached out to his Aiwan companion.

"*Kypa,*" Neil hissed mentally.

Kypa stopped and cast him a questioning look.

Neil tilted his head slightly and whispered to the droid, "What is it?"

Using its photoreceptors, Ten-Tee projected a blue hologram map of the tunnel before them. Two pulsing, white dots depicted Kypa and Neil in their current location—approximately halfway to the refinery. Zooming into an area up ahead, Ten-Tee displayed the collapsed section ahead, blocking their passage.

"*That doesn't look good,*" Neil murmured.

Kypa sighed. "*No, it does not.*"

Stepping closer to the hologram, Kypa studied the layout for a long moment in silence. Undeterred, he said with unwavering resolve, "*Our objective is still in front of us.*"

Kypa pointed to a gaping hole in the tunnel wall near the collapsed section. Unfortunately, Ten-Tee's scan only displayed visible obstacles in the tunnel, not any hidden dangers that may be lurking about in the uncharted areas.

"*When we reach the collapsed section,*" Kypa said decidedly, "*we will detour through this side opening.*"

Ten-Tee swiveled its tiny head toward Neil as if gauging his reaction. If the droid could scan through his nanosuit, it would have detected Neil's increased heart rate.

Seeing no alternative, Neil agreed with a curt nod and gestured forward with his blaster.

"*Age before beauty,*" he quipped, trying to mask his apprehension.

Kypa forced a tight-lipped grin, appreciating the levity while inwardly sharing Neil's unease. Taking a calming breath, he crept onward, venturing deeper into the tunnel. The tension mounted as they neared the collapsed section, each step echoing ominously in the suffocating silence.

The quiet was suddenly shattered by a sharp whistle from Ten-Tee, causing both Neil and Kypa to nearly jump out of their skin. Kypa spun around, ready to deliver a scathing rebuke—only to find the droid no longer perched on Neil's back. Before he could speak, Kypa spotted Ten-Tee scurrying ahead toward a nearby archway.

He and Neil exchanged a tense glance, their eyes wide with alarm and disbelief, silently asking each other, *Did that just happen?*

They turned their attention to the droid hopping up and down, seemingly excited about something. Cringing, Neil swiftly tiptoed forward, praying Ten-Tee would quiet before attracting unwanted attention.

"Shh," he hissed softly.

Ten-Tee fell silent but kept stomping in place like it desperately needed to pee.

Neil crouched beside the droid and whispered, "What is it?"

In response, Ten-Tee projected a beam of light onto a rusted control panel on the wall. Curious, Neil straightened and stepped forward to inspect it. Kypa joined him.

The Aiwan's eyes narrowed as he quickly diagnosed the issue, confirming the droid's warning.

"*I see,*" Kypa muttered with disappointment. "*This is the shield barrier the worker spoke of. With the refinery offline, there is no power running to it.*"

Kypa scanned the area warily, then turned his attention to Ten-Tee. When his eyes landed on the droid, Ten-Tee recoiled, taking a cautionary step backward. But Kypa disarmed the droid by crouching and laying his hand out on the ground, palm up, to invite it closer.

Ten-Tee accepted, shuffling forward.

Kypa rose, lifting the droid to eye level. "It was a good idea," he whispered, "but we need you to stay quiet. Understood?"

After Ten-Tee nodded in affirmation, Kypa handed it off to Neil. The droid scurried along Neil's arm, perching comfortably behind his shoulder once again.

Kypa observed the interaction, intrigued. It reminded him of the bond between Earthlings and their pets—something he read about once while at Groom Lake. Aiwans neither kept pets nor relied on droids, especially for tasks they could easily handle themselves. Yet, during his limited space travels, Kypa came to realize that droids had their place in the universe, and this particular unit possessed a uniquely developed personality.

"*The collapsed section is close,*" he cautioned Neil. "*Ready?*"

Neil nodded, then took a deep breath before falling in step behind Kypa.

Pressing onward, they continued a few moments longer in silence before Kypa slowed and signaled Neil to hold up. Up ahead, the soft glow of lights lining the tunnel abruptly ended, swallowed by a wall of darkness.

Kypa activated his helmet's night vision, bathing the tunnel in an eerie green glow to reveal the collapsed section ahead. A wall of debris piled high from floor to ceiling blocked the rail line. As he feared, the cave-in looked impassable—a dead end in more ways than one.

On the left, Kypa spotted the opening in the side wall. Enhancing the image with his HUD, he realized the tunnel's collapse did not cause the gaping hole; it was the opposite. Something massive had burrowed through the planet's crust and broken into the tunnel—likely causing the cave-in. Kypa's stomach tightened as he guessed the culprit—a gracylai. If he was right, this creature was enormous.

Kypa waved Neil forward. Leaning close, the Aiwan whispered to Ten-Tee, "Scout ahead and scan for life signs. Do it quietly," he reiterated. "No noise."

The droid accepted its order with a vigorous nod, then tapped Neil's shoulder to let it down. Neil dropped to one knee and allowed Ten-Tee to run down his arm. He stood and watched along with Kypa as their fearless little scout scurried toward the borehole.

Before entering, Ten-Tee activated its repulsors and hovered at the base of the opening. Scanning the interior, it detected no threats and then disappeared inside.

Neil and Kypa waited anxiously, hoping the droid would not compromise their position. Much to their relief, Ten-Tee reappeared moments later—alone. The tiny droid landed at their feet and projected a hologram diagram of its findings. According to the display, the borehole extended approximately thirty yards through solid rock and then opened up into a cavernous magma chamber, complete with a wide river of lava.

Kypa examined the projection from different angles, his gaze narrowing as he took in the details. The lava flow posed a significant risk, but additional boreholes, each as large as the one in front of them, troubled him even more. However, Ten-Tee highlighted one, in particular, that offered a way forward. The tiny droid projected a narrow path running parallel to the molten river. It bypassed the collapsed section and led to a second opening in the tunnel wall.

A wave of relief washed over Kypa. "*We are in luck,*" he told Neil, pointing to the display. "*Ten-Tee found us a way around. We should be able to re-enter the tunnel here without losing much time.*"

Neil lowered to one knee, inviting Ten-Tee to climb back on. "Good work, Tee," he whispered. When he straightened, Neil found Kypa gesturing toward the borehole with an expectant glint in his eye.

"*Youth before wisdom?*" Kypa teased with a raised eyebrow.

Neil dropped his shoulders and frowned. "*I think I like you better without a sense of humor.*"

Kypa smiled thinly as Neil took the lead. Pausing at the opening, he stared down the long tube and could see the faint orange glow of magma in the distance.

Swell, he grumbled inwardly.

Neil cautiously climbed inside on all fours, then straightened. The borehole's towering height allowed him to stand upright—an unsettling reminder of the sheer size of the gracylai that created it. The thought of a creature that large, one that could likely swallow him whole, sent a chill down his back.

Pushing that grizzly thought aside, Neil focused instead on the path ahead. He carefully moved forward, flinching as every flicker of light seemed to threaten the presence of a lurking predator.

As Neil neared the end, the light ahead grew brighter, revealing a vast chamber beyond. A river of molten lava snaked through the immense chamber, radiating intense heat from its searing flow.

Straight out of Paradise Lost, Neil thought grimly.

Standing on the precipice, he scanned the chamber. Additional boreholes riddled the walls, but to his relief, there was still no sign of the creatures.

Peering down, Neil spotted the narrow path hugging the river's edge. Just as Ten-Tee had shown, the trail led directly to an adjacent borehole. But reaching it would be challenging. The drop from his current position to the slender path was about two feet, with zero margin for error. One misstep, and they were going swimming.

Neil holstered his weapon and waved Kypa forward. As soon as his friend joined him, Neil pointed down to the path.

"*That first step's a doozy*," he warned.

As Kypa surveyed the chamber, his face paled at the sight of the precarious route. He patted Neil's shoulder for encouragement and said, "*You got this.*"

"*Gee, thanks,*" Neil replied as Kypa turned his back to check their six.

Choosing not to prolong the inevitable, Neil sat on the floor, dangling his feet over the edge. Ten-Tee hopped off and watched anxiously from the side. Meanwhile, Kypa stowed his weapon and positioned himself behind Neil, ready to pull him up by the armpits at the slightest sign of trouble.

Praying the ledge could bear his weight, Neil lowered himself feet-first down to the narrow path. Facing the lava flow, he immediately felt the heat radiating through his suit. Despite the rising temperature, his nanosuit compensated well, keeping his body cooled at a tolerable level.

With his arms shaking from the strain, Neil blindly felt for the trail beneath his feet. Finally, his toes grazed the surface. He prodded the ground, testing its stability, as beads of sweat began trickling down his forehead. The path felt solid, but the real test would come when he shifted his full weight onto it.

"Ready?" he grunted, breaking the silence.

Squatting behind Neil, Kypa looped his long arms around his friend's chest for support.

"Ready," he replied.

Closing his eyes and hoping for the best, Neil lowered himself onto the path. For a fleeting second, panic surged as his feet shuffled in the loose gravel, but when the ground held firm, a wave of relief washed over him.

Neil exhaled deeply, only then realizing he had been holding his breath. Cocking his head sideways, he gave Kypa a thumbs up.

"I'm good," he said. "Hop on, Tee."

As soon as the droid was situated atop his shoulder, Neil carefully began side-stepping to his right along the narrow path with his back pressed to the wall. Behind him, Kypa kept a watchful eye, bouncing his attention between Neil and the borehole behind them. He waited until Neil was safely across before following.

With his long arms and legs, Kypa's descent to the path went much smoother, though equally stressful. Making his way steadily along the river's edge, Kypa had neared the end when, suddenly, the ground began to shake beneath his feet. He froze as a loud rumble echoed throughout the chamber as if a distant eruption was taking place.

Standing nearby, Neil braced himself as dust and debris cascaded from the ceiling, plunging into the lava river with a fiery splash.

"Come on!" he urged Kypa.

Kypa did not hesitate, quickening his pace along the narrow path to join up with Neil and Ten-Tee. Together, they followed the trail as it curved away from the river toward the opening that led back into the tunnel. Upon reaching it, they climbed inside and sprinted through, fearing the borehole might collapse at any moment.

By the time they re-entered the tunnel, the tremors had subsided, leaving an unsettling stillness in their wake. Dust hung in the air, drifting slowly as if the smallest sound might disturb the fragile calm. They paused, bracing for aftershocks that, to their surprise, never came. Yet, the silence felt heavy, reminding them of the other dangers still lurking about.

Neil and Kypa drew their blasters and scanned the tunnel, sweeping over every crevice for signs of movement. Only after they were sure it was clear did they dare to exhale, allowing themselves a brief moment to catch their breath.

As Kypa examined the collapsed section of the tunnel from this side, Neil whispered, "Thunder God."

Kypa turned, giving him a puzzled look.

Neil pointed to the ceiling and continued in a hushed tone. "Back on Earth, there's a mountain range in Arizona called the Superstition Mountains. According to myth, the Apaches believed a thunder god resided under the mountains, probably because of the volcanic activity."

Kypa's cocked his head. "Do you believe in myths?" he asked, genuinely curious.

"Not really," Neil admitted, "but if that tremor was anything like what the Apaches experienced, I'd be superstitious, too."

Accepting Neil's response, Kypa turned his attention to the tunnel ahead. On this side of the cave-in, he was relieved to find their path illuminated once again by the emergency lights.

Kypa gestured forward with his blaster. "This way."

Neil took a step to follow but halted as something crunched under his feet, echoing loudly throughout the tunnel. He froze, instinctively scanning the ground to figure out what he stepped on.

Kypa approached and crouched beside him, retrieving a handful of thin, pale shards. He straightened and held out his palm for Neil to see.

"It looks like eggshell," Neil remarked.

Kypa sent a neural command to his suit. "*Computer, identify.*"

His HUD flickered as the AI scanned the fragments in his hand. The results came back almost immediately.

"Not eggshells," Kypa clarified. "Bones."

Neil recoiled; his face twisted in disgust. "The workers?" he hissed.

"Mm," Kypa affirmed, brushing the remnants from his hand. "The undigested parts."

Neil's body tensed as his eyes darted around the tunnel. "Kypa," he muttered fearfully, "I've got a bad feeling about this."

30
HONEY TRAP

Planet Earth
Satipo, Peru

Deanna, Mathias's trophy girlfriend, stood half-naked in the master bathroom of the billionaire's private suite. Staring at her reflection in the mirror, she noted the tired shadows beneath her eyes.

"Blondes have more fun?" she scoffed, absently tugging at a strand of her pale hair, once vibrant but now dulled by countless dyes and restless nights.

The phrase, so frivolously tossed about, felt like a slap in the face after years of pretending to be something she was not.

"Bollocks," she concluded, her voice dripping with disdain.

Deanna eyed the line of cocaine laid out on the sink next to her. She craved an escape that did not involve taking off her clothes. It was nearly nine o'clock in the morning, and Edmund was off making final preparations for his high-profile return to the United States, leaving Deanna to her own devices.

Edmund insisted she not make the trip, a decision Deanna vehemently protested. Despite their diplomatic immunity, he knew that legal protection meant little when staring down the working end of an M-16. President Fitzgerald was unpredictable and could easily renege on their deal, seizing him and Luna the moment they set foot on American soil. Bringing Deanna along only complicated matters, so leaving her behind made sense to him.

But not to her. Their wicked fight the night before was epic, though it ended with Edmund offering her a shopping spree on Carnaby Street as a peace offering—that, and a night of raunchy make-up sex—as if that ever satisfied her.

In reality, Deanna's whining and arguing were all for show. She had no desire to go to the United States, but if she did not play the part and make Edmund feel like he would be missed, he might grow suspicious. Ultimately, Deanna got what she wanted—a first-class ticket home to England. But, as always, it came at a price. Lately, that price weighed heavier on her, evidenced by her increased drug use.

Just this once, she promised herself again.

Snorting a single line from her Italian-made pocket mirror, Deanna savored the tingling sensation in her nostril for a long moment, then checked her face for signs of residue. Satisfied, she washed the mirror thoroughly, ever mindful there would be drug-sniffing police dogs at the airport.

Stashing the mirror in her purse, Deanna entered her spacious walk-in closet. She dressed quickly in the designer pantsuit she had already selected. Standing in front of the tall mirror, she pirouetted several times, straightened her outfit, then pumped up her bra for good measure to ensure enough cleavage was visible in her low-cut, V-neck blouse. The "girls" always helped to create a natural distraction—one of her many tricks for breezing through customs.

Deanna returned to the bedroom to finish packing. She intended to travel light and return with at least one or two new pieces of luggage filled with London's latest fashions.

If I return, she corrected herself.

This assignment was nearing its end, one way or another. Deanna, aka Agent Colleen Addison of His Majesty's Security Service, had done her bit for king and country. As a member of ULTRA—a highly secretive British counter-espionage unit that dated back to World War II—Agent Addison's devotion to duty had exceeded all expectations. To say she had gone above and beyond the call of duty was an understatement, and sleeping with the enemy had extolled a heavy psychological price.

Akin to female Russian spies known as sparrows, Addison thought she had the mental fortitude to handle the emotional load that came with using seduction and sexual appeal to extract information, gain leverage, and manipulate targets. She was wrong. This "honey trap" had taken its toll, and her sense of patriotism and duty could no longer carry her. It was time to move on before this assignment destroyed her.

But there is still work to do, she reminded herself.

Addison eyed her carry-on. Beneath the neatly folded clothing and toiletries lay a hidden compartment. Inside was an encrypted, solid-state drive filled with images of Edmund's private files, stolen from his wall safe less than ten feet away. Deanna had not accessed the safe in weeks, but Edmund had been quietly rummaging around earlier while she pretended to be asleep.

What happened next would haunt Colleen Addison to her dying day. Perhaps it was the drugs or the thought of starting a new life that clouded her judgment, but the ULTRA agent committed a rookie mistake when she failed to check the bedroom door before opening the safe. Had she looked through the peephole, she would have seen a team of guards waiting outside in the hallway. Instead, Agent Addison retrieved the SSD and a Ziplock baggie from her carry-on. Inside the baggie was a strip of lifting tape used by forensic technicians at crime scenes. The tape contained Edmund's fingerprints.

Moving to the wall safe, she slid aside a framed painting mounted on rollers. Behind the painting was the door to the safe. Agent Addison held Edmund's copied thumbprint up to the scanner. A light turned from red to green, followed by the sound of the door unlocking. She opened the safe, and her mouth dropped.

Empty!

Just then, the bedroom door burst open, startling Colleen. Her head snapped sideways in a panic as two guards rushed toward her pointing Glock 17 pistols at her.

"Freeze!" the lead guard shouted.

Caught red-handed, Agent Addison clenched the fingerprint strip in her fist. She flicked her eyes toward her purse just a few feet away on the bed. Inside, Colleen kept a cyanide capsule, but she quickly dismissed the thought; the guards would shoot her before she could even reach it. Besides, suicide was an extreme reaction. She had every confidence that she and "the girls" could talk their way out of this.

Without missing a beat, Agent Addison demanded, "What's the meaning of this?"

Keeping his weapon trained on the suspect, the lead guard shouted over his shoulder toward the door, "Clear!"

Edmund poked his head inside, locating his soon-to-be ex-girlfriend held at gunpoint. Colleen spotted Mathias in the doorway, wearing his trademark smirk. Their eyes met, and at that moment, Addison knew her game was up. But she clung to her act, refusing to surrender.

"Eddie, what is this?" she asked, her voice trembling with simulated fear and confusion.

Edmund ignored her performance, stepping calmly between the guards. He glanced at the open safe and shook his head in disappointment.

"Tsk, tsk," he clicked with disapproval. "Such a sad way for things to end."

Addison darted her eyes at the safe. "What?" she scoffed. "I didn't take anything—you left it open," she argued.

"Aux contraire," Edmund corrected, shaking his finger. "I locked the safe before I left … just after I emptied it," he added in an accusatory tone.

Edmund held out his hand, palm up, silently demanding she hand over his stolen fingerprints.

A tenuous silence followed. Agent Addison stared at Edmund's outstretched hand, her mind racing. For an instant, she considered arguing her innocence further, but the cold finality in Edmund's eyes told her it was useless. Besides, she was exhausted from the charade, and the thought of dragging it out any longer to spite him felt like a hollow victory.

With a sharp exhale, Addison huffed in frustration, then slowly uncurled her fist. She released the crumbled piece of tape into his hand.

Edmund hmphed, then pocketed the tape. "Thank you, Deanna … or should I say, Agent Addison of the British ULTRA unit?"

Addison glared at him. "How long have you known?"

"Not long enough," Edmund admitted. Eyeing her cleavage, he added in a rare moment of honesty, "I guess I deserved it, though. Every man has a vice, but you, my dear, are exceptional at what you do, I'll give you that."

Unfazed by the lewd remark, Addison arched her brow. "So, what now?" she asked impatiently. "If you're going to kill me, best get on with it."

Edmund chuckled in delight. It was the first time Addison ever stepped out of character, revealing her British accent.

"Bravo, Miss Addison." He clapped slowly, mockingly amused. "Truly an Oscar-worthy performance."

Addison remained silent; her lips pursed as she fought to suppress the icy dread creeping up her spine. But a slight tremble in her hand betrayed her. Edmund noticed. His smile thinned, relishing the crack in her composure before his expression darkened.

"When I discovered your betrayal, my first inclination was to put a bullet in your head," he said matter-of-factly. "But that would be too easy. Then I realized—you could serve a relevant purpose. My super soldiers haven't been properly field tested. So, what better way to prove my force enhancement serum works than by using you as the demonstration?"

Edmund stepped back, signaling the guards to take Agent Addison into custody. She resisted, and a spirited scuffle ensued. The ULTRA agent landed a punch to one of the guards' faces before being tackled from behind by the second man. He slammed her to the ground with a heavy thud. Yet, Addison kept fighting. She thrashed and clawed, wildly kicking as they grappled on the floor. But the guards' combined strength proved too much for her. With their weight pressing down, they pinned Agent Addison face-down to the floor.

Chest heaving from the struggle, she hurled curses at them—and at Edmund—while the guards zip-tied her wrists and ankles. After rolling Addison onto her back, the guards stepped away, leaving her sprawled on the floor.

Edmund approached slowly, standing over his former lover with a smug smile of satisfaction. Addison, defiant to the last, spat at him with venom in her eyes.

Witnessing this, one of the guards reached into her luggage and retrieved a pair of pink silk panties—a gift from Edmund. The guard stuffed them into Addison's mouth to shut her up.

Ignoring her muffled protests, Edmund stepped aside to clear a path to the door.

"Take her downstairs," he instructed as the guards lifted Addison off the floor. As they passed, Edmund said to her with a sly grin, "I've got someone special I want you to meet."

The guards hauled Agent Addison unceremoniously down the hall, ignoring her protests as they made their way to the west end fire escape. As they descended the stairs, their priority was discretion—avoiding the attention of workers as the late afternoon shift approached.

Reaching the ground floor, two more guards arrived, grabbing Addison's legs. Now carrying her face-down with Edmund bringing up the rear, they headed toward a door directly across the hall from Mr. Renzo's dojo where Dr. Vlachos awaited. Standing beside him was a stone-faced man with a bald head dressed in black combat fatigues.

Addison lifted her head, her eyes filling with terror at the sight of the doctor's latest test subject. She screamed in her gag, but her muffled cries only fell on deaf ears.

Edmund stepped forward, unlocking the door using his personal access code. He held it open as they carried Addison inside. They crossed the unused storage room to an emergency exit door.

Squinting in the morning sunshine, the guards stepped outside onto a patch of freshly mowed grass separating the compound from the jungle. They set their prisoner upright, though with her hands and feet still bound, they had to hold her steady.

Breathing heavily through her nose, Addison darted her eyes about in a frantic attempt to get her bearings. She had never been outside of the compound on this side, facing the dense jungle. The isolation struck her—there was not a soul in sight, and even without her gag, she doubted anyone would hear her scream.

Edmund stepped forward to the jungle's edge, pausing as he closed his eyes to take in Amazonia's natural symphony. The rhythmic chatter of wildlife soothed him, and he lingered in the moment, inhaling as if trying to feed his senses.

But the tranquility was fleeting. Edmund snapped his eyes open, the serenity replaced by a wicked grin. He turned to Addison and strode up to her with the confidence of a dangerous man. Before getting right up in her face, one of the guards wisely grabbed a fistful of Addison's hair, yanking her back just in case she entertained the idea of headbutting Mathias.

Edmund and Addison locked eyes.

"You know what? I'm feeling generous today," he said, gently running his finger down the crease of her cleavage. "Because of our history together, it seems only fair that I give you a fighting chance to escape."

Edmund stepped back, motioning the guards to cut her loose. The moment Addison's hands were free, she pulled the panties from her mouth. Her arm reared back to fling them at Edmund, but a guard quickly seized her wrist.

"That wouldn't be the first time you've thrown those at me," Edmund chuckled, drawing laughs from the guards.

Dr. Vlachos, unsettled by what was about to happen, remained silent while his test subject stood impassive and devoid of emotion.

Addison cursed Edmund, lacing her words with colorful metaphors and telling him exactly where he could shove the panties. Edmund did not bother responding, his amusement fading.

"So, here's the deal," he said bluntly. "We're going to play hide and seek. You get a one-minute head start to run into the jungle. Then I set him loose." Edmund gestured to the test subject.

Addison turned to face the man, his expression disturbingly calm, a picture of complete detachment. Her defiance faltered, giving way to a chilling tremor of fear. The reality of her situation hit—*I'm going to die out here.*

"Eddie, please," she cried, her voice cracking. "Don't do this. I'm sorry, okay? I was just doing my job."

Edmund stepped aside, clearing her path to the jungle, and tapped his watch face. "The clock is running, my dear. You best get on with it," he said, mocking her British accent.

Addison's lip curled into a snarl, but before she could hurl another insult, the guards shoved her from behind, forcing her to stumble into the outer thicket of the jungle. She quickly regained her balance and turned back to Mathias. He grinned, showing no mercy. Addison flipped him off in defiance, then broke into a light jog, disappearing into the jungle.

Lucky for her, she was wearing flats instead of heels. Ducking under branches and skirting trees, Addison's flight instinct took over. Running the race of her life now, she knew she had to put as much distance between herself and the man hunting her while simultaneously plotting a way out of this mess.

Meanwhile, Edmund watched the final seconds tick away on his watch. Satisfied he had lived up to his word, he turned to the test subject.

"I want proof of death," he instructed.

The man acknowledged the order with a curt nod, then tore off into the jungle, pursuing his prey.

"Make it quick!" Edmund called after him. "I have a plane to catch!"

With the force enhancement serum coursing through his veins, the test subject sprinted through the thicket, vaulting over fallen tree limbs, until Mathias's facility faded from view. He halted, allowing his eyes to adjust to the shifting light while scanning for movement among the foliage. He listened attentively, distinguishing between the jungle's ambient noises and the elusive footsteps of the female he hunted.

A distant twig snap caught his attention. The test subject whipped his head to the left, his enhanced hearing picking up the faint rustling of leaves, confirming his suspicion. Without hesitation, he broke into a sprint, chasing the sound's source. Each stride made him feel more alive than ever—stronger, faster, and fueled by limitless stamina.

Up ahead, Addison ran in a panic and with less grace. Jogging on an indoor treadmill was her forte, not trail running, and without the support of a sports bra, "the girls" were working against her now. Despite this, she pressed on. Branches lashed against her designer clothing as she fled, desperate to outrun an unseen pursuer.

After running for what felt like an eternity, the pinch on Addison's side became unbearable, and she had to stop to catch her breath. Chest heaving, she looked about with dismay. The jungle seemed to stretch endlessly in every direction, its oppressive sameness only intensifying her sense of isolation and desperation. It offered no clue to a way out.

She rounded sharply at the sound of snapping twigs behind her. Through the foliage, she spotted the test subject in the distance, approaching fast. Addison's eyes widened in panic as the man zigzagged through the twisted vines and branches in cold pursuit.

With a surge of adrenaline, Addison ran for her life. Ignoring the pain, the sound of her ragged breath played counterpoint to the beat of her racing heart.

Moments later, she reached the bank of a murky river, dashing her hope of escape. Addison skidded to a halt, her feet sinking in the mud. Cursing her bad luck, she hesitated, scanning the water. The opposite shore was only twenty yards away, and despite the fast-moving current, she was certain she could make it across.

Then, she froze.

An eight-foot crocodile basked in the sun on the opposite bank. Spotting Addison, the enormous reptile quietly slid into the river, its unblinking eyes protruding slightly above the waterline, conveying a sense of ancient, primal menace. The croc began its predatory crossing with the silent and deliberate motion of its armored tail.

Realizing she was trapped, Addison's breath quickened. She spun in a tight circle, frantically searching for an out. But there was none. Caught between her pursuer and a prehistoric beast, Addison realized she had reached the end of the line. She had no choice but to face what she thought was the lesser of two evils and hope for the best.

She backed away from the shore, grabbed a nearby stick off the ground, and readied herself for combat. The test subject quickly covered the distance between them, having barely broken a sweat.

Heart pounding with fear, Addison tightened her grip on the stick with both hands as she came face to face with her pursuer. When the man stepped toward her, she juked to the right, deliberately moving away from the river. The man moved with her. Undeterred by Addison's weapon, he lunged at her with relentless focus. Addison quickly thrust the stick in his face, looking to gouge his eye, but the man dodged the attack with a head bob. Addison pulled the stick back quickly, and in one fluid motion, she made a roundhouse spin, switching her grip down low like on a baseball bat and swinging downward with all her might.

The man raised his arm just in time, deflecting the strike with his forearm. The stick shattered with a sharp crack, snapping in half.

Addison hissed in frustration and hurled the broken piece at him. It struck his mouth, splitting his lip, but he wiped away the blood with casual indifference before moving in for the kill.

With no other option, Addison charged, making a guttural growl as she met him head-on. She threw a flurry of punches, but none found their mark. The man swatted them aside effortlessly as though playing with her. Then, he lunged in a flash, locking his hand around her throat in a vice-like grip.

The crushing force of the man's death grip took Addison by surprise. A strangled gasp escaped as her eyes widened in horror and desperation. Cold and ruthless, the man lifted Addison off her feet with one arm, his strength uncanny.

Addison clawed and kicked, trying to free herself, but her efforts were futile. The man was too strong. Her gaze lifted toward the sky as her face turned blue. Sunlight shimmered through the treetops in a serene glow as if beckoning her home. Her vision blurred, and her eyes rolled back in her head as the world around her faded.

Then, suddenly, she was free.

Violently released from her assailant's grip, Addison crashed to the ground like a discarded rag doll. She coughed hoarsely, gasping for air, as chaos erupted around her. Two bodies tumbled over her, locked in a furious struggle. Her mind raced to the crocodile, but reality snapped back into focus, and she could not believe her eyes.

Luna!

The Aiwan had appeared out of nowhere, ambushing Mathias's super soldier from behind and catching him entirely by surprise. Luna clamped her oversized hand over his bald head and attempted to establish a telepathic connection. But something was off. His mind was a whirlwind of chaos, too wild to subdue.

Forced to his knees, the man resisted with a ferocity unlike anything Luna had ever encountered—on Earth or Aiwa. Straining to maintain her hold, Luna stole a glance at Addison. Their eyes met, Addison's shell-shocked expression filled with disbelief and gratitude for the Aiwan's intervention.

"Run!" Luna commanded firmly, grimacing from the exertion. "I cannot hold him much longer!"

The urgency in Luna's words jolted Addison into motion. She scrambled to her feet, steadying herself as she regained her balance. Just as she prepared to dash away, she hesitated, turning back to Luna.

"What about you?" she asked.

"I will handle this," Luna growled through clenched teeth. "Now go!"

At the Aiwan's insistence, Addison reluctantly took a few steps back. She gave Luna a small, appreciative smile before turning to leave, trusting the Aiwan to fend for herself.

Once Addison disappeared into the brush, Luna finally released her grip. She staggered backward, exhausted from the effort, while the test subject collapsed onto all fours, gasping for air.

The reprieve was short-lived. Despite the mental disorientation, the man slowly rose to his feet, his determination unyielding. His sharp gaze locked onto Luna, who clutched her head, visibly drained from the effort.

Her presence unnerved him; Luna was unlike anything he had ever encountered—or even imagined existed. But it was irrelevant. She had interfered with his mission and stood between him and his target.

Narrowing his eyes, the man drew a six-inch blade from behind his back and assumed a combat stance. He pressed his thumb on the spine of the blade in what was known as a Filipino grip, ready to finish the fight.

Seeing the blade, Luna shook off the effects of her splitting headache. Then, with a fierce snarl, she crouched low, spreading her arms as she fully extended her razor-sharp claws.

The combatants squared off, circling one another with lethal focus. Luna struck first, unleashing a flurry of wild slashes, but the super soldier was too fast. He evaded each strike with inhuman reflexes, effortlessly blocking and deflecting her blows. Then, he countered with unrelenting rage, driving Luna back on her heels, only to have her recover and go back on the offensive.

They went toe-to-toe, back and forth in a deadly dance for several minutes until the fight reached its climax. With a guttural roar, the super soldier charged, knife raised high, sunlight gleaming off the blade. The flash blinded Luna for an instant, breaking her focus. As the knife arced down, she grabbed the man's wrist, halting the blade inches from her aquasuit. But the force of his momentum sent them both tumbling backward. Luna lost her footing in the muddy riverbank, and they plunged into the water with a violent splash.

Beneath the surface, their struggle continued—but now they were not alone. The commotion drew the attention of additional crocodiles on the opposite bank, who propelled themselves forward with startling speed and disappeared under the water.

Swept downstream by the current, the combatants became separated in the murky depths. Despite near-zero visibility, Luna was in her element and sensed the man thrashing nearby. But the fast-moving crocodiles were the closer threat now, the first of which was on her immediately. As the croc lunged with its massive V-shaped mouth open wide, Luna grabbed its upper snout and established an instant telepathic link. She calmed the beast long enough to redirect its head into the steel-trap jaws of a second croc. As the two beasts fought, Luna saw an opening and retreated to shore, kicking powerfully through the water.

Once safe on dry land, she paused, scanning the river for any signs of pursuit. Then, a high-pitched, gargled scream pierced the air. Luna looked downstream to see Mathias's super soldier caught in the grasp of a crocodile. The reptile thrashed violently, dragging him under before initiating its death roll and drowning him with brutal efficiency as more crocs swarmed in to take part.

Luna grimaced at the gruesome sight and turned away. Taking a deep breath, she checked herself for injuries and exhaled in relief—she and her suit remained intact and unharmed.

Glancing skyward, Luna realized she had been gone too long; soon, the guards who had grown accustomed to her daily walks outside the compound might grow suspicious.

Making her way back to the facility's main entrance, Luna chose a circuitous route to avoid being seen by Edmund. Along the way, she briefly considered tracking down Deanna—whose true identity remained a mystery, their telepathic connection never established—but it no longer mattered. Hopefully, Deanna would escape the jungle and finally be free from Edmund Mathias once and for all.

Twenty minutes later, Edmund checked his watch and sighed heavily.

"She couldn't have gotten that far," he said impatiently.

Dr. Vlachos shifted uneasily, sharing the same concerns. The test subject should have accomplished his mission by now. Even with the jungle's dense cover and Agent Addison's training, she was no match for his enhanced abilities. The most likely explanation for the delay seemed grim: Addison had fallen prey to one of the jungle's predators, and the test subject was still searching for her remains—which may never be found.

"He has a locator chip," Vlachos offered. "I can go inside and track his whereabouts."

Disappointed, Edmund puffed out his cheeks and exhaled, his lips fluttering in a light, rippling sound. "Do what you have to do," he replied with a flippant wave. "I've got a flight to catch."

"Yes, sir," Vlachos said as Mathias headed back inside. "I'll let you know as soon as he returns."

Edmund did not respond.

Vlachos turned his attention back to the jungle, narrowing his gaze in hopes of spotting some movement, but the landscape remained still.

What if he doesn't return? he wondered.

The unsettling thought struck him. Going AWOL seemed unlikely, given the recent tweaks to the serum. The test subject had responded favorably, exhibiting no signs of defiance—only complete obedience. However, the possibility lingered that both Addison and the test subject had perished in the unforgiving jungle.

Vlachos shook his head to dispel the grim notion. Yet, as the minutes ticked away, it became evident that something was wrong. The morning heat and humidity were also intensifying, conditions that did not agree with Vlachos.

He turned to the guards. "Stay here and keep an eye out," he instructed, frustration evident in his voice. "I'm going inside to see if I can locate him."

Edmund made his way to the rooftop pool. Crossing the deck, he found Luna sitting in her customary spot at the bottom of the deep end. He stood at the edge, waved to get her attention, and she rose to the surface.

Edmund tapped his watch. "Hey Luna, time to head to the airport," he said, a hint of edginess in his voice.

Luna picked up on this. As she swam to the side, she gave him a curious look. "Is everything alright?" she asked.

Other than the fact I need to find a new girlfriend? he thought bitterly. But instead of voicing his angst—he hated unresolved matters—he shifted his frustration to the murky pool water.

"How can you swim in that?" he said with disgust.

Luna's heart skipped, fearing a different kind of discovery. "Swim in what?" she asked, feigning ignorance.

"That," Edmund snapped, pointing to the pool. "The water looks filthy. You shouldn't be swimming in that muck."

"Oh," Luna responded innocently. She climbed out of the pool, water dripping off her mud-free aquasuit as she reached for her towel on the nearby chair.

Edmund retrieved his handheld radio. "Hey, get the freakin' pool boy up here pronto," he barked into the receiver without identifying himself. "This pool is disgusting, and if I find it like this again, he'll be looking for a new job. Got it?"

"Yes, sir. Right away, sir," stammered a voice over the radio.

"I swear, I have to do everything around here," Edmund grumbled as he lowered the radio. Turning to Luna, he exhaled in frustration. "Sorry about that. I'll make sure it doesn't happen again."

Luna breathed a sigh of relief—her secret was safe.

31
SPOOFING

Planet Earth
Central Intelligence Agency, Langley, Virginia

Jessica Aguri entered her new office for the first time since her promotion to Deputy Director of the CIA's National Clandestine Service. Since returning from Sanhe, China, she had hit the ground running, her hectic schedule a blur of flights and meetings, crisscrossing the country with hardly a moment to breathe.

She closed the door behind her and took a moment to absorb the view from a new perspective. A wave of nostalgia, excitement, and apprehension washed over her as she realized the office space no longer represented authority above her but was now a testament to her accomplishments.

Embracing the weight of her new responsibilities, Jessica crossed the room to her desk. As she passed the coffee bar, a 5x7 notecard caught her eye—folded into a tent with her name scribbled on the front. Opening it, she smiled at her boss's messy handwriting. The note read: *You got this!*

Appreciating the affirmation and the gift bag of Highlander Grog coffee beans that came with it, Jessica placed the note in her desk's top drawer. Her eyes shifted to the cardboard box on the desk, filled with the few personal items from her old cubicle. She set the box on the floor behind the desk and settled into her plush leather chair.

Just as she exhaled, the phone rang. Jessica straightened, noting the caller ID—her boss, Brett Brenham. She quickly cleared her throat before picking up the receiver and answering, "Yes, sir?"

"Drop what you're doing and meet me by the elevator," he said, his tone cutting through the air with urgent authority.

Before Jessica could reply, Brenham hung up, and the line went dead. She replaced the receiver and stood. Grabbing her planner, Jessica took a deep breath and quipped, "And away we go."

Jessica reached the elevators just as her boss arrived. They did not exchange words, but all signs indicated something serious was going down. Jessica's suspicions were confirmed when Brenham pressed the up button to call the elevator. They entered the empty car, and Brenham used his access card to select the top floor. They were headed to see Maxine Ratliff.

As soon as the doors closed and they started moving, Jessica broke the silence. "Thanks for the coffee, by the way."

Brenham chuckled. "Good stuff, that is. Carried me through many a day at this place."

Jessica smiled thinly, then turned serious. "Any idea what this is about?"

"I know as much as you," he said with a heavy breath, "but the director asked for you personally."

Taken aback, Jessica's mind started racing. *Me? What'd I do?*

Sensing her uncertainty, Brenham offered a reassuring glance. "Relax. If you were in trouble, I'd know about it already."

Jessica let out a breath of relief as the elevator arrived. The doors slid open, and she followed her boss down the hall to CIA Director Maxine Ratliff's office.

The director's executive assistant spotted them approaching and quickly notified her boss. As Brenham and Jessica reached the reception area, the assistant gestured to Ratliff's office with one hand while discreetly pressing a button under her desk to unlock the director's door.

"The director will see you now," she said, offering a polite smile.

Brenham and Jessica entered the director's office to find Ratliff with her back to the door, carefully placing a saucer of water beneath a potted Venus Flytrap on the windowsill. Following her boss's lead, Jessica quietly approached Ratliff's desk.

Turning away from her carnivorous plant, Ratliff swiveled her chair to face them and gestured toward the open chairs in front of her desk. Brenham and Jessica sat.

Ratliff cut right to the chase. "The Russians sunk a British sub," she announced bluntly.

Jessica's jaw dropped, but Brenham merely frowned as if the revelation was not unexpected.

He exhaled deeply. "So, the rumors are true?"

Ratliff did not bother asking how Brenham knew—it was his job to know such things. She nodded and added, "It happened two days ago. Fortunately, it was an autonomous sub, no crew onboard. But as you can imagine, the Brits are pissed." She flashed Jessica a brief, cordial smile. "Hi, Jessica."

"Good morning, ma'am," Jessica replied, returning the smile before asking, "Where?"

"Challenger Deep," Ratliff replied. "Needless to say, tensions have amped up considerably."

"Have the Russians accepted responsibility?" Brenham followed up.

"Not directly," Ratliff answered. "But confirmation came from Edmund Mathias himself. He called the president personally and told him everything—while I was in the room," she added, still stunned by the man's audacity. "He's not even trying to hide his intentions and is using the Russians as muscle to keep us away."

Jessica recalled her conversation with General Garza—he had warned that Mathias's ambitions centered on his activities in Peru.

"Mathias is developing a so-called 'force enhancement serum,' and the Kremlin is just one of his many buyers," Jessica stated. "Could protecting Mathias's deep-sea venture be part of the deal?"

"I wouldn't put it past either of them," Ratliff admitted. "But here's the kicker—NASA has detected an Aiwan probe in orbit. It hasn't committed any overt acts of aggression, yet, but it's there, just watching and waiting."

"To what end?" Jessica asked, glancing between Ratliff and Brenham.

"Prince Kypa warned us that off-world harvesters would eventually come for our crystals," Brenham replied. "Maybe the probe is watching for new arrivals."

"And Mathias is getting nervous?" Jessica speculated.

"Exactly," Ratliff confirmed. "His phone call to the president served two purposes. First, it was a warning to stay out of his way. Second, he wants to make a deal."

Brenham and Jessica leaned in, awaiting the details.

"Luna, the second Aiwan who is now Mathias's—quote-unquote—business partner, presented an idea to the president. She claims she can reprogram

Kypa's old escape pod to send a jamming signal through our military satellites, projecting it out into space. The idea is to deceive enemy sensors, making it seem like Earth has no crystals. In theory, it should deter any harvesters from targeting us."

"Access to our military satellites … is he crazy?" Brenham said, incredulous.

"Actually, not just ours but Japan, Germany, and Britain as well," Ratliff clarified. "And I agree, it all sounds ludicrous, but Luna's idea has merit. Earth could be facing a major invasion, and this might be our only way of avoiding it."

Jessica shifted in her seat. "What does Mathias get in return?"

"Unhindered access to Challenger Deep," Ratliff answered. With a skeptical expression, she added, "Apparently, he plans to take his operations intergalactic, but there's a deal on the table where he has to allow inspectors and share a portion of the harvested crystals."

Brenham leaned back, shaking his head in disbelief. "This feels like hiring a fox to guard the henhouse," he muttered.

"The president doesn't like it any more than you, but he's playing the hand he was dealt," Ratliff responded. "He's invited our allies to Camp David. They should be arriving today to discuss the proposal. If they agree, Mathias will be granted diplomatic immunity to re-enter the United States and accompany Luna to Groom Lake where she'll begin work on the jamming signal." Ratliff pointed to Jessica. "That's where you come in."

Jessica straightened. Feeling her cheeks flush, she said, "Ma'am?"

"I want you to fly to Atlanta and pick up Dr. Landry—by order of the President," Ratliff made clear. "If this deal with Mathias goes through, we'll need Dr. Landry's help to get to Luna."

"I've already spoken to Rose—she's willing to help us," Jessica affirmed, though a part of her hated dragging her friend back into this mess.

Ratliff nodded with approval. "Good. By the way, I shared Kypa's beacon with the president. It was sent to Groom Lake for analysis. If Kypa contacts Dr. Landry, the president wants to be informed immediately."

"Understood," Jessica replied. "Speaking of Dr. Landry, she's requested we remove her security detail. She wants her life to return to some semblance of normalcy."

Ratliff glanced at a framed picture of her grandchildren on the desk. Leaning back with a heavy sigh, she admitted, "I don't blame her. But I'm convinced Mathias was behind the hit on Paul Wiggins. Just thinking of that bastard being back on American soil makes my skin crawl," Ratliff said with disdain. "One way or another, Mathias will face the consequences of his actions.

But until justice is served, the detail stays—for now."

Camp David
Frederick County, Maryland

Since the days of Franklin Roosevelt, Camp David served as the president's country residence. Formally known as Naval Support Facility Thurmont, this secluded retreat is nestled within Catoctin Mountain Park in Frederick County, just a thirty-minute helicopter ride from the White House. For this reason, President Fitzgerald chose it as the site for today's meeting. Bringing the leaders of Japan, Germany, and the United Kingdom away from the capitol to discuss Mathias's proposed alliance required careful diplomacy. The serene setting of Camp David provided an ideal backdrop to discuss the controversial situation.

Named after Eisenhower's grandson, Camp David spanned 125 acres of wooded hills. The main cabin, Laurel Lodge, served as the venue for meals and meetings, while the nearby Aspen Lodge housed bedrooms, a swimming pool, and access to a single golf hole—all connected by scenic walking trails ideal for private, one-on-one negotiations.

Fitzgerald and his three counterparts from the international Group of Seven gathered at Laurel Lodge in the main living room. Seated in front of a large stone fireplace, each of the G7 members reclined on plush leather couches, sipping coffee and tea as they exchanged friendly conversation, reacquainting themselves.

The president glanced at his watch, his anxiety mounting. At 1400 hours, Zulu, Edmund Mathias, and the Aiwan female, Luna, were scheduled to address the group via video conference. Fitzgerald had until then to break the news to his guests and convince them to hear Mathias out.

Fitzgerald set his coffee down on the side table and cleared his throat, silencing the room. With their undivided attention, he began his pitch.

"My friends, I appreciate you accepting my invitation on such short notice. I realize our relations have been strained lately, especially with the arrival of Prince Kypa and the Aiwans, but what I'm about to share concerns all of our security interests."

His opening words had the desired effect. The mood in the room shifted, growing more serious and somber.

"I've chosen to shrink the room a bit and not invite the other G7 members because what I am about to propose does not directly affect them," he continued. "So, let's get to it, shall we?"

With no objections, Fitzgerald gestured to the large screen television hung above the hearth.

"In about fifteen minutes, we will be joined by the founder and CEO of Mathias Industries, Edmund Mathias."

At the mention of Mathias's name, British Prime Minister Amelia Acker tensed in her chair, and her eyes narrowed with anger. Before she could voice her objection, Fitzgerald raised his hand, silently urging her to hold her protest until he had finished.

German Chancellor Wagner Koch and Japanese Prime Minister Botan Tanaka noticed Acker's reaction. Exchanging confused glances, they turned to Fitzgerald for an explanation.

"Let me be perfectly clear, Edmund Mathias is not a man to be trusted," the president stated emphatically. "Personally, I'd love nothing more than to see him behind bars, but our planet is facing an unprecedented threat—"

"—This is about the crystals," Acker cut in sternly, locking eyes with Fitzgerald. The president responded with a curt nod. Acker turned to Tanaka and Koch and added, "Two days ago, the Russians sank one of our autonomous submarines near Challenger Deep. They were acting on Mathias's orders. He's using them to protect his interests so he can exploit the crystals."

"Amelia is right," Fitzgerald confirmed. "Mathias is working with Polokov and just about every other terrorist state to fund his undersea mining operations. But according to Mathias, your sub wasn't attacked to stop you from reporting on him—he's made no secret of his intentions with the crystals—rather, it was to keep your sub from interfering with his efforts to hide those crystals from off-world harvesters."

"I'm not buying it," Acker shot back, arms crossed. "Our sub was nowhere near Challenger Deep when it was attacked—this was an act of war."

Before Fitzgerald could respond, German Chancellor Koch raised his hand to intervene. "I hear you, Amelia," he began, offering a nod of support, "but what exactly do you mean by hiding the crystals?"

"As you may or may not know, Mathias is harboring a second Aiwan in Peru," Fitzgerald replied. "Her name is Luna, and she built a cloaking device to mask the presence of the crystals from deep-space sensors. The hope being that this will fool others from coming to Earth to harvest his, rather, *our* crystals. However, the cloaking device only covers a small area—a cave inside Challenger Deep to be precise—and more crystals are located throughout the world. For Mathias's plan to work, he needs to cloak the entire planet before the competition arrives, which, it just so happens, has begun."

"You are referring to the alien probe in orbit," Tanaka clarified.

"Yes," Fitzgerald confirmed. "We don't know if the probe is friend or foe. Prince Kypa has not contacted us to explain its presence, nor has anyone else reached out or made demands. But someone is watching us, and Mathias has a plan to dissuade any harvesters from taking an interest in Earth."

"Leave it to him to turn self-interest into mutual interest," Acker remarked snidely.

"I can't argue with that," Fitzgerald seconded.

"I'm almost afraid to ask, but how does this involve us?" Chancellor Koch interjected, cutting through the rhetoric.

Fitzgerald leaned forward in his seat and replied, "Luna, the Aiwan, wants to send a signal into space that essentially disrupts the long-range scanners used by alien ships. To do that, she needs access to Prince Kypa's escape pod, which is currently held at Groom Lake, and …" he hesitated, readying himself for the inevitable backlash, "… access to a select number of military satellites controlled by each of us."

"Preposterous," Acker exclaimed, glancing around at the others in disbelief. "We're not handing over top secret equipment to him—or to an alien race."

"I'm with Amelia," Koch added firmly. "My constituents would never support this."

Their reaction did not surprise Fitzgerald; he knew this would be an uphill battle. He let the tension simmer in silence before turning to Tanaka. "Thoughts?"

The Japanese Prime Minister did not rush to respond. With his brow furrowed, he carefully weighed Fitzgerald's plan from a different angle. Tanaka was a national hero—a former astronaut who had once spent time aboard the International Space Station. His journey from space to politics carried him to Japan's highest office. Though Tanaka had a deep passion for space exploration, his concerns were more grounded. Closer to home, he worried about the looming threats from Russia, China, and North Korea in the Sea of Japan.

"Spoofing," Tanaka said finally, drawing curious looks from his counterparts. "That is what we're talking about here."

"Forgive me, I am unfamiliar with that term," Acker replied, puzzled. "What is spoofing?"

Fitzgerald chuckled, not at her confusion, but in acknowledgment of Tanaka's simplification of Luna's plan.

"You're right," he said with a smile. "Spoofing is what Russia does to dodge our sanctions. Their cargo ships, especially oil tankers heading to China, send out fake location signals to evade detection."

"Or they just turn off their transponders entirely," Tanaka added.

"Exactly," Fitzgerald nodded. "We call it the shadow fleet."

"And if I'm understanding Luna's proposal correctly," Tanaka continued, "she intends to disrupt the sensors of alien vessels coming to Earth, making them think there are no crystals, correct?"

"That's the idea," the president confirmed. "Once we re-task a few satellites to blanket the planet, Luna will transmit a signal from Kypa's escape pod, which our satellites will then beam into space."

"And she's convinced it will work?" Koch asked, softening his stance.

"You can ask her yourself," Fitzgerald replied, checking his watch once again. "But to answer your question, yes, Luna believes she can spoof the harvesters."

"And what's to keep her from hacking our satellites and disabling our defenses?" Acker pressed.

Fitzgerald nodded slowly. Her concerns were valid—this proposal posed an ethical dilemma of the highest order.

"It's a risk," the president granted, "but part of the agreement is that we review and approve every line of code embedded in the signal. If necessary, we can add extra firewalls to ensure Luna's signal doesn't compromise other systems."

Still unconvinced, Acker asked, "But can our programmers really outcode an Aiwan?"

Tanaka shrugged. "Who can say for sure?" he said bluntly. "In cybersecurity, achieving complete invulnerability is nearly impossible. But the pendulum swings both ways—this plan gives us a chance to examine Luna's coding logic up close."

Acker had not considered that angle and reluctantly acknowledged its merit, though she kept it to herself. In a wary tone, the British Prime Minister asked pointedly, "And what else does this deal entail?"

"In exchange for access to our satellites and agreeing not to interfere with Mathias's operations in Challenger Deep," the president explained, "we get half of the crystals he harvests."

"And what good will that do us?" Acker posed. "We don't have the technology to harness the power of these crystals. If Luna's plan fails, any alien harvesters coming to Earth will trace the crystals right back to us. We'd be putting our heads in a noose."

"Good point," Koch agreed.

"Listen, this is our best option to save the planet," Fitzgerald argued, his voice charged with conviction. "I understand your concerns, I do, because I share them. But this is bigger than individual nations and we have to do something—now."

A brief silence settled over the group, the weight of the president's words hanging in the air. Fitzgerald looked to the three foreign leaders, awaiting their reactions. But all eyes naturally shifted toward British Prime Minister Acker. Given her country's recent attack, it felt right to defer to her.

Sensing this, Acker tapped her teacup rhythmically, the soft clink echoing her contemplation.

Finally, she said wryly, "You're good at selling hope, Mr. President. I'll give you that."

Fitzgerald chuckled, appreciating the levity. "Thank you, Amelia. I'll try to remember that next year when I launch my re-election bid."

Turning to Tanaka and Koch, Acker's response was firm. "If I were to agree to this, I would insist that each of us has our best engineers on-site at Groom Lake to oversee this coding."

"Absolutely," Fitzgerald interjected, his tone leaving no room for doubt. "I made that condition non-negotiable with Mathias."

Koch leaned forward, pinching his brow. "And how will we know if Luna's plan is successful?"

"Good question," the president acknowledged, checking his watch. "And your timing is impeccable. I'll let Luna answer."

On cue, the television above the hearth came to life, displaying the Seal of the President of the United States. All eyes turned to the screen as a countdown timer appeared at the bottom, ticking away the final seconds until the meeting began.

The presidential seal disappeared, replaced by a live video feed aboard Mathias's private jet. Edmund sat side by side with Luna, facing the camera. He brightened with the shallow grin of a used car salesman.

"Greetings," he began, his voice brimming with an air of superiority. "We've all met before, so I won't bore you with me. Instead, allow me to introduce you to my partner Luna—our savior."

32
SICARIO

Planet Earth
Nellis AFB, Nevada

"Close your mouth, Dear, you look like a trout," Marlana remarked as she retrieved her suitcase from the closet.

Hector Nunez closed his mouth, though his displeasure at his wife's unexpected travel plans was evident. "But the election is tomorrow," he reminded her. "You said you'd be here."

Marlana let out a heavy sigh. With less than ninety minutes to catch her flight, Hector's impending HOA election was the furthest thing from her mind. Yet a pang of regret tugged at her heart; she knew how much tomorrow night meant to him.

Turning to face her husband, Marlana gently touched his arm.

"Hey, don't worry," she said earnestly, lifting his chin to meet her gaze. "I'll be back tomorrow, and I promise I'll be right by your side when they announce you're the winner."

As much as he hated it, Hector knew the drill—duty came first. With a crooked frown, he nodded in reluctant understanding and pulled his wife into a warm embrace.

Marlana grabbed his butt cheeks firmly with both hands and playfully sang in her best Marilyn Monroe voice, "Happy Birthday, Mr. President."

Hector laughed. "You're so bad," he said, patting her rear before stepping back so she could finish packing.

Hector sat on the edge of the bed as his wife retrieved her service dress uniform. After a moment of silence, he asked with uncertainty, "Do they really think Min and Rose are still in danger?"

Marlana pulled a pair of dark blue slacks from a hanger and folded them carefully on the bed. "Honestly, I think Mathias is capable of anything."

Hector's eyes dimmed as his mind replayed haunting scenes—two Army assault helicopters landing outside Mathias's Peruvian compound. He could still feel the tension of sitting in the back of a vehicle with Paul Wiggins and Eduardo Salazar, watching as Operation Bold Fortress unfolded. Both men were now dead, murdered by Edmund Mathias.

After blinking back to the present, Hector's eyes refocused on his wife. His voice softened as he made her swear, "Just promise me you'll watch your six."

Moved by his concern, Marlana circled the bed and kissed his forehead tenderly. "I promise."

Marine Logistics Ship, *Zaragoza*
Port of Progreso, Mexico

Captain Gallardo stood outside, leaning on the railing of his ship's bridge wing. A refreshing breeze touched his face as his eyes tracked Mr. Renzo debarking the ship. The savage man murdered two of his crew members with his bare hands. Renzo's fit of primal fury was the most terrifying display of violence he had ever witnessed, and he felt a deep sense of relief as the man finally set foot on the pier.

He watched the killer with a mixture of revulsion and morbid curiosity, wondering what could drive a man to such ruthless brutality. The answer came to him as if whispered by the wind—*The Devil*. Only a soul steeped in darkness could abide such evil. The captain crossed himself for good measure.

Just as Gallardo was about to return to the bridge, a flash of motion caught his eye—a white SUV barreling across the crowded pier. Its bright gold trim and matching rims gleamed obnoxiously in the sunlight, demanding attention. Dock workers scattered, diving out of its path to avoid being hit. Yet, no curses or obscene gestures followed. Everyone knew that SUV. They also knew better than to challenge it. Heads down and steps hurried, they resumed their tasks, unwilling to draw the ire of the Sinaloa Cartel.

From his vantage point, the captain watched the SUV screech to a stop in front of his ship, where Mr. Renzo was waiting. A man exited the front passenger seat, holding a long carrying case. Captain Gallardo exhaled sharply, his unease growing as the cartel man handed the case to Renzo with a broad smile. Renzo accepted it, and they exchanged a few brief words before opening the SUV's back door. Without hesitation, Renzo climbed inside, and the vehicle sped off moments later.

Relieved to see them go, Captain Gallardo shook his head and silently prayed that Renzo would never set foot on his ship again.

Renzo was greeted by two other cartel men inside the SUV—the driver and another backseat passenger to his left. Resting his new blowgun on the floorboard between his legs, Renzo quietly surveyed the interior, noting the location of the door locks and handles in case a quick exit became necessary. While he remained silent, his three Sinaloa companions joked and laughed in Spanish, their voices filling the car as he subtly took their measure.

If he had to guess, Renzo suspected they were brothers. Their features—charcoal black hair, dark brown eyes, and medium complexions—made the resemblance unmistakable. Each wore a flashy tracksuit adorned with matching braided gold chains and carried identical gold and nickel-plated revolvers tucked into shoulder holsters.

Inwardly, Renzo scorned their appearance, especially the absurdly large, diamond-encrusted crucifixes hanging around their necks. The irony was never lost on him people in their line of work, men and women alike, wore such symbols of faith while spawning violence and crime. The hypocrisy amused him, though he kept his thoughts to himself. Despite their wannabe gangster appearance, the Chachapoyan knew better than to underestimate them. Even a blind squirrel finds a nut now and then. These men worked for one of the world's most ruthless drug cartels, and they would not be transporting him to the U.S.-Mexico border if their bosses did not trust them.

The man seated to Renzo's left—Jesus—gestured to the case and asked in Spanish, "Do you approve?"

Taking this opportunity to inspect his new two-piece, big-bore blowgun, Renzo unzipped the case and began inventorying the contents. He removed the two blow tubes and a shorter middle piece that connected them. Satisfied, he noted it was the exact four-foot carbon fiber model he had requested. With practiced precision, Renzo screwed the three sections together firmly. The assembled weapon spanned half the length of the back seat.

"Very good," he replied, nodding with terse approval. "Thank you."

"Inside, you will find the darts and the drugs you requested," Jesus added.

Renzo retrieved a hard plastic container from the carrying case. He opened it to find thirty-six 0.625-caliber mini broadhead darts, along with two vials—one of Ketamine and the other of Cyanide. Renzo placed the items back in the case and began dismantling the blowgun.

"You're the first sicario we've seen use a weapon like this," Jesus said with a chuckle. "Very old school, my friend."

Renzo nodded thoughtfully. He knew the term *sicario* well; it came from the Latin word *Sicarius*, which literally meant "dagger bearer." In modern times, it referred to cartel hitmen—assassins like himself, plucked from the slums at a young age and trained to be ruthless killers. For them, killing was not personal—it was business.

"This is the weapon of my ancestors," Renzo stated. "It is primitive, yes, but effective."

Jesus patted the pistol in his shoulder holster and grinned, revealing a mouth adorned with gold grills, and shrugged. "I prefer Betty here."

Renzo dipped his chin, respectfully acknowledging the man's choice of weapon. Not surprisingly, the three cartel soldiers made no offer of a firearm to their guest. That was not part of the agreement. For all they knew, the sicario—or whatever Renzo was—might be planning to eliminate them once their journey together reached its end.

"How far to the border?" Renzo asked.

"We should arrive in Nuevo Laredo tomorrow afternoon," Jesus replied. "That's if we drive through the night, but if you want to stop, we can."

Renzo shook his head. The North Koreans were expecting him on the U.S. side of the border tomorrow night.

"No, thank you. I have friends waiting." *If you could call them that*, he did not add.

Jesus accepted Renzo's response without question and tapped the driver on the shoulder. Their eyes met in the rearview mirror.

"¡Vamos!" Jesus prodded his brother. "Our friend has business in Texas!"

33

MANTA

Planet Aiwa
Supra, Realm of Eos

Agent Vylara waited anxiously, hoping to get eyes on the Cirran refugee known as Manta. Acting on a hot tip from her friend, Hera, Vylara set up a stakeout in the shadows across the street from a dilapidated structure on the edge of the refugee camp. She monitored the front entrance from her position, noting the steady flow of unsavory-looking figures coming and going. It was clear from the start that Hera's lead was solid—a gathering was underway, and the hulking lookout stationed outside signaled that only those invited would be allowed in.

Manta—the primary person of interest in King Loka's murder investigation—was inside. Vylara knew this for certain, but it had been some time since she last saw him. Still, the activity within the building was undeniable. Even from a distance, she could pick up the raw, unfiltered telepathic voices resonating from the meeting. Their tone, at times heated and raucous, charged the atmosphere around her, keeping Vylara alert, her muscles tight with anticipation.

Vylara's stakeout took an unexpected twist when a royal patrol arrived. The lookout at the front entrance tensed at the sight of two riders approaching on xipos, the seahorse-like creatures used by the royals. He subtly tapped the commlink on his wrist, warning those inside of the impending trouble.

Vylara ducked further behind a stack of storage crates, her six-chambered heart pounding as she watched the scene unfold.

Just keep moving, she silently willed the riders, hoping they would pass without incident and not compromise her stakeout.

Instead, the patrol halted at the door and telepathically exchanged words with the lookout. Vylara wisely locked out that part of her mind to avoid detection, which made it difficult to discern their exchange. However, the lookout did not appear to resist the riders' inquiry. He lowered his mental defenses just enough to engage in what seemed to be a casual conversation—standard etiquette for Aiwans—but avoided physical contact. Without establishing a telepathic connection through touch, even the most skilled telepath could not pry deeper into someone's mind.

Suddenly, the front door slid open, and six imposing Cirrans emerged from the building—Manta among them. They moved quickly, encircling the patrol, their sudden appearance startling the xipos, which shifted nervously beneath their riders.

The riders gripped their reins tighter, steadying their unsettled mounts. The lead rider squared his shoulders and addressed the group with authority.

"*Disperse at once,*" he ordered firmly. "*This gathering is violating curfew.*"

Manta swam forward, calming the rider's xipo with a soothing stroke along its snout. "*You are not welcome here,*" Manta replied calmly. "*Now, be on your way and leave us in peace.*"

"*By order of the king, I command you—*"

"*—And which king would that be?*" Manta interrupted, glancing around theatrically. "*I do not see Loka or Kypa, or even your young princess.*" He scoffed. "*Seems like you are fresh out of rulers.*"

The riders exchanged uneasy looks, sensing the tension rising. They were outnumbered and trapped.

The lead rider gave a decisive nod to his partner before addressing the group, his voice calm but firm. "*Clear the street and return to your homes, or we will return with an entire regiment.*"

Manta locked eyes with the lead rider in a standoff, his unwavering gaze showing no signs of backing down. His followers looked to him eagerly, awaiting the command to strike. But instead of escalating, Manta defused the situation.

Manta grinned knowingly. Then, without a word, flutter-kicked out of the way, signaling his followers to stand down. Seizing the opportunity, the riders quickly departed without further incident.

"*You see, Krunig was right,*" Manta declared to his followers with fervor and determination. "*We will always be slaves to the other realms unless we take back what is rightfully ours.*"

His followers echoed the sentiment, raising their fists and chanting support telepathically.

Manta quieted them and added, "*Our time has come. You have your assignments—now go and await my signal.*"

As Manta's followers dispersed, Vylara remained hidden, calculating her next move. She had to report this to Boa, but Manta's instructions to his followers gave her little to work with. Aside from claiming allegiance to Krunig, there was no direct evidence tying this group to the king's death. Bringing Manta in for questioning seemed premature. Doing so might spook his followers and send them into hiding. Yet, from what she had just overheard, these fanatics were mobilizing. Something dangerous was on the horizon, and Vylara had to uncover it—before it was too late.

Patience, she counseled herself.

Vylara waited a moment longer and then stole a glance across the street. The others were gone except one, and her eyes widened.

Koba!

Vylara's heart sank at the sight of Hera's son. Watching Manta chum it up with the impressionable youth made her skin crawl. Every instinct told her to blow her cover and confront them, just as Hera had done earlier, but she held back. Koba had fallen under Manta's spell, blinded by his dangerous lies. Then, inspiration struck.

Koba is your angle, Vylara told herself. *He will tell you what Manta is planning.*

The more she watched Manta engage Koba, the more she despised him. She pressed her lips together with renewed determination—she could not wait to bring him down.

"*I have complete confidence in you,*" Manta reassured Koba. "*You will do fine.*"

Bolstered by Manta's support, Koba nodded gratefully. A mischievous grin spread across his face. "*Then, will I get to meet her?*" he asked eagerly.

Manta chuckled at Koba's one-track mind and shook his head. "*You will if you do as I say,*" he replied, affectionately patting Koba's head. "*Now, get home before your mother discovers you are gone,*" he added, shooing the youth away. "*I will see you tomorrow.*"

As Koba swam away, Manta remained, watching him depart with a satisfied grin. He then set off in the opposite direction.

Vylara instinctively covered her mouth to stifle a gasp. *Tomorrow*!?

Her heart raced as she wrestled with a decision: alert Boa, confront Koba with his mother, or tail Manta. In the end, Vylara chose to follow Manta. She could always circle back to press Koba for answers if this trail led nowhere.

Edging toward the alley entrance, she peeked around the corner and spotted Manta slipping away up the street. A glance to her left confirmed that Koba had already vanished from sight. Steeling herself, Vylara set off after Manta.

Staying at a safe distance, she moved carefully from one building to the next, blending into the shadows. This covert work was not what she had imagined when she agreed to help Commodore Boa track down Major Gora's accomplices. Now, alone in unfamiliar territory, every sound heightened her nerves. Yet beneath the tension, the surge of adrenaline was thrilling.

As they neared the camp's outskirts, Vylara grew increasingly suspicious of where Manta was leading her. Beyond the city limits was nothing but the energy shield and the open sea.

Vylara kept her telepathic presence masked, but her instincts screamed of a trap. She stopped at the edge of the last structure, her eyes tracking Manta as he swam across the open ground toward the shimmering energy barrier in the distance.

What are you up to? she asked herself.

Vylara remained still, watching as Manta passed through the shield. She still had eyes on him, but her window of opportunity was closing fast. She would have to risk exposing herself in the open water if she wanted to continue the chase.

Determined as ever, Vylara decided to gamble and made her move. She surged out of the shadows in one swift, fluid motion, kicking hard toward the shield, praying Manta would not glance back.

Vylara passed through the shield without slowing and quickly ducked behind a rock formation, pausing just long enough to check her six. No one from the camp seemed to be following, so she reacquired Manta in the distance. He was swimming away and still unaware of her presence.

Relieved to have made it this far, Vylara resumed her pursuit. Manta traced a path along the energy barrier, skirting the edges of the capital. Before long, they arrived at a reef glowing with vibrant, phosphorescent algae. Vylara watched as Manta slipped sideways into a narrow crevice between the rocks and disappeared from view.

Pulling up, she crouched behind a coral garden that provided perfect cover and concealment while offering a clear line of sight to Manta's location. With visual contact lost, Vylara quickly activated the commlink on her wrist, pulling up a hologram display of the reef. As expected, this undeveloped area around the capital had been mapped for defense, and even better, she discovered there was only one way in or out of the reef. Manta could not leave without her knowing.

Settling in, Vylara waited for his next move—which took longer than expected. However, when Manta finally emerged, he was not empty-handed. He held something in his right hand.

Vylara's heart nearly skipped a beat. *A teleporter puck*!

As he swam past, Vylara ducked out of sight; he was heading back toward the camp. Alone again, she briefly considered following him but felt her curiosity tugging her back to the reef.

After watching Manta disappear, Vylara abandoned her cover and swam toward the narrow opening in the reef. Sliding sideways through the tight passage, it opened up into a cave tall enough for an Aiwan to stand upright.

Vylara cautiously entered the cave and scanned the area. It was a dead end—empty, with just a sandy floor and algae-covered walls.

What were you doing here? she wondered, frustration growing.

One thing was clear: Manta had not entered the cave carrying a teleporter puck. He had come to retrieve it. But what gnawed at her was the amount of time Manta had spent inside retrieving the simple device.

Acting on a hunch, Vylara began inspecting the walls, feeling for any nooks or hidden compartments where Manta might have stashed the device. Methodically, she ran her hands over every inch of the cave's interior but found nothing.

Still convinced there was more to uncover, she shifted her focus to the sandy floor. Vylara sifted through the sand in a grid pattern on her hands and knees, determined to find whatever Manta had hidden.

Her persistence paid off. Moments later, she unearthed a metal disc. Vylara's eyes widened in disbelief—a second teleporter puck.

Confused by this discovery, the temptation to examine it closely was strong, but her instincts warned her it was time to leave. Manta could return at any moment, and she had no intention of facing him alone and unarmed.

For a moment, Vylara hesitated. Taking the device could alert Manta and jeopardize their investigation. But leaving empty-handed was not an option, either.

Thinking fast, she activated the scanner on her commlink and began interfacing with the teleporter. It was a delicate task—one wrong move could trigger a failsafe, wiping the puck's memory or alerting Manta and his followers to the breach. But with a mix of skill and creativity, Vylara successfully accessed the data she sought: the usage report.

Her heart pounded as she read the results. Now it made sense why Manta had taken so long—he had used the teleporter to go off-world. But something did not add up. According to the log, Manta had traveled to Pria-12, Aiwa's most distant moon.

This cannot be right, Vylara thought, questioning the data. *And what was the second puck for?*

Frustrated and out of time, Vylara reluctantly buried the teleporter in its hiding spot under the sand. Armed with this critical new evidence, she slipped out of the cave. Determined more than ever, she swam straight toward the palace to meet Commodore Boa, eager to share her findings and finally unravel the motives driving Manta and his followers.

34
LEVERAGE

Planet Rogantu

Ava squeezed her eyes shut, trying to project her thoughts with all her might.

"*Reggie, can you hear me?*" she tried again, willing the words across the void and hoping they materialized somehow in the sentient mind of her ship's computer.

But her telepathic efforts to connect with Reggie only led to frustration. With an exasperated breath, Ava sat on the cramped closet floor, contemplating how to bridge the communication gap. To make matters worse, Toma had fallen silent, too. She used to sense his presence even when he slept, but now there was nothing. It was as if Toma had vanished.

Fearing the worst, Ava pushed herself to stay strong. "C'mon, Suntan, think. You can figure this out."

With her wrists bound tightly behind her back, Ava stood carefully and began high-stepping in place. She always thought better on her feet, and with the closet walls pressing in, any movement was better than none.

Drawing on her military training, Ava conducted a quick situation assessment. Her first task was to escape her bonds and find a way out of this suffocating closet. But even if she accomplished those Houdini-like feats, freeing

Toma would be no easy task. Overpowering two bounty hunters and the slicer on her own seemed like slim odds. And if, by some miracle, she could free Toma without confronting their captors, the Reaper was still trapped. Taking off would be impossible as long as the freighter remained grounded.

Reggie was her best hope.

Why can't we connect? Ava pondered with frustration.

Though less advanced than Toma or Kypa, her newfound telepathic abilities were likely the culprit. Perhaps the freighter's walls and distance from the Reaper inhibited her abilities? She likened it to the poor Wi-Fi reception in her old barracks back in Djibouti.

Another hypothesis crossed Ava's mind: what if telepathy only worked between organic beings? While seated in the pilot's chair aboard the Reaper, Reggie could read her thoughts, but Ava had to communicate verbally with her friend when roaming the ship.

My friend?

That profound realization gave her pause. She had never used those words to describe her relationship with Reggie before. Yet, her connection to the sentient lifeform had grown. Reggie was no longer simply her ship's main computer—devoid of emotion—but a self-aware, valued crew member with genuine feelings.

Looking up at the ceiling, Ava spoke softly, "But you're even more than that, Reggie. You're family."

Reggie's sentience was nothing short of a miracle. How it happened was beyond her comprehension and deserved to be explored much deeper—once they were free. For now, Ava needed to stay focused on the task at hand and find a way out.

Actually, it found her a few moments later when Smythe opened the closet door.

"This way," the bounty hunter ordered, motioning with his blaster as he backpedaled into the corridor. "And don't try anything stupid. Your suit can't stop a blaster now."

Ava complied, heading aft as directed. She had no idea where the passage led, but any place seemed better than that tiny closet. And even though she was technically still in captivity, walking about inside the bounty hunter's ship felt liberating.

Ava's SERE training kicked in, and she scanned for survival, evasion, resistance, and escape opportunities. At the end of the corridor, a blast door blocked their path. She rounded on Smythe with an expectant look.

The bounty hunter stepped forward, pressing the barrel of his weapon against Ava's chest, and pressed a button on the wall panel. The blast door slid open, revealing the freighter's cargo hold—Ava's breath hitched. The Reaper was less than fifty feet away, suspended in the clutches of two massive overhead mechanical arms. Her ship was immobilized, locked in place to prevent any escape.

"Keep moving," Smythe barked, shoving her forward with a rough nudge.

Ava shot a venomous glare over her shoulder as she moved into the cargo hold. She followed a grated catwalk to a set of steps leading down to the main deck. With each step, Ava reached out with her telepathy, desperately trying to connect with Toma and Reggie.

"*Ava?*" Toma responded finally, his mental voice groggy but recognizable.

"*Toma!*" Ava blurted, relieved beyond words to hear from him. "*Where are you? Are you safe?*"

"*Yes, I am fine,*" Toma replied, sounding disheartened. "*Sorry, Ava.*"

Before Ava could respond, a sharp jab from Smythe's weapon broke her concentration.

"Stop here," the bounty hunter commanded.

Ava held up short of the Reaper's boarding ladder. Her eyes darted about, trying to anticipate what was coming next.

"Gort!" Smythe called up to his partner.

"Here, boss," Gort replied, his voice echoing distantly from inside the Reaper. His frog-like head then appeared in the opening above.

"We're coming up," Smythe said. "If she so much as twitches, kill the Aiwan."

Ava's shoulders slumped; her worst fear had come true—they found Toma.

Smythe grabbed Ava's arm and spun her roughly to face the ladder. He leaned in close from behind. "Don't test me," he warned in her ear.

Ava heard a distinct click, and the cuffs loosened around her wrists. Her arms fell limply to her sides, and a tingling sensation flowed from her aching shoulders down to her fingertips. As she wrung her hands, the bounty hunter nudged her from behind.

"Get moving," Smythe snapped.

Ava ascended the ladder, her mind racing to devise a plan. But now that they had Toma, she felt powerless. Climbing aboard the Reaper, she entered the engineering section. Her gaze fell on the wet bath, and for a fleeting second, she selfishly yearned for the comfort of a hot shower.

Pushing that thought aside, Ava turned to find Toma kneeling in front of Hiromi and Gort. Their eyes met, and Ava's heart softened at the remorse etched on Toma's face.

"*Just stay calm,*" she reassured him as Smythe shackled her wrists once again. "*I'll handle this.*"

"Over there," Smythe nudged her forward. Ava moved without protest. "On your knees."

As she knelt, facing Toma, he reached out to her.

"*Sorry, Ava. My suit has been glitchy ever since we landed,*" he explained, guilt heavy in his voice. "*That was how they found me.*"

"*It's okay,*" Ava responded. "*Mine's been acting up, too. Must be something about this planet.*"

Gort glanced at Smythe. "So, what now?" he asked, growing impatient.

Before Smythe could answer, Ava scoffed, her voice dripping with defiance. "Let me guess—you want my ship?"

"That's right, and you're going to give it to us," Hiromi replied, her cold tone politely menacing.

Ava glanced at the cyborg slicer, taking in her appearance for the first time. Hiromi's doll-like features and intricately adorned exoskeleton drew an amused smirk.

"I had a toy like you once when I was a kid," Ava said mockingly.

Hiromi took a step toward Ava with an unsettling grace, her expression eerily calm. She looked the fragile human over and then asked in a genteel voice, "Could your toy do this?"

Without warning, the cyborg's metal hand whipped across Ava's cheek, the force sending her crashing to the floor.

Toma reacted immediately, struggling against his cuffs to intervene. "I wouldn't do that," Smythe warned, aiming his blaster at Ava.

The threat halted Toma. He froze, his jaw set as he glared at the bounty hunter.

Smythe smirked. "Wise choice."

Ava stirred, stars dancing in front of her eyes as she blinked back into focus. The right side of her face throbbed. She coughed hoarsely—the copper taste of blood on her lips.

"Ava, are you okay?" Toma said with concern.

Ava shook off the effects and gingerly tested her jaw. Once she gathered her wits, she rolled onto her back, nodding silently to reassure him.

Smythe's shadow fell over Ava as he stood over her. She turned to him as he said in a low voice, "Enough games. Deactivate your ship's security protocols."

"I told you before, I'm never handing over my ship to you," Ava said defiantly, then hocked a bloody loogie on the insectoid's boot.

Smythe hmphed, then gave Gort a curt nod. Without hesitation, his partner raised the electrode—the same device Ava once used to kill an obercai—and jabbed it into Toma's back. The young Aiwan's body seized up instantly, his teeth clenched as spasms of pain wracked him.

"Stop!" Ava shouted. "He's just a boy!"

Smythe watched with cold detachment, allowing the torture to continue a moment longer before giving Gort a subtle, dismissive signal to stop. Toma collapsed forward, his convulsing body landing at Ava's feet.

"Toma," Ava gasped, her voice breaking with panic.

"Ready to cooperate?" Smythe asked calmly.

Ava glared at the bounty hunter with burning intensity. Her lips quivered, aching to spit out a storm of curses, but she bit them back.

"No?" Smythe said, his voice dripping with smug indifference. "So be it."

He signaled Gort to resume the torment. His partner grimaced as he activated the electrode, delivering another jolt to Toma's leg. The Aiwan screamed in agony.

"Stop! Please!" Ava begged, tears spilling from her eyes. "Just stop."

Gort exchanged a glance with Smythe before retracting the device and stepping backward.

"I'm not going to kill your friend," Smythe revealed. "He's worth too much. But next time, we'll hurt him permanently. Now, are you ready to hand over your ship?"

Ava's resistance crumbled. Her face, streaked with tears, twisted in defeat. "Okay, you win," she whispered. "I'll do it."

"Finally," Gort muttered impatiently, earning him a sharp glare from Smythe.

Ava swallowed hard, fighting to compose herself as she forced out the words she swore she would never say. Her throat felt like sandpaper. "Reggie," she rasped, "deactivate security protocols."

Reggie responded instantly with a hint of concern in her feminine tone. "Captain, I am detecting heightened stress levels. Are you under duress?"

Hiromi and the bounty hunters exchanged glances, surprised by the AI's sudden presence.

"It's okay, Reggie," Ava assured her. "Do as I say. Everything will be fine."

A tense silence followed before Reggie replied, "Order confirmed. Security protocols deactivated."

"Good," Smythe affirmed. "Now transfer control of the ship to Grawn Krunig."

Ava shot him a look of disbelief. "What?"

"That's right," Smythe replied with a twisted smile. "I know Kypa switched out the blue crystal, and while I cannot deliver that, I can at least hand over you and your ship," he boasted. "I'm guessing he'll take great pleasure in making you suffer for all the trouble you've caused him."

Ava sneered. "I don't give a mother-effing-doodoo what you think, bughead."

Smythe paused, briefly admiring her unwavering defiance, even in defeat. He then shifted his gaze to Toma, and his tone grew darker.

"And as for you," he continued. "With you as his prisoner, Krunig will have all the leverage he needs over your father."

Toma grimaced as he lifted himself off the floor. Tears welled in the adolescent's eyes as Smythe's words rang true to his heart. The bounty hunter was right; his father would have to choose between saving his son's life and risking Aiwa's fate. It was an impossible decision that Toma refused to let his father make.

Suddenly, Smythe felt a sharp stabbing sensation in his head. His body jerked involuntarily as the pain escalated to an excruciating level. He stumbled backward, clutching his skull, just as Toma let out a guttural roar.

The young Aiwan's face contorted with pure rage, unleashing a torrent of telepathic energy aimed at the bounty hunter.

Smythe dropped his weapon, clutching his head with both hands as if it was about to explode. The agony was unbearable, like a searing blade twisting in his skull. He cried out and dropped to his knees, writhing in pain.

Gort froze, uncertain what to do, before Hiromi sprang into action. She delivered a decisive karate chop to the base of Toma's neck. The blow instantly severed the telepathic connection to Smythe, sending a jarring shock through Toma's body. He collapsed to the floor, staring up at the ceiling, dazed and confused.

Gort stepped forward, leveling the electrode at Ava's face. He stole a glance at Smythe, who was on one knee, groaning as he shook off the disorienting effects of the attack.

"You okay, boss?" he asked.

"I think so," Smythe stammered a reply, clutching his aching head. He holstered his blaster before coming carefully to his feet and turned to Hiromi. "Thanks, I owe you one."

"You're welcome," the cyborg replied, focusing more on inspecting the back of her hand for scuffs than on the bounty hunter's gratitude.

Smythe turned his attention to Toma, noting the chaotic storm of delirium swirling behind the young Aiwan's eyes.

"Aiwans are lethal, I'll give 'em that," he muttered, catching his breath. Realizing Toma's incapacitation would not last long, he added, "We can't risk another outburst like that."

Smythe placed his hand over Toma's face, secreting a web-like substance laced with a paralytic toxin. The webbing quickly took effect, rendering Toma unconscious.

"Uh-oh," Gort interrupted, glancing at his commlink. "We got company."

Smythe snapped to attention, his first thought being the gracylai. "Where?"

"Ship approaching," Gort replied grimly.

Smythe quickly checked his commlink, projecting a hologram of an ominous warship entering Rogantu's atmosphere. He recognized the shark-finned vessel instantly.

"It's Krunig," he uttered, his two stomachs tightening. "He found us."

Smythe shot a suspicious glare at Gort, who shrugged innocence. His eyes then darted to Hiromi, but her face was unreadable. Yet, his instincts sensed betrayal. Smythe reacted, reaching for his blaster.

But Hiromi was faster.

With a series of smooth, mechanical clicks, the cyborg's nimble, articulated hands transformed into cylindrical gun barrels, locking their sights squarely on Smythe and Gort. The fluidity of her transformation stunned the bounty hunters. Realizing she had them dead to rights, Smythe slowly raised his hands in surrender as Gort dropped the electrode.

"And your holsters," Hiromi prodded.

Smythe and Gort reluctantly obeyed, unbuckling their holsters and allowing them to drop to the floor.

"Was this your plan all along?" Smythe asked.

"No," Hiromi replied casually. "I intended to honor our agreement, but once it became obvious our cause was lost, prudence demanded I revert to my backup plan."

"But you were in the clear," Smythe argued. "We were going to deliver the Reaper to Krunig as planned, and you would've been paid."

"Krunig is no fool," Hiromi explained. "The moment you delayed delivery, he issued a bounty on both your heads, but curiosity got the best of me. The opportunity to slice Aiwan tech seemed too good to pass up ... until it wasn't.

Krunig's paying me triple what you were offering."

Smythe's expression pleaded for understanding. "But the ship is worthless without the blue crystal."

Hiromi shrugged. "That's not my concern. All I know is that Krunig is here to claim the Reaper and deal with you."

A rare shiver of fear ran down Smythe's spine.

"And as for you," Hiromi added, turning her gaze to Ava, "Smythe was right—Grawn Krunig is quite eager to make your acquaintance."

35
REFINERY

Planet Rogantu

Neil and Kypa advanced cautiously in the underground tunnel, gripping their blasters tight. Following the shadowy rail line, they had yet to encounter a gracylai. Still, the evidence of their presence was undeniable: piles of half-digested bone fragments littered their path and, later, patches of sloughed reptilian skin. The question was no longer *if* they would face the creatures but *when*.

"We have to be close," Neil whispered anxiously to Kypa, who was on point.

Kypa activated his HUD and checked their location on the hologram map. "It is not much further," he replied, equally unsettled. He pointed. "There is a stairwell up ahead."

"Thank God," Neil muttered. "This place is giving me the creeps."

No sooner had he conveyed his misgiving than Kypa stopped abruptly. The Aiwan's fist shot up, halting Neil in his tracks. Neil froze, breath catching, as Kypa raised a finger to his mouth, signaling for silence.

Neil dared not to move, his eyes darting around the tunnel in search of hidden threats.

Kypa remained still, his ears straining, trying to discern whether he heard something or if his mind was playing tricks. After a few tense moments of silence, he relaxed and turned back to face Neil.

"Never mind," Kypa said in a low tone. "I thought I heard something."

Neil dropped his shoulders, and he let out a nervous chuckle. "Man, you had me going there for a second. C'mon, let's …"

His thought trailed off as Ten-Tee began tapping his shoulder urgently. Neil cocked his head sideways to answer and caught a faint noise in the distance. He rounded sharply toward the source, eyes widening in alarm. From the shadows emerged a six-foot-long creature, its orange-glowing eyes fixated on them. The centipede-like beast snaked toward them with frightening speed, its many legs skittering across the rail line, filling the air with a rhythmic clatter that grew louder as it approached.

"What the fu—!?" Neil exclaimed.

But his words were drowned out by the recoil of blaster fire. Beside him, Kypa unleashed a continuous barrage aimed at the elusive creature.

Acting on pure adrenaline, Neil followed Kypa's lead, raising his weapon with shaky hands. Panic surged as he squeezed the trigger, firing wildly into the tunnel. The first shots sprayed the area, missing the mark as the creature slithered and weaved with unnerving agility, its serpentine movements proving difficult to anticipate. Desperation mounted as the creature closed the distance alarmingly fast. Neil kept firing in a panic, his aim growing more erratic with each shot.

Kypa landed the first direct hit. His blaster bolt struck true, severing the creature's body in half and sending its upper half tumbling against the far wall.

Neil fired two more shots in quick succession—one hitting the creature's writhing remains in the middle of the tunnel, the other missing high. A brief lull followed, but the reprieve was short-lived. As Neil shifted his aim toward the creature's upper half, he realized, to his horror, that it had already righted itself.

With a blood-curdling screech, the creature bared rows of needle-like fangs and launched its second attack, more enraged than ever.

Neil and Kypa opened fire, working together to create a web of overlapping fire that gave the creature no chance to escape. They finished it quickly, blasting the creature to bits across the tunnel floor.

As the firing ceased, Neil and Kypa kept their weapons poised, sweeping the area in search of more creatures. Their hearts pounded as they stood tense, watching and waiting. An eerie silence followed, save for the crackling sound of the creature's charred remains a few feet away.

The silence stretched longer until Kypa finally exhaled and cautiously lowered his weapon.

"I think we are safe now," he whispered to Neil.

Kypa glanced at his friend and noticed Neil remained in a rigid fighting stance, his weapon still aimed down the tunnel and his hands trembling slightly.

"Neil?" he repeated.

But Neil did not respond. He kept his grip on the weapon tight, knuckles white with tension. His wide, unblinking eyes reflected the shock of his first taste of actual combat.

Kypa gently placed his hand on Neil's blaster, encouraging him to relax. Neil snapped back to the moment. He turned sharply to Kypa, who met his gaze with a reassuring smile.

Realizing the fight was over, Neil lowered his weapon with a sharp exhale. "Sorry," he said, embarrassed. "That was pretty intense."

"No apologies necessary," Kypa said in a hushed tone, clapping his friend's shoulder. "You fought well."

Neil responded with a small grin, then glanced at the creature's smoldering carcass, wrinkling his nose at the acrid stench.

"Is that what killed the workers?" he hissed.

"Probably," Kypa answered quietly, keeping a wary eye on the tunnel for more creatures. "The gracylai are harder to kill than I imagined."

Gracylai, Neil mused, imagining a swarm of the nasty creatures and grimaced. Just one proved near impossible to stop, and the thought of facing more sent a chill through him.

"Well," Neil said with a sigh, "if they didn't know we were here before, they do now."

Kypa nodded, sharing the same grim thought. "We should keep moving."

They pressed on, reaching the tunnel's end a few minutes later. A stairwell loomed ahead, identical to the one they descended back at the outpost. Ten-Tee detached itself, hopping off Neil's back. Just before hitting the ground, the tiny droid activated the repulsors under its feet and came to a hover. It then floated effortlessly toward the stairwell and ascended the steps.

Kypa followed, blaster ready. Neil trailed behind, covering their backsides as he ascended the steps cautiously.

Ten-Tee waited for them at the top of the landing—no longer airborne. The tiny droid jittered in place, bouncing up and down in an unmistakable display of alarm. Kypa froze mid-step, his instincts flaring. Neil, unprepared for the sudden stop, stumbled into him from behind. He caught himself, narrowly avoiding a noisy misstep. Kypa glanced back to ensure he was alright, then raised a long finger to his lips, his gaze sharp with a silent command for absolute quiet.

"*Stay here*," Kypa communicated, reverting back to telepathy.

Neil nodded vigorously, shooting a glance at Ten-Tee, who stepped back and swiveled its head toward an unseen threat. Neil swallowed the lump in his throat as Kypa crept slowly up the steps.

Reaching the top of the stairs, Kypa immediately understood Ten-Tee's warning. The pocket door was partially ajar, its metal frame mangled and warped as though something massive had forced its way through. Deep gouges scarred the door, the jagged marks telling the tale of a fierce struggle.

Kypa signaled Ten-Tee to stay put, then tentatively approached the door. Leading with his blaster, he peeked inside the twisted doorway and found the adjacent corridor empty. Yet, the blood-spattered walls confirmed his worst fears. An intense battle had raged here. The walls were scorched with blaster fire and blackened from explosions. But even more troubling was the absence of bodies—the fallen were gone.

Eaten, Kypa surmised.

Taking a calming breath, he summoned his courage to proceed inside. Contorting his tall and lean body, Kypa carefully ducked through the mangled threshold. He placed his feet precisely, avoiding the shards of glass littering the floor, and tip-toed his way to the end of the corridor.

Heart pounding, Kypa approached a second door, which also showed signs of forced entry. He paused, examining the damage. Whatever had breached the facility was far larger than the creature they had encountered in the tunnel. A chill ran through him as he realized how unprepared they were to face a threat of this magnitude.

Kypa peered through the gap in the door, discovering it led to an empty control room. He entered cautiously, sweeping every nook and cranny with the barrel of his weapon. Satisfied the room was clear, he relaxed slightly and moved toward a large, shattered window overlooking the refinery's main production floor. From this vantage, Kypa took in an array of hulking machinery—stone-crushing grinders and long conveyor belts stretching into the distance. Above, dormant cranes with oversized metal claws hung like giant hands, ready to move massive boulders from one end of the refinery to the other.

"*Neil, it is safe to proceed*," Kypa called telepathically. "*Beware the glass on the floor, and remember, no noise.*"

Moments later, Neil poked his head inside the corridor. He spotted Kypa at the opposite end, waving him forward. Neil nodded and started toward him, with Ten-Tee again perched on his back. Wincing as he carefully navigated the glass-strewn floor, Neil could not help but feel a bit like *Indiana Jones* in a temple filled with booby traps.

Reaching the end, he sidestepped through the doorway and entered the control room. Inside, he found Kypa standing in front of a long, rectangular console adorned with buttons, switches, and inactive screens and lights. Neil joined him and gazed out the broken window to the production floor. He noted the thick layer of volcanic dust coating every inch of the refinery's interior, a clear testament to its long-abandoned state. Yet, the eerie stillness only heightened his unease.

Kypa craned his neck, glancing out the broken window to the production floor's vaulted ceiling. Several glass panels were shattered or missing, exposing Rogantu's blood-red sky beyond.

"At least the storm has passed," he whispered, grateful for small mercies.

Neil did not reply. He was too distracted by the empty chairs at the console, imagining the workers attacked by the gracylai.

Kypa turned his attention to the production floor below, where he counted ten rows of massive storage bins in the middle of the expansive room. Several bins were still filled with rocks, left behind by the company in its rush to escape the facility.

Parallel to these bins were large conveyor belts, each extending the length of the production floor and angled upward at a forty-five-degree angle. Feed hoppers connected to the conveyors at the lower end. Working out the process, Kypa assumed rocks were extracted from the bins and dumped into the hoppers to be broken into manageable chunks. The rocks were then fed onto the conveyors and transported to the grinders at the opposite end, three stories up.

Kypa tracked the conveyors' path from right to left above the production floor. The awaiting grinders crushed the rock into tiny pebbles at the high end before pushing them into a hydrocyclone. This machine blasted the pebbles, pulverizing them into dust with a high-pressure vortex of water. In this process, the overflow of water and dirt was separated from the dense minerals and ores and pumped out. The heavier materials were then collected and readied for off-world shipment.

Kypa turned to Ten-Tee and whispered, "Scan the area for life signs."

The tiny droid's twin photoreceptors lit up as it began scanning the refinery in a systematic grid pattern. Ten-Tee chirped excitedly upon detecting lifeforms in the adjacent landing bay, but Kypa quickly hushed it. Obediently, Ten-Tee fell silent, projecting a hologram of the entire facility, highlighting five beings nearby.

Kypa brightened at the digital projection of Ava and Toma. They were alive but being held at gunpoint outside the bounty hunter's freighter—and they were not alone in captivity. Kypa recognized the insectoid he fought on the Aiwan beach. The bounty hunter was on his knees beside Ava, Toma, and a frog-like creature—all four held at bay by a gentle-looking being with blasters for hands.

"It's them!" Neil hissed. "But who are the others?" he asked, puzzled by seeing additional hostages.

"This one is the bounty hunter," Kypa replied, pointing out Smythe. "The other one must be his partner. It looks like a deal gone bad," he speculated, adding another layer of complexity to their mission.

"Ten-Tee, any sign of gracylai?" Kypa whispered.

Ten-Tee conducted a quick scan, then shook its head to indicate negative results.

"What do you think?" Neil asked.

"Two of us against three of them," Kypa mused. "Those are good odds."

"Yeah, well, as Mike Tyson used to say, everyone's got a plan until you get punched in the face," Neil joked.

Kypa started to reply when the entire facility suddenly began rumbling. The decrepit refinery's steel beams groaned as dust fell from the rafters. Bracing himself, Kypa instinctively glanced at the console, assuming the machines had come to life, but they remained inert.

"More tremors?" Neil asked, holding onto one of the chairs for support.

For a moment, Kypa thought the same—until a massive shadow swept over them, plunging the factory floor into darkness. Kypa looked skyward and spotted a menacing warship through the refinery's glass ceiling. He recognized the ship immediately and realized the unsettling truth: Grawn Krunig had arrived.

Recalling the warship from the space battle at Aiwa, Neil said quietly, "Is that who I think it is?"

Kypa did not answer; his mind was already at work. He retrieved two explosive grenades from his vest and handed them to Neil. "Take these," he urged. "We do not have much time."

36
PARADISE RANCH

Planet Earth
Groom Lake, Nevada

The pilot of the Airbus ACJ319neo waited patiently near the aircraft's forward exit, occasionally flashing an apologetic smile at the increasingly annoyed United States Secret Service agent positioned in the open doorway. The agent's frustration was evident as he glanced toward the rear of the aircraft, where Edmund Mathias, the plane's owner, casually passed the time. With Luna and Ms. Diaz seated near him, Edmund scrolled through his phone, humming to himself as he checked the outside temperature—upper 70s and clear skies.

The luxury jet had touched down fifteen minutes earlier at the Nevada Test and Training Range—once called Paradise Ranch to entice workers to the facility, but now it was commonly referred to as Area 51 by UFO enthusiasts. Since its arrival, the aircraft had remained parked at its designated location on the tarmac, surrounded by Secret Service and a cadre of U.S. Air Force security personnel. Though the engines had long since powered down and the boarding stairs moved into place, Edmund purposely held off deplaning for one simple reason: President Fitzgerald.

Outside, the president stood in the mid-day sun at the end of a long red carpet that stretched from his position to the base of the stairs beside Mathias's plane. To his left were the leaders of Japan, Germany, and Great Britain, with Secretary of State Bill Nguyen at the far end. Ernie Gutierrez, General Dukes, Admiral Donnelly, and Colonel Marlana Nunez stood on the president's right. They, too, were growing equally impatient.

Resisting the urge to glance at his watch, Fitzgerald recognized this delay as Mathias's subtle display of his power.

Petty and predictable, the president mused.

Ernie leaned close and asked, "Mr. President, shall I go see what the holdup is?"

Fitzgerald opened his mouth to reply when he spotted the Secret Service agent inside the aircraft starting down the stairs.

"Standby, Ernie. Looks like he's finally going to grace us with his presence," the president commented sourly.

Around him, the official welcome party straightened. The international delegation anxiously awaited the arrival of Aiwa's second visitor to Earth. However, their anticipation tempered slightly when Mathias, not Luna, emerged first from the aircraft.

Locating the president below, Edmund waved from afar with a cocky grin.

"Look at that smug SOB, waving to us like he just found Wonka's golden ticket," Fitzgerald muttered, eliciting a chuckle from Ernie.

"You can't polish a turd," Nunez chimed in, loud enough to draw attention.

In unison, heads turned to her—except for General Dukes, who closed his eyes in mortified silence, cringing at his subordinate's blunt remark.

Down the line, Fitzgerald smiled wryly, appreciating Nunez's levity and spot-on assessment of Mathias.

"Sorry, sir," Nunez said, suppressing a smirk, "just something my grandpa used to say."

"Your grandfather deserves a medal," he replied. Joking aside, Fitzgerald refocused on Mathias. "Okay, everyone, let's get this over with."

Taking his cue, the president strode down the red carpet accompanied by the other heads of state. At the foot of the stairs, a pair of Air Force officers assigned to Air Force One stood at attention. The senior of the two raised a crisp salute, which Fitzgerald returned swiftly.

Edmund lingered at the top of the stairs, watching the four world leaders take their places below. As he began his descent, Mathias's eyes swept the rooftops, noting the snipers perched on the nearby buildings. He grinned, confident in the knowledge they could not touch him.

Reaching the last step, Edmund paused, savoring the warmth of the Nevada sun on his face. He took a deep breath, taking in his triumphant return to American soil, then hopped off the final step. He landed squarely in front of Fitzgerald with a flourish.

"Aah," Edmund exhaled, grinning. "It's good to be home."

Edmund extended his hand to the president, who glanced at it briefly before turning his attention back to the aircraft's opening.

"Aren't you forgetting someone?" Fitzgerald asked, his tone dripping with sarcasm.

Edmund pouted theatrically. "What, no love for the prodigal son's return?" Frowning, he shifted his gaze to the other leaders. "Aren't you going to introduce us?"

"Cut the crap," Fitzgerald snapped. "We're not here for you. This is a marriage of convenience. Nothing more."

Edmund clicked his tongue in mock disappointment. "And here I thought we'd let bygones be bygones."

"Not a chance," the president shot back, his patience wearing thin. "Now, where's Luna?"

Edmund held Fitzgerald's gaze, clearly enjoying how much he was getting under the president's skin.

"You're such a killjoy," Edmund joked. "No wonder I didn't vote for you." He wiggled his finger at the pilot, signaling him to send the others down. "Very well," he said with a heavy breath. "I hope you're happy."

The first to appear in the doorway was Ms. Diaz. After a quick scan of the surroundings, she started down the steps. Luna followed. Pausing at the top of the stairs, she took in the scene—the soldiers posted around the hangar, the dignitaries lined up along the red carpet, and the sense of tension hanging in the air.

Luna narrowed her gaze as she scanned the crowd. The one person she longed to see was Rose, but she was nowhere in sight. Suppressing a flicker of disappointment, Luna made her way down the steps.

Meanwhile, Edmund was busy introducing Ms. Diaz to the world leaders. Fitzgerald greeted her with a distracted nod, his focus shifting to Luna. As the Aiwan descended the stairs, she and Fitzgerald locked eyes in a moment of historical significance. Their smiles were friendly but curious, signaling a mutual understanding of how important this meeting was for both of their worlds.

When Luna reached the bottom of the stairs, Edmund stepped in front of the president, extending his hand to Luna. She accepted, and Mathias guided her onto the red carpet.

"Mr. President," Edmund announced with exaggerated pomp, "it is my distinct honor to introduce you to my dear friend and business partner, Luna, from the planet, Aiwa."

Fitzgerald bowed his head respectfully. Keenly aware of the Aiwan's telepathic abilities—a detail Ernie reminded him of no fewer than ten times during the flight from D.C.—he refrained from physical contact.

"Luna, welcome to Earth and to the United States of America," he said warmly. "We are honored by your presence."

Luna dipped her chin in acknowledgment. "Mr. President, it is a pleasure to meet you. On behalf of all Aiwans, I extend my gratitude for your willingness to bridge our worlds in partnership during this time of great need."

"Indeed," the president affirmed. He then introduced the leaders of Japan, Germany, and Great Britain. After they exchanged salutations, Fitzgerald added, "Today marks a continuation of the friendship we began with your esteemed leader, Prince Kypa. I pray that you will soon be reunited with him and your people."

The sincerity of Fitzgerald's words struck a chord with Luna. Although she could not connect with him telepathically, her first impression aligned with what Rose had shared back in Peru—the president was an honorable man. Fitzgerald's kind treatment of her beloved prince and dear friend, Kypa, would not be forgotten.

Luna bowed her head again, deeply appreciative.

Fitzgerald gestured to the far end of the red carpet. "This way, please. I'd like to introduce you to the rest of my leadership team before we take you to Kypa's escape pod."

Luna fell into step beside Fitzgerald, followed by the other three heads of state, with Edmund and Ms. Diaz trailing behind. The group made their way toward the hangar, where Fitzgerald went down the line, introducing Luna to his team, starting with Secretary Nguyen. Introductions continued, with everyone visibly captivated by the Aiwan's presence. Like Prince Kypa, Luna exuded a dignified grace, and her command of the English language was remarkable, considering how little time had passed since her crash in North Korea.

Mathias received a far less enthusiastic welcome. He introduced himself alongside Ms. Diaz, but their reception was icy. Yet, Edmund remained unfazed, relishing the discomfort his presence stirred among the group.

Things got interesting when Ms. Diaz met Marlana. Both women exchanged polite smiles.

"Colonel Nunez," Diaz greeted, offering a handshake.

Nunez glanced at Diaz's hand cursorily but kept her own pinned at her sides. Her brow furrowing, she asked, "Have we met?"

"Not formally, no," Diaz remarked, smirking at the slight and retracting her hand. "I recognized you from the security footage in Satipo."

Edmund, who was about to follow Fitzgerald and the others out of the hangar, halted at the mention of Peru. His interest piqued, he paused, listening as the conversation unfolded.

Nunez's forced smile tightened. "I'm afraid I don't know what you're talking about."

"Come now," Diaz cooed, her voice sickly sweet, "we all have blood on our hands here … including your husband, Hector."

Marlana locked eyes with Diaz. She pictured relieving Edmund's assistant of a few teeth, but self-restraint prevailed.

"Sorry, not ringing a bell," Nunez said coolly. "Although, I did hear about what happened in Peru … such a shame," she added, shaking her head with mock sympathy. "But while you're tidying up, you might want to think about restocking your cleaning supplies."

Diaz's eyes flashed with fury beneath her composed exterior; she understood the barb all too well. Nunez had infiltrated Mathais's facility under the guise of a housekeeper. She and the traitor, Lalo, pulled off a flawless diversion that facilitated the rescue of Rose Landry and Choi Min-jun.

"Ah, Colonel Nunez," Edmund interjected smoothly. "No longer one of Garza's puppets, I see." He noticed Marlana's jaw clench slightly and grinned. "By the way, thanks for the tip. I'd share it with your friend, Senōr Salazar, and … oh, what's the name of that sweet old housekeeper of his?" he asked Diaz, pretending to struggle to remember.

"Camila," Diaz replied icily.

"Ah yes, Camila," Edmund said, smirking. "I was truly saddened to hear that she and Eduardo—along with your soldier friends — are no longer with us."

Marlana's fists balled at her sides, and she was on the verge of throwing down when General Dukes stepped between her and Mathias, his massive frame blocking the confrontation.

"We're done here," Dukes said with a stone-cold glare. "If you've got more to say, you say it to me."

Edmund looked up at Dukes towering over him, the top of his head barely reaching the brigadier general's chest ribbons. He scoffed at the physical disparity, knowing he made more in a day than this career officer earned in a year.

With a feigned air of boredom, Edmund took his assistant's hand. "Come along, Ms. Diaz. We've had our fun—the natives are getting restless," he said, leading her away.

Fitzgerald and Luna missed the tense exchange. They were already on their way to the president's limousine. As they arrived, a Secret Service agent opened the back door. The foreign leaders joined them, along with Edmund, who insisted on staying close to Luna.

Diaz climbed into the front seat of the trailing SUV while Ernie and the others settled into the back for what turned out to be a brief drive across the base. The six-vehicle motorcade, flanked by the president's security detail, arrived minutes later at a beige Quonset hut that looked right out of the 1950s.

After parking, the group of VIPs followed General Dukes inside, where the base's longest-tenured employee greeted them, Ms. Norma Jean Stanton. Her genial smile showed no sign of being fazed by the presence of Luna.

President Fitzgerald approached Norma Jean warmly. "Hello again, Ms. Stanton. Long time, no see."

Norma Jean flashed a flirtatious smile. "Good to see you again, Mr. President," she said, winking playfully.

Following protocol, Norma Jean retrieved a plastic bin from beneath the counter and placed it in front of the president, along with a logbook dating back to the Eisenhower administration. Raising her voice slightly so she would not have to repeat herself, Norma Jean instructed the group, "Please sign in and leave all electronic devices in the bin. Thank you."

One by one, the group stepped forward, signed the logbook, and deposited their devices in the bin. Once they passed through security, they entered an elevator that took them down to the underground levels of Area 51. From there, they boarded Segway PUMAs to traverse the massive tunnel leading to Area S4, the ultra-secretive site that housed the United States' most advanced technologies.

Exiting the tunnel, General Dukes led the group through a series of sterile corridors, his spit-shined Corcoran dress shoes echoing off the walls. At the rear of the procession, Mathias fondly recalled the years of U.S.-funded cloning and force enhancement experiments he once conducted here at Groom Lake. That research alone was poised to make Mathias Industries the largest publicly traded company in the world, with a market cap estimated to be around four trillion USD.

Surveying his old stomping grounds, Edmund called up to Dukes,

"Perhaps Luna would like to see the cell, er rather, the *quarters* where Prince Kypa stayed?"

Dukes stopped at a T-junction and glanced at the president for guidance.

"Luna, are you interested in seeing where Kypa stayed?" Fitzgerald asked.

Luna nodded. "Yes, please. That would be most kind."

"As you wish," the president replied, gesturing for Dukes to proceed.

Dukes turned left instead of right, leading the group down a narrow hallway until they arrived at room T101. Holding the door open, he ushered them into an observation area. Before them, fogged, shatterproof windows concealed the view. Dukes stepped up to the control panel on the wall and pressed a button, causing the glass to clear and reveal Kypa's former room.

"Shame it's empty," Edmund said with mock disappointment. "I was hoping to say hello to Garza and Sizemore while I was here. Oh wait, I forgot," he corrected himself, pretending to slap his forehead. "They both cut deals to testify against me … but I guess that's a moot point now, huh?"

Fitzgerald did not take the bait. While Mathias's diplomatic immunity shielded him from prosecution on American soil, the president knew nothing could stop the United States from aiding other nations in building a criminal case against him.

"This is where Prince Kypa was held?" Luna asked, running her hand along the protective glass.

Fitzgerald sighed. There was no sense denying the truth. "It is," he admitted solemnly. "I'm ashamed to say two individuals acting under my command unlawfully detained your prince. They had help, of course," he added, casting a sharp look at Mathias, "but thanks to the brave actions of people like Colonel Nunez here, your prince was freed."

"Water under the bridge. Right, Luna?" Edmund chuckled nervously.

Luna did not reply. She knew the truth about Mathias's involvement in Kypa's detention as well as his twisted ambitions to splice Aiwan DNA with animal and human genomes—all to create a force enhancement serum. And it was only a matter of time before he moved on to a hybrid clone. But like the American president, Luna was bound in a fragile alliance. She could not tip her hand too soon or risk turning Edmund against her. She had to play the long game.

"Speaking of water," Nunez interjected, breaking the tense silence, "would you like to see Kypa's private pool?"

The change of subject was a welcome reprieve. Luna accepted with a graceful bow.

"Perfect," Nunez replied, suppressing a knowing grin. She gestured to the door. "This way."

Marlana led them back into the corridor to an adjacent room just one door down. She held the door open for Luna, allowing her to enter first.

Inside, Luna could not help but notice the large, above-ground pool that dominated the center of the room. Her gaze quickly settled on two women standing beside the ladder—one with long dark hair pulled into a ponytail and the other sporting curly red locks. Both women had their backs to the door when Luna entered.

Jessica Aguri turned to the sound of footsteps echoing in the room. Upon recognizing the VIPs, especially Luna, she grinned and tugged at her friend's sleeve.

Luna's eyes lit up in surprise as she immediately recognized the red-haired woman. Excitement bubbled within her at the sight of her dear friend, Dr. Rose Landry.

37
STRIKES AND GUTTERS

Planet Earth
Area S4, Groom Lake, Nevada

Rose brushed away unexpected tears as she hurried toward Luna. Just as she reached out, Luna paused, stopping short of the embrace. Rose froze, momentarily puzzled, before she understood Luna's intent. Their eyes met, a silent agreement passing between them to maintain their charade and avoid physical contact.

Still, Rose could not keep her feelings contained. "I should've never left you behind," she whispered, her voice unsteady as fresh tears threatened to spill. "Everything happened so fast."

In response, Luna re-established their telepathic connection, her mind reaching out to soothe Rose's turmoil.

"*It is alright,*" she said gently. "*We are both safe, and you made it home to your family. That is all that matters.*"

Rose hesitated, realizing what Luna had done, and mentally switched to their incognito mode. "*But you're alone,*" she silently replied, guilt wrapping around her thoughts. "*I never should have left you.*"

Luna responded with a chuckle. "*And yet, here we are—together again in another underground lab.*"

Rose nearly guffawed when Edmund interjected. "Are you two just going to stand there, staring at each other? C'mon, time is money," he said, tapping his watch. "Let's pump the brakes on this Hallmark moment and get back to business, shall we?"

President Fitzgerald shook his head at Mathias's jerk remark. Stepping forward with a gentle smile, he offered Rose his handkerchief. "Nice to see you again, Dr. Landry."

Rose flushed with embarrassment as she accepted it. "Sorry, Mr. President."

Fitzgerald waved dismissively. "No apologies necessary," he said warmly. "The bond you two share is a testament to the friendship Kypa envisioned."

"Blah, blah, blah," Edmund mocked, turning his hand into a talking puppet. "But, in all sincerity, it's good to see my dear old friend, Dr. Landry, once again."

He stepped forward, arms outstretched, as if to hug Rose, but she took a deliberate step back to rebuff him. Edmund froze mid-motion and left with his arms awkwardly suspended, like a mannequin caught in a forced pose.

"This must be a 'No Hugging' zone," Edmund remarked, his grin faltering as he lowered his arms and stepped back.

Rose's eyes swept the group until they landed on Ms. Diaz, the only other representative from Mathias Industries. "So, where's your henchman?" she asked, her tone pointed.

Edmund's eyes narrowed as he studied his former mentor. Rose met his gaze, her stare unwavering. The tension between them swelled, thick with unspoken animosity. Rose's words were not a casual jab but a calculated blow. She knew how much Renzo meant to Edmund and was all too aware that the Chachapoyan died badly at the hands of her friend, Min-jun.

At least, she was meant to believe so.

Edmund managed a tight-lipped smile, remaining silent. But as he watched Rose side with Fitzgerald, her eyes gleaming with a sharp, hostile edge, the fragile hope for her approval shattered within him. The realization struck harder than he expected—it was time to let the past go. Rose was no longer just a sweet old grandmother or a former colleague; she was the enemy now.

He responded with unshaken confidence as though his armor remained undented.

"Yes, losing Mr. Renzo was a bitter pill to swallow," Edmund admitted, "as was the damage to my facility. But fortunately, I found an extra twenty million dollars lying around to cover the repairs."

Rose barely reacted, shrugging as if his words held no weight. "I never wanted your blood money to begin with," she snapped.

Edmund opened his mouth, ready to retort, but President Fitzgerald cut him off sharply. "I suggest we move on," he said. It was not a request.

The room fell silent for an uncomfortable moment, and then General Dukes' deep voice broke the tension.

"Hangar 17 is this way," he said, gesturing toward the exit. "If you'd kindly follow me, I'll take you to Kypa's escape pod."

The tension between Edmund and Rose remained a moment longer, then with a casual shift, Edmund turned his attention to Luna.

"Shall we?" he said, offering her his arm, a clear reminder of their partnership.

Luna did not hesitate to accept, knowing her choice might hurt Rose. As she turned to leave, Luna's eyes briefly met Rose's. "*It will be okay*," she discreetly assured her friend.

Though Rose remained unconvinced, she said nothing as she watched them depart. Her worry for Luna's well-being deepened when Edmund glanced back, flashed a smug grin, and stuck out his tongue at her.

Fury boiled to the surface as Rose parted her lips to hurl an expletive in response, but Fitzgerald gently placed a calming hand on her shoulder, stopping her before she could speak.

The president leaned in and whispered low and steady in her ear, "Don't give him the satisfaction."

Caught between duty and friendship, Rose nodded, suppressing her rising emotions. Whenever Edmund cozied up to Luna, it grated on her nerves like fingernails on a chalkboard.

Taking a deep breath, Rose composed herself and followed the procession down the corridor. A short time later, they arrived at Hangar 17. General Dukes approached the cipher lock on the door just as the familiar, whimsical notes of *Magical Mystery Tour* by The Beatles resonated through the walls.

Dukes smiled sheepishly at the president. "That would be Dr. Persons," he said with a hint of apology. "He's a bit of a fanatic."

"So am I," Fitzgerald admitted with a chuckle.

The door unlocked, and a buzzer sounded—its sharp tone drowned out by the music. Dukes entered, holding the door open for the president and their distinguished guests.

The enormity of the underground hangar caught Luna by surprise, but her breath caught at the familiar sight of the Aiwan escape pod. The last time she saw it was aboard the crippled mothership, watching Prince Kypa—injured and unconscious—jettisoned to Earth. The helplessness of that moment had haunted her for months, compounded by the guilt of not knowing if he was dead or alive. Rose had eventually set her straight, but now Luna's heart ached for home more than ever.

Noticing Luna's captivated expression, Fitzgerald asked, "Look familiar?"

Luna nodded. "Yes, the last time I saw Prince Kypa, he was in that pod."

"We recovered it off the coast of Kauai," the president explained as they walked. "Dr. Landry mentioned you were searching that area when Mathias captured you."

Edmund raised his finger in point of contention. "Rescued, actually," he clarified. "Luna's always been free to come and go as she pleases."

Fitzgerald glanced at Luna, gauging her reaction to Mathias's claim. She remained mum on the subject, choosing not to contradict Edmund.

"I searched everywhere for my prince," Luna offered instead. "Several sea dwellers in the area pointed me to the location where Kypa landed, but by the time I arrived, he had already been rescued."

"Sea dwellers?" Fitzgerald repeated, sounding incredulous. "You mean you spoke to dolphins and whales?"

Luna shrugged and responded, "Of course. Who else would I ask? It is their home."

Feeling foolish, Fitzgerald nodded understanding. Inwardly, the gravity of Luna's profound words began to sink in. It was apparent to Fitzgerald that his worldview needed to evolve. He had already believed that humanity was destroying the planet, but this new awareness toward ocean dwellers underscored a broader responsibility to all living creatures.

The music abruptly cut off, the last notes echoing faintly through the cavernous hangar before gradually fading into silence. As the group crossed the hangar, Dr. Persons emerged from behind a cluster of research equipment. He was flanked by the rest of the project team, each wearing a white lab coat. They approached the delegation in front of the pod.

"Mr. President ... distinguished guests, it is an honor to have you here," the mop-haired scientist greeted. Dr. Persons then cast a wary glance at Luna. His last encounter with an Aiwan involved Kypa threatening to use mind control on him after thwarting an arrest attempt made by General Garza. Swallowing hard, he addressed Luna. "Welcome, I'm Dr. Richard Persons, he began. "I'll be leading Operation Nightshade alongside my esteemed colleagues from Japan, Germany, and Great Britain." He gestured toward the team, each offering excited nods of acknowledgment.

Luna bowed cordially, her presence exuding calm despite the scientist's evident nerves. "Greetings, Dr. Persons, and to all of you." she said warmly, her gaze sweeping across the group. "Tell me, what is your impression of Aiwan engineering?"

"Remarkable," Persons exclaimed, his enthusiasm breaking through. "Studying your designs has been the highlight of my career."

"That is kind of you to say," Luna replied graciously. "I look forward to collaborating with each of you, and merging human and Aiwan technologies against our common enemies."

Her words were met with a round of applause from Persons and his team, their enthusiasm palpable as they expressed their support.

Luna turned to President Fitzgerald. "With your permission, I think it would be best if we began immediately."

"By all means," the president agreed, stepping aside. "You heard her, everyone—let's make ourselves scarce so they can get to work."

As Fitzgerald and the others made their way to the exit, the atmosphere buzzed with excitement. The foreign leaders were already briefed on Operation Nightshade and given a tour of the pod, so now it was up to their technical teams to re-task the military satellites for the mission. Under Dr. Persons' supervision, they would oversee Luna's access to the top-secret equipment. And despite the looming concerns over cybersecurity—an ever-present, four-ton elephant in the room—the atmosphere was charged with a spirit of cooperation and shared purpose. Everyone was eager to contribute to a higher cause.

Everyone except Rose.

As the VIPs departed, Dr. Landry hesitated, her thoughts lingering on Luna. She wanted to share so many unspoken words, but above all, she dearly missed her Aiwan friend.

Dr. Persons noticed Rose standing by herself. Puzzled, he asked politely, "Dr. Landry, did you forget something?"

As Luna started toward the computer stations, surrounded by the technical team, she overheard Dr. Persons and halted abruptly. She rounded to find Rose alone in the middle of the hangar. Concerned, she excused herself and approached her friend.

"Rose, what is wrong?" Luna asked.

Rose initially tried to brush it off, but her fidgeting hands betrayed her unease. Embarrassed, she stuffed them in her pockets. "Sorry," she chuckled nervously, rolling her eyes.

"No need to apologize," Luna said gently, sensing Rose's distress. "You look troubled."

Taking his cue, Dr. Persons silently excused himself and rejoined the team, steering them back to work.

As Luna stepped closer, Rose met her gaze on the verge of tears. "I know I'm being ridiculous, and you can handle yourself, but I can't stand by and watch you with him. You're not alone in this," she said earnestly.

They both knew she was referring to Mathias.

Lowering her voice, Luna replied, "I can handle Edmund. Just know that I am right where I need to be. Trust me."

Rose looked into Luna's striking blue eyes and saw a determined glint. Yet, despite Luna's confidence, Rose could not shake the worry for her friend and whatever endgame she was planning.

"Be careful," Rose cautioned softly.

"*Always,*" Luna replied telepathically. "*There is something you can help with—can you get word to the British government?* Rose nodded slightly. "*Edmund's mate, Deanna, is a British agent. He tried to have her killed, but I helped her escape. She is on her own in the jungle outside Satipo. Can you help her?*"

Taken aback by this revelation, Rose imagined Deanna running through the jungle, alone and defenseless. But there was no time for questions.

"*I'll tell Jessica,*" Rose replied. "*She can help.*"

"*Thank you,*" Luna said, a flicker of worry crossing her face. "*I hope it is not too late.*"

"Doctor Landry!" General Dukes called from across the hangar.

Snapping back to the moment, Rose turned to find the president and the others waiting near the exit. Realizing she was out of time, Rose faced Luna and asked, "When can we talk again?"

The urge to reach out and take Rose's hands in hers was tempting, but Luna resisted. "Soon, I promise," she assured her friend. "But first, I must focus on building this array while there is still a chance to stop the harvesters."

Later that evening, Rose sat alone on the bed in the same room Captain Tan had occupied months earlier during Operation Sundiver. She stared distantly at her closet door, her mind light years away. As much as she worried about Luna, Rose's thoughts drifted to her other friends halfway across the galaxy.

They had not heard so much as a peep from Ava, Neil, and Kypa since they departed Earth. But what troubled her most was the silence after activating Kypa's beacon. He had sworn he would come if she pressed it. Yet, his lingering absence only fueled her growing fears that something bad had happened to the three of them.

A sudden knock at the door jolted Rose from her thoughts. When she opened it, she found Jessica standing in the hall with a mischievous grin on her face.

Rose smiled, welcoming the distraction. "Tell me you brought alcohol," she said, her tone almost pleading.

Jessica chuckled. "Nunez had a hunch you'd say that," she replied. "C'mon, grab your things. We're going out."

Rose gave her a curious look. "I'm almost afraid to ask."

"Marlana's husband won some election, so we're going to her place to celebrate," Jessica explained. "She's waiting for us topside."

"What the hell," Rose said with a shrug. "I don't have to work tomorrow."

Rose grabbed her coat and purse and followed her friend to the elevator. The doors closed, and she broke the silence as they ascended to the top floor. "I'm glad we have a moment alone," Rose said, her tone slightly hesitant. "I've been meaning to talk to you. I need your help."

Jessica turned to her, curiosity piqued. "Of course. What's going on?"

"Can you get word to the British government?"

Jessica blinked in surprise. "I can, but why? Are you in trouble?"

"Not me," Rose assured her. "I'm asking for Luna. She helped Mathis's girlfriend escape his facility in Peru. Apparently, Edmund tried to kill her—turns out she's a British spy."

Jessica's draw dropped. "He tried to kill Deanna?"

Rose raised an eyebrow, impressed but not surprised that Jessica knew. "You know her?"

"Not personally," Jessica answered, "but the Brits were pissed about how your rescue went down. We had no idea they had an asset in place, and Deanna was there when the choppers moved in. Luckily, she wasn't hurt in the crossfire, but they sure let us hear about it."

"Well, I think they'll appreciate the gesture," Rose said. "I just hope Deanna's okay."

"Yeah, me too," Jessica replied somberly, knowing the odds were against her. "I'll make a call."

"Thank you," Rose said, grateful to support Luna, even in a small way.

A bell chimed, signaling their arrival. The doors opened, and they stepped into the lobby. Norma Jean had their cell phones ready and handed them over when they signed out.

"Colonel Nunez is waiting outside," Ms. Stanton said warmly.

As they stepped out of the Quonset hut, they spotted Nunez waiting in her Honda CR-V with the window rolled down and a yacht rock tune blaring.

"Hop in, chicas!" she called out, punctuating her words with a playful honk of the horn.

Suppressing a laugh, Rose raised an eyebrow and warned Jessica, "Just remember, this was your idea."

They climbed into the vehicle and sped away toward the main gate. As the excitement died down, Rose gazed out the window from the back seat. The sun dipped behind the jagged summit of Worthington Peak, painting the sky with brilliant oranges, pinks, and purples that cast a warm glow over the desert. Wildflowers were starting to bloom, signaling the arrival of spring. Normally, this was Rose's favorite time of year—gardening season—but with everything happening, it did not feel like renewal.

Still in disbelief that she was back at Area S4, Rose exhaled heavily and said, "I thought I was done with this place after Kypa left."

Sitting up front, Jessica twisted in her seat to face Rose. "Well, hopefully, your part will be over soon, and you can go home."

Rose sighed. "God, I hope so. I think it's time to retire and go play in the dirt full time."

Jessica grinned. "A gardener, huh?"

"Yeah, it's my happy place," Rose replied, her smile softening. "Strawberry season is my favorite; they are the first fruits to ripen. Unfortunately, the chipmunks like them, too. I try to plant enough to share, but sometimes those critters drive me crazy." She turned back to Jessica. "But I could talk about strawberries and chipmunks all day. What about you? How are things at the CIA?"

"Oh, you know, strikes and gutters," Jessica said with a shrug.

Marlana gave her a curious look. "Strikes and gutters? Are you a bowler or something?"

Jessica chuckled. "Not me, but my dad was. Whenever you'd ask him how things were going, he'd reply, 'Strikes and gutters—good and bad.'"

Rose grinned, appreciating the simple metaphor. "I haven't bowled in years. Back when Joe and I were dating, he'd take me to the bowling alley on campus. It was free, thank goodness—we didn't have a nickel between us."

"Aw, that's sweet," Jessica said with a kind smile. "My dad worked midnight shifts his whole career, so we didn't see him much. But every Saturday morning as soon as he got home, he'd stay up and take me and my sisters to the bowling alley." Her face lit up with a fond grin. "We loved it because they had free donuts." She chuckled. "It was his way of spoiling us, but honestly, the best part was just having him all to ourselves. Those mornings? I wouldn't trade them for anything."

Moments later, they pulled into Marlana's neighborhood and parked in the driveway of her modest, ranch-style home. A "Hector for President" sign was planted on the front lawn while *Don't Stop* by Fleetwood Mac filled the street with an upbeat melody.

As the others began to climb out of the vehicle, Jessica's phone lit up. She stayed seated, her gaze fixed on the screen. Reading the message, her expression grew darker with each passing moment.

Seconds later, Marlana's phone buzzed. She reached into her purse and pulled it out, her attention shifting to the message with the same intensity.

Rose's eyes flicked between them, the timing too deliberate to be coincidental. Sensing something was off, she asked, "Strike or gutter, ladies?"

In perfect unison, Jessica and Marlana answered with a frown, "Gutter."

38
SMOKING GUN

Planet Aiwa
Supra, Realm of Eos

High in the upper levels of the royal palace, Maya had just put Arya and Fraya down for the night. The children drifted off immediately, but their mother remained in the doorway, watching them sleep peacefully while her thoughts drifted to Kypa and Toma.

There was still no word from her mate, which only deepened Maya's fears. It was increasingly difficult to maintain a brave face when the girls asked about their father and brother daily. Kypa swore to bring Toma and Ava back safely, but Maya's faith was wavering. With tensions escalating in the capital, her concerns for her family's safety weighed heavily on her heart.

A soft bell chime interrupted her thoughts. Curious about the late-night visitor, Maya turned toward the living room and saw Princess Seva on her way to greet whoever was calling. She had stopped by earlier to help with the children's night routine. Seva and Queen Qora had been pillars of support while Kypa was away, providing comfort and care to her and the children.

Maya closed the girls' door and moved to the living room. There, she was surprised to find Seva conversing in a low tone with Commodore Boa and a female Aiwan she had never met. Maya clutched her chest, fearing the worst.

Seeing her distress, Boa raised his hands to reassure her. "It is okay," he whispered. "There have been no updates from Kypa or Toma yet."

Maya dropped her shoulders as she exhaled with relief. "Thank you, Commodore. For a moment, I thought …"

"I did not mean to alarm you," he said softly. "Please forgive the intrusion, but it was imperative that we speak with you immediately."

Though his tone was calm, Boa's urgency and the mystery surrounding his visit created an unsettling vibe in the room. Maya gestured for them to sit, sensing that whatever they had to say was not good.

"Thank you," Boa said as they sat. "This is Agent Vylara. She is one of my most-trusted officers."

Vylara dipped her chin respectfully.

Boa cleared his throat and began, "We have uncovered more accomplices in the king's murder," he said bluntly. "The evidence points to an even larger conspiracy. Thanks to Vylara, we now know how the assassins boarded the royal yacht undetected."

Seva knitted her brow, processing this new information. "How?" she asked.

Vylara, eager to explain, leaned forward. "Teleporter pucks," she replied. "The assassins used a personal teleporter to transport onto the yacht after it arrived at Cirros. They attempted to destroy the puck after their attack to cover their tracks."

"Have you made any arrests?" Maya followed up, her voice steady but tense.

"Not yet," Vylara replied, "but we are close. Our investigation is still ongoing, but the evidence has taken a troubling turn."

Maya's expression tightened, sensing this was the reason for their visit. "What do you mean?"

Vylara glanced at Boa, deferring to him.

"Maya, were you aware Kypa kept a secret laboratory off-world?" he asked delicately so as not to sound accusatory.

Maya's cheeks flushed. Sworn to secrecy by Kypa, she shifted her gaze from Boa to Vylara and then to Seva, torn between whether to reveal the truth.

Sensing her hesitation, Boa added, "Kypa is not in any trouble, I promise. He took me to Pria-12 before leaving with the human, Dr. Garrett, and personally showed me where he built the Reaper."

Maya studied Boa's face, initially skeptical, but seeing the sincerity in his eyes, she finally relented and quietly admitted, "Yes, I knew about the lab."

"I see," Boa acknowledged, his tone understanding. "Before he left, Kypa told me his reasons for hiding it from me, and honestly, I cannot blame him," Boa admitted candidly. "However, now I regret not asking him how he managed to thwart our security for so long."

Seva sat back, folding her arms and giving Boa a disapproving look.

"There was nothing you could have done," Maya asserted. "Kypa is incredibly clever, you know. He sliced into the defense network and showed me a route out of the palace that exposed every gap in coverage to avoid being detected."

Boa could only smile at the prince's ingenuity, acknowledging he had been outplayed. He leaned forward and asked pointedly, "Then, you know about the cave?"

"I do," Maya admitted. "Kypa led me to it, and we teleported to his lab a few times. He insisted I know how to find my way there in case of an emergency."

"What kind of emergency?" Vylara asked.

"Kypa did not construct the lab just to build Reapers," Maya replied matter-of-factly. "He received countless death threats after what happened in Cirros. Everyone blamed him—"

Boa's expression softened with regret. "—Including me."

"Yes," Maya said evenly.

Although Boa had publicly recanted his scathing remarks against Kypa and supported his claim to the throne, Maya still harbored resentment for the stress and pain Boa caused her mate.

After pausing briefly to collect herself, Maya added, "Kypa built the teleporters so he could leave Aiwa discreetly if the threat against our family became unbearable."

"I understand why neither of you came to me sooner with this," Boa said somberly. "But I am here now, and I will do everything in my power to protect your family and this kingdom."

Maya's eyes filled with tears, and her voice trembled as she met Boa's gaze and charged him with a straightforward task: "Just bring Kypa and Toma home safely."

"You have my word," Boa assured her. Then, returning to his line of questioning, he asked gently, "Is there anyone else who might have known of Kypa's plans?"

Maya shook her head. "Not that I am aware of. Why?"

Vylara and Boa exchanged uneasy glances before Vylara spoke.

"Tonight, our chief suspect led me to Kypa's cave," she explained. "He used a teleporter puck to visit the lab."

Maya darted her eyes between Boa and Vylara, then scoffed. "Kypa would never aid terrorists."

"Agreed," Boa seconded. "That is why we are here. If Kypa could evade detection for so long, I doubt he would have revealed his lab to just anyone."

"What about Luna?" Seva suggested.

Boa paused, considering this angle. He knew of Luna and her relationship with the royal family, but their paths rarely crossed. However, she was Cirran, he recalled, which gave her a motive.

"Kypa might have confided in her," Boa granted. "But Luna died on Earth, long before the king's murder."

"Even so," Seva pressed. "Luna could have passed this information to Gora and his accomplices."

"Fair point," Boa conceded. "We cannot rule anyone out."

Maya refused to believe Luna would betray Kypa but kept it to herself. She turned to Boa and asked, "What is your next move?"

"The cave is under constant surveillance," Boa replied. "We plan to visit Kypa's lab after this meeting. There is a good chance the assassins obtained the teleporters there—without Kypa's knowledge," he clarified. "In fact, it is possible they used Kypa's lab as a jumping point to the king's yacht."

He stopped there, reluctant to share more details until he had conclusive evidence.

Seva stood abruptly. "I am coming with you," she declared, surprising Boa and Vylara. "I need to see my brother's lab for myself."

With all the tact he could muster, Boa said gently, "My princess, we do not know what we could be walking into. It would be wiser for you to stay in the palace, where it is safe. I promise I will contact you as soon as—"

"—Nonsense, Commodore," Seva cut him off. "Prudence be damned, I am going, whether you like it or not. Take whatever precautions you deem necessary."

Against his better judgment, Boa relented. There was no point arguing. Besides, Seva was the acting Warden of Eos, and her authority overrode his.

"Very well," he said, poorly masking his disapproval. He stood with Vylara and Maya. To Maya, he said, "Thank you again for your help. Your cooperation is greatly appreciated. I will contact you as soon as I have more information, or hear from Kypa."

Maya nodded. "Thank you, and be careful … all of you."

With that, Boa, Seva, and Vylara departed, taking the private lift to the palace's lower levels. While en route, Boa contacted Captain Nova, Keeper of the Royal Vault and interim Commander of the Royal Guards, informing him that the princess would be traveling off-world. Nova's hesitancy mirrored Boa's reservations. Allowing Seva to leave the capital, let alone Aiwa, was a tactical risk. But like Boa, Seva overruled Nova—end of discussion.

Moments later, they reached the hangar bay. Boa and the others crossed the flight deck toward a heavily armored, fast-attack Aiwan corvette. They waited at the base of the boarding ramp, along with Captain Areda, the ship's captain, as final preparations for departure were underway. Soon after, Captain Nova and a squad of shoretroopers jogged across the deck to meet them.

Nova greeted Seva and Boa with a customary bow, then ordered his troops to board.

"My apologies for the short notice," Boa offered.

"No need, sir. We are always ready," Nova replied, clearly proud of his troops' efficiency. He turned to Seva. "Princess, with your permission I will leave you with Commodore Boa and my troops."

"You are not coming with us?" Seva asked, surprised.

"Regrettably, duty calls elsewhere," he explained, bowing respectfully. "But you are in capable hands, I promise."

"Very well," she replied, trusting Nova's judgment. As he departed, Seva turned to Captain Areda. "Shall we get underway before we are missed?"

"At once, Your Highness," he replied, gesturing to the ramp. "After you."

As soon as they were on board, Captain Areda retracted the boarding ramp and sealed the hatch before making his way to the cockpit.

Within moments, the corvette was underway, lifting off the flight deck and exiting the hangar to begin its ascent to the surface. The twin-engine starship swiftly accelerated after passing through the energy shield protecting the capital, leaving Supra in its wake.

Meanwhile, the passengers sat in tense silence. Vylara glanced aft to the seated shoretroopers. She could tell by their expressions that they anticipated trouble at Kypa's lab, each warrior mentally preparing for whatever dangers lay ahead.

A short time later, the corvette broke through the ocean surface and rocketed skyward. Clearing Aiwa's upper atmosphere, it passed Commodore Boa's heavily damaged battlecruiser hovering in orbit. Surrounded by maintenance and supply vessels, the flagship was amid a rapid refit as crews—Aiwan and robotic—worked feverishly to make repairs and get the battlecruiser back in service as soon as possible.

The corvette immediately jumped to lightspeed, headed for Aiwa's most distant moon. Their journey was brief. Upon arrival, Boa, Seva, and Vylara moved aft to join the shoretroopers before making their way to the ship's landing bay. There, they boarded a shuttle similar to the one Boa had recently used to transport Kypa and Dr. Garrett to the prince's secret lab. Feeling a sense of déjà vu, Boa climbed behind the flight controls and brought the main systems online. Soon after, he powered up the engines, and the shuttle departed for Pria-12.

Following the exact flight path as before, Boa piloted the shuttle into a vast crater on the moon's surface and descended into a narrow cave. The shuttle's exterior running lights cast eerie shadows along the cave's interior as they ventured deeper into the moon's core. When they reached a dead end, Boa stopped the shuttle and deactivated the holographic rock wall, revealing Kypa's hidden lab.

"Scanning for lifeforms," Boa said to Seva, seated beside him in the co-pilot's chair. He was not taking any chances of walking into an ambush. The results appeared instantly. "No signs of life inside," he reported.

"Excellent," Seva said with a satisfied smile. "Set us down."

The shuttle passed through the containment field and settled on the landing platform inside the lab. As a precaution, Boa shut down the engines but kept the internal systems online.

"Wait here while we clear the lab," he told Seva. She nodded in agreement.

As Boa moved aft to speak with the shoretroopers, the princess rotated her chair to face Vylara.

"Do you really think we will find evidence linking other Cirrans to my father's murder?" Seva asked, skeptical.

Vylara raised her eyebrows and took a measured breath. "The evidence led us here, Your Highness. Our suspect and his followers are definitely up to something, and this could be the link that ties it all together. With any luck, we can end this threat once and for all."

Seva regarded Boa's agent with admiration. "Vylara, you are a loyal and dutiful servant to the crown. I will see that you are rewarded appropriately."

Vylara regarded her warmly, appreciating the praise. "Thank you, Your Highness. That is very generous, but unnecessary. I am just doing my duty."

Seva returned the smile before shifting her attention to the exit door, which hissed open, and the boarding ramp descended. The shoretroopers poured out in a disciplined formation, quickly fanning out around the lab. Boa remained in the doorway, his posture tense as he awaited their findings.

The sweep of the facility was swift and thorough. Moments later, the senior trooper reappeared at the base of the ramp. "All clear, sir," he reported crisply. "The lab is empty."

Boa signaled to Vylara and Seva that it was safe to disembark. When he reached the base of the ramp, the shoretrooper pointed to the far end of the bay.

"Sir, we found a permanent teleporter pad over there."

Boa nodded, then turned to Vylara. "Check the logs and see when it was last used," he instructed.

Before she set off, another shoretrooper approached, holding a teleporter puck. He handed it to Boa. "Sir, we found this in a storage container. There were slots for three more, but they were empty."

Boa examined the device. "It matches the damaged unit we found aboard the king's yacht," he noted, confirming his suspicions.

"There is still one unit buried in the cave, and Manta has one on him," Vylara stated. "That would account for all of them."

"Mm," Boa muttered. Yet, one last piece of evidence remained. "Check the log," he repeated. "If the assassins used this lab to teleport onto the king's yacht, I want to know."

"Right away, sir," Vylara replied, barely containing her excitement.

She ran off toward the teleporter pad, eager to get started, while Boa joined the shoretroopers searching the back rooms. Left to her own devices, Princess Seva wandered the surrounding area, seemingly marveling at her brother's creation with a deep sense of awe.

Meanwhile, Vylara accessed the permanent teleporter pad. It was unencrypted, allowing her to pull up the usage log quickly. The most recent entry confirmed what she already knew—Manta was the last person to use the teleporter, transporting roundtrip from the cave to the lab and back again. As she scrolled through the entries, Vylara stopped on one entry, and her heart nearly skipped a beat.

"Commodore Boa!" she called urgently.

Boa emerged from the back rooms in a rush, accompanied by the shoretroopers. "What did you find?" he asked, hurrying toward her.

"I found it," she said, her voice trembling with excitement. "The log shows several teleports took place on the day of the king's assassination. I count ten entries, all originating here and traveling to Cirros—precisely where the king's yacht had moored."

Boa stepped forward to see for himself, nodding affirmation as he read through the entries. "It appears only one assassin returned to the lab after the attack, and then teleported to the refugee camp."

"It has to be Manta," Vylara guessed. "Shall I have him and the others in the camp rounded up?"

Before Boa could reply, an electronic barrier activated, partitioning the landing bay in half and cutting Seva, Boa, and Vylara off from the shoretroopers. The containment field's emergence shocked everyone at first, and for a moment, it seemed like a malfunction—until the shoretroopers noticed Seva off to the side. Boa followed their eyes, rounding sharply to find the princess standing in front of a control panel.

"Seva, what are you doing?" he asked in disbelief.

Without saying a word, Seva deactivated the outer containment field, exposing the shoretroopers to the unforgiving vacuum of space. Their desperate cries filled the lab as they were torn from the ground and wrenched out into the void.

"No!" Boa shouted, helplessly watching his troops face a swift and brutal end.

An eerie silence settled over them, heavy and suffocating. Shell-shocked, Boa and Vylara stood momentarily frozen, their expressions etched with horror and confusion.

Fists clenched, Boa turned and started toward Seva. "Why?" he choked out, his voice hoarse.

With a cold fury burning in her eyes, Seva reached into a nearby weapons locker and retrieved a blaster. She aimed it steadily at Boa and Vylara, holding them at bay.

"I lost everything because of what happened to Cirros," she hissed, her voice quivering with rage. "You advised my father to overharvest despite Kypa's objections, just to keep your war machine running. And for what—to see it destroy your own people? Moorga lost his kingdom because of you, and you exiled him for speaking out against my father. You ruined everything, and now you will pay."

Seva pulled the trigger.

Boa instinctively braced himself for the blast—but the pain never came. Then, Vylara's sharp gasp broke the silence.

Turning to face her, Boa found Vylara staggering backward against the wall. She had her hands pressed against her blood-soaked abdomen, her eyes wide with shock and fear.

"Vylara!" Boa cried, rushing to her side as she collapsed. He caught her just before she hit the ground and eased her onto her back.

Cradling Vylara's head in his lap, he watched helplessly as her breath grew shallow, her eyes glazing over. With a final, ragged breath, Vylara's eyes rolled back, and her body fell limp.

Boa pulled her close and held her tight. "Forgive me," he whispered.

"By the way, I was the one who planted the teleporter puck aboard the yacht, not Gora," Seva said coldly.

Her callous words struck Boa like a dagger to the heart. He carefully lowered Vylara and gently closed her eyes with his trembling hand before rising to his feet. Boa shook his head in disappointment.

"Even if you kill me, Seva, Aiwa will never stop fighting."

"Oh, I am counting on it," she replied with a twisted smile. "But they will not be fighting me. Like a decaying tree rotting from the inside out, the remaining realms will destroy each other, squabbling over the ruins of a dying world. A new Cirros is rising," she declared, steadying her aim at Boa. "Too bad you will not live to see it."

A shot rang out, striking Boa square in the chest. The force of the blow sent him sprawling backward, collapsing onto the cold floor.

Without hesitation, Seva activated her commlink.

"Yes, Your Highness," came Manta's immediate response.

"Change of plans," she stated coolly, approaching Boa's motionless form. "Boa was onto you, so I had to eliminate him."

"Boa is dead!" Manta blurted. "How?"

"It does not matter now. Once his body is discovered, they will lock down the camp and arrest you and the others."

Manta's mind raced for options. "What do we do?"

"We proceed as planned," Seva replied. "Gather a small group of your best warriors and meet me at the cave right away."

Perplexed, Manta asked, "The cave?"

"Yes, we need to commandeer a transport," Seva explained. "But watch out, Boa has the cave under surveillance. Do not move against the guards until I give you the signal. Understood?"

"Yes, Your Highness," Manta affirmed, already devising an assault plan in his head.

"Hurry," Seva ordered. "I am teleporting to the cave now. Contact me as soon as you are in position."

Manta did not question Seva's command. They were improvising now with a sense of chaotic urgency.

"Understood," he replied dutifully. "We are leaving the camp now."

Seva ended the transmission and maneuvered over Boa and Vylara to get to the teleporter's control panel.

"Excuse me," she said, oddly polite.

Activating the teleporter, Seva entered the coordinates to the cave outside the palace. As soon as she stepped onto the pad, the teleporter hummed to life, and Seva vanished in a flash of white light.

39
BANG AND BURN

Planet Aiwa
Supra, Realm of Eos

As soon as the transmission with Seva ended, Manta leaped into action. Boa's discovery of their scheme turned everything on its head—time was no longer on their side. Fortunately, their original plot was already in motion; only a few adjustments were needed, which the princess handled. Manta focused on mobilizing his followers with renewed urgency.

He quickened his pace, slicing through the water and hoping to avoid any patrols. Soon, he reached the group's meeting place on the camp's outskirts.

Inside, nearly a hundred Cirrans awaited him with hushed anticipation. Their anxious expressions reflected the weight of the impending rebellion, and whispers filled the space with the zeal of their cause.

Manta raised his hand, quieting the group. "Listen up," he began in a steady voice. "It is time to act. Seva struck the first blow … Commodore Boa is dead!"

The group had mixed reactions—most cheered while others felt fear and uncertainty at the shocking news. One thing was clear: there was no turning back now. They had to see this through to the end or die trying.

The chatter faded to silence as Manta continued. "There is not much time.

When Boa is discovered, soldiers will swarm the camp. We must accelerate our plans—that includes commandeering a ship from the palace."

A murmur rippled through the crowd. As Manta's followers absorbed the shift in strategy, an unshakeable sense of purpose settled in the room, his people were ready to confront any challenges ahead.

Nodding with approval, Manta added. "Our first objective is to eliminate a surveillance team nearby. I will lead that mission with a small team. The rest of you will stay here and wait for my signal. When the chaos begins, you must move quickly and without hesitation. Understood?"

The group responded with resounding agreement, fully aware of the stakes.

Manta pulled two of his lieutenants aside and began choosing the members for the assault team. Each selected Cirran, a former soldier in Loka's regime, stood armed and battle-ready. Manta gathered them to the side and outlined the operation. Upon receiving Princess Seva's signal, their objective was to ambush the surveillance team outside the cave and prevent them from sounding the alarm.

Clear in their purpose, Manta assigned one lieutenant to stay behind with the rest of their followers, then led the assault team outside. They sliced through the water, reaching Supra's protective shield moments later. Manta watched his team pass through before glancing back to ensure they were not followed.

Satisfied, he lifted his gaze and followed the arc of the capital's protective barrier, its curvature leading to the distant central core. His thoughts shifted to Koba—the young Cirran he had mentored. Their fate now rested on his shoulders.

Inside the central core, Koba stood before a terminal in the main control room, his thoughts consumed by the betrayal he was about to commit. Guilt gnawed on him as he gazed through the power station's transparent ceiling, captivated by the twelve sinuous armatures towering above, swaying gracefully in the ocean's perpetual currents.

Acting as control rods, these armatures channeled energy from a crystal-powered reactor buried deep beneath the ocean floor. The energy coursed upward through each arm, culminating in dish-shaped emitters at their tips. Together, the armatures projected a dazzling lattice of golden beams, forming the capital's shimmering, protective dome.

Koba pictured his mother, Hera, whom he would never see again. His vacant stare betrayed his inner turmoil. A part of him yearned to abandon this deadly plot, to slip away quietly and rush back to her without anyone knowing.

But Koba knew better. He was already in too deep. If he failed, Manta would come for them both. This way, at least, his mother had a fighting chance.

Koba's chest tightened. *I hope she survives.*

Resolving himself to his chosen path, Koba focused on the task ahead. When Manta's signal arrived, he would have to move fast to access the main terminal and bypass a series of security protocols. It would not be easy, but Koba felt confident in his cunning.

For weeks, he had discreetly sabotaged the controls, laying the groundwork for this moment. In hindsight, it had been surprisingly simple. No one had paid much attention to a lowly apprentice, and certainly, no one suspected the young Aiwan of being capable of such treachery.

Koba had covered his tracks well, and his slicing efforts went unnoticed. Now, it was just a matter of triggering a series of catastrophic failures that, once in motion, would send workers chasing phantom alarms, buying him precious time to flee. The teleporter puck provided by Manta was stashed in the adjacent room, primed and ready for his quick getaway. All Koba had to do was await Manta's signal and be prepared to act. Once the core shut down—cutting off energy to the five realms and leaving them utterly defenseless—anarchy would reign across the planet.

Seva found herself in a similar holding pattern. Having teleported from Kypa's lab, she materialized inside the darkened cave on the capital's outskirts. Now completely alone, she waited and prayed that the Aiwan soldiers surveilling the cave decided not to venture inside and discover her before Manta arrived.

Hiding in shadows was not her style, which made the urge to peek outside almost unbearable. Yet, Seva resisted the reckless impulse. As far as she knew, the soldiers believed the cave to be empty—they expected intruders to enter it, not exit. Her best choice was to stay out of sight and wait, but that was proving more challenging than expected.

Seva envisioned her next move if the soldiers found her. Instinctively, she began crafting an alibi but quickly dismissed it. When Boa and Vylara's bodies were discovered, along with his troopers, all evidence pointed squarely at her. There was no denying her involvement, and begging for mercy was beneath her. She would rather die a martyr than betray her cause for self-preservation.

Feeling the weight of inevitability pressing down on her, Seva tightened her grip on the blaster and waited, the seconds stretching into what felt like an eternity. To occupy herself, she plotted how to sneak Manta and their Cirran followers into the palace, accomplish their primary objective, and hijack a transport.

It could work, she told herself, visualizing each step of her plan. *It has to work.*

But just like Manta's mission to eliminate the Aiwan guards outside the cave, Seva's escape plan relied entirely on taking down the central core. Without that diversion, they were all as good as dead.

Suddenly, a telepathic voice reached out to her in the darkness. *"Seva!"*

Seva's breath hitched, startled by Manta's calling. *"Manta?"*

"Yes, Your Highness. You may come out now," he replied. *"We have eliminated the guards."*

Seva's shoulders dropped with relief. For the first time, she dared to hope. *This is going to work!*

Pria-12

Multiple alarms sounded inside the Aiwan corvette's cockpit when all six shoretroopers simultaneously flatlined. Captain Areda and his co-pilot, Lieutenant Roka, exchanged panicked looks. One alarm could be mistaken as a glitch, but all of them triggering at once spelled trouble.

"Commodore Boa, this is Captain Areda! Do you read me?" he called urgently.

No reply.

"I repeat. Commodore Boa, this is Captain Areda. Please respond," he said, his voice growing more desperate. Still, there was no reply. "Princess Seva … anyone? Please respond."

"What do you think happened?" Roka asked, fearing the worst.

Areda ran a quick scan of the crater's opening with negative results. "Something is definitely wrong," he said, not daring to speculate. "Call it in and request backup," he ordered as he came out of his seat.

"Yes, sir," Roka replied. Opening a channel to the controller back on Aiwa, the co-pilot began to speak but hesitated when he noticed Areda leaving. "Where are you going?"

"Someone has to go down there and find out what happened," Areda replied firmly. "Stay here. If you do not hear from me in one quarter Solaar, return to base immediately. That is an order. Understood?"

"But, sir—" Roka objected.

"Do it!" Areda snapped over his shoulder as he departed.

Moving aft, Captain Areda opened a storage closet and pulled out a one-piece space suit. He quickly climbed into it and attached the helmet.

"Comm check," he said, activating the suit's commlink.

"I read you," Roka confirmed, adding, "Sir, I notified Control. They are dispatching a response team. Maybe you should wait until they arrive?"

"No time," Areda shot back, fastening a gun belt around his waist. He checked the blaster's charge before holstering it. "I am leaving the ship now."

He retrieved a personal propulsion unit from storage. The device would give him the thrust and maneuverability needed to descend rapidly inside the moon's crater.

Areda stepped into the airlock and sealed the hatch behind him. The chamber slowly depressurized, and moments later, a green light blinked above the outer door, indicating it was safe to exit. He opened the hatch, revealing a sea of endless stars. Standing on the threshold, Areda gazed down into the vast crater below; a shadow of doubt flashed in his mind. But he shoved it aside. Summoning his courage, Areda stepped forward and leaped into the boundless void of space.

Drifting weightlessly, he gripped the propulsion unit firmly with both hands. Areda thumbed the activation button, feeling it hum to life, and held on as he squeezed the throttle. Righting himself, he steered toward the dark crater, the unit's lone headlight piercing the blackness with a narrow beam of light.

Entering the crater, Areda's breath echoed loudly inside his helmet, heightening his unease. As the walls passed by in shadowy blurs, a sinking feeling settled in his gut—what if they were all dead?

As he tried to shake the thought, he spotted the faint glow of the lab's exterior lights ahead.

"I see the lab," he reported to Roka. "I—"

Areda suddenly found himself face-to-face with the frozen corpse of a dead shoretrooper. Releasing an involuntary cry of horror, he panicked and nearly lost his grip on the propulsion unit. He managed to steady himself, though his heart pounded furiously in his chest. Taking a deep, calming breath, Areda set his jaw as more lifeless figures emerged in the cold light. Six shoretroopers in total, their silent forms hauntingly adrift.

"Roka, come in!" he gasped hoarsely.

"Here, sir," the co-pilot responded instantly.

"Dead!" Areda stammered, his voice trembling. "All of them … dead!"

A heavy silence followed; Roka was stunned. Then his voice came through, thick with urgency. "Sir, you need to return to the ship immediately," he insisted. "Do you hear me? Return at once."

But Areda set his sights on Prince Kypa's lab. "I see the shuttle," he responded, determination overriding his fear. "I am moving in for a closer look."

Roka objected, but Areda ignored him. Throttling forward, he switched off the headlight, relying on the soft glow of the lab's interior to guide him. As he approached, his attention was immediately drawn to the deactivated energy barrier on the shuttle's side of the bay.

A fatal error? he speculated, wondering if perhaps the troopers had accidentally dropped the shield, sealing their fate.

But then, Areda noticed a second barrier partitioning the lab right down the middle, which was still active. It looked deliberate. As he neared, his heart sank. Commodore Boa lay in a pool of blood with Vylara's crumpled form beside him.

At the sight of his fallen comrades, Areda's stomach churned with dread, and his mind raced with possibilities. Something terrible had happened, and Princess Seva was nowhere to be found.

Captain Areda entered the lab through the open half of the landing bay and set down beside the shuttle. He activated his suit's magnetic boots with a tap on his forearm control pad. Drawing his blaster, Areda cautiously moved to the back of the bay and located a control panel. Within moments, he reactivated the containment field and lowered the middle partition, restoring life support and artificial gravity to the lab.

With the environment stabilized, Areda hurried aboard the shuttle, searching for hostiles, but found it empty. His heart pounded as he rushed across the bay to Boa and Vylara. Kneeling between them, he checked Vylara for a pulse and found none. Despair washed over him. Softly touching Boa's neck, he expected the same result but found a faint pulse. Boa moaned.

"Sir!" Areda exclaimed with a start.

Gently rolling Boa onto this back, Areda gasped at the unsightly scorch mark on the commodore's chest.

"By Gwaru's good graces, you are alive," he said in disbelief, then added, "Try not to move. Help is on the way."

Boa struggled to speak, his voice barely a whisper. Areda leaned in close, straining to catch his words.

"Say again, sir," Areda urged, pressing his ear near Boa's mouth. "Who did this?"

Boa's eyes shot open, a flicker of fire rekindling in their depths. Summoning the last of his strength, he stared at the ceiling, his voice thick with raw emotion as he forced out a single, damning name, "Seva!"

Planet Aiwa
Supra, Realm of Eos

"Are you going to answer that?" a stern voice cut through Koba's daydream.

Lost in the thought of finally getting to meet Princess Seva, his idol, Koba blinked and snapped back to reality. His supervisor stood beside him, arms crossed and in a foul mood. Koba shot him a puzzled glance until his supervisor gestured toward his belt. Only then did Koba realize his commlink was chirping.

Flustered, Koba cleared his throat, stammering, "Thank you, sir ... sorry, sir."

When his supervisor walked away, Koba snatched the commlink off his belt. Realizing this was the call he had been waiting for, he stared at the device for a long, hesitant moment before finally answering.

"Koba, are you ready?" Manta's voice crackled through.

"I ... I am, sir," Koba replied, his voice shaky.

"You know what to do," Manta urged. "Complete your mission, we are standing by to receive you. Understood?"

Fear gripped Koba's chest like a vice, but with a reluctant nod, he acknowledged the order and ended the transmission. What followed felt surreal, as though he were watching from outside his own body. He walked to a nearby terminal with unsettling calm and executed the heinous act flawlessly.

As soon as the core shut down, alarms activated. Chaos erupted around him as workers scrambled in response to the emergency, allowing Koba to slip away to the adjacent storage room. Inside, he opened a locker and retrieved the teleporter puck. Pre-programmed with the coordinates to the cave outside the palace, Koba placed the device on the floor and activated it.

Suddenly, Koba's supervisor burst into the room, startling him. Pausing in the doorway, he eyed Koba suspiciously.

"Koba, what are you doing in here?" he demanded.

Koba froze, his throat tightening as a tense silence settled between them. His supervisor's gaze fell on the teleporter puck, confusion shifting to a slow, dawning realization—Koba was up to something.

"Hold it right there!" the supervisor ordered.

A defiant grin creased the corner of Koba's mouth. Before his supervisor could draw nearer, Koba stepped onto the teleporter and vanished in a flash of light. A fraction of a second later, the puck began to smoke and exploded in a shower of sparks.

On the opposite side of the capital, Seva was leaving the cave when the teleporter puck on the sandy floor behind her activated. Startled, she whirled around, instinctively raising her blaster and firing as Koba materialized before her. His eyes filled with surprised delight at seeing her—just as the shot landed. The blaster bolt struck him square in the chest, burning a fatal hole straight through. Koba's gaze grew distant, then faded as his eyes closed forever.

Seva gasped, her heart sinking as she realized her mistake too late. She stared in horror at the young Aiwan's lifeless body, floating eerily in place.

A soft touch on her shoulder caused Seva to scream. She spun around, raising her blaster in a panic, only to have her wrist seized in a firm grip. She struggled briefly before recognizing her assailant's face: Manta.

He relaxed his grip once Seva regained her composure, though his stern expression did not waver as he glanced at Koba's body.

"*What happened?*" he demanded.

Seva's panicked eyes softened to remorse. "*He caught me by surprise,*" she confessed. "*I fired—*"

Her explanation was cut short as the cave shook violently. Tremors rocked the ground, sending shockwaves through the water and stirring silt and debris while the walls groaned under the strain.

Seva froze, wide-eyed with fear. Manta braced himself against the wall. Then, he realized this was no quake—it was the successful completion of Koba's mission.

Without wasting another second, Manta grabbed Seva by the wrist and led her out of the cave. They emerged just in time to witness Supra plunge into darkness and the domed shield collapse.

40
PALACE RAID

Planet Aiwa
Supra, Realm of Eos

Moments after Koba sabotaged the central core, an eerie stillness enveloped the capital. The once vibrant cityscape, now shrouded in darkness, had ground to a halt. A tension filled the waters as if the entire city held its breath, bracing for what was to come.

The calm before the storm, Manta mused with a smug grin.

He looked south toward the central core. Despite the power outage, the faint glow of phosphorescent algae provided scant illumination—enough to observe Koba's handiwork. Once gracefully swaying with the currents, the core's massive armatures lay lifeless on the ocean floor. With the protective shield gone, Supra was exposed, vulnerable to sea predators and off-world threats, leaving the neighboring realms equally defenseless.

Manta stood momentarily speechless, his chest swelling with pride as he savored their accomplishment. But he knew this was only a partial victory. The capital would soon erupt in panic, and the royal government would move swiftly to contain the chaos. They had to act quickly to seize the advantage this diversion had created.

Without a word, Manta led Seva over a rocky slope to join the awaiting assault team. Ignoring the two dead bodies from Boa's surveillance team, Manta turned to his squad, who stood transfixed by the sight of the darkened capital, their faces lit with triumph.

The squad gathered around Manta and Seva, exchanging congratulations and greeting the princess. They could barely contain their excitement. Then, a female Cirran noticed something was off.

"*Where is Koba?*" she asked, glancing toward the cave.

"*Koba is dead,*" Manta replied solemnly. "*He was shot while trying to escape the station and died in the cave.*"

Seva's jaw clenched, but she held her tongue as the group fell silent, shocked and saddened by the loss. Manta acknowledged Koba's immense contribution to their cause, exchanging a brief, knowing look with Seva—an unspoken agreement to keep the truth buried.

They both had blood on their hands. Manta's carelessness allowed Boa's agent to tail him, forcing Seva to reveal her true intentions prematurely. Had Krunig been here, such a blunder would have been punishable by death. But Manta redeemed himself by protecting Seva. Now, they were even.

"*Listen up,*" Manta said, quieting the group. "*Koba's loss is tragic, and we will honor him later, but our mission is not over. We still have much danger in front of us.*" Pointing to his best soldier, he said, "*Fara, go back to camp and bring the others. We do not have much time.*"

"*Yes, sir,*" she replied and swam off quickly.

Manta turned to the others. "*The rest of you, hide these bodies in the cave. It will not be long before they are missed.*" Without hesitation, the team began the grim task of concealing Boa's dead soldiers.

Manta turned to Seva. "*How long do you need to accomplish your task?*"

"*Not long,*" Seva replied with confidence. "*But I should go alone.*"

Manta considered the situation carefully. He did not like the idea of the princess—soon to be wanted for murder—running through the palace alone and unprotected. Despite his concerns, Manta knew she was right and reluctantly agreed.

"*Very well. You will lead us inside, then we will split up and I will take a small team to the hangar to commandeer a transport. Meet back here and we will make our escape.*"

Seva nodded in agreement. Together, they synchronized the timers on their commlinks. When the group tasked with disposing of the dead bodies returned from the cave, Manta briefed them on the plan and hand-picked three followers.

"You will come with me to the hangar bay," he directed. *"The rest of you stay here and await Fara and the others. Keep out of sight and be ready to cover our escape. Understood?"*

The group nodded, their eyes conveying a mutual commitment to completing their mission at all costs.

Manta signaled Seva to take point. She moved to the front, leading the five-member team toward the palace in tight formation. They passed the area where the protective shield once stood, its absence a fleeting victory that heightened their vigilance. As they entered enemy territory, each member braced for an ambush, half-expecting spotlights to suddenly illuminate an army of Aiwan soldiers lying in wait.

Seva guided the team to a rocky alcove against the palace's exterior. The formation barely reached waist height, with a narrow gap separating it from the palace wall. Nestled in the shadowy nook, an artificial rock lay concealed.

Seva swam to the rock and reached behind it.

"There is an activator switch back here somewhere," she explained, grunting with effort as she searched blindly for the well-hidden button.

Seva grinned triumphantly as she located the switch and pressed it. She moved away as the rock glided backward on rails, revealing an access hatch. The hatch opened automatically as soon as the rock was clear, exposing a flooded chamber below.

"Follow me," Seva urged, gesturing inside.

One by one, the team descended feet-first into the chamber. Inside, Seva operated the control panel on the wall, sealing the overhead hatch and draining the seawater. When the chamber pressurized, a warm red light activated, drying the occupants. Once complete, the exit door slid open, revealing a small room beyond. The team filed out, with Manta bringing up the rear.

They stood at the landing of a long, spiral stairwell that wound up to the tower where the royal family resided. Seva knew this passage all too well. It was the route Kypa had often used to sneak out of the palace unnoticed, bypassing the alarms with a skill that masked his movements—but never from her.

There was an express lift beside the stairwell, but it was off-limits. Even if it had power, using the lift would attract immediate attention, so walking was their only option.

"Four flights up is the exit to the main level," Seva explained to the group.

Suddenly, an alarm klaxon sounded, echoing in the stairwell.

"Right on time," Manta affirmed. "Now listen, when we reach the exit, expect chaos. Ignore everything and follow me straight to the hangar. They are not looking for us, so stay calm and do not attract attention. But if we run into trouble, fight your way to the hangar. I picked each of you because you know how to fly," Manta said, fixing them with a hard stare. "Commandeer the nearest transport—something big enough for all of us—and get off-world."

"Where will we go?" one of the team members asked.

"Rogantu," Seva answered, revealing their secret rendezvous point for the first time. "Krunig is waiting for us there."

A palpable sense of anticipation rippled through the group as they reacted to this news.

"Time to go," Manta prodded. "May Gwaru smile down on us."

The team echoed his words, and then a hush fell over the group as they followed Seva up the stairwell. Four flights later, she stopped at a door leading into the palace. Seva entered her passcode, and the door hissed open, revealing King Loka's private chamber, undisturbed since his passing.

Seva led them inside, crossing the darkened room to a second door. She opened it and peered into the reception area. Finding it empty and unguarded, she breathed a sigh of relief and guided them through.

At the reception area's main doors, she turned to the team. "I will go first. Wait until I am clear, then go."

Manta nodded in agreement.

Seva swept her eyes over each team member one last time, her gaze brimming with pride. The determination on their faces mirrored her own. Nothing more needed to be said.

Rounding to face the double doors, Seva rolled back her shoulders and lifted her jutted chin in a regal stance—one she had perfected since childhood. But then, she caught herself, remembering the blaster in her hand. With an exasperated breath, she placed the weapon in the open hands of a nearby statue of her father. Smirking at the irony, Seva regained her composure. She opened the doors, revealing a bustling crowd shrouded by red emergency lights. A wave of frantic energy hit her as she watched frightened Aiwans rush through the corridors. The city-wide alarm blared in the background, intensifying the sense of urgency and chaos in the air.

With a subtle, chilling smile, Seva silently relished the crowd's terror—a taste of what the Cirrans had endured.

Moving with purpose, Seva slipped into the adjacent corridor, but her presence did not go unnoticed. The noisy crowd, hurrying with animated chatter, collectively realized their leader was among them. Seva's presence disrupted the traffic flow as passersby slowed down and began calling out her name. But she ignored them, swiftly carving her way through the clamoring Aiwans seeking reassurance, information, or both.

Two guards picked up on the disturbance and hurried to aid the princess.

"Take me to the vault," Seva instructed over the noise.

Without question, the guards cleared a path, guiding Seva to a heavy door nearby guarded by a wall of sentries. Recognizing the princess as she approached, the guards created an opening to allow Seva to pass, then closed ranks around her.

One of her escorts activated the panel on the wall, opening the door. Seva entered alone and proceeded down a long corridor. At the far end, two sentries stood watch in front of a private lift.

They retracted their energy pikes and stepped aside, granting Seva passage. She pressed her long hand firmly against the scanner on the wall panel, and the lift's door slid open with a hiss.

"Let no one pass," she commanded.

Without hesitation, the sentries put their backs to the lift, adopting a defensive stance. Seva entered, the door sealing shut behind her. She exhaled slowly, steadying her nerves as the lift descended to the sub-levels.

Moments later, the doors parted to reveal a shimmering energy barrier blocking her path. Beyond the translucent field, she spotted Captain Nova standing at the entrance to the royal vault, engaged in a low conversation with two guards. One of the guards stiffened, his gaze snapping to Seva, alerting Nova to her presence.

Surprised by the princess's unannounced visit, Nova said, "Lower the barrier," and quickly approached her.

Seva's chest tightened, but she maintained her calm façade. As the barrier lowered, she stepped forward to meet him.

"Princess Seva, forgive me," Nova said with a respectful bow. "I was unaware you had returned from Pria-12."

"We landed just before the outage," she lied smoothly. "Boa should have notified you."

Nova's brow creased slightly; such an oversight was uncharacteristic of Commodore Boa. "I received no message," he said, though it no longer mattered. Shifting his focus, he added, "Your Highness, it might be best if you returned to your residence. It would be safer—"

"—In a moment," she interrupted. "I need to check the vault first."

Nova hesitated, preparing to insist, when his commlink chirped. He glanced at the urgent transmission, his expression darkening.

"What is it?" Seva asked.

"Trouble at the central core," Nova replied grimly. "I must go, and so should you. The vault is secure, Princess."

"Then so am I," she countered firmly. "Now, go where you are most needed, Captain. That is an order."

Recognizing the unyielding resolve of Queen Qora reflected in Seva's eyes, Nova relented. With a sharp bow, he snapped to attention. "Yes, Your Highness." Turning to the guards, he issued firm instructions. "Call for reinforcements. Once the princess is finished, escort her safely to her residence. Understood?"

"Yes, sir," the guards replied in unison.

Nova stepped into the lift, the doors sliding closed behind him. His final glimpse was of the princess accessing the vault.

With a deep rumble, the heavy panels parted, revealing a containment field within the vault. Seva stepped inside. As the doors sealed behind her, the barrier flickered and deactivated, leaving her alone in the silent chamber.

Confident that no one was watching, Seva shifted her focus to her objective: the blue crystal.

Meanwhile, Manta and his three followers maneuvered through the crowd, heading toward the main hangar. Hugging the corridor's edge, they moved against the traffic flow to avoid attracting attention. Their eyes continually scanned the crowd, watching for royal guards.

When they reached their destination, Manta was relieved to find the hangar entrance unguarded. He halted the team outside, and they huddled close.

"So far, so good," Manta said, his relief tempered by the knowledge that the most challenging part of their mission was still ahead. His eyes darted around, noting that the passersby seemed unaware or uninterested in their presence. With a quick motion, he discretely handed his blaster to one of his team members, who stowed it away without a word.

"Stay here," Manta instructed. "I will go alone and find us a transport."

The team nodded assent, then fanned out, looking inconspicuous while Manta entered Seva's personal code on the control panel. The doors slid open with a soft hiss, and he slipped inside the hangar. He found it deserted and unnervingly still. Aiwan vessels lined either side of the bay, their crews nowhere in sight.

Manta's gaze swept to the far end of the expansive hangar, where the containment field shielding the sea entrance still shimmered. A grim smile tugged at his lips. Koba's sabotage of the central core affected almost everything, but he had kept this barrier intact, as planned.

He then located the ideal transport for their escape—the royal yacht. Manta turned to fetch his team but stopped abruptly, his breath catching as he stood face-to-face with a royal guard.

"Hold it," the guard ordered, gripping his energy pike tighter. "This is a restricted area."

Manta's hands shot up reflexively. His heart raced as he scrambled for words.

"What are you doing here?" the guard demanded.

"I—I was told to evacuate and report here," Manta lied, feigning fear and confusion.

Suspicious, the guard scanned the area for signs of foul play and replied, "No evacuation orders have been given. Who told you that?"

Manta's eyes darted to the exit just as his team appeared. He nodded in their direction and said casually, "They did."

The royal guard spun around to discover three armed intruders closing in fast. He reacted a moment too late. As Manta dove for cover, two of the Cirrans raised their blasters and fired in unison, both striking the guard. He was dead before he hit the ground.

Suddenly, an alarm sounded inside the hangar, its piercing tone triggered by the weapons fire.

"Move!" Manta barked, motioning his team forward.

"Halt!" a booming voice bellowed from above as they sprinted toward the yacht.

The Cirrans did not slow, prompting the guards funneling out of the hangar's elevated control room to start shooting. Blaster fire erupted as Manta led his team up the yacht's boarding ramp. Ducking enemy fire, he dashed inside the ship. Behind him, one of his followers got hit in the back and went down hard, collapsing face-first at the base of the ramp. The remaining two members leaped over the body without stopping. They boarded the yacht and sealed the hatch as more blaster fire rattled the hull.

Manta wasted no time getting to the cockpit. He pressed a button by the door, and matching holographic pilot seats materialized before him. Taking his place in the crescent-shaped chair on the left, he activated the HUD and initiated the ship's emergency start-up sequence.

A female Cirran joined him, taking the co-pilot's chair. She immediately raised the yacht's shields.

"Clear the moorings," Manta instructed as he assumed manual control of the ship, placing his hands and feet inside the four orbs.

"Moorings clear!"

Manta expertly manipulated the controls, lifting the yacht off the deck. A barrage of blaster fire peppered the forward viewport, but the guards' efforts to prevent their escape proved futile—the small arms fire bounced harmlessly off the yacht's shields.

Rotating the ship toward the hangar exit, Manta spotted a problem—the containment field was glowing red instead of blue. With the barrier locked down, nothing could pass in or out of the hangar.

With a swift neural command, Manta used Princess Seva's code to override security and deactivate the barrier. A crushing wall of seawater surged into the hangar as he slammed the throttle forward. The yacht splashed through the surging tide, slicing its way out of the flooding hangar. Behind them, the guards, pummeled by the overwhelming force of the water, had no chance to escape.

Meanwhile, Princess Seva exited the vault with the prized blue crystal concealed behind her back. The two guards flanking her were none the wiser. They rode the lift to the main floor and stepped out. With alarms echoing throughout the palace, the guards naturally veered left to take the princess to her residence, but Seva had other plans.

"Wait," she commanded, stopping the procession. "I need to retrieve something from my father's chambers."

The two guards exchanged uneasy glances.

"Your Highness," the senior guard began cautiously. "With respect, Captain Nova's orders were clear—he wanted you escorted directly to your residence. It is safer there. Perhaps I can retrieve the item—"

But Seva had heard enough. Time was of the essence, and she had to get moving. She set off through the crowd, weaving her way to Loka's chamber.

"Princess!" the senior guard shouted, but it was already too late. He lost sight of her in the crowd, which had intensified with panicked chatter about the flooded hangar.

The guards set off in pursuit, elbowing past the clamoring Aiwans, yelling, "Make way!"

Seva reached Loka's chamber moments later. She clutched the blue crystal with both hands, her grip so tight that even a full-grown obercai would struggle to pry her fingers apart. Hearing the guards calling to her in the distance, she dared not look back.

The princess slipped inside the reception area and sealed the door just as the guards arrived. Pounding fists and muffled shouts echoed behind her as Seva hurried across the room to her father's private chamber. She made a beeline for the far wall and activated the hidden door. Before stepping through, Seva paused, glancing back at the empty chamber. A bittersweet smile tugged at her lips—a blend of sorrow and joy. Seva stepped into the secret passage and sealed the door, closing that chapter of her life for good.

Nearly a hundred Cirrans had gathered near the cave outside the palace. By the time Seva arrived, most had already boarded the royal yacht.

Manta lingered anxiously at the base of the boarding ramp, his tension dissolving into a wave of relief as the princess appeared. When Seva reached his side, Manta's eyes were drawn to the blue crystal glistening in her hands. Their eyes met, and they exchanged triumphant smiles.

With a sweeping gesture toward the yacht, Manta bowed humbly. *"My princess, destiny awaits."*

41
CHAOS ON AIWA

Pria-12

Commodore Boa grimaced, his face contorted in pain, as he struggled to prop himself up on one elbow. Each movement sent a sharp jolt through his fractured ribs, drawing a ragged gasp from his lips. Captain Areda hovered beside him, carefully avoiding the pool of blood while trying to assist.

"Please, sir, you have to lay still," Areda cautioned. "You have lost a lot of blood."

"The blood … is not mine," Boa rasped, his breath labored. "I am wearing a protective suit under my uniform."

"Protective suit?" Areda repeated, raising an eyebrow. "I did not realize we had such tech."

"We do not," Boa replied. "Prince Kypa made it for me using nanites. Lucky for me, he insisted I wear it."

Areda glanced at Vylara with a pained expression. "I still cannot believe Seva did this," he said, shaking his head in disbelief. "No one could have seen this coming."

Maybe Areda was right, but Boa felt the weight of yet another security failure. All he could do now was try to mitigate the damage. Rolling over onto all fours, Boa slowly came to his feet, brushing off Areda's attempt to help him.

Areda's commlink chirped. "Go ahead," he answered.

"Captain, I am picking up multiple distress calls on Aiwa," Roka replied, his voice trembling with urgency.

Boa snapped toward Areda, sending a sharp stab of pain through his torso. "The palace?"

Hearing Boa's gruff voice in the background, Roka responded. "Yes, sir. The transmissions are coming from Eos and the other realms. Wait, I have new information coming in." There was a brief pause. "Sir, there has been an incident at the central core. It is completely offline," he reported grimly. "All realms are operating on reserve power, and the shields are down."

Seva! Boa fumed. The magnitude of her deception was growing painfully clear. This attack was her doing—hers and the Cirran refugees she had fought so fiercely to protect. Now, he knew why.

Boa's frustration intensified with the helplessness of being isolated here on Pria-12 instead of in Supra.

"Prep the shuttle for takeoff," he told Areda. "We need to get home immediately."

Planet Aiwa
Rhanda, Realm of Fonn

Aiwa's undersea realms were in grave peril. The domed shields protecting each capital city collapsed abruptly when the central core went offline, leaving them dreadfully exposed. Vulnerable to attack, they now faced threats from off-world harvesters and Aiwa's deadly ocean predators.

In the realm of Fonn, the situation deteriorated rapidly. Once the shield dropped, a school of carnivorous gnashfish swarmed into the capital unchecked. The predatory fish attacked ferociously, catching the unsuspecting Aiwans off guard. With razor-sharp teeth and powerful jaws, the gnashfish unleashed carnage upon anyone caught outside.

An epic clash unfolded as a cavalry of Fonn riders charged into battle, their energy pikes glowing like spectral lances in the gloom. Mounted atop swift and agile xipos, the riders engaged the gnashfish head-on in a coordinated assault, their movements a seamless blend of bravery and skill. Diving and weaving in intricate maneuvers, the riders flanked their enemies and struck with practiced precision. Energy pikes flashed and crackled with power in the murky depths as the riders methodically hunted the gnashfish, impaling them with well-aimed thrusts.

Gradually, the tide turned in Fonn's favor as they drove the remaining predators from the city—or so they thought. Just as the battle appeared to be over, the gnashfish circled back and charged toward the city.

The Fonn riders formed a tightly knit skirmish line bristling with pikes and shields. Their eyes fixed ahead, they steeled themselves to repel the wave of gnashfish surging toward them—only to realize, in chilling clarity, that the gnashfish were not attacking them but fleeing something far more terrifying.

From the depths emerged a colossal zemindar, *the* apex predator of the deep. Its unblinking, phosphorescent eyes cast an eerie glow across the battlefield while luminescent stripes pulsed rhythmically down the length of its serpentine body. Like a giant eel, the creature slithered forward, undulating with deadly grace as it sized up its new hunting ground, teeming with potential prey.

Primal fear swept through the ranks of the Fonn riders. Even the most seasoned warriors—male and female who had faced countless foes—felt an involuntary chill creep up their spines. They were no longer the hunters but the hunted, standing before a predator of legend.

But as the initial shock wore off, their fear hardened into a fierce resolve. Each rider gripped their weapons tighter, a look of defiance replacing the dread. With a rallying cry that echoed up and down the line, the Fonn riders charged forward, answering the monster's arrival with a surge of courage.

As the battle raged outside, Lord Zefra remained within her council chamber, nestled deep in Fonn's Acropolis. She sat on a throne of dark obsidian, its polished surface gleaming like glass, elevated on a central dais that underscored her commanding presence. Encircling Zefra were her trusted advisors, their faces tense with the weight of the conflict. Before them, Commodore Boa's holographic figure materialized, his image marred by faint static.

"Commodore Boa, what is happening?" she demanded. "Our shield is down, and we are under attack!"

Clutching his aching ribs, Boa forced his words through gritted teeth. "Lord Zefra, we have been betrayed—by Princess Seva herself. She killed seven warriors and even attacked me."

Zefra and her advisors froze, their expressions shifting from shock to disbelief.

"Seva … it cannot be," Zefra murmured, her voice wavering as if the words themselves were too heavy to bear.

Boa gave a grim nod, still grappling with the truth himself. "It is true," he confirmed. "Princess Seva, alongside a band of Cirran rebels, sabotaged the central core."

"This does not make any sense," Zefra refuted, her eyes darting back and forth, searching for motive and reason. "Why would she do this?"

"Seva blames me and her father for what happened to Cirros," Boa explained, his voice laden with regret. "She also holds us responsible for ending her engagement to Moorga."

Zefra nodded slowly, recalling the exiled Cirran prince. Her brow furrowed. "But if what you say is true, then Seva conspired to kill her own father and ..."

Her voice trailed off as the painful reality of Seva's betrayal sank in. Zefra's son, Commander Rega—betrothed to the princess after Moorga—died in the attack on King Loka. At the time, it was inconceivable to think Seva was involved. Yet, in this universe, one never truly knows the evil lurking in another being's heart until it is too late.

Zefra's expression turned stone-cold. Seva would pay for her crimes but now was not the time. There were more significant problems to contend with.

"Does the queen know?" Zefra asked. "Or worse, could she be an accessory to this insurrection?"

"I do not know," Boa admitted, having considered the possibility himself. "But I trust Prince Kypa. His mate, Maya, assisted with our investigation into your son's death. We traced the assassins to the Cirran refugee camp outside Supra and uncovered how they boarded the king's yacht undetected."

"Yes, the teleporters," she said, recalling Boa's briefing to the High Court. "Did you find more?"

"We did," Boa affirmed. "They acquired the devices from Kypa's secret lab on Pria-12 before carrying out the attack."

He paused to catch his breath as Zefra's thoughts turned to Kypa's recent testimony about using an off-world lab to build the Reaper.

"The teleporter was the crucial piece of evidence that tied it all together," Boa continued. "Once our investigation linked the assassins to the Cirran refugee camp, we knew we were close—then Seva revealed herself." Boa grimaced, then added, "My lord, we must assume the princess is in league with Grawn Krunig and this was a calculated strike to destabilize the Five Realms."

"Without the central core, we are defenseless against the harvesters," Zefra stated. "My people are warriors, Commodore, we can protect our realm from sea creatures but not attacks from space. See to it the central core is restored at once, or we are all dead."

Aiwan Corvette
En route to Aiwa

Boa bowed, straining from the effort as the transmission flickered to an end. Alone with his thoughts, he revisited Seva's motive, reflecting on her remarks about the rise of a new Cirros. But why now? And why like this? She could have helped Cirros by working with the other realms, not destroying them. Then, a chilling realization struck him—Krunig was bent on taking Aiwa's crystals, and Seva had to know as soon as the planet's defenses were down, Krunig would come for the rest.

"Or just one," Boa muttered. *The blue crystal.*

Panic surged through him as he reached for his commlink to warn the guards at the royal vault. But before he could speak, the device chirped in his hand, alerting him of an incoming message.

Now what? he thought with dread.

"Sir, orbital defenses just tracked an unauthorized vessel leaving the system," Captain Areda reported. "It is the royal yacht, and it is ignoring our hails."

Boa stiffened. "It has to be Seva!"

"There is more, sir," Areda continued. "The ship is emitting an unusually large energy signature."

Boa's chest tightened—he was too late. Sabotaging the central core was just a diversion so Seva could raid the vault. His lip curled into a snarl.

"Stop that ship at all costs!" he ordered. "Destroy it if you must!"

A brief silence hung in the air before Areda's voice returned, laced with regret. "I am sorry, sir, but the ship jumped into hyperspace. It is gone."

Boa's knees buckled, and he sank into a nearby jump seat. He sat silently for a long moment, staring blankly at the floor, utterly demoralized. If his assumptions were correct, Grawn Krunig would soon possess the blue crystal, leaving him powerless to defend Aiwa.

"Sir?" Captain Areda's voice crackled through the commlink. "What are your orders?"

The sound snapped Boa back to the present. He straightened in his seat, considering how he would break the news to Lord Zefra and the rest of the High Court.

"Take us back to Supra," Boa replied somberly. But then, an idea sparked in his mind. His eyes narrowed, and a new plan began taking shape.

"Wait, Areda," he said, his voice sharpening. "Locate Captain Nova. I have a mission for the two of you."

42
DIVERSION

Planet Rogantu

Grawn Krunig's shark-finned warship loomed over the refinery, blocking the sun and casting a menacing pall over the dormant facility. A smaller gunship emerged from the underbelly, its running lights piercing the darkness as it descended toward the surface. Though the storm had passed, a thin veil of dust swirled when the gunship touched down outside the refinery's landing bay.

The side door slid open as soon as the landing struts settled. Six Madreen fighters stormed out, led by Skargg—a hulking brute with mahogany skin and a white mohawk sprouting from his bald head. His fiery red eyes burned with a vicious hunger for blood.

Brandishing blaster rifles, Skargg and his fighters charged into the landing bay.

"In here!" Hiromi called out as soon as she heard them approaching.

The Madreen swept inside, fanning out to secure the area.

"Search the ships!" Skargg barked, his voice thick and gravelly.

He approached Hiromi, his keen eyes swiftly taking in the scene. She stood in the center of the hangar with dual blasters extended from her cyborg arms. Four captives kneeled in front of her, their hands bound tightly behind their backs.

"As promised," Hiromi said matter-of-factly, "both bounty hunters, the Reaper's captain, and one Aiwan prince."

Skargg scrutinized the prisoners before his gaze settled on Hiromi. His eyes flickered with uncertainty as he took in her peculiar blend of heavy armament and refined demeanor.

"We'll take it from here," he said.

"As you wish," Hiromi replied, retracting her blasters and morphing her petite hands back to their original form. She glanced at the hangar entrance with curiosity, noting Krunig's absence. "Your boss is not coming?"

"First things first," Skargg responded. He snapped his fingers, summoning one of his subordinates. "Search the prisoners—and be thorough about it, especially these two," he added, waving the barrel of his weapon at Smythe and Gort.

Starting with Smythe, the subordinate vigorously searched every inch of the insectoid, acutely aware that the bounty hunter could hide weapons anywhere. Skargg watched him begin, then shifted his gaze toward Toma. He recognized an adolescent Aiwan when he saw one, but that did not make Toma any less dangerous. Despite his lanky frame, Toma's fully developed claws were lethal at this age. But what truly set him apart was his bloodline.

Skargg sneered at the young prince, who withstood his scrutiny in silence. Toma struggled to shake off the lingering effects of the paralytic toxin Smythe had used to knock him out. Though the webbing had dissolved, a stabbing headache and queasy stomach remained.

Then there was Ava—the so-called "fleet killer." Skargg studied her closely. Despite her fearsome reputation, her bruised face and petite frame failed to intimidate the battle-hardened marauder.

As they searched her—more invasively than necessary—Ava locked eyes with Skargg. Her eyes blazed with a defiance that challenged his very existence.

Unmoved, Skargg held her glare with a cool, indifferent stare. "With that charm, you'll make a lousy prostitute," he jeered, then added, "but our clients will work that out of you."

With her hands still bound, Ava struggled against her restraints as she spat out a profanity-laced retort that was only ignored. When she quieted, the Madreen fighter finished his search, pushing Ava's head down as he stood, his fingers digging into her scalp.

"They're clean," he reported.

Skargg gave a curt nod, then bobbed his head toward the bounty hunters' freighter. "Go help the others," he ordered.

Skargg and Hiromi remained outside as the search of the ship continued, waiting in silence for the results. Moments later, one of the Madreen fighters emerged from the freighter.

"The ships are empty," he reported. "No signs of life."

"What about the Reaper?" Skargg asked.

"It's here," the fighter confirmed. "The internal systems are online and as far as I can tell, the security protocols are deactivated."

Skargg turned to Hiromi. The cyborg shrugged. "Told you so," she remarked.

Satisfied, Skargg tapped a sequence of buttons on the commlink strapped to his forearm. "You held up your end of the bargain," he acknowledged, releasing the agreed-upon funds to the cyborg. "This concludes our business."

For an instant, Hiromi's mechanical eyes glowed slightly brighter as she accessed her bank account and confirmed her finder's fee deposit. The glow faded to normal as she asked, "So, I am free to go?"

"By all means," Skargg replied. "My master thanks you for your service and hopes we can do business again in the future."

Hiromi dipped her chin. "Tell him the feeling's mutual."

With that, the cyborg took her leave. As she passed Smythe and the other prisoners, Hiromi noticed their desperate stares, but her faceplate remained cold and unmoving. Self-preservation was her top priority now; their fate was of no concern. The sooner she left Rogantu, the better.

Returning to her ship, Hiromi wasted no time getting underway. As soon as she took her place at the flight controls, she powered up the systems and activated the maneuvering thrusters. The starship kicked up a cloud of dust as it lifted off, clearing the hangar and lurching skyward.

Steering away from Krunig's warship, Hiromi aimed for deep space as soon as she escaped the planet's gravitational pull. The cyborg slicer then charted a course for Starhaven before engaging the hyperdrive and departing the system in a flash.

Stars elongated into sweeping trails outside the cockpit windows, creating a serene, spiraling tunnel that enveloped the viewport. Hiromi leaned back in her seat, reflecting on a job riddled with setbacks. Slicing the Aiwan ship had proven far more challenging than expected—but she was alive and well-paid, which was all that truly mattered. Now, with her newfound credits burning a hole in her virtual pockets, she set her sights on a week of pure indulgence at a luxurious spa—and blissful, uninterrupted silence.

Back in the refinery's landing bay, Skargg activated his commlink, ready to send for Krunig, when Smythe interrupted.

"Let's not be too hasty," the insectoid cautioned, making Skargg pause. "Before you call your boss, perhaps you and I can come to some arrangement?"

A flicker of curiosity crossed Skargg's face as he weighed the implications. Sensing an opportunity, Smythe pressed on.

"My partner and I have access to a large nest egg," he enticed. "You and your friends here would be set for life. Take our ship and leave the Reaper behind for Krunig. All we ask is safe passage. Drop us off on a habitable world, and I'll transfer the funds, then we part ways."

For a moment, it seemed as if Skargg was seriously considering the offer. But then he scoffed. "Do you take me for a fool, bounty hunter?" Skargg sneered. "Or should I say, *ex*-bounty hunter," he added mockingly. "Grawn Krunig never forgets—and certainly never forgives."

Without further hesitation, Skargg raised the commlink to his lips. "My lord, we have the prisoners and the Reaper."

"Good work," Krunig replied immediately. "You know what to do."

"Understood," Skargg affirmed.

Ending the transmission, Skargg lowered his arm and cast a taunting glance at the bounty hunters. He clicked his tongue, shaking his head with a smirk, as he raised his blaster at Smythe.

Overlooking the refinery from high above, Neil clung to a metal ladder bolted to the side of a dormant smokestack. His grip tightened as his HUD zoomed in on the landing bay in the distance.

"Whatever you're going to do, you better do it fast," he urged Kypa, struggling to keep his voice steady despite the dizzying height. A knot of unease tightened in his gut—something bad was about to go down.

"Go now!" Kypa instructed, his voice crackling over the commlink.

Inside the landing bay, Ava and Toma experienced a subtle yet familiar itch in the back of their minds—a sensation they knew all too well.

"*Ava ... Toma!*" Kypa called them, his clear and unmistakable voice resonating in their heads.

Toma's eyes widened at the sound of his father's voice. "*Father!*" he responded mentally, his tone brimming with barely contained excitement.

"Kypa!" Ava gasped, the name slipping from her lips before she could stop it.

Skargg's head snapped toward her, his weapon swinging from Smythe to zero in on Ava. His nostrils flared as he demanded with a dangerous growl, "What did you just say?"

Ava's face flushed with panic and embarrassment. "Nothing," she stammered, shaking her head vigorously.

Skargg's suspicious gaze lingered on Ava. Something was off. His eyes methodically swept across the landing bay, probing for hidden threats. Sensing their leader's heightened awareness, Skargg's team instinctively followed his lead, swiveling their heads as they scanned the area, weapons ready.

Ava and Toma exchanged knowing looks while their captors were distracted—they were not alone, after all.

But their moment of hope quickly dissipated. Skargg's attention snapped back to Smythe, and without a second's hesitation, he pulled the trigger.

Neil had never witnessed an execution before. The shock of the violent act caused him to recoil. As he did so, a sudden wave of vertigo overwhelmed him, making the ground below spin. Neil faltered and nearly fell. Clutching the ladder with all his strength, he pressed himself tightly against the rungs, his heart pounding.

"Neil, what happened?" Kypa asked in alarm. "I heard a shot."

Gathering his composure, Neil answered in disbelief, "They shot one of the bounty hunters."

Inside the hangar, Ava turned away sharply at Smythe's sudden demise, squeezing her eyes shut as the insectoid's body crumpled to the floor.

"Now you, my green friend," Skargg said, swinging his barrel toward Gort.

Panic surged through Ava as the realization struck her like ice water—they were going to die before being rescued. But then, as if time stood still, she glimpsed movement out of the corner of her eye. Narrowing her focus to the far wall, she spotted a tiny droid hiding beneath the freighter's boarding ramp, hopping up and down, trying to get her attention.

Ava blinked, wondering if she was hallucinating—then the ground shuddered beneath her, growing into a steady, unsettling tremor. Ava's body tensed, her muscles straining to keep her upright as the floor vibrated.

Dust cascaded from the open ceiling throughout the hangar, shaken loose by the refinery's sudden awakening. Machinery that had lain dormant now roared to life, filling the once-still air with a cacophony of sound. Massive furnaces ignited with a thunderous whoosh, sending an eerie orange glow flickering across the walls. The rhythmic thump of industrial pumps and the grinding of rusty gears reverberated throughout the facility, echoing the refinery's relentless, mechanical heartbeat.

Ava shifted on her knees to get a better look at the unfolding chaos. Turning toward the refinery, she glanced up and saw steam and smoke billowing out of the towering stacks. And there, clambering down an access ladder from high above, she spotted a lone figure.

Her breath caught in her throat. *Neil!*

43
PROMISES

Planet Rogantu

The refinery's sudden startup caught Skargg off guard, but his confusion quickly faded. Already sensing foul play, his suspicions were confirmed when he followed Ava's gaze toward the smokestacks. There, he spotted a figure hurrying down an access ladder.

Skargg growled in frustration. "Secure these two onboard," he ordered, waving the barrel of his blaster between Ava and Toma. "And prep the ship for take-off."

"Yes, sir," came the synchronized reply from the two fighters closest to him.

As they hauled Ava and Toma to their feet, Gort turned to Skargg, his eyes wide with panic. "What about me?" he mumbled. "It wasn't my fault; it was his idea," he said, nodding at Smythe's motionless body.

Skargg checked the charge on his weapon before aiming it at Gort's temple. "Tell that to your partner," he said with cold detachment, then pulled the trigger.

The close-range shot sent Gort's head snapping back as blood and brain matter exploded outward, leaving a gaping hole. His body crumpled beside Smythe.

Ava recoiled, cringing as smoke curled from Gort's cauterized head wound, the stench of burning flesh assaulting her nostrils. The horrific scene conjured memories of a North Korean soldier crushed to death aboard the Aiwan mothership back on Earth—the grossest thing she had ever seen … until now.

"Move!" Skargg commanded, shoving Ava and jolting her back to the present. "The rest of you, follow me. We've got company."

As Skargg's last word hung in the air, a single shot echoed through the landing bay. He whipped around just in time to see one of his fighters fall to his knees at the far end, his chest cavity exposed from being shot in the back. The abruptness of the kill froze Skargg and his crew—not from grief for their fallen comrade but from the sight of the one responsible: Prince Kypa of Aiwa.

For a heartbeat, time stood still, and a tense silence charged the air. Skargg and Kypa locked eyes, caught in a deadly standoff while the remaining fighters remained rooted in place.

Skargg stole a glimpse at Kypa's weapon—aimed directly at him. A thin wisp of smoke rose from the barrel. Kypa had him dead to rights.

Then, out of the corner of his eye, Skargg saw movement—one of his fighters shifted slightly. Kypa reacted with lethal speed, shattering the stillness as he fired again, dropping the fighter with one shot.

Skargg and his remaining team immediately returned fire. Kypa peeled away just in time, vanishing into an adjacent corridor that led to the refinery while the Madreen fighters advanced. Firing at the space where Kypa once stood, they hit nothing but shadows.

The firefight died down, and Skargg was about to give chase when he heard the freighter's boarding ramp closing behind him. He spun around just as the ramp sealed shut. Ava and Toma were gone.

Skargg's face twisted with rage. "Idiots! You let them get away!" he fumed, aiming his frustration at the two fighters responsible for guarding the prisoners.

The fighters exchanged accusatory looks, each scrambling for an excuse. In truth, they were so caught up in the firefight that they forgot all about their prisoners.

"Get them back," Skargg snarled. "If that ship escapes, you die!"

Both fighters nodded vigorously before double-timing it back to the freighter. Their departure reduced Skargg's ground team to three: Drago, Larsk, and him.

"Maybe we should call for reinforcements?" Drago proposed, his eyes darting between Skargg and Larsk as if hoping for a sign of approval.

Skargg sneered. "And announce our failure to Krunig? Are you mad, or just stupid?"

Drago's jaw tightened with a flash of anger, but he quickly saw the futility of his suggestion and dropped it.

"Listen," Skargg continued. "There can't be more than a few of them, or they would've overrun us by now. It's a trap. They're trying to draw us into the refinery," he said with certainty. "We'll split up. I'll take the middle. Drago, you go left. Larsk, you cover the right. We'll push them back and box them in. Got it?"

Both fighters nodded in agreement.

"And set your blasters to stun," Skargg added sharply. "We need Prince Kypa alive."

Inside the freighter, Ten-Tee activated the miniature repulsors under its feet, gracefully lowering itself to the floor after closing the ramp. Ava and Toma exchanged glances, impressed by the tiny droid's resourcefulness. But they did not have a moment to lose.

"Nice work," Ava said with a wry grin. "Did you lock it?"

Ten-Tee responded with a series of excited chirps and beeps—none of which Ava, or the AI in her helmet, could decipher. She shot a questioning look at Toma for his take. He responded with a shrug, equally perplexed.

"Okay, we'll take that as a yes," Ava replied. "Listen, we don't have much time," she said urgently. "Can you get these off?"

Ava turned her back, presenting her bound hands. Ten-Tee nodded eagerly and beeped a two-syllable reply that sounded uncannily like "Sure thing."

"Perfect," Ava said, carefully lowering to her knees.

Ten-Tee opened a small compartment in its torso. A tiny arm extended outward, tipped with a tool that resembled a lockpick. Once Ava was in position, she held her hands out, giving the droid the space it needed to work.

While Ten-Tee picked the lock on her cuffs, Toma anxiously shifted his weight, keeping a wary eye on the exit. He expected Krunig's troops to storm the freighter at any moment. And if they did, he and Ava were powerless to stop them.

"We need weapons," he said, scanning the area for anything that might qualify.

"I agree," Ava said over her shoulder. "See anything?"

Before Toma could answer, Ava heard a distinct click and felt the cuffs loosen around her wrists. Her arms dropped limply to her sides as the binders fell to the floor with a metallic thump. She was free at last.

"Yes!" Ava said with excitement and relief. She wrung her hands and turned to Ten-Tee, gently patting its head. "Thank you, friend. You have no idea how good this feels."

Ten-Tee chirped contentedly, leaning into her touch, much to Ava's delight.

The tender moment was fleeting. Ava stood, rubbing her aching wrists. "Your turn," she said to Toma.

Toma dropped to one knee and held out his wrists for the droid to reach his restraints. Ten-Tee made short work of the binders, freeing Toma within moments.

"C'mon, we need to get to Reggie," Ava urged, gesturing up the corridor to where the Reaper was held.

Toma hesitated, planting his feet. "Wait, my father is out there," he said, gesturing to the exit. "He needs our help."

Ava paused; her shoulders slumped as she sighed. "I know, Neil is with him," she said reassuringly. "We'll help them—I promise. But first, I need to—"

A loud popping sound abruptly cut her off. Ava and Toma rounded sharply to find the control panel by the exit ramp smoking. Krunig's troops were trying to force their way inside.

Thinking fast, Ava grabbed Toma by the wrist. "This way!"

She pulled him along, weaving through the corridor to the freighter's cargo hold. Seeing the Reaper again was a welcome sight, but it was still held securely by docking claws.

Ava veered toward her ship, but Toma pulled up, freeing his wrist from her grasp.

"Ava, we do not have time for this," he implored.

But Ava was determined to contact Reggie. She continued toward her ship and replied over her shoulder, "I'll be right back. Try contacting your father— tell him where we are and find out what he's planning."

Toma opened his mouth to object but hesitated, realizing Ava was going regardless. She was already starting up the ladder to board the Reaper. Frustrated by her decision, Toma cast a worried glance back down the corridor. The passage was empty, but for how long remained to be seen. By the time he turned back, Ava had disappeared inside the Reaper.

Reading Toma's worried expression, Ten-Tee emitted a low, mournful beep, echoing his concern.

Toma shook his head, muttering with annoyance, "Adults."

Inside the Reaper's engineering compartment, Ava called to her ship's computer, "Reggie, you there?"

"Greetings, Ava," Reggie responded in her usual, calm cadence.

Ava paused, catching her breath before sighing with relief. "Oh my god, it's good to hear your voice, Reg. Are you okay?"

"All systems nominal," Reggie answered dutifully.

Ava chuckled softly. "That's good, but I meant how are you *feeling*?" she clarified.

Reggie hesitated, her programming grappling with the new concept. "I... I am not sure how to respond," she admitted. "Can you restate the question?"

Ava's smile softened, and a surge of protectiveness swelled in her chest. She placed her hand on the bulkhead and replied, "We'll figure it out later, I promise. But right now, I need your help. We're in a bit of a pickle."

Scanning the room as she spoke, Ava noticed the electrode Gort had used to torture Toma. She took the device in her hands and activated it. A blue arc of electricity crackled at the tip, evoking memories of her mission to North Korea. Operation Sundiver felt like a lifetime ago, but the haunting yellow eyes of the beast she killed with this weapon would haunt her forever.

Deactivating the electrode, she spoke into the air. "Reggie, listen, I hate to do this, but I have to leave you again. Toma's outside, and Neil and Kypa are here mounting a rescue. They need our help. Can you hold on just a bit longer?"

"Hold on? Here in dry dock?" Reggie replied, her voice carrying a hint of playful sarcasm.

Ava exhaled, her shoulders slumped at the weight of her own words. "Right. Sorry, Reg—stupid question. I'll be back soon to free you, I promise."

As she turned to leave, Reggie's voice followed her, filled with innocence and sincerity, "Good luck, Captain."

Biting her lip, Ava wrestled with the guilt of leaving Reggie behind once again. But duty called. Pulling herself away, she descended the ladder, determined to keep her promise—as soon as she helped Neil and Kypa.

Outside, she found Toma pacing anxiously, making animated hand gestures as he muttered to himself. Ten-Tee mimicked his movements, marching back and forth like a toy soldier.

Toma heard Ava climbing down. Their eyes met, and he held up his finger, signaling her to wait. Ava paused, watching him curiously, noting the deepening furrow in his brow. Then, suddenly, his expression shifted to frustration. Toma clenched his fists, trembling with barely contained anger.

"What is it?" Ava asked worriedly.

"My father wants us to stay here," Toma replied, still fuming.

"Stay here? That's crazy," Ava shot back. "Tell him Krunig's men are right outside. They're coming for us."

"I tried, but he cut off our connection before I could explain."

Ava handed him the electrode. "Here, take this. Do you know how to use it?"

"All too well," Toma said wryly. He held the weapon firmly with both hands, then activated the electrical arc and added, "The pointy end goes in the enemy, right?"

"Damn straight," Ava affirmed. "Now, c'mon and follow me."

Toma hesitated as he watched Ava depart. "Ava, wait," he called out. "My father wants us to stay here."

She glanced back, fiery determination flashing in her eyes. "You can stay if you want, but I'm done playing the victim."

Inspired by Ava's resolve, Toma tightened his grip on the electrode, steeling himself. Drawing a steadying breath, he rushed to catch up with her.

44
COLLATERAL DAMAGE

Planet Rogantu

Skargg entered the refinery's production floor with a predator's grace. His heart pounded with the thrill of the hunt as he crept silently between the rows of machinery and massive storage bins. Every step was deliberate and measured as he ventured deeper into the expansive workspace in search of Prince Kypa.

With his blaster at the ready, Skargg paused often, ever mindful that he was as much of a target as Kypa. Since the mechanical din of the refinery impaired his hearing, he relied heavily on his vision, scanning every shadow and corner for the slightest hint of his prey.

Skargg sensed he was close. He knew Aiwans were highly intelligent, but he was a skilled tracker. Skargg would pursue his quarry with patience and discipline, ready to strike like a coiled spring when the moment was right. Kypa would never see the attack coming.

Drago and Larsk, however, lacked skill and experience and were far less careful. Upon entering the refinery, Drago went left while Larsk climbed a metal stairwell leading to a maze of catwalks above the production floor. Their heavy footfalls and poor light discipline telegraphed their movements.

Skargg rolled his eyes. *Amateurs.*

Still, Larsk and Drago's flaws played to Skargg's advantage, serving as perfect bait to lure their targets.

As Skargg moved forward, he glimpsed a fleeting shadow near the edge of a storage bin ahead. He froze, gripping his blaster tighter, and glanced up at the overhead conveyor. Though empty, the rotating belt kept churning as if it carried rocks to the grinder several stories above.

The shadow moved again, a subtle flicker drawing Skargg's attention. His lips curled into an ugly smile, revealing rows of yellow, crooked teeth. He inched closer, careful not to give his position away—one misstep could turn him from predator to prey.

Skargg sprang into action at the corner, rounding the edge and raising his blaster, finger tense on the trigger. But Kypa was nowhere in sight—only an old rag tied to a ladder rung, swaying in the draft from one of the refinery's shattered windows.

He exhaled in frustration, lowering his blaster as he approached the flapping cloth. Then Skargg spotted a device hidden behind the fabric, secured to the bin. A row of red lights blinked in sequence, counting down to detonation.

Skargg's eyes widened in a panic. He dove for cover just as the device exploded. The blast sent him airborne, slamming against the neighboring bin. Pain erupted in his skull, and he crumpled to the ground, dazed from the bone-jarring impact.

He lay sprawled on the floor, coughing in the smoke-filled air as the world spun around him. Gradually, his senses returned, and the sounds of battle pierced his mental fog. Looking up, Skargg saw blaster fire flashing like lightning through the haze above. He spotted Larsk on the catwalk, advancing while firing his weapon. Skargg followed his line of fire to the far end of the catwalk and saw Larsk's target darting for cover. He blinked, not believing his eyes.

Another human!

Adrenaline surging, Skargg grabbed his blaster and forced himself to his feet. Shaking off the lingering effects, he hurried to join the pursuit, determined to crush Kypa's rescue attempt before Krunig noticed anything amiss.

After his harrowing ordeal on the smokestack, Neil finally reached the refinery's third floor, where Kypa crouched behind a massive stone grinder, engaged in a fierce firefight with Drago. Neil dove for cover beside his friend as Larsk fired repeatedly, his shots ringing out in a relentless attempt to cut him off. Scrambling onto all fours, Neil muttered a curse, his words lost in the deafening chaos around them.

Kypa reacted instantly to Larsk's incoming fire. Shifting to stand over Neil, he fired two shots at Larsk, both narrowly missing. Suddenly, a blaster bolt whizzed past Kypa's face from the opposite direction, making him recoil. He pivoted sharply to his right, where Drago was firing relentlessly through the shattered control room window.

Crouching behind the grinder, Kypa shouted in Neil's ear, "Take the one on the catwalk!"

The urgency sent a shiver through Neil, but there was no time for hesitation. With blaster fire raining down from both sides, he sprang into action.

Glancing around the corner of the grinder, Neil spotted Larsk charging toward him. He paused for a split second, drew a steadying breath, then surged to his feet and stepped out into the open.

"Freeze!" Neil shouted, taking aim.

Larsk ignored the command and continued firing. In a panic, Neil squeezed his eyes shut and pulled the trigger.

Time seemed to stand still as his shot's echo faded into the machinery's din. Then, a heavy thud reverberated on the catwalk. Neil's eyes shot open, and he blinked in disbelief. His shot had found its mark—Larsk's headless body lay sprawled across the metal grating.

Neil winced at the grisly sight, his stomach twisting as he hastily patted himself down for injuries. To his astonishment, he was unscathed.

"Move!" Kypa barked, gripping Neil by the back of the neck and directing him behind cover. A split second later, an errant shot from Drago whizzed past Neil's face, missing him by inches.

Moving swiftly, Kypa darted back to his right to reacquire Drago. He peeked around the corner of the grinder and spotted him in the control room, adjusting his weapon. Seizing the opportunity, Kypa opened fire, blasting through the shattered window. The barrage forced Drago to retreat and disappear.

A brief silence followed, and Kypa scanned the control room for movement. Just as he began to relax, Drago reappeared, unleashing a series of salvos.

Kypa ducked behind the machinery, blaster bolts impacting all around him. As he prepared to counterattack, something about the last exchange struck him as odd—the enemy's blaster fire had a different ring. Then, it clicked. Unlike previous shots, the recent energy bolts dissipated harmlessly on impact.

Stun blasts.

Kypa's eyes narrowed as he grasped his enemy's shift in tactics. Krunig's forces were trying to capture him now, not kill him. Whether that order extended to Neil was uncertain, but Kypa had no intention of finding out.

With renewed urgency, Kypa swung his weapon around and aimed at the control room—only to find it empty. Drago had vanished. Scanning the area with the barrel of his weapon, Kypa found no sign of the enemy. Thinking fast, he hustled back to Neil, keeping low and ready for anything.

"We need to move," Kypa said, extending his hand. "They are trying to flank us."

Neil took his friend's hand and pulled himself up. Feeling the concern in Kypa's gaze, he responded with a quick nod of reassurance. The initial shock of his first kill had faded, and he was ready to press on.

Accepting this, Kypa glanced past Neil to the nearby catwalk, estimating its length. The elevated walkway spanned approximately three hundred yards from their current location to the landing bay at the far end. Traversing it would leave them dreadfully exposed, but it was the fastest route.

"It is time to spring our trap," Kypa said, leaning close to Neil to be heard over the noise. "Toma and Ava are free. They are waiting for us in the landing bay. Can you run?"

Neil eyed the catwalk and nodded.

Kypa pointed to their destination, spurring Neil into action. "Go now—all the way to the end, and do not stop!"

With a firm nudge, he urged Neil forward, and the two sprinted toward the nearby catwalk. Neil vaulted over Larsk's remains, shoving the horrible image out of his mind as he ran. But before they could gain much ground, blaster fire erupted from below.

Skargg lay in wait, biding his time as Drago flushed out their quarry. The moment Neil passed, Skargg launched his ambush, firing a stun blast that struck Kypa in the upper arm and knocked him off balance.

Kypa nearly plunged over the railing but caught himself just in time. Righting himself, he shook off the effects of the stun blast as another shot narrowly missed him. Inspecting his arm, Kypa noticed a disturbance in his nanosuit. The impact had caused the nanites to glitch, leaving a gap that exposed his olive-green skin. Without hesitation, he pinched the material together, allowing the nanites to realign and seal the breach.

"Kypa!" Neil shouted urgently.

Kypa looked up and spotted Neil up ahead, anxiously waving him forward. Pressing on, Kypa took a step forward when another bone-jarring blast hit him in the chest. The impact lifted him off his feet and sent him sprawling onto his back. He landed hard, rattling the catwalk.

Skargg swiftly dodged as Neil opened fire from above. Blaster bolts erupted around the Madreen fighter, but Skargg was quick and elusive, weaving through the barrage. He kept moving, eyes locked on Kypa, searching for an opening to reposition and take another shot.

Neil lost sight of him in the maze of bins below and held fire. Seconds later, Skargg emerged underneath Kypa, firing a concussive blast that struck the Aiwan while on his back, still stunned by the previous hit. However, the catwalk's grated metal walkway dissipated most of the blast, and Kypa's nanosuit absorbed the rest. He rolled over onto all fours, grimacing with pain, and looked up to find Drago standing over him, wearing a victorious smirk.

Drago had Kypa in his crosshairs, his blaster aimed squarely at the Aiwan's head. Kypa began to surrender when Drago suddenly gasped. His body convulsed violently as thin tendrils of smoke rose from his ears, nose, and mouth. His eyes rolled back, and with a final shudder, he collapsed to his knees and fell face-first onto the catwalk.

Toma stood over Drago's lifeless remains, gripping the electrode tightly, with Ava by his side. Seeing the pair, Kypa managed a pained smile.

"Father!" Toma cried, rushing toward him.

But before they could reunite, a fresh volley of blaster fire erupted. Another stun blast from below rattled the catwalk, halting Toma. Ava quickly pulled him to safety as more shots rang out, though these were from Neil. Leaning over the railing, he was firing down at Skargg, trying to drive him away.

"Neil!" Ava shouted.

Neil stopped firing and turned at the sound of her voice. When his eyes found Ava, a fleeting smile spread across his face.

Taking advantage of Neil's distraction, Skargg quickly adjusted his blaster to a lethal setting while moving between bins and then returned fire. He caught Neil out in the open and fired several shots—one striking him in the leg.

The sharp sting to his thigh grabbed Neil's attention. He looked down at his leg and found the shot had only grazed him, but the nanosuit around the wound flickered, revealing a patch of reddened skin. Neil's eyes widened in surprise at the sight of the superficial burn. Realizing his suit could no longer protect him, he panicked and fled towards the landing bay.

Thinking quickly, Ava snatched up Kypa's blaster and fired at Skargg, creating enough cover for Neil to slip away. Skargg retreated, vanishing amongst the storage bins. Once he was gone, Ava turned to find Toma helping his father to his feet.

With no time to waste, she gestured toward the back stairwell leading to the production floor. "C'mon," she urged. "We have to help Neil!"

Aboard Grawn Krunig's warship, a persistent alarm drew the attention of a bridge technician. Silencing the alert, he frowned as he traced its source. Puzzled by the results, he ran a diagnostic check on his equipment to confirm his findings. With certainty, he called to Draxx, the ship's acting first officer.

"Yes, what is it?" Draxx asked, annoyed by the interruption.

"Sir, I'm detecting unusual activity on the planet's surface," the technician reported, his voice steady despite Draxx's impatience. "It's the refinery, sir. Sensors show a massive energy signature—I believe the facility has powered up."

Draxx scoffed. "Powered up? Nonsense. That refinery's been dormant since before you were born."

"See for yourself, sir," the technician replied, sliding his monitor over.

Draxx's brow knitted together as he scrutinized the display. "That's impossible," he muttered, searching for answers. "Contact Skargg and find out what's going on down there."

Spurred into action, the technician repeatedly hailed Skargg and the ground team but received no response. After numerous failed attempts, he had no choice but to relay the troubling news to Grawn Krunig.

His superior's reaction was immediate. Krunig stormed onto the bridge moments later, demanding answers in a thunderous voice. When Draxx failed to provide any, Krunig's rage flared. He ripped a sickle from his armored chest plate and raised it to strike.

"My lord, incoming message from the ground team!" the technician interrupted, freezing the crime lord mid-swing.

Seething behind his faceless mask, Krunig slowly lowered his weapon. "Put it on speaker," he growled.

"Ground Team to Control, we are under attack. Repeat, we are under attack by an Aiwan assault team," came the frantic report. "We have visual confirmation of Prince Kypa and are attempting to apprehend him."

"What!?" Krunig bellowed, stepping closer to the comm station. "Identify yourself!" he demanded.

Recognizing Grawn Krunig's angry voice, one of the Madreen fighters tasked with capturing Ava and Toma in the freighter stammered a reply.

"M-My lord, this is Wolfgar," he answered. "The bounty hunters are dead, and we've secured their ship, but Prince Kypa's son escaped along with the female human. Skargg and the others are in pursuit."

"You have the Reaper?" Krunig asked, his tone sharpening.

"Yes, my lord. It's secured onboard the bounty hunter's freighter."

"Very good," Krunig said, his anger momentarily tempered. "Bring me the freighter, I want both ships. Understood?"

"Yes, my lord. We're leaving now."

Krunig ended the transmission and turned to Draxx. "Deploy every foot soldier we have to the surface," he ordered. "I want Kypa captured alive!"

Neil sprinted across the catwalk, frantically evading Skargg. At the catwalk's end, he hurried down a metal staircase to the ground floor, then bolted through the archway leading to the landing bay. He arrived just as the bounty hunter's freighter lifted off.

Thinking fast, Neil located an exit to his left and started in that direction, hoping to circle back outside and re-enter the refinery elsewhere. But as he stepped into the landing bay, the high-pitched whine of decelerating engines froze him in his tracks. Neil looked up to find three Madreen dropships descending on his position.

They spotted him, too. The side door of the nearest transport slid open, and a door gunner appeared. He immediately zeroed in on Neil, spraying the area with heavy cannon fire.

Neil dove back inside as the walls around him disintegrated. He scrambled to safety on all fours, then came to his feet and sprinted back into the refinery. Skidding to a halt, chest heaving, he frantically scanned the production floor. His friends were nowhere in sight. Uncertainty gripped him as every path ahead seemed equally perilous.

"Don't move!" Skargg shouted, emerging from the shadows to Neil's left, his blaster leveled.

Neil's shoulders sank in defeat; the fight drained from him as he let his weapon clatter to the floor. He then slowly raised his hands.

Skargg sneered. "Now, call your friends."

Neil nodded in acknowledgment. But just as he opened his mouth to speak, Ten-Tee fell from the sky. The tiny droid had jumped off the catwalk above, igniting the repulsors in its feet, inches from Skargg's bald head. The sudden burst of heat scorched the top of his skull, singeing his mohawk. Skargg cried out in anguish as he swatted at the menacing droid.

Seizing the moment, Neil lunged at Skargg with a linebacker's tackle, knocking the blaster from his hand. Momentum carried them both backward until Skargg's heel caught the base of a conveyor. He tripped, and they tumbled together onto the moving belt.

The conveyor lurched into motion, carrying them toward the ominous stone grinder in the distance. Skargg rolled, pinning Neil beneath him. He then threw a punch at Neil's face, only to cry out in pain as his fist collided with the human's invisible helmet. The impact sent a sharp, jarring pain shooting up Skargg's arm, but he quickly shook it off. His face contorted with fury, and he wrapped his thick hands around Neil's throat, squeezing with all his strength.

Neil's eyes bulged, and a strangled gasp escaped his lips. Unable to move under Skargg's crushing weight, he struggled to break free, but the Madreen's powerful grip was like a steel trap. Neil's mind raced for an escape as he tried clawing desperately at Skargg's face, but his fingers fell short. He then threw several feeble punches with little effect. Choking, Neil's face gradually turned a deep shade of purple, and his vision blurred—the fight in him started to slip away.

Ten-Tee returned just in time. Undeterred by the danger, the droid attacked Skargg from behind. Extending an armature from its torso, Ten-Tee jabbed the electrode into Skargg's lower back and zapped him with a full charge of electricity.

Roaring in pain, Skargg released Neil and twisted around to swat at the pesky droid. Ten-Tee dodged the brute's swing, retreating enough to stay out of harm's way.

Neil's reprieve was brief. Clutching his throat, he drew a ragged breath, followed by a deep, shuddering inhale as his lungs gratefully filled with air. Coughing and gasping, he barely had time to regain his focus before Skargg's massive hand clamped down over his face, pressing him firmly to the conveyor.

Holding Neil in place, the Madreen reached behind his back and drew a dagger. Skargg activated the blade's carbon edge in one swift motion, energizing it with a monomolecular laser capable of piercing most armor. A vicious snarl curled Skargg's lip as he raised the weapon overhead, bringing it down in a deadly arc.

Panic flashed in Neil's eyes at the sight of the descending blade. He flung his arm up in a desperate attempt to defend himself, deflecting the thrust just enough to avoid being impaled. The blade scraped against the side of Neil's holographic helmet before embedding itself in the conveyor.

Skargg growled, his rage mounting, and drew back for another strike. Thinking fast, Neil had an epiphany. With Skargg's hand still clamped over his face, Neil grabbed Skargg's wrist, and in an instant, the nanites from his right sleeve surged onto the Madreen's hand.

A look of confusion crossed Skargg's face, quickly turning to alarm as the swarm of black nanites crawled up his arm. He frantically swatted at the foreign substance, trying to brush it off, but the nanites climbed higher. As they spread from Skargg's neck to his face, the nanites tightened over his nose and mouth like a suffocating shroud, cutting off his breath.

Skargg released the dagger, his muffled screams growing more frantic as he clawed desperately to free himself.

At that moment, Ava, Kypa, and Toma rushed in. Ava gasped as she spotted Skargg atop Neil overhead, the conveyor carrying them closer to the grinder's rolling jaws of death.

She raised her blaster, looking for a clear shot at the Madreen, but found none at this angle.

"Neil!" she cried out helplessly.

Ava's voice registered, but Neil was too engrossed in the moment. With the grinder looming, he wriggled downward between Skargg's legs and rolled over the side just as the conveyor fed the hulking thug into the machine. Hanging precariously by one hand, Neil heard Skargg's high-pitched scream as the grinder's spinning blades devoured him.

"Hang on! We're coming!" Ava shouted as she sprang into action.

But it was already too late. As Neil threw his free hand up, trying to latch onto the conveyor, his nanosuit glitched unexpectedly. Neil's breath hitched as his grip faltered, and suddenly, he was falling.

Kypa elbowed his way past Ava, attempting to catch his friend. But Neil slipped past his outstretched arms and crashed onto the unforgiving floor, striking his head.

"No!" Kypa's voice broke as he immediately dropped to his knees beside Neil. He shook his friend's crumpled body urgently. "Neil, can you hear me? Neil!"

There was no response. Kypa gently rolled Neil over, cradling his head, but Neil remained unconscious, his eyes closed and his body still.

Ava stood back, her hands over her mouth, tears streaming down her cheeks. Beside her, Toma gently touched her shoulder, offering silent comfort.

Kypa deactivated Neil's helmet and pressed his long fingers against his neck. "He has a pulse," Kypa announced with a glimmer of hope in his voice. "It is weak, and his breathing is shallow, but he is alive. We need to move quickly to stabilize him."

Ava hastily wiped away her tears. "Tell me what to do."

"Gather up," Kypa instructed, glancing around for Ten-Tee. The tiny droid stood a few feet away, looking almost like a frightened child. "Come here, little one," Kypa said, waving it closer. "He needs your help, too."

45
OVERRUN

Planet Rogantu

Neil Garrett's life hung by a thread as he lay unconscious on the refinery's production floor, surrounded by his friends. Kypa worked frantically to save him while Ava and Toma watched anxiously.

With Neil's nanosuit missing on the right sleeve, Kypa used Ten-Tee's lockpick to adjust the settings on Neil's nano-ring. The hope was to repair Neil's faulty suit and use it to stabilize him for transport.

"There, that should do it," Kypa muttered, setting the tool aside. He then gently removed Neil's tactical vest and handed it to Toma. "Here, put this on," he instructed his son.

Toma did so without question.

"Do you think this'll work?" Ava asked, desperation evident in her voice.

Kypa lifted his gaze, offering a reassuring smile. "In theory, yes. But we will not know the full extent of his injuries until we can get him back to the ship."

Turning back to Neil, Kypa placed his hand on his friend's exposed arm. He then issued a neural command to his own suit's AI, instructing it to transfer ten percent of his nanites to Neil's suit. Suddenly, a shimmering effect spread across Kypa's body from the neck down as a wave of nanites flowed down his arm and transferred onto Neil's flesh. The old and new nanites seamlessly merged within seconds, forming a sleeve from Neil's shoulder down to his elbow.

Kypa turned to Ava. "Now you."

While Ava and Toma did their part, Kypa used the lockpick to adjust his nano-ring. With the planet's interference continuing to wreak havoc on their suits—and the dwindling supply of nanites—there was no guarantee their suits would stay intact long enough to get back to the ship.

Kypa pushed that thought aside as Ava and Toma finished their transfers. With Neil's body fully covered again, the nanites reconfigured, encasing Neil in a protective cocoon—like an ancient Egyptian sarcophagus. During the process, the nanites expelled Neil's bag of credits onto the floor.

"What's that?" Ava asked.

"Neil found some credits at the outpost," he replied, picking up the bag and tossing it to Toma. "Hold onto this for him, would you?"

Toma caught it with one hand and tucked it inside his vest pocket.

"Neil should be stable now," Kypa said with some satisfaction. He straightened and gestured to Ava's nano-ring with the lockpick, "May I?"

"Yeah, of course," she replied, craning her neck to give him room to work. Ava glanced at Neil's cocoon as Kypa reset her nano-ring, restoring its defensive capabilities. "You even added carrying handles," she noted with a hint of amusement.

"Yes," Kypa replied. "I thought they would help us move faster."

When he was finished, he stepped back. Wasting no time admiring his handiwork, Kypa started on Toma's hardware.

"Well, at least we don't have to carry him very far," Ava remarked, her expression hardening with a war planner's focus. "There's still one or two more bad guys in the hangar. If we take them out, we can move Neil to the Reaper and get out of here."

Toma's brow furrowed. "What do you mean? The Reaper is gone."

Ava snapped her gaze at him. "Come again?"

"I thought you already knew," Toma replied, surprised by her reaction.

Kypa finished his task and stepped back, joining Ava. Both of them looked at Toma, waiting for an explanation.

"Right after we got separated from Neil," Toma continued, nodding toward the shattered skylights above. "I saw the bounty hunter's freighter take off."

Ava's gaze shot upwards, seeing nothing but Krunig's menacing warship. She gripped Toma's arm, her eyes boring into his with unspoken urgency. "Toma, are you absolutely sure? Did you see Reggie?"

Toma blinked, taken aback, and replied innocently, "Well, no ... but it was the freighter, I am sure of it."

Ava's hands curled into tight fists as she fought back the urge to scream. Despite her frustration, she forced herself to stay composed, pressing her lips together into a thin, unyielding line.

"Ava," Kypa began gently, but she cut him off with a sharp wave of her finger, silencing him before he could say more.

"Don't, please," she said curtly. Taking a deep breath, she turned to Toma. "I'm sorry, this isn't on you—it's on me," Ava admitted, her tone softening. "My ship, my crew ... they're my responsibility. I promised Reggie I'd come back for her." Her voice faltered, then hardened with anger. "And now Krunig's stolen her from me ... *again.*"

"We will find Reggie," Kypa assured her. "But first, we must help Neil."

Accepting the harsh truth, Ava nodded in agreement. Reggie would have to wait.

"It is too dangerous to stay here," Kypa said. "We need to leave before more troops arrive."

"Can we make it to your ship?" Ava asked, wondering how far they would have to carry Neil.

"Yes, but the distance is considerable," Kypa replied. "If we hurry, we can make it before nightfall. Toma and I will carry Neil. You provide cover."

Ava gripped Kypa's blaster tighter, ready to do her part. Just then, she spotted movement in the distance. Her eyes widened as Krunig's forces poured into the refinery through the landing bay.

"Uh oh," she muttered.

Kypa followed her eyes, his gaze sharpening at the sight of the four-armed, crimson-armored figure leading the charge.

Krunig locked onto Kypa and his companions. "Seize them!" he bellowed.

Without hesitation, Kypa scooped up Ten-Tee and shouted to the others, "Move!"

Ava raised her blaster and opened fire as Kypa and Toma hoisted Neil's cocoon from the floor. Gripping the handle nearest Neil's head, Kypa took the lead, guiding their escape toward the far end of the refinery.

"Where are we going?" Ava called out, firing haphazardly to keep Krunig's forces at bay.

"Outside!" Kypa responded without breaking stride.

Passing the final storage bin, Kypa slipped through an open doorway into a barren corridor. He veered left and pressed on, mentally mapping their path while running calculations in his head.

At the end of the corridor, they reached an open door that led outside. Kypa burst out of the refinery, racing across the rugged, volcanic terrain. Ava and Toma caught their first glimpse of Rogantu—a barren, desolate wasteland—but there was no time to linger. Kypa kept them moving at a frenetic pace, driving them away from the facility with purpose.

"Hop off," he instructed Ten-Tee.

The tiny droid leaped out of his hand, using its thrusters to land on Neil's cocoon.

With his hand free, Kypa reached into his vest pocket and pulled out a detonator. Trusting his guesstimates, he pressed the activate button. A series of thunderous explosions followed. The grenades Neil had planted on the smokestacks ignited behind them, and the deafening booms reverberated across the landscape.

Startled by the explosions, Ava and Toma glanced back to find thick plumes of black smoke rising from the base of each stack. As the towering structures began to topple onto the refinery, Ava realized this was Neil's doing—he had rigged the charges to cover their escape.

She grinned wryly. *Chalk one up for NASA.*

Inside the refinery, the shockwave from the three explosions brought Krunig's fighters to a standstill. The blasts shattered the remaining rooftop windows, raining down razor-sharp glass. The stacks began to fall with a dreadful screech of twisting metal. Three looming shadows engulfed the fighters, paralyzing them with indecision—until panic took over, and they turned to flee.

Krunig surveyed the chaos and instantly realized his troops were doomed. Without hesitation, he retreated to the landing bay, flanked by two grenadiers close on his heels. As they reached the entrance, the stacks collapsed onto the facility with a thunderous crash. The refinery shuddered as clouds of dense smoke and dust billowed outward, shrouding the destruction in a thick haze.

The shockwave slammed Krunig and his guards to the ground as one of the dropships parked outside the landing bay flipped over. Its fuel cell ruptured in a violent explosion, engulfing a neighboring vessel and triggering a second explosion.

Struggling to his feet, Krunig tripped over the grenadiers sprawled at his feet—their dead bodies twisted in unnatural positions. He activated the HUD inside his helmet. It flickered on, and he scanned the area through the churning cloud of dust and smoke. His sensors detected a few survivors pinned beneath a mountain of rubble. But any hope of rescuing them vanished moments later as Krunig picked up additional life signs. What began as minor movements where the refinery's control room used to stand rapidly multiplied. Within seconds, the facility was teeming with activity.

Krunig's scan identified the lifeforms: gracylai—centipede-like carnivores native to Rogantu. Realizing the situation was beyond salvage, he headed for the last dropship. As Krunig emerged from the dust cloud, the side door slid open. Two fighters jumped out, providing covering fire while he climbed aboard. Once they were all inside, the dropship lifted off.

Krunig wasted no time and made his way to the cockpit.

"Circle the compound," he ordered. "Fly low and look for survivors."

"Yes, sir," the pilot replied, adjusting course.

The transport swung around the northern end of the compound, where the smokestacks used to stand. Krunig surveyed the devastation. Through the forward viewport, he glimpsed the gracylai swarming the facility.

"Lower!" he barked. Convinced Prince Kypa had survived, Krunig was determined to capture him before those creatures got to him first.

"My lord, I'm detecting three life signs on foot," the pilot reported. "Looks like they're heading for the outpost."

Krunig peered out the cockpit window. He zoomed in on the targets using his HUD: two Aiwans and a human female sprinting across open ground. Grinning behind his helmet, he shifted his gaze to the long, black object they were carrying, which had a small droid riding on top.

Intrigued, he asked the pilot, "What are they carrying?"

After a brief scan, the pilot responded, "Inconclusive, sir. Shall I open fire?"

"Negative," Krunig replied. "Take us down. I want them alive."

"Kypa, where are we going?" Ava shouted in frustration, trying to keep pace with the Aiwans.

"We are almost there," he responded over his shoulder. "Just a bit further!"

Moments later, Ava heard the roar of the Krunig's dropship. She glanced back, her eyes widening as the snub-nosed spacecraft descended rapidly on their position.

"Incoming!" she cried out.

Ava instinctively ducked as the dropship buzzed overhead, whipping up dirt and ash as it streaked by. Undeterred, she kept running, firing two salvos and missing before the transport moved out of range.

"Whatever you're going to do, do it fast!" she urged as the dropship slowed in the distance and lowered its landing struts.

Kypa slowed as they reached a maintenance hole, half-buried in volcanic ash. Ten-Tee jumped off as they set Neil down. Kypa knelt beside the cover. Brushing off the manual release lever, he gave it a good yank. The rusted cover slid open with a loud screech, revealing a ladder leading directly to the underground tunnel.

"Hurry," Kypa said urgently to Ten-Tee. "Go down and scan for threats."

The tiny droid beeped dutifully. It peered over the edge into the maintenance hole, then hopped inside, lowering itself in a controlled descent using its miniature thrusters.

As soon as Ten-Tee was gone, Kypa followed. Climbing inside, he turned to his son. "Quick, lower Neil down to me."

Toma nodded and then glanced toward the dropship. As Krunig's vessel landed, three soldiers jumped out, advancing on their position. Kypa and Toma exchanged anxious looks, both thinking the same thing: they were running out of time.

Kypa peered down the ladder to check on Ten-Tee's progress. The droid had reached the bottom and scanned the tunnel with its photoreceptors.

"All clear?" he called down.

A confirming whistle echoed up the shaft, which Kypa interpreted as the all-clear signal. Without hesitation, he continued down. Toma set aside the electrode and started dragging Neil's cocoon into place with Ava's help.

"Ready?" Toma called down to his father.

"Ready!" Kypa replied.

Lowering Neil inside turned out to be trickier than expected, even with Ava's help. Toma maneuvered the cocoon feet-first into the opening, then lifted the opposite end and let gravity do the rest.

Suddenly, blaster fire rang out as Ava opened fire on the advancing Madreen fighters, trying to buy her friends time. The noise startled Toma, causing him to lose his grip and nearly drop Neil onto his father. But he recovered just in time and steadied the cocoon.

"Let go!" Kypa called up. "I have him!"

Toma released his grip, leaving his father to bear the full brunt of Neil's weight. Once Kypa stabilized himself on the ladder, he continued down one rung at a time.

Wasting no time, Toma climbed into the maintenance hole. With just his head sticking out, he checked on Ava, who was still engaged in the firefight.

Toma looked to the dropship and spotted a foreboding warrior dressed in crimson armor waiting outside the ship—Grawn Krunig.

"Ava, time to go!" he called to her.

Ava caught sight of Toma just as he waved her over. In one swift motion, he seized the electrode and disappeared into the maintenance hole. That was her signal—it was time to leave the battlefield.

Breaking off contact, she holstered her weapon to make her getaway. A stun bolt struck Ava from behind just as she reached the opening. The impact knocked her to her knees. Shaking off the effects, she scrambled on all fours to the hole, enemy shots skipping off the dirt around her. Climbing inside, she yanked the release handle, sealing the hatch shut overhead and casting the maintenance hole into darkness.

"How do I lock this thing?" Ava called down to Kypa.

Kypa had reached the bottom of the ladder and was lowering Neil to the ground. Glancing up the shaft, he shouted, "Shoot the control panel!"

Ava moved further down and hooked her left arm through the ladder rung, gripping it tightly. She drew her blaster and aimed at the panel, wincing as she turned away and pulled the trigger. The panel exploded in a shower of sparks. When the smoke cleared, she found it was completely fried.

"Got it!" she said, holstering her weapon before starting her descent.

Outside, Krunig's fighters reached the maintenance hole. Noticing a tendril of smoke rising from the control panel, they were not surprised when the hatch failed to open.

"My lord, they disabled the hatch," the ranking foot soldier reported. "It will take time—"

"—Get it open!" Krunig snapped back.

As his grunts went to work on the hatch, Krunig surveyed the horizon, looking for Kypa's ship. The abandoned outpost was a speck in the distance, but he knew from previous scans it was empty. Besides that, there was nothing but volcanic mountains and lava rivers as far as the eye could see.

Just then, his commlink crackled to life. "Yes?" Krunig answered tersely.

"My lord, three Aiwan corvettes just emerged from hyperspace," Draxx reported. "They're on an intercept course."

Krunig clenched his fists in rage, a growl of frustration escaping his throat. He was so close to capturing Kypa that abandoning the chase boiled his blood. Yet, remaining on the surface with enemy warships bearing down on them was too great a risk. Kypa would have to wait—for now.

"Prepare for battle," Krunig ordered as he boarded the transport. "I'm returning to the ship."

As the dropship lifted off, Krunig cast a final glance at his fighters, still attempting to open the hatch. He sneered, vowing to himself that he would destroy both Aiwan princes at all costs.

Even if I have to reduce this planet to rubble.

Deep underground, Kypa, Toma, and Ten-Tee waited at the ladder's base as Ava rejoined them.

"That was close," she said, catching her breath. Looking up and down the tunnel with evident concern, she asked, "Now what?"

"This tunnel leads to an abandoned outpost," Kypa replied, pointing ahead. "We have a ship waiting nearby, but we will be vulnerable out in the open."

"We'll cross that bridge when we get to it," Ava remarked optimistically. "Let's just hope Krunig doesn't find it first."

Kypa nodded in agreement. "There is one more thing …"

His voice trailed off at an unmistakable shuffling sound in the distance. The trio rounded sharply in the direction of the refinery. Sensing danger, Kypa and Ava instinctively raised their blasters while Toma assumed a fighting stance with the electrode. They stood frozen, hearts pounding, searching in the darkness for any sign of movement.

"*We are not alone down here,*" Kypa warned Ava and Toma telepathically. "*Switch your helmets to infrared.*"

With a neural command, their visual displays flickered to life, bathing the tunnel in an eerie green glow. They collectively gasped as a massive heat signature came into view—a swarm of gracylai skittering toward them at high speed along the floor, walls, and ceiling.

Kypa fired haphazardly at the creatures as he lifted one end of Neil's cocoon.

"Run!" he shouted.

Toma seized the other end and set off with his father while Ava laid down covering fire. She loosed several shots but quickly realized it had little effect. Peeling away, Ava sprinted for her life. Her breath came in ragged gasps as she raced after her friends. Behind them, the gracylai closed in, their high-pitched screeches slicing through the air.

Her heart pounding, Ava caught a flicker of movement to her left—a fast-moving shadow. A wave of panic hit her, but when she glanced over, she saw Ten-Tee hovering beside her at eye level. The sight was so unexpected it almost made her laugh.

"Nice wheels," she managed between breaths.

Ten-Tee beeped cheerfully and then zipped ahead to take point.

"They're gaining!" Ava shouted, firing wildly over her shoulder.

Up ahead, Kypa spotted a faint, flickering light to his right; they were approaching the collapsed section of the tunnel. In their haste, he had forgotten all about sidetracking along the lava river—it would be treacherous and slow them down considerably.

Kypa's mind raced for a solution. He still had two grenades, but detonating them risked collapsing the entire tunnel on top of them. Desperate, he settled on the only option that might give them a chance.

"*Ava … Toma, listen to me,*" he said telepathically. "*We will not make it to the end. We must stop and cocoon ourselves like Neil, then wait for the creatures to pass.*"

Not liking the sound of that idea, Ava shouted, "Are you sure?"

"Yes," Kypa replied, his pace slowing. *In theory*, he did not add.

Kypa stopped abruptly and dropped Neil without ceremony. Spinning around, he aimed his blaster and began firing. Chest heaving, Ava joined in as Toma activated the electrode and stood ready to fight. As the gracylai drew closer, Kypa and Ava made every shot count, determined to kill as many creatures as possible.

"On my mark …" Kypa shouted over the blaster fire. "Get ready …"

Without warning, a shimmering wall of energy suddenly materialized before them, spanning the tunnel's cylindrical archway from floor to ceiling. Startled, Ava and Kypa ceased firing when their shots dissipated in the energy barrier. But the gracylai kept coming, wave after wave, crashing into the impenetrable wall at full speed, only to be repelled with a painful shock that sent them recoiling with angry hisses.

Ava and Kypa exchanged incredulous looks, baffled by this unexpected turn of events. They traced the barrier's source to Ten-Tee, hovering off to the side by the control panel.

A wide grin spread across Ava's face. "Aren't you full of surprises?"

Ten-Tee beeped cheerily, giving a modest shrug of its little legs as if to say, *It was nothing.*

"Of course," Kypa realized. "When the refinery powered up, it must have energized the tunnel." To Ten-Tee, he added, "Nice work, little one. Neil would be proud."

Ten-Tee chirped appreciatively.

As the gracylai continued to pound against the barrier, dirt trickled from the ceiling. Ava's smile faded when the creatures redirected their efforts to the side walls. Several gracylai began clawing through the tunnel's artificial material, burrowing into the rock.

"Guys, we need to keep moving," she urged.

Kypa nodded vehemently. "This way."

Picking up Neil, they pressed on, reaching the collapsed section of the tunnel within moments. Kypa wasted no time steering them toward the borehole that led to the magma chamber. He and Toma hoisted Neil inside, then passed through with Ava right behind.

Emerging on the far side, Toma and Ava climbed out after Kypa. They surveyed the ominous cavern, their gaze lingering on the foreboding lava river.

"Mind your step," Kypa cautioned, taking up his end of Neil's cocoon. "The trail narrows by the river."

As soon as Toma was ready, Kypa led the way.

Before following, Ava glanced over her shoulder. The gracylai's distant screeches echoed faintly through the borehole. She hoped the energy barrier would hold, but a sinking feeling told her the creatures were not going to give up their pursuit so easily.

Pushing that grim thought aside, Ava hustled to catch up to the others. She felt the intense heat radiating from the molten flow as they made their way along the narrow path. Beads of sweat formed on her brow as her depleted nanosuit struggled to regulate her body temperature. Yet, despite the annoyance, she resisted the urge to deactivate her helmet to wipe her face. The gurgling gas bubbles breaking the lava's surface served as a constant reminder to stay sharp and focus on the path.

Reaching the opposite borehole at the trail's end, Kypa and Toma carefully muscled Neil inside. As they climbed in after him, Ava checked their six once more.

"Now you," Kypa said to her, offering Ava his hand.

She placed her weapon inside the borehole and took Kypa's hand, allowing him to pull her up. With everyone regrouped, they pressed on. Moving through the passage, Ava noted its striking symmetry and realized it was not manufactured—something enormous had burrowed it out.

Reaching the end, she waited while they unloaded Neil, and then climbed out feet-first, her back to the others.

"Well, that wasn't so hard," Ava half-joked as she planted her feet on solid ground.

She brushed herself off and turned around—only to find herself staring straight down the barrel of Smythe's blaster. Her breath hitched, and she froze.

"Drop your weapon," the insectoid commanded.

Struggling to comprehend how the bounty hunter could still be alive, Ava tossed her weapon and raised her hands. Inching away from the borehole, she bumped her foot against something on the ground. Ava glanced down to find Ten-Tee lying motionless at her feet, offline, alongside Kypa's blaster and Toma's electrode. Her heart sank at the sight of the helpless droid.

"Move," Smythe prodded, motioning Ava with his weapon toward Kypa and Toma.

Ava joined her friends, their grim expressions reflecting the same dread she felt. Then she noticed the bounty hunter clutching his chest. It seemed impossible that Smythe had survived a shot at point-blank range. Yet here he was—proof of his exoskeleton's resilience. But the way he favored the wound hinted at serious damage.

"Where's your ship?" the bounty hunter asked.

"On the surface," Kypa replied, purposely vague.

"Take me to it," Smythe demanded, aiming his weapon at Toma. "Alone."

"I am not leaving without them," Kypa insisted. "You will never find the ship without me, and those creatures are coming. We need to keep moving—all of us."

Smythe's jaw tightened, acknowledging the truth in the Aiwan's words. With a frustrated sigh, he pointed at Neil's cocoon. "What's inside?"

"Our friend was injured," Kypa explained. "The suit he is wearing created a protective shell to keep him stabilized."

"He'll slow us down," Smythe growled.

"No more than standing here arguing," Kypa countered. "He comes with us."

"Fine," Smythe grumbled. "Load him onto the sled."

As Kypa and Toma hoisted Neil onto the back of the sled, Smythe shifted his gaze to Ava. Their eyes met, and her glare left no doubt about her hatred for him.

Smythe smirked. "Looks like bughead wins after all," he sneered.

Ava started to form a rebuke when movement caught her eye. She furrowed her brow as the rock wall behind Smythe shimmered, and loose dirt trickled to the floor. Ava's curiosity quickly turned to horror as she realized the gracylai were burrowing through.

Smythe picked up on her reaction and spun around. His eyes widened in fear as a large gracylai—the queen—emerged. The creature's massive head pushed through the crumbling wall, locking its glowing yellow eyes onto Smythe. Opening its jaws, the queen spat a sticky, lime-green substance with a force that knocked the bounty hunter off his feet, pinning him to the wall. Smythe struggled to free himself, but the green goo instantly hardened, incapacitating him.

Ava quickly snatched Ten-Tee off the ground and hurried to the sled as the queen wormed into the tunnel.

"Go, go, go!" she shouted.

Kypa jumped behind the controls as Toma and Ava scrambled aboard. Just as the mammoth queen righted itself and reared back to strike, the sled surged forward, racing up the tunnel. Ava looked back in terror as more gracylai poured into the tunnel. Their queen shrieked in fury, then shifted its focus to Smythe as the swarm enveloped him. Ava turned away in disgust, unable to watch as the bounty hunter's final scream echoed through the tunnel.

They rode in silence for several minutes until Kypa stopped the sled at the tunnel's end. He and Toma quickly unloaded Neil while Ava nervously kept watch, clutching Ten-Tee in her arm like a football. Without wasting a second, Kypa led them up the flight of stairs to the outpost. At the top of the landing, they heard the unmistakable sound of the approaching swarm.

"They're coming," Ava said in a panic.

"Move!" Kypa urged, leading them inside.

Entering the outpost, they snaked through the back corridor to the control room. Kypa did not slow, heading straight for the exit. He paused to open the front doors, his heart pounding as the piercing screeches grew louder.

The outer doors slid open, flooding the room with daylight. Shielding their eyes, Kypa, Ava, and Toma stepped out onto Rogantu's daunting landscape and sealed the door behind them, for what it was worth. They had a considerable distance to cross over open ground, followed by a treacherous climb—all while carrying Neil with the gracylai in hot pursuit.

Realizing they would never outrun the swarm, Kypa reconsidered cocooning themselves. It was their only hope. Then, static crackled inside his helmet.

A garbled voice interrupted his panic. "Prince Kypa, do you read me?"

Recognizing Captain Nova's voice, Kypa's heart nearly skipped a beat.

"Yes, I read you!" he shouted back with excitement. "Hurry, we need immediate evacuation!"

With unexpected hope, Ava and Toma searched the skies for Nova's ship. But their moment of anticipation shattered as a thunderous crash erupted behind them, followed by the grating sound of tearing metal. The gracylai were attacking the doors.

"Run!" Kypa ordered.

The trio bolted across the plains, desperate to distance themselves from the outpost as much as possible. They dared not look back as the relentless creatures forced their way through the doors. But the dreadful clamor of their pursuit soon gave way to the roar of engines.

Kypa glanced upward just as an Aiwan gunship swooped low overhead. Seated behind a heavy, six-barreled cannon, the door gunner unleashed a torrent of disruptor fire that tore into the gracylai emerging from the outpost. However, the aerial assault had minimal effect; the voracious swarm only grew, advancing toward the fleeing survivors.

The gunship landed in front of Kypa and the others, stirring up dust. As the door gunner continued firing, Captain Nova and three shoretroopers leaped out, rifles blazing to provide cover fire. Kypa, Ava, and Toma rushed to the transport, loading Neil aboard swiftly before they jumped in.

Nova ordered his troopers back onboard, and then climbed inside. He shouted over the weapons fire to the pilot, "Go, go, go!"

The gunship lifted off just as the gracylai reached them. The door gunner continued raining fire down on the swarm as the transport gained altitude and banked away from the outpost. Once the creatures' haunting screeches faded, he secured his weapon and slid the door shut. Leaning back in his seat, the gunner exhaled, grateful to leave that nightmare behind.

A somber stillness settled inside the cabin. Ava, Kypa, and Toma sat back in their seats, catching their breath, as the overhead lights cast a pale glow on their exhausted faces.

Sitting across from Kypa, Captain Nova leaned forward to check on the passengers. "Is everyone alright?" he said over the sound of the engines.

Slouching in their seats, Ava and Toma nodded wearily, managing faint, exhausted smiles.

"Thank you, Captain," Kypa said, his voice filled with gratitude. "Your timing was impeccable."

Nova dipped his chin respectfully. "Our pleasure, Your Highness. Welcome aboard."

"We have one seriously injured," Kypa added, gesturing to Neil's cocoon. "He is in stable condition but requires medical attention."

Nova nodded. "I will alert Captain Areda."

Taken aback, Kypa asked, "Areda? Where is Commodore Boa?"

Noticing the prince's confusion, Nova explained, "Aiwa has been attacked. Commodore Boa ordered us to bring you home."

"Attacked! By whom?"

Before Nova could reply, the pilot called over the comms, "Sir, it looks like Krunig is retreating," he reported, sounding surprised.

Nova stood and headed for the cockpit, accompanied by Kypa. The pilot pointed out the viewport toward an aerial skirmish above the refinery. Just as the pilot described, Krunig's warship was retreating, disengaging the three Aiwan corvettes.

Despite being outnumbered, the crime lord's vessel still outgunned the smaller corvettes, making Nova question Krunig's tactics.

"What is that?" the co-pilot asked, pointing to a small projectile dropping from the underbelly of Krunig's warship. The mysterious object fell in a deliberate arc, headed straight for the refinery.

A chill swept through Nova as he realized Krunig was not dumping his trash—it had to be something far worse.

"Hurry, contact Areda," he said to the pilot. "Tell him to break off contact immediately and rendezvous at our location."

"Yes, sir," the pilot responded, quickly signaling the co-pilot to relay the orders.

Kypa leaned over the pilot's shoulder and pointed to the nearby mountain ridge. "There, take me to my ship," he ordered.

Without hesitation, the pilot adjusted course. Seconds later, they crested the ridge, only to find the area deserted. The pilot's brow furrowed. "My prince, are you certain this is the correct location?"

"Positive," Kypa affirmed before issuing a neural command to Prototype II's onboard computer to initiate emergency startup procedures.

Sitting in the back, Ava stared distantly at Neil's cocoon on the floor. Processing the shock of the day's events, she clutched Ten-Tee in her lap. Suddenly, a glint of light outside drew her attention. She peered out the window and spotted the second Reaper materializing below. Ava blinked in disbelief, then brightened with a wide grin.

"Kypa, it's Reggie!" she said excitedly.

From the cockpit, Kypa cast a quick glance over his shoulder and said gently, "I am afraid not, Ava. That is Prototype II—a near replica of your ship. This was its maiden voyage."

Ava's hopeful expression faded to a crooked frown, a painful reminder of her lost ship and crewmate.

Kypa quickly turned his attention back to the prototype, watching as the twin nacelles powered up. The maneuvering thrusters then activated, kicking up a swirl of volcanic dust as the vessel lifted off.

Captain Areda's corvette appeared overhead, casting an ominous shadow over the area. The other two corvettes assumed flanking positions on the port and starboard sides.

Suddenly, a brilliant flash lit up the sky. Ava and the others instinctively turned away as the windows automatically polarized to shield against the blinding light.

Blinking away the white spots dancing before his eyes, the gunship pilot narrowed his focus on his HUD readouts. "Detonation to the east!" he reported with alarm.

Kypa and Nova looked outside. What they saw left them speechless.

Krunig's Blazecaster projectile had struck the refinery, detonating with a deafening roar. The explosion unleashed a flash of blue light so intense that it outshone the sun, casting stark, eerie shadows across the volcanic plains. A massive bubble of raw energy blossomed from ground zero, rising ominously into the sky while twin shockwaves expanded outward, vaporizing everything in their destructive path.

"Take your seats!" the pilot ordered, abandoning formalities. "Everyone, brace for impact!"

As Kypa and Nova hurried aft, the pilot acted with cool command. "Control, prepare for emergency landing," he told the flight controller aboard Areda's corvette.

Confirmation came immediately, and the gunship's pilot throttled forward. With expert precision, he initiated an emergency approach, bypassing the assistance of the corvette's tractor beam. He manually guided the gunship into the corvette's docking bay and touched down safely on the flight deck.

"Clear!" the pilot relayed to the flight controller.

With a series of loud sonic booms, the three corvettes and Prototype II rocketed away in rapid succession, escaping the area just as the blast waves arrived, obliterating the mountainside.

46
OPERATION NIGHTSHADE

Planet Earth
Groom Lake, Nevada

Approaching the main gate to the Nevada Test and Training Range, Marlana Nunez slowed her Honda CRV as a large crowd of protesters blocked the entrance. Helicopter blades thudded overhead, the aircraft's spotlight cutting through the dark to illuminate the sea of raised signs and angry faces.

"Lucy, you got some splainin' to do," she quipped.

Seated next to her in the passenger seat, Jessica Aguri squinted at the protesters' handwritten signs. "*Fitz: Silence is Violence*," she read aloud. "That doesn't sound good."

Marlana scoffed and pointed. "What about that one? '*The only thing we have to fear is … ALIEN INVASION*,'" she recited with exaggerated drama.

"They're not wrong, you know," Rose commented flatly from the backseat. "Everyone's scared, and it's only going to get worse."

Marlana glanced at Rose in the rearview mirror, catching the tension in her friend's eyes. "You wanna talk about it?" she asked, raising an eyebrow.

Rose's jaw tightened, and she let out a frustrated breath. "Mathias is using Luna to blackmail the world, and, no offense, our government is letting him." Her voice trembled as she continued. "It's what he does, and it's really pissing me off."

"I hear you," Marlana agreed emphatically. "Mathias is a pig, and that hussy assistant of his, Diaz ..." she continued her thought, spitting out a fierce string of profanity-laced threats in Spanish that left Rose and Jessica momentarily speechless. "... And I'm not kidding, I'll do it," Nunez concluded, gripping the steering wheel like she was squeezing the life out of Diaz herself.

A tense silence settled in the car before Jessica calmly said, "These are dangerous times, no doubt," she acknowledged, watching the raucous crowd warily. "I don't claim to know the president's reasons, but sometimes peace requires strange bedfellows."

Outside, the atmosphere grew more charged, and the protesters' chants escalated. Jessica could sense the tension building toward a boiling point.

"I think we should get out of here before this gets ugly," she suggested.

Marlana did not need convincing. She threw the vehicle into reverse and backed away from the gate, steering toward the highway. A few miles down the road, they passed their favorite alien-themed diner. The packed parking lot and the Reaper replica mounted in front drew a chuckle from Jessica and Nunez, but Rose's frown deepened. They had not heard a peep from Kypa, Neil, and Ava since their departure, and the silence troubled her.

As they drove on, the diner faded in the distance, and the road stretched out into the pitch-black desert.

"Are we heading back to your place?" Jessica asked.

"Not yet ..." Marlana replied, her voice trailing off as she slowed the vehicle and scanned the shoulder for a familiar landmark.

"What are you doing?" Jessica asked, glancing over with a puzzled expression.

"It's around here somewhere," Nunez muttered, then pointed to a nondescript dirt path off the highway. "There it is!"

She turned off the pavement, steering onto a dirt road that led toward a massive rock formation. The ride grew bumpy, and dust kicked up around the CRV as Marlana navigated to the rear, where a second rocky outcropping loomed. She eased the vehicle into the narrow gap dividing the two formations, bringing it to a halt. Shutting off the engine, Marlana killed the headlights, shrouding them in darkness.

Jessica shot her a bewildered look. "Uh, Nunez? What are we doing here?"

A sharp knock on the front passenger window made Rose and Jessica jump; their startled screams echoed inside the vehicle. Both shrank at the sight of a dark-clad figure standing outside the window.

Snickering, Nunez lowered the front windows. "Relax, it's just base security," she said calmly.

A second figure appeared at Marlana's window. A tactical flashlight clicked on, casting a red glow across the vehicle's interior.

Both airmen wore camouflage fatigues, their faces obscured by paint. They each had 9mm pistols strapped to their legs and carried Sig Sauer XM7 rifles—the next-generation squad weapon replacing the old M4.

Airman Shaw, the guard on Marlana's side, greeted her with a respectful nod. "Evening, ma'am … ladies," he added, his gaze flicking between the three women.

"Hey, Billy," Nunez replied, offering her security badge. "Sorry for the unannounced visit, but there's a lot of commotion at the other gates. Can you let us in?"

Airman Shaw took her badge, carefully reviewing Colonel Nunez's credentials before scanning the barcode on the back with a handheld device. While he verified her access rights, his partner walked around the vehicle, conducting an exterior inspection using a handheld backscatter X-ray imager—the same kind of device the U.S. Border Patrol used to detect contraband entering the country.

"Thank you, ma'am," Shaw said, returning Marlana's badge. "Ladies, I'll need to see your IDs, too."

Jessica and Rose produced their security badges, which Shaw studied individually. After confirming their privileges, he returned their items with a grateful nod.

"You're all set," Shaw said, glancing at his partner for the all-clear signal.

"They're good," his partner affirmed.

Shaw nodded confirmation. He spoke into his lapel mic and said, "Sierra-Six to Control, I've got one vehicle with three occupants cleared to enter."

"Copy that," came the reply. "Standby one."

Shaw turned to Nunez. "Ma'am, you know the drill—take it slow and stop at the checkpoint inside."

"Got it," Nunez replied. "Thanks, Billy."

"Sure thing," Shaw replied with a nod. "Go ahead and start your vehicle," he instructed, "but leave the headlights turned off."

As Nunez turned the ignition, the ground twenty yards ahead lowered, revealing a hydraulic ramp leading underground. Illuminated by dim red lights, the hidden passage was wide enough to accommodate an armored personnel carrier three times bigger than Marlana's CRV.

Jessica chuckled. "You gotta be kidding me."

"Pretty cool, right?" Nunez replied.

When the entrance finished opening, Shaw stepped back and waved Nunez inside. "You're all clear, ma'am. Have a good night," he said, punctuating his words with a crisp salute.

Nunez smiled, returned a friendly wave, and drove forward.

As the vehicle descended the steep incline, Rose inhaled sharply. "This is why I hate roller coasters," she said, tightening her grip on the seat.

"It's all good," Nunez assured her, leaning forward in her seat, hugging the steering wheel as she peered over the hood.

Behind them, the entrance closed with a heavy thud; the sounds of the engine and tires on concrete echoed in the enclosed passage. Every seventy-five feet, they rolled over retractable traffic spikes that could be raised at a moment's notice to stop any unauthorized vehicle from reaching the bottom.

Moments later, the passage leveled out at the first checkpoint, where a thick metal door blocked their way. Nunez brought her vehicle to a stop as beams of infrared light scanned it from all angles, confirming three occupants. The lights cut off, and a warning alarm sounded as the entrance door slowly swung open.

Inside, two airmen awaited—one male and one female—both wearing camouflage fatigues with sidearms strapped to their thighs. The female sergeant directed Nunez to a designated parking space, and as she parked, the heavy door closed behind them with a resonating clang.

"Evening, ma'am," the sergeant greeted. "Please leave your keys in the ignition and step out of the vehicle."

Nunez, Rose, and Jessica climbed out. They joined the sergeant on the driver's side, producing their IDs. Each badge was scanned again and access confirmed.

"Thank you," the sergeant said, returning their items. "I'll need to collect your mobile devices, please. You can pick them up with Norma Jean at the front desk when you leave." To Nunez, she added, "We'll bring your car around for you."

Quick body scans followed. As soon as the sergeant cleared them, the women proceeded to a nearby elevator. At the lowest level, the doors opened to reveal the familiar tunnel leading to Area S4. Nunez and Rose shared a Segway PUMA, while Jessica followed in a separate vehicle.

After parking, they went directly to Hangar 17. Inside, they found the cavernous space buzzing with teams of engineers from the United States, Japan,

Germany, and Great Britain. A web of fiber optic cables sprawled across the floor, linking portable workstations to select military satellites in orbit—all of which Luna had jerry-rigged to the Aiwan escape pod.

A palpable tension hung in the air, heightened by the presence of President Fitzgerald and the other world leaders. Everyone understood the stakes: the success of this test would determine whether Earth's combined military satellites could generate a spoofing signal strong enough to keep the planet's crystals hidden from detection.

Trust—or the apparent lack of it—only added to the tension in the room. Despite a façade of cooperation, sharing control of their top-secret military satellites left Fitzgerald and his counterparts feeling vulnerable, not only with one another but especially with Mathias and Luna. Only a fool would believe she could not outcode every human programmer in the room and subtly hack into their networks.

For this reason, each nation assigned someone to shadow Luna's every move, monitoring every keystroke. Yet, the real uncertainty lay in the Aiwan technology. Once the escape pod linked with the satellites, the vulnerabilities were endless. No one could foresee what Aiwan artificial intelligence might do—even without Luna's direct influence.

To mitigate these risks, teams of experts deployed robust cybersecurity measures, utilizing multi-layered defenses to protect against any hacking attempts. The technical specifics were beyond the president and his fellow leaders, who could only discuss issues in general terms. But one thing was clear: they were in this together and had to trust that Mathias and Luna would not betray them.

As Jessica broke away to report to Directors Ratliff and Brenham, Nunez and Rose crossed the hangar to join General Dukes.

"Evening, sir," Marlana greeted. "You rang?"

"Yeah," Dukes replied, noticeably tense but grateful to have his XO at his side. "Sorry to have to recall you on Hector's big night, but things are progressing faster than expected."

"It's getting pretty hairy outside, too," she added.

"Tell me about it," the towering one-star general replied gruffly. "The good news is that your Aiwan friend has made quick work of integrating the pod with our satellites. If this initial test succeeds, I'm told Air Force One will be wheels up before daybreak." He sounded hopeful. "Maybe once those protestors see him leave, they'll pack it in."

"Let's hope so," Nunez said, glancing around the hangar. She chuckled at the sight of two engineers—one Japanese and the other German—engaged in a spirited exchange, struggling to solve a problem in broken English. They navigated their philosophical differences with careful diplomacy, managing to stay civil. But as they parted ways, each shook their head in exasperation, muttering in their native tongues.

While Dukes and Nunez continued talking, Rose scanned the area for Luna. Amid the sea of people and equipment, she spotted her Aiwan friend as Luna ducked inside the escape pod. Excusing herself, Rose headed in that direction to wish her good luck.

At the pod's entrance, she crouched and called inside. "Luna?"

"Rose?" Luna responded immediately, poking her head around the corner. Her face lit up at the sight of her friend, and she waved Rose inside. "Please, come in."

Crawling on all fours brought back memories of Rose's last visit inside the pod. Kypa and Neil had blindsided her with a proposal to help Kypa escape. It felt like a lifetime ago, though it had only been just over a month. So much had happened, yet here she was again, back in the pod, ready to help another Aiwan friend.

Once inside, Rose straightened and prepared to greet Luna with a warm embrace. This reunion was their first private moment together since parting ways in Peru. But as Rose opened her arms, Luna hesitated, her gaze flicking upward to a CCTV camera mounted to the pod's inner hull—a silent reminder they were not truly alone.

Rose rolled her eyes and nodded understanding, then asked with concern, "How are you?"

Luna exhaled, looking weary. "Busy," she admitted, "but I feel confident about the plan ... as long as no harvesters decide to drop into Earth's atmosphere, that is."

"What do you mean?"

"The signal we are broadcasting will only work on long-range sensors, including the Aiwan probe currently in orbit," Luna explained. "But if that probe—or any other ship—enters Earth's atmosphere, the signal will be useless. All the effort to hide the crystals will have been in vain."

Rose nodded slowly, digesting the implications, then cringed to ask, "Just please tell me you're not helping Mathias use our satellites against us."

Luna looked affronted. "Of course not. Why would I do such a thing?"

"I'm sorry," she said emphatically. "It's just ... Mathias can't be trusted, and I'm worried for you. Edmund is a master at manipulating people."

"Ouch, that hurts," came a familiar voice from behind them. Startled, Luna and Rose turned to see Mathias kneeling by the exit, his trademark smirk plastered across his face.

Rose's gaze hardened, her arms crossing in distaste. "What do you want?" she asked, her words dripping with disdain.

Edmund arched an eyebrow as though the answer was glaringly obvious. "What do I want?" He scoffed. "The same thing everyone else wants, my dear—to get this party started. How much longer?"

"I am almost ready," Luna replied calmly. "Five more minutes."

"Good," Edmund said, his gaze flitting between Rose and Luna with a hint of suspicion. "Save the gossip for later. We've got a show to put on."

"Right away," Luna answered, dipping her chin obediently.

Satisfied, Mathias climbed out of the pod, leaving Luna to continue her work. As soon as they were alone, Rose turned back to her friend.

"See what I mean?" she whispered urgently. "He's taking advantage of you."

Sensing the need for privacy, Luna connected to Rose telepathically. "*Rose, I understand your concerns, I do,*" she assured her friend. "*I am doing this for all of us, not just Mathias.*" She shot a worried glance toward the exit. "*Listen, there is more to all this, but I cannot explain right now. Just trust me, I know what I am doing.*"

Seeing the determination in Luna's eyes, Rose accepted her friend's explanation with some reserve. Still concerned, she added, "*Just remember, you're not alone. I'm with you, no matter what.*"

With a tender smile, Luna said softly, "Kypa chose his friends well … and so did I." With that, she bobbed her head toward the exit and added with a playful grin, "Now go. We must not keep our audience waiting."

Rose caught the glint in Luna's expression and sensed the Aiwan was up to something. Their knowing look confirmed it, but Rose decided to let it go for now.

"Good luck," she said, anxious to see what Luna had planned.

"Thank you, Rose. We will talk again before this is over, I promise."

Luna watched her friend leave, then refocused on the task at hand. She spent the next few minutes verifying that the pod was communicating with the designated military satellites. Inwardly, she marveled at how primitive human technology seemed compared to Aiwan advancements—and much of the galaxy, for that matter. Hacking Earth's global network would be simple, but that was not her aim.

Once all systems were ready, Luna announced to those eavesdropping, "I am ready to begin the test."

Outside the pod, communications officers from each country confirmed her signal before giving Dr. Persons the go-ahead to proceed.

Persons turned to Fitzgerald. "Mr. President, we're ready to commence Operation Nightshade."

Fitzgerald looked to each of the foreign leaders. One by one, Tanaka, Acker, and Koch nodded their approval. Last in line was Mathias, who exchanged a calculating look with the president before offering a sly smile. For a brief moment, Fitzgerald entertained thoughts of nixing the operation altogether. He knew he was taking a big gamble, but it was not Mathias he trusted; it was Luna.

Ernie Gutierrez, sensing the president's hesitation, nudged him. "Sir?"

Fitzgerald drew a deep breath and exhaled sharply. "Let's hope this works," he said. "Proceed."

Persons grinned with excitement. He leaned toward the intercom, pressed the microphone button, and said, "Luna, we're ready when you are. You may begin."

"Thank you, Dr. Persons," Luna responded. "I am activating the signal now."

A hush fell over the room as all eyes turned to a large monitor displaying a digital image of Earth with the selected military satellites and their orbital trajectories highlighted. As Luna initiated the signal, an animated graphic appeared, illustrating the Aiwan pod's connection to each satellite. One by one, they linked together, forming a global network. Once fully synchronized, the jamming signal then beamed outward into space.

Silence hung in the air as everyone held their breath, anticipating something spectacular to occur. After a few tense moments, Mathias's voice shattered the stillness, his tone laced with annoyance.

"Is that it?"

47
DRAVEN

Planet Earth
Groom Lake, Nevada

The project team's anticipation dissolved into disappointment and confusion as Operation Nightshade concluded without visible signs of success. Eyes shifted between one another and the static display, searching for answers that were not there. Then, Luna emerged from the pod. Everyone turned to her, breaths held in suspense.

Sensing their anticipation, Luna hesitated before announcing softly, "It worked."

After a moment of stunned silence, the room erupted with shouts of joy and nervous laughter. Relief washed over the room, and they exchanged hearty handshakes to celebrate the first Human-Aiwan collaboration against the harvesters.

"Congratulations, Luna," President Fitzgerald said, beaming with excitement. "Thank you so much for what you've done to help protect our world and yours."

Luna dipped her chin modestly, though a flicker of hesitation lingered in her eyes—she was not ready to declare they were safe by any measure.

Cozying up beside Luna, Edmund clutched his chest with exaggerated drama, a mock pout on his face. "What am I, chopped liver?" he teased, flashing a playful grin at Fitzgerald. "I'd like to think I played a pretty big role in this, too."

A dozen biting retorts flooded the president's mind as images of CIA Station Chief Paul Wiggins and the fallen soldiers in Peru flashed before his eyes. The temptation to renege on their deal and lock Mathias away in Kypa's former cell was overwhelming. Even if his confinement only lasted a short while, it would be worth seeing the look on his face.

Fitzgerald resisted the urge. With all eyes on him, he swallowed his anger and focused on the bigger picture. As he raised his hand to offer Mathias a congratulatory handshake, Admiral Donnelly called out loud enough for all to hear.

"Mr. President, NORAD is tracking an inbound spacecraft!"

All eyes shot to Donnelly. Standing by one of the workstations, she held a landline pressed to her ear, listening intently to the voice on the other end from Peterson Space Force Base.

"Is it the Reaper?" Rose asked, daring to hope.

Donnelly's expression darkened. She covered the mouthpiece and shook her head to the contrary. "No, it's much bigger."

After exiting hyperspace near Mars's moon, Phobos, Grawn Draven's warship proceeded on an intercept course to Earth. Moments later, the vibrant blue-green world loomed large outside the main viewport of the crime lord's private chamber.

Clad in his distinctive crimson armor, Draven stood with his hands clasped behind his back, both within easy reach of the battle axe strapped between his shoulder blades. He surveyed the primitive world below with the eyes of a conqueror.

Draven turned to Vekka, who stood quietly at his side. "With no planetary defenses, Earth appears ripe for the taking," he observed confidently. "Let's see if your master's claims hold true."

"Yes, my lord," Vekka replied smoothly, unfazed by Draven's intentions.

With his hands concealed in the flowing sleeves of his tunic, Vekka held his cool composure. But despite the calm exterior, there was cause for concern. This mission carried significant risk—first and foremost to Vekka's life. They were here to validate Krunig's claim that Earth held no harvesting potential for the syndicate. If the claim proved accurate, Vekka had nothing to fear. Draven would be satisfied, Krunig would be vindicated, and the matter forgotten.

But if Krunig had lied—which Draven wholeheartedly suspected—Vekka would pay the price for his master's deception, which most assuredly included a one-way trip out the nearest airlock.

With Earth growing outside the window, the moment of truth had arrived.

"Bridge, begin scanning the surface for crystals," Draven ordered, speaking into his commlink. "I'm on my way."

"Yes, sir," Captain Rugar replied, the ship's first officer.

Ending the transmission, Draven started toward the door. "Come along, Vekka. You won't want to miss this."

Vekka followed closely, his movements fluid and unhurried.

As Draven crossed the room, he discreetly checked the HUD display inside his helmet. The data, fed from his chamber's security sensors, measured Vekka's vital signs—heart rate, blood pressure, perspiration—searching for any indicators of heightened fear and possible aggression. Yet, Vekka's vitals remained unnervingly steady, suggesting confidence in Krunig's claim.

Then, the sensors picked up an anomaly—Vekka gracefully extended both arms outward in a non-threatening manner, palms open. Draven's instincts flared even though his suit detected no weapon or ill intent. He spun on his heel to face Vekka, hand already reaching for his axe.

"What are you doing?" he demanded.

Vekka halted abruptly. Facing Draven, arms outstretched, his expression twisted into a sneer. Without a word, he slowly brought his hands together, palms out, forming a pyramid with his thumbs and index fingers. Draven's gaze narrowed as he noticed the intricate tattoos engraved on Vekka's palms and fingers. His suit's onboard systems automatically scanned the patterns— springing Vekka's trap.

Inside the sleek confines of Draven's armor, the world blurred into chaos as malicious code surged through his systems. The HUD flickered ominously, controls became unresponsive, and a series of urgent alerts flashed before his eyes. Draven tried to react, but his armor fought him, each movement a struggle against an invisible force. With his senses assaulted by a dizzying display of failing systems, Draven said in a panic, "What did you do to me?"

Before Vekka could reply, Draven's suit ejected him, hurling the green-skinned, three-eyed being face-first onto the floor.

Disoriented and exposed, Draven struggled to collect himself, but Vekka immediately pounced. Pinning Draven's frail form beneath him, he struck the sides of Draven's neck with pinpoint precision, targeting the auditory glands.

The crushing impact rendered the crime lord helpless—his vision swimming and his voice silenced, unable to call for aid.

Vekka was not finished. He coiled his thickly braided hair around Draven's throat and yanked it tight in one swift motion. Draven's eyes bulged in terror as he fought to free himself, legs thrashing and hands clawing for purchase. The struggle was vicious and desperate; the tighter Vekka pulled, the weaker Draven's resistance became. In moments, Draven's movements grew sluggish and then ceased entirely as death claimed him.

Even as the ex-crime lord's body fell limp, Vekka maintained his stranglehold, ensuring there was no doubt. He released his grip after a long moment, letting the motionless form slump to the floor. Vekka rolled off, breathing heavily as he surveyed the lifeless heap before him. There was no satisfaction in the kill, only grim acknowledgment of necessity. It was the way of their chosen profession—kill or be killed.

Picking himself up, Vekka tossed his braid over his shoulder and turned his attention to the open suit of armor. A slow grin spread across his face as he surveyed his prize.

Before claiming the suit and assuming his new role as Grawn Draven, Vekka had one more task. He methodically stripped off his clothes, dressing the corpse in his discarded garments. The process was cold and impersonal—a final act of erasure. Vekka felt no pity for the being he had manipulated; his primary concern now was to avoid the mistakes of his predecessor and remain a step ahead of his enemies.

Finishing that ugly business, Vekka steeled his nerves as he stepped backward into the empty suit. Once situated, a red sensor activated, scanning his body to verify the fit. Vekka's physiology was one reason Krunig had targeted Draven—he and Vekka had similar builds. How his master obtained this knowledge—and the occupant's true identity—remained a mystery to Vekka, but it worked. After passing the check, a black nanite material rose from the base of the suit, enveloping Vekka's bare body from his feet up to his neck.

With his nanosuit in place, the armor pieces locked into position with a mechanical click, encasing Vekka in his new protective shell. The HUD flickered to life, projecting vital data across his visor. The sensation was a peculiar fusion of comfort and power.

"Welcome, Grawn Draven," the suit's AI intoned.

Vekka's vision sharpened, enhanced by the suit's sensors, as he felt the AI integrating with his thoughts. He tested the suit's flexibility—clenching and unclenching his fists and twisting his torso. The suit moved seamlessly with him, light and balanced, like a second skin. It was no longer just armor. It was a weapon—his weapon.

Vekka seized the dead being by the collar and dragged him to the nearby airlock. Opening the hatch, he effortlessly tossed the remains inside and sealed it shut.

"Enjoy your journey to the afterlife," he said icily.

Vekka pressed the eject button, sending the body tumbling into the cold vacuum of space. Without a second glance, he rounded sharply and headed for the door. Pausing before it opened, he drew a steadying breath.

Vekka is dead. You are Grawn Draven now.

With that resolved, he strode out of his private chamber and made his way to the bridge. When he arrived, the command center was buzzing with activity. To his right, he noticed Captain Rugar leaning over the science officer's shoulder, studying the data on his display.

Rugar recognized Grawn Draven's unmistakable footfalls approaching. He straightened just as his superior arrived.

"Master Draven," he began with a bow, "our initial scans of the planet are complete. There is no trace of magnetarite."

Grawn Draven masked his surprise. "Is that so?" he replied coolly.

"Yes, my lord," Rugar affirmed. "We're continuing our scans, but Grawn Krunig's claim appears accurate."

"Mm," Draven muttered. Sensing deception, he turned his attention toward the giant viewport and quietly surveyed Earth.

Rugar shifted uncomfortably as his leader's silence left him unsettled.

Had they overlooked something in the scans? he wondered, questioning the crew's thoroughness.

Rugar cast a wary glance down the corridor, expecting to see Vekka, Krunig's representative. The absence of the long-haired albino struck him as peculiar, considering Vekka's presence was crucial for this moment.

Pushing that thought aside, Rugar waited expectantly for orders while his master contemplated their next move.

After a brief silence, Draven rounded to face Rugar. "The crystals are there, I know it," he declared. "Continue scanning, and report to me the moment they're found."

"Yes, my lord," Rugar bowed dutifully. "Shall I speak with Vekka? Perhaps he can provide insight—"

"—Vekka is no longer with us," Draven said flatly, the finality in his tone leaving no doubt about the albino's fate. "Contact Grawn Krunig. Inform him that I must speak with him immediately. I will be in my chambers."

"Yes, sir," Rugar replied, a cold shiver prickling his spine.

As Draven strode off the bridge, hands clasped behind his back, he cocked his head sideways and said, "Locate those crystals, Captain, or I will find someone who can."

Rugar swallowed the lump in his throat. His leader's abrupt mood shift felt out of character, though understandable considering the circumstances. Murdering Vekka, a trusted aide of another grawn, was risky. Such an act was a direct challenge to Krunig himself. And if Earth turned out to be unharvestable, as Krunig claimed, Draven would face the syndicate's wrath for his bold defiance.

48
TACTICAL PAUSE

Planet Earth
Groom Lake, Nevada

Fitzgerald and the operations team stood silently before the large monitor, watching in awe. On the screen, a grainy image revealed a massive warship, its ominous silhouette hovering over Earth. The weight of dread settled heavily on the room as the team remained transfixed, their silence laden with unvoiced questions.

Luna turned to Fitzgerald, her expression grim. "Mr. President, that is not an Aiwan vessel."

Rose squinted at the image, pointing to a symbol emblazoned on the warship's hull. "I've seen that symbol before," she remarked, searching her memory. Then it came to her, a frightening moment months ago when Kypa drew that very symbol on the fogged glass inside his cell, etched in Neil's blood. "That's a harvester ship!"

A frenzy of anxious murmurs erupted among the team. After witnessing the destruction of the International Space Station, they were all too aware of their limited defenses.

"Quiet … everyone!" Ernie snapped, his voice cutting through the chatter.

As the room fell silent, Luna spoke again. "Dr. Landry is correct, but that is not any ship. That is a Madreen flagship, and it belongs to one of the grawns." Her tone deepened with worry. "This is very bad."

Director Ratliff's eyes narrowed on the image. "Grawn, you say? What does that mean?"

"The Madreen Crime Syndicate is the most feared criminal organization in the galaxy," Luna explained. "Their sector leaders are known as grawns, each overseeing a designated territory and answering to Grawn Supreme, their chosen leader." She turned back to Fitzgerald, her voice steady but grave. "If a grawn has come this far into deep space, it means they are very interested in exploiting Earth."

Fitzgerald absorbed Luna's warning, his jaw tightening as he processed the implications.

Admiral Donnelly, still on the line with Space Command, said calmly but urgently, "Mr. President, I recommend DEFCON 1."

Fitzgerald glanced at her, then nodded decisively. "Do it. Initiate DEFCON 1." As Donnelly carried out the order, the president returned to the warship on the screen. "So, which grawn are we dealing with?" he asked Luna.

"I do not know," she replied, massaging her hands nervously. "The grawn who attacked Aiwa was named Grawn Krunig."

"Krunig, huh?" Fitzgerald echoed, his eyes fixed on the display, searching for any sign of the enemy's next move. "What's he doing now? Did Nightshade actually work?"

"It's called a tactical pause, Mr. President," came a familiar, gruff voice from the back of the room.

Fitzgerald spun sharply, his gaze hardening. The project team stepped aside, revealing retired General Anthony Garza, the former Chairman of the Joint Chiefs of Staff. With his usual air of authority, Garza stood tall in a tailored, dark brown suit reminiscent of his Army dress uniform, an American flag pinned to his lapel. Beside him stood Senator Georgia-Berry Hawthorne, Fitzgerald's long-time political rival, and Edmund Mathias, whose folded arms and smug grin only added to the tension.

Caught off-guard by Garza's unexpected arrival, the president did not mince words. "What the hell are you doing here?" he asked in a low, controlled tone.

Edmund stepped in, smirking as he gestured to Garza. "General Garza, *retired*, is now consulting for me," he announced. Catching Fitzgerald's glare, Edmund feigned innocence and shook his head. "What? You said I could bring a few guests."

"He wasn't on the list," Ernie shot back.

"No, but I was," Senator Hawthorne interjected. "I invited him."

As chairperson of the Armed Services Committee, she had the authority to grant Top Secret-SCI clearance, including access to Groom Lake.

"We don't have time for this," Fitzgerald said impatiently. "I'm still the president and I say he goes." Turning to Ernie, he ordered firmly, "Get him out of here."

"With pleasure," Ernie replied, starting toward Garza, clearly eager to eject the disgraced officer.

Before he could, Edmund stepped in his path, raising his hands to stall the moment.

"*Mister* Garza—fully pardoned by you, I might add—may be tardy to the party, but his expertise is second to none," Edmund argued, loud enough for the entire group to hear. "Given the circumstances, I think it's in everyone's best interest to hear what he has to say. Don't you agree?"

Before Ernie could respond, Garza pointed to the monitor. "Like I said, Mr. President, in the field, we call that a tactical pause—a deliberate halt to reassess the situation before planning our next move." Garza squared his shoulders and added, "If I were this grawn fella, and came all this way expecting to find crystals, I wouldn't give up so easily. Nightshade may have bought us some time, but I'd bet my bottom dollar this grawn is just getting started."

Admiral Donnelly agreed and added, "Mr. President, if that ship discovers our signal, they could trace it back here. Groom Lake would be their first target."

"Sir, we should get you and the others out of here," Ernie suggested.

Fitzgerald huddled with the three foreign leaders, along with Ernie, Donnelly, and Secretary Nguyen. A heated discussion ensued, ranging from preemptive military options to diplomatic outreach and sheltering-in-place strategies. Voices clashed, and tempers flared, but as the debate escalated, Mathias shifted his gaze to the monitor. Staring at Draven's warship with obvious greed, his eyes gleamed with something far from fear. To him, the grawns were the key to his grand scheme—his ticket into the lucrative intergalactic harvesting trade.

Ignoring the squabbling around him, Edmund envisioned the vast wealth and power within his grasp. A grin of perceived superiority spread across his face as he glanced around at the bickering fools. Their shortsightedness only confirmed what he already believed: he was destined for greatness, and this was his moment. Fitzgerald's ship was sinking, and it was time to make his move.

"I believe our work is done here," he said to Garza, brushing his hands as though dusting off the entire debacle around him.

Ms. Diaz took her cue, moving forward through the crowd to escort Luna and Senator Hawthorne. However, their departure did not go unnoticed. As Mathais's entourage began to make its way toward the exit, the operations team fell silent, already missing Luna's keen insights.

Ernie was first to react and whispered to the president, "Sir, Mathias is leaving."

Fitzgerald rounded sharply, peering over the crowd and spotting Luna among the departing figures. "Where do you think you're going?" he called out.

Edmund turned around, casually walking backward with arms outstretched. "I know a lost cause when I see one, Mr. President," he said with a grin. "But don't worry about me—my destiny lies up there."

Edmund pointed to the ceiling, his expression brimming with confidence and hinting at the bright future he envisioned for himself. Before Fitzgerald could retort, Rose's voice cut through the tension.

"Luna!" she called out.

Luna halted at the sound of her name. She turned sharply to see Rose pushing through the crowd, which parted just enough to let her through.

Rose emerged with frantic urgency, her wide, pleading eyes locking onto Luna's. Heart racing, she steadied herself and implored her friend, "Please, don't go."

The hangar fell into a sudden, heavy silence. Rose's desperate plea lingered in the air, her words a last, fragile hope that Luna might abandon her alliance with Mathias. All eyes turned to Luna, waiting for her response as if watching the deciding moment of a high-stakes match.

Standing beside Luna, Mathias smirked, gently taking the Aiwan's hand in his as a silent declaration of their unity. But Rose's gaze never wavered. The way she leaned forward, almost reaching out, was an unspoken appeal for her friend to stay.

Luna's expression softened. Even without reading Rose's mind, she could feel the love and concern radiating from her human friend.

"I hear you, Rose," she communicated telepathically, her mental tone imbued with warmth and gratitude. *"Your strength and support gives me the courage I need to see this through. It will be alright, I promise."*

Realizing Luna intended to leave, Rose's eyes began welling, her lips quivering with emotion. Nunez quickly moved to her side, wrapping her arm around Rose's shoulder in comfort.

Severing the telepathic connection, Luna gave Edmund's hand a reassuring squeeze. Then, with a calm finality, she spoke aloud to Rose. "Goodbye, Rose. I hope we meet again."

With that, Edmund led his entourage out of the hangar. As he reached the door, he said confidently under his breath, "Nothing can stop us now."

British Embassy
Miraflores, Peru

At first glance, the Embajada Británica en Lima could easily be mistaken for a five-star hotel rather than a diplomatic mission—and in many ways, it truly was. Situated in Miraflores, one of Lima's most affluent districts, this foreign consulate stood apart from any other in the world. There were no imposing concrete barriers or armed guards patrolling the perimeter. Instead, the British Embassy resided within Sea Park Tower, a seaside luxury hotel and casino overlooking the ocean.

The building's design showcased a seamless blend of British and contemporary Peruvian architecture. Its sleek lines and refined façade made it a distinctive landmark in the city. With its privileged view of the bay, Sea Park Tower's office and commercial space spanned twenty-three floors connected by six high-speed elevators, ensuring quick and efficient movement throughout. An A-plus-rated structure, the building was also equipped with discreet and effective high-level security measures, combining elegance, functionality, and safety to make it an ideal diplomatic base.

Yet today was anything but business as usual. The cool breeze blowing in from the ocean failed to soothe the growing tension outside the bustling hotel. News of an alien warship in Earth's orbit had sparked widespread panic, sending guests into a frenzy to cut short their trips and flee the city.

A line of yellow taxis and luxury automobiles snaked along the entrance drive, honking impatiently. Amid the chaos, bellhops darted between vehicles, hurrying to load luggage into trunks as they did their best to expedite anxious departures.

Suddenly, all activity came to a screeching halt—literally. The crowd collectively winced, clutching their ears against a piercing noise. The culprit: a beat-up pickup truck making a sharp turn into the hotel's roundabout. Its worn-out rubber tires strained against the asphalt, emitting a high-pitched squeal that cut through the air like nails on a chalkboard.

As the vehicle lumbered up the drive, the noise tapered to a rattling clatter. Rust-speckled and sputtering thick black smoke, the pickup sent chicken feathers fluttering from the wire coops stacked in its bed. Its muffler dangled precariously while the engine wheezed and groaned.

Ignoring the line of awaiting vehicles, the driver brought the pickup to a grinding halt in front of the hotel. A loud bang backfired from the engine, startling everyone in earshot.

"Move that truck!" the valet shouted tersely.

The driver, a middle-aged Peruvian farmer, smiled sheepishly and waved apologetically as he climbed out of the cab and made his way to the rear of his pickup. There, wedged between the tailgate and a dozen wire chicken coops, was Agent Colleen Addison of His Majesty's Security Service. The driver lowered the gate and helped her down.

"Gracias, Miguel," she said with genuine gratitude, spitting out a stray white feather.

Agent Addison breathed a sigh of relief as her feet touched solid ground. After a grueling journey from Satipo, she was thankful for the lift—and even more so for being alive. Following her narrow escape from Mathias's test subject—thanks to Luna—Addison spent two days in the bush, evading jungle predators and avoiding local thugs. By sheer luck, she met Miguel and his grandson, who were on their way to the markets in Lima and agreed to give her a ride.

Now, she was safe in her element, but her appearance drew more than a few sideways glances. Addison was a filthy mess—her designer clothes ruined, and her wild hair tangled together in sweaty clumps. She stank of body odor, chicken droppings, and jungle musk that made anyone downwind gag.

She paid no mind to the gawkers. Exhausted, dehydrated, and famished, she was in no mood to care. Turning to Miguel, Addison raised her hand, signaling for him not to drive off.

"Wait here, I have something for you," she said in perfect Spanish.

With his sun-weathered skin and sturdy frame from years of labor under the Andean sun, Miguel nodded and returned her smile with a toothless grin.

"Perfect," Addison replied, managing a weary smile.

She made her way to the hotel entrance, drawing the concierge's immediate attention. He stepped into her path to block her way and gave her a quick, scrutinizing look. Despite the grime and disarray, there was no mistaking the remnants of her expensive clothes and blond-highlighted hair—she was clearly not a local villager. Yet the stench was overpowering, forcing him to wrinkle his nose as he fought to keep his composure.

Assuming she spoke English, he asked snidely, "Excuse me, are you a hotel guest?"

Addison exhaled in exasperation. "Not yet ... *Pablo*," she replied, reading his name tag with a hint of sarcasm. "I have an appointment with the British embassy."

Pablo's smirk faltered slightly. "I see. Well, if you'd kindly wait here, I will notify the embassy that Miss …"

"Coulter," she lied, straight-faced.

"… that Miss Coulter has arrived," he finished with a forced smile.

"Don't bother, Pablo, I know the way," she said with a dismissive flick of her wrist as if brushing him aside. She strode past with a "talk to the hand" gesture as the hotel doors automatically slid open to grant her passage.

Her entrance was nothing short of dramatic, akin to Moses parting the Red Sea. As she marched through the lobby, patrons covered their noses and cast judgmental glares her way, but Addison did not break stride, her chin held high in defiance.

Predictably, the stench helped secure her an entire elevator car to herself. As it ascended to the twenty-second floor, she felt a sense of relief settling in. When the doors opened, and she saw the Union Jack proudly displayed outside the embassy's front entrance, she dropped her shoulders, and the tension melted away.

Three people stood in the lobby awaiting the elevator. Addison's gaze flicked between them, sizing them up in an instant. Expecting that the hotel might have notified the embassy of her arrival, she quickly concluded that these three were not here to intercept her—judging by their beachwear.

Tourists.

The beachgoer's reaction to her appearance was priceless. As Addison exited the elevator, their faces twisted with nausea, recoiling at the stench that hit them like a tidal wave.

Addison grinned mischievously as she strode past and uttered, "For King and Country."

Inside the embassy lobby, the reception was no warmer. The office manager quickly approached, buttoning his tweed jacket. Taking in Addison's grimy appearance, his expression quickly shifted from polite curiosity to thinly veiled disgust. He forced a tight-lipped smile, unsure what he was dealing with.

"Miss Coulter, I presume," he said, his eyes assessing her mud-caked clothes and messy hair. "Do you require medical assistance?" The question carried a veneer of professionalism, but his tone betrayed a hint of underlying concern.

Addison let out a dry chuckle. "Nothing a hot shower and a spa treatment won't fix."

"Very well," he replied, adjusting his tie. "Then, if you could enlighten me as to the nature of your visit."

"Of course." Addison leaned closer, lowering her voice. "Tell your gardener, I'm here to see to your vegetable patch."

The manager's brow furrowed in confusion, but his expression softened with recognition as the meaning behind the coded phrase sank in. His gaze met Addison's, and he saw the gravity etched on her dirt-streaked face—this was no ordinary visit.

"I-I see," he stammered, quickly regaining his composure. "How may I assist you, mum?"

"You can start by delivering my message," Addison replied evenly. "You know which number to call?"

The manager nodded vigorously. "It will be done. Straight away." He rounded sharply to leave but hesitated. Pivoting back toward her, he added, "Where are my manners? The embassy keeps a block of rooms here at the hotel. I'll fetch a key and escort you up myself."

Addison's lips curved into a tired smile. "That would be divine," she replied, relief washing over her. As he turned to leave, she added, "And one more thing—does the embassy keep spare quid for emergencies?"

The manager's expression tightened, and there was a flicker of suspicion in his eyes. "Yes, mum," he said slowly, uncertain of her intentions.

"Perfect, there's a rusty pickup parked out front with a man named Miguel inside. The Crown owes him a great debt—he saved my life," she explained. "See to it he is well compensated. Two years' wages should suffice."

The manager's mouth opened to object, but Addison cut him off. "And do be a good chap and call room service. I'd kill for a proper English breakfast and a cup of Earl Grey."

He nodded obediently, signaling to his staff. Addison watched them hustle off to carry out his instructions, amused at how he probably thought she was some Double-O agent.

Ten minutes later, she and the manager arrived at the hotel's top floor. He led her to room 2410 at the end of the hall and slid the keycard into the door lock. The green light flashed, and the door unlocked. Ignoring the lingering stench, the manager stepped inside and held the door open for her.

Addison wiped her feet on the hallway carpet before entering. She crossed the spacious living room, silently reserving judgment as she moved directly to the far wall, where floor-to-ceiling tinted windows framed a breathtaking view of the bay. The sun sank toward the horizon, casting a warm glow over the water.

After savoring the sight for a long moment, Addison circled the room, taking in the tasteful décor and luxurious furnishings. Her gaze swept critically over every detail before she finally nodded in approval.

"This will do nicely," she declared.

"Excellent, I think you'll find the rest of the accommodations to your liking," the manager responded confidently. "The fridge is fully stocked. Feel free to help yourself—compliments of the embassy. And your room service will be up shortly."

"Thank you," Addison replied, returning to the front door. "Your hospitality is much appreciated."

The manager handed her the room key. Addison graciously accepted, placing it on a slender console table nearby. Then, without a hint of hesitation, she began stripping off all her filthy clothes. The manager's eyes widened in disbelief and immediately averted his gaze.

"I beg your pardon," he exclaimed, clearly affronted.

Unfazed, Addison stood boldly naked on the tile entryway and gathered her soiled garments into a bundle. She thrust them into the manager's arms.

"See to it these are burned," she instructed. "The sooner, the better."

Speechless, the manager accepted the bundle. Before he could react further, Addison gently steered him towards the door, closing it decisively behind him. As he lingered outside, still reeling from the unexpected encounter, the memory of her figure flashed in his mind. It stirred a naughty thrill, but the rank odor emanating from the clothes quickly snapped him back to work. Grimacing, he held the foul bundle at arm's length and made his way down the hall to the maid's closet, where he could dispose of them properly.

Half an hour later, refreshed and invigorated from a glorious hot shower, Addison answered a knock at her door. She was clad in a comfortable white robe and matching slippers, her hair wrapped snugly in a towel, looking every bit the pampered guest. As she opened the door, a room service staffer stood in the hall with a cart filled with hot food and tea. His polite smile faltered when he glanced over his shoulder at the two stern-looking men standing behind him. Addison immediately recognized them as British Intelligence.

Addison pulled the door open as she stepped back and invited the hotel staffer inside with a welcoming smile. "Park it anywhere," she said, polite but brisk.

As the attendant passed, Addison cast a quick sideways glance at the agents in the hallway. The thinner of the pair—Deputy Director Neville Grayson—was a man in his forties with a receding hairline. He tapped his watch impatiently, a silent prod for her to hurry.

Addison turned her attention to the attendant, who parked the food cart beside the dining table. As he lifted the plate cover, the savory aroma of eggs, sausage, bacon, baked beans, and fried tomatoes filled the room. Addison nodded approvingly. The attendant then saw himself out, exiting quietly and leaving the bill settled.

The moment he was gone, she turned to the men outside.

"Hello, Grayson," Addison greeted, addressing her superior.

"Addie," he responded, his tone indifferent to her appearance. "Back from Satipo earlier than expected," he noted, raising an eyebrow. "I trust there's a good reason."

"You could say that," she replied flatly. With her stomach growling and her energy fading, Addison waved them inside, saying impatiently. "Well, don't just stand there like lemons. We've got a lot to discuss, and my breakfast is getting cold."

49
RED NOTICE

Planet Earth
Missoula, Montana

Choi Min-jun sat on the creaky front porch of the FBI safehouse, gently rocking in an old wood chair with his eyes closed and a serene smile on his face. In the distance, the sun dipped slowly behind Blue Mountain, casting a warm, golden hue over the landscape.

He pulled the colorful Native American throw blanket tighter over his lap, savoring the comforting texture and the last rays of daylight. The cool evening air hinted at the approaching night, but for now, he basked in the tranquility of the setting sun, feeling a rare moment of peace.

"Are you sleeping?" Ji-eun's soft voice broke the silence as she practiced her English.

Min-jun's eyes fluttered open to find Ji-eun standing beside him, holding a tray with two steaming cups of tea. His smile widened at the sight of her. Well into her second trimester, Ji-eun glowed with the unmistakable radiance of an expectant mother. Even with her oversized hoodie, her growing belly was now showing.

Min-jun straightened in his seat. "Not asleep. Enjoying the …" He paused, searching for the word.

"Calm," Ji-eun offered with a warm smile.

Min-jun nodded. "Yes, enjoying the calm."

Ji-eun set the tray down between them and then handed him his cup. Since arriving in the United States, she made a habit of serving him tea as they watched the sunset together—a small gesture of gratitude that had taken a deeper meaning since his return. Min-jun was nearly healed from his physical injuries, though the origins of his cuts and bruises remained a mystery to Ji-eun. She never asked about them, and it did not matter. He was home, and together, they could continue their journey in this foreign land.

They sat in blissful silence, sipping their tea, until two black and white SUVs rumbled up the gravel driveway. Both vehicles bore the insignia of the Missoula County Sheriff's Office.

Min-jun and Ji-eun set down their teacups, exchanging a tense glance.

FBI Special Agent Geisert, recently assigned to their protection detail, stepped out of the house to meet the visitors. Min-jun and Ji-eun did not know the sheriff's visit had been expected, and their anxious expressions betrayed their surprise.

"It's okay," Geisert said, raising a hand to stay put. "I invited them."

As Agent Geisert stepped off the porch, Sheriff Whitaker and his deputy climbed out of their vehicles, the crackling chatter of the police radio breaking the stillness. Min-jun recognized the sheriff immediately. They had met several weeks ago in the men's restroom at Annie's Axes, a local sports bar. That night, Whitaker had intervened just in time to stop a group of hooligans—led by an oversized parolee nicknamed Bull—who sought revenge after Min-jun bested him in an axe-throwing contest. That evening, the sheriff's blend of friendliness and professionalism had left an impression on Min-jun—he was trustworthy.

Min-jun and Ji-eun watched as Geisert exchanged firm handshakes with the sheriff and his deputy. After a brief conversation, Whitaker nodded and began walking toward the house. Ji-eun's breath hitched, and she instinctively placed one hand on her belly, the other reaching for Min-jun. He took her hand and gave it a reassuring squeeze before standing, bracing himself for whatever news the sheriff had brought.

"Ma'am," the sheriff greeted warmly, tipping his cowboy hat.

Ji-eun's heart raced as she gave a curt nod and lowered her gaze. Min-jun, still holding her hand, bowed respectfully.

"Sheriff Whitaker and his deputy just stopped by to introduce themselves," Geisert explained. "There's been a development since your return."

Min-jun's brow furrowed. "What do you mean?"

Geisert hesitated, knowing the weight of the news she was about to deliver. However, there was a reason Min-jun and Ji-eun were under federal protection, and she had to be transparent. Stepping closer, she handed Min-jun her phone. The screen displayed an INTERPOL red notice, the name Lorenzo "Renzo" Condori emblazoned in bold. Beneath it, Edmund Mathias was listed as Renzo's last-known associate.

"Do you recognize this man?" Geisert asked, her eyes studying Min-jun's reaction to the photograph.

Min-jun's chest tightened at the sight of Renzo's grainy image—the man he was sure he had killed. Memories of their brutal fight came flooding back. He could still feel phantom pains from the blows they exchanged and the strain of the chokehold he had used to end Renzo's life—a move he thought left no room for doubt.

Min-jun's gaze lingered on the image before shifting to Geisert, then Whitaker. He handed back the phone, nodding in confirmation.

"That photo was taken two days ago at a port in Mexico," Geisert continued. "Lorenzo Condori is alive."

Min-jun's expression hardened. "Is he coming for us?"

Deep down, he already knew the answer. Min-jun could almost see Renzo's menacing eyes—cold, unforgiving, and filled with a relentless thirst for vengeance. Renzo was a man driven by bloodlust, a killer who would not rest until he had his retribution.

Geisert shrugged, trying to alleviate their fears. "To be honest, we don't know Renzo's current location. He entered Mexico illegally, but not before killing two crewmen aboard a container ship ... not to mention what he did to you."

Ji-eun's head snapped up, her eyes brimming with shock as she turned to Min-jun. Their eyes met, and, in that instant, the pieces fell into place. Now, she understood what happened during Min-jun's absence and the reason behind his injuries. As fear took hold, Ji-eun absently began massaging her belly.

Min-jun's face softened with regret as he knelt beside her. "Forgive me," he whispered, lowering his head in shame. "I never meant for this to happen."

Ji-eun glanced from Min-jun to the officers, searching for the right words yet seeking assurance that they would not allow harm to befall her, Min-jun, or the baby.

"Listen, folks," Sheriff Whitaker interjected in a calming voice. "I'm sorry for dropping this news on you and spoiling your evening. I know this isn't what you wanted to hear, but try not to worry. Every law enforcement agency in the country is looking for this guy, including my department. We won't let him get anywhere near you, trust me."

Slaughter Park
Laredo, Texas

The shortest distance between two points is a straight line—a principle the Sinaloa Cartel embraced when it secretly constructed an underground tunnel beneath the Rio Grande River. Completed six months ago, this multi-million-dollar project linked the cities of Nuevo Laredo, Mexico, and Laredo, Texas—ground zero in the war on illegal immigration and drug trafficking between the United States and Latin America.

Renzo was seeing the tunnel firsthand. After being dropped off at a safe house in Nuevo Laredo, his cartel hosts led him downstairs to a bathroom, where the bathtub lifted on hydraulics to reveal a staircase leading underground.

Renzo descended the steps and entered the narrow tunnel. The passage was damp and musty but well-lit. Its concrete walls were wide enough for two people—typically drug mules trying to pay off their debts to the cartel. But the passage was primarily designed for a single rail line, which allowed bricks of narcotics to be loaded into a rail-fixed mining cart and transported under the river to a cartel safehouse on the Texas side of the border. On the return journey, the cart was filled with stacks of cash wrapped in cellophane, destined to be laundered and funneled back into the cartel's coffers.

Renzo made the fifteen-minute trek through the tunnel alone. When he emerged on the other side, he climbed a set of stairs into yet another bathroom. Waiting for him with wary eyes were four cartel enforcers, their shaved heads and tattooed bodies giving them a menacing appearance.

Despite being searched before crossing, Renzo endured another pat-down. Once the enforcers were satisfied, they led him through the single-story house to the attached garage, where a lowrider Cadillac Escalade awaited. The eldest of the Sinaloans opened the tailgate and gestured for Renzo to get in.

Renzo complied without question, understanding that this precaution was for everyone's safety. He unslung his blowgun case and climbed in back, laying sideways with his head resting on his arm. As the tailgate lowered automatically, the enforcers piled into the front seats.

Mexican rap music blasted from the speakers when the engine roared to life. A deep, thumping bass rattled the vehicle as the driver opened the overhead garage door, allowing sunlight to filter through the SUV's dark-tinted windows.

They departed the safehouse, weaving through the Chacon neighborhood and past Slaughter Park before merging onto US-83 North, then I-35 North. Traffic was moderate, and thirty minutes later, the SUV exited the highway onto a frontage road that wound into the foothills of San Ramon.

As they neared their destination, the driver turned off the music. In the back, with no view of his surroundings, Renzo heard the unmistakable sound of the Sinaloans loading magazines into their weapons and chambering rounds. The atmosphere in the vehicle grew tense as they rode in silence for the next two miles until reaching a dead end. Awaiting them, out in the middle of nowhere, was a sleek Porsche Panamera 4 Hatchback.

The Escalade rolled to a stop twenty feet away. For a moment, the occupants of both vehicles watched one another through tinted windshields—a standoff of mutual suspicion, each side waiting to see who would make the first move. Finally, the passenger-side doors of the Porsche sedan swung open.

A pair of North Korean assassins stepped out, while a third remained behind the wheel. The two men moved with precision, one circling to the front of the vehicle, the other to the rear. They were nearly identical in build and appearance, both with pale skin, clean-shaven faces, and neatly cropped black hair. Their attire matched down to the smallest detail: black, single-breasted suits, crisp white dress shirts, black ties, polished shoes, and identical dark sunglasses that completed their uniform.

They buttoned their jackets as they approached the Escalade, keeping their empty hands in plain sight. In response, the Sinaloans remotely opened the tailgate.

Renzo climbed out and slung the blowgun case over his shoulder. Peering around the back of the SUV, he quickly sized up the situation and then glanced back at the Sinaloans. Seeing how they remained in their vehicle, he took this as a good sign.

Sitting in the back seat, the ranking cartel enforcer met Renzo's gaze and offered an affirming nod.

"Gracias, amigos," Renzo said before closing the tailgate.

Starting toward the North Koreans, Renzo approached with his hands raised to show he was unarmed. Neither side spoke at first as they stood face to face, but the North Koreans recognized Renzo from his dossier. The assassin on the left extended his hand, indicating Renzo's case. He handed over the blowgun, which the man opened and inspected thoroughly. Meanwhile, the other assassin stepped forward and conducted a thorough frisk of Renzo. Once satisfied, he stepped back and gave his partner a curt nod.

After returning the blowgun, the North Koreans motioned Renzo toward their vehicle. Before following, the Chachapoyan turned and gave a thumbs-up to the Sinaloans. Rap music blasted from the SUV almost instantly, echoing through the foothills. Their task completed, the Sinaloans turned the vehicle around and sped off, kicking up a cloud of dust as they disappeared down the road.

One of the North Koreans returned to the front passenger seat while his partner led Renzo to the rear of the sedan. When the trunk opened, Renzo half-expected they would want him to climb inside. Instead, the North Korean threw back a blanket, revealing an arsenal of weapons. Inside lay an assortment of small arms, AK-47s, and even a rocket-propelled grenade launcher—all meticulously arranged and ready to use.

"My name is Hoon," he said evenly, his English clear but measured. "The targets we seek are under federal protection."

Renzo nodded, unsurprised. "Do you know their location?"

Hoon pulled out his phone and opened a map, revealing a farmhouse near Missoula, Montana. It was isolated, with no other homes for miles around—a perfect setting for what Renzo had in mind.

"If you please," Hoon said politely, gesturing toward Renzo's blowgun.

The Chachapoyan agreed and gently placed his weapon in the trunk. Hoon covered it with the blanket before shutting the trunk with a decisive thud. Their eyes met, and an unspoken understanding passed between them—a temporary alliance forged in pursuit of a shared goal.

Both men then moved to their respective sides of the sedan. As Renzo reached for the door handle, his hand trembled unexpectedly. He recoiled slightly and clenched his fist. Flexing his hand open and closed several times, he willed the tremor to stop, hoping no one had noticed.

Hoon, preoccupied, climbed in without a glance.

Taking a steadying breath, Renzo shook off the lingering effects and opened the car door. He climbed inside and settled into his seat. Keeping his fists clenched, Renzo began contemplating the long drive ahead. The serum's side effects were resurfacing—a bitter reminder that his time was running out. All he could do was hope to survive long enough to exact his revenge on Choi Min-jun.

50
CROSSROADS

Aiwan Corvette
Somewhere in hyperspace …

Ava sat inside the Aiwan gunship, tapping her foot incessantly as her eyes remained fixed on Kypa. He stood outside on the corvette's flight deck in deep conversation with Captains Nova and Areda. From Kypa's tense expression, the news was not good.

Beside her, Toma passed the time by inspecting Ten-Tee, who remained offline. Turning the tiny droid over in his hands, he examined it carefully and realized it had not been damaged by the bounty hunter after all, only deactivated. Spotting a switch on the back of Ten-Tee's binocular-shaped head, he flipped it.

With a soft whir, Ten-Tee powered up, its photoreceptors glowing as it straightened itself on Toma's lap. The droid swiveled its head in a full circle, taking in its surroundings and confirming the absence of danger. It beeped cheerily, then noticed Neil's cocoon lying on the floor. Hopping down, it tapped Ava's foot and emitted a soft, electronic sigh.

Ava's gaze broke from Kypa's conversation, irritation flashing briefly before she registered the droid's concern. She exhaled and softened her tone.

"It'll be okay," she said gently. "We won't let anything happen to him."

A sudden shout echoed from outside, startling Ava and Toma.

"No, that cannot be!" Kypa's voice thundered through the bay. "Seva would never do that!"

Ava and Toma turned abruptly to see Kypa pacing in tight, agitated circles; fists clenched as he fought to contain his fury. Empathizing, Nova and Areda stepped back, giving the prince space to process the devastating revelation about his sister.

Ava had never seen Kypa so unhinged. She stood quickly, stepping outside with Toma close behind.

"Kypa, what's wrong?" she soothed, trying to calm him.

Kypa stopped pacing and turned to face her, tears glistening in his eyes. He looked at his son, who watched him with quiet, anxious concern. Kypa's mouth quivered, his words caught in his throat as he teetered on the verge of breaking down.

Without hesitation, Toma rushed forward and wrapped his long arms around his father's waist in a fierce embrace. The gesture seemed to unravel Kypa, and he sank to his knees, overcome with grief.

Ava stepped closer, resting a gentle hand on Kypa's shoulder. He responded with a grateful touch, taking her hand in his and pulling her down to huddle with him and Toma. Kypa held them close for a long moment, then, after a long, grinding silence, he took a deep breath. Steeling himself, Kypa shared the dreadful news.

"Aiwa has been attacked again," he said, his voice edged with grave concern. "The central core was sabotaged, cutting off the power grid and disabling the protective shields in every realm."

Taken aback, Ava and Toma exchanged uneasy glances, their apprehension mirrored in each other's eyes, before turning their attention back to Kypa. They searched his expression intently, hoping to find even a glimmer of hope.

"What about Mother?" Toma inquired, fearing the worst.

"She is safe," Kypa assured him. "As are the queen and your sisters."

"Krunig?" Ava spat, her voice laced with contempt.

Kypa's jaw tightened, a flicker of rage flashing across his face as he gave a curt nod. "The attack was orchestrated by a group of Cirran refugees aligned with Krunig."

"What could they possibly hope to gain?" Ava asked, shaking her head in disbelief.

She knew enough about war to understand that terrorists could not operate on idealism alone; they needed money to fund their movement. Perhaps that was Krunig's angle: buy the allegiance of traitors and use them as instruments to disrupt Aiwa from the inside. But unless anarchy was the endgame for both sides, how could the Cirrans hope to start over and reclaim their homelands with the other realms turned against them?

Kypa hesitated, reluctant to place yet another burden on his son. But Toma's resilience, the strength he had displayed in the face of recent trials, changed his mind. His son had been tested beyond his years, forced to confront danger head-on. Realizing Toma would one day lead Aiwa, Kypa understood that shielding his son would only hold him back.

"Princess Seva is among the traitors," he added. "She helped them steal the blue crystal."

"What!?" Ava blurted, startling those within earshot.

Kypa lifted a hand, signaling her to listen closely. "I cannot believe it myself," he admitted, "but Seva murdered several Aiwan soldiers before she turned on Commodore Boa. He survived, but the attack on the central core was a diversion to steal the crystal. Seva succeeded, and then escaped off-world."

Kypa shifted his gaze to Toma, who seemed lost in sad reflection. His son's tormented expression revealed the inner conflict brewing within. Kypa and Ava exchanged a glance, then he gently rested his hand on Toma's arm, a quiet offer of strength.

Toma raised his eyes, his voice steady but tinged with simmering anger. "Seva killed grandfather," he stated, not as a question but as a hard truth.

Kypa's heart sank as he saw the anguish in his son's eyes. With a heavy sigh, he nodded, acknowledging the painful reality.

"We have to stop her," Toma said firmly.

Ava jumped in without a moment's pause. "Toma's right. If Seva delivers that crystal to Krunig, he'll be unstoppable."

"We must assume Krunig already has it, or soon will," Kypa replied.

"And Reggie … don't forget her," Ava said sharply.

Kypa's expression softened with empathy. The fire in Ava's eyes reflected the anger he harbored for his sister. He never imagined Seva could be capable of such atrocities, not just against her people but against their own family.

"Right now, what matters most is protecting Aiwa," Kypa said, his resolve hardening. "I must return home and try to undo the damage Seva has caused."

"And what about Neil?" Ava asked, panged with guilt for nearly forgetting about him. "Neil's dying in there."

Kypa exhaled heavily as he focused on the cocooned figure inside the gunship. Standing beside Neil, Ten-Tee met Kypa's gaze, its photoreceptors widening in anticipation. The sight of the droid sparked an idea in Kypa's mind.

"Neil's suit cannot sustain him indefinitely," Kypa conceded, "and with Aiwa's power grid offline, our physicians may not be able to save him, either. You must go elsewhere for help."

"Earth?" Ava said skeptically, shaking her head. "We're not that advanced."

"Not Earth," Kypa corrected, his eyes narrowed as a plan formed. "You could take him to Starhaven."

"Starhaven?" Ava repeated, unfamiliar with the term. "What's that?"

"It is a floating space station that caters exclusively to the galaxy's elite. Starhaven offers rejuvenation treatments for every lifeform imaginable … if you can afford it," Kypa explained. "I know someone there—Vespa Rune. She helped me obtain parts for both Reapers. Vespa owes me a favor and can connect you with an augmenter who specializes in cybernetics."

"Wait, you mean implants?" Ava questioned skeptically.

"Yes," Kypa answered. "Neil has suffered a traumatic brain injury, far beyond my skills. An implant might be his only chance. Will you take him?"

Ava's chest tightened, but she did not hesitate. "Of course. What do I have to do?"

"Ten-Tee!" Kypa called. The tiny droid stepped forward to the edge of the gunship's doorway. "Does your programming include a celestial chart with coordinates to Starhaven?" Ten-Tee chirped confirmation. "Good," Kypa continued. "You will go with Ava and show her the way. Understood?"

Ten-Tee beeped cheerily, hopping up and down, eager to get underway.

A smile tugged at Ava's lips. "Ten-Tee, huh?"

"We found him back at the outpost," Kypa explained. "He has taken a liking to Neil and has proven to be quite resourceful."

Ten-Tee chirped in agreement.

"Father, I am going with Ava, too," Toma declared, his voice firm.

Kypa turned to his son in mild surprise, raising an eyebrow. Remembering his promise to Maya, he was poised to disagree outright, but Kypa held back. Setting aside his protective, fatherly concerns, the realist in him recognized that Ava stood a better chance of success with Toma at her side.

"Very well," he replied, a glint of pride in his eyes. "Your mother will have my hide for this, but Neil deserves all the help he can get." He turned to Captain Nova. "You will accompany them as well."

Nova straightened. Without hesitation, he stepped forward, eager to redeem himself after Seva's betrayal. "As you command, my king."

My king, Kypa mused silently.

The idea of succeeding his father had weighed heavily on him since Loka's passing, but the urgent needs of the Five Realms overshadowed his personal doubts. Nova's pledge of loyalty cleared the last of those reservations. It was time to embrace his destiny, return home, and take his place as rightful heir.

Ava, trying not to sound presumptuous, asked coyly, "And how will we be getting to Starhaven?"

With a wry grin, Kypa turned to Areda. "Captain, signal the fleet to drop out of hyperspace."

"Yes, my lord," he replied.

Without hesitation, Areda relayed the order to the bridge and trailing ships. Moments later, the small fleet exited hyperspace and returned to normal space.

Kypa summoned the second Reaper prototype using the commlink in his helmet. The sleek vessel appeared outside, then passed through the landing bay's shimmering containment field before touching down gracefully on the deck. Kypa then instructed the ship's computer that Ava would assume command. Once the order was confirmed, Kypa turned to Ava.

"Consider it a loan until we rescue Reggie," he stipulated.

Ava chuckled, eyeing the familiar starship. It was a mirror image of her beloved Reaper, though she reminded herself it was *not* the same—not without Reggie.

"I assume it has all the bells and whistles," she said.

"It does," Kypa confirmed, then added with a hint of allure, "including a cloaking device."

Taken aback, Ava grinned slyly. "Seriously? Like in the movies?"

Kypa caught the reference to Earth's pop culture and nodded with a knowing smile. Neil had always been a big fan of films, especially those set in outer space, and often shared his enthusiasm during their time at Groom Lake. Kypa's gaze drifted to Neil's cocoon, prompting him to refocus on the mission at hand.

"You can learn more about the cloaking device after you get underway," Kypa said. "Also keep in mind that your personal preferences will have to be reprogrammed. This ship's AI does not know you the way Reggie does."

"Right," Ava murmured, wondering what Reggie was experiencing at this moment. She quickly pushed that thought aside, reminding herself, *First, we save Neil, and then we get Reggie back … somehow.*

A brief silence hung in the air as Ava and Kypa's eyes met, an unspoken understanding passing between them. They were at a crossroads, each about to set out on divergent paths with uncertain outcomes ahead. Ava wrapped her arms around his waist in a grateful hug.

"Thank you for coming for me," she whispered, holding him tight.

Kypa gently patted her back. "That is what friends do," he said softly before adding with a playful smirk, "Now we are even."

Ava chuckled softly, thinking back to when she risked everything to help Kypa escape Area S4. She stepped back, her gaze locking with his dazzling blue eyes, their intensity a stark reminder of their bond. "Good luck back home," she said, her voice earnest and steady. "I hope everything works out."

"It will," Kypa said with conviction. "It has to."

Ava offered a reassuring smile, then gestured toward Toma. "And don't worry about him," she said. "As soon as we take care of Neil, we'll return to Aiwa. I promise."

Kypa dipped his chin in gratitude. "May Gwaru illuminate your path and protect you on your journey."

Ava nodded appreciatively. "And to you," she replied.

With that, Ava stepped away, turning to face her makeshift crew. "Alright," she said, drawing a deep breath. "Time to get underway. Nova, you and Toma get Neil loaded." Pointing to Ten-Tee, she added, "And you're with me. Let's go introduce ourselves to the ship's computer."

As Ava departed with Ten-Tee following close behind, Captain Nova nodded farewell to Kypa, then boarded the gunship to tend to Neil. Captain Areda took his cue and discreetly stepped away, leaving Kypa and Toma alone.

Father and son stood in silence. For Kypa, the moment was bittersweet—pride mingled with the sorrow of parting. He struggled to find the right words, but Toma saved him the trouble.

His son lowered his head in shame. "Father, the last time we were together, I said things … behaved in a way unworthy of our family. Forgive me."

Kypa gently placed his long index finger under Toma's jutted chin and lifted his head. Looking into his son's eyes, he said sincerely, "There is nothing to forgive. We may not always see eye to eye, but I will *never* be ashamed of you."

Toma's face brightened with a grateful smile.

"Now get going before I change my mind," he added with a wry smile. "When this is all behind us, I look forward to swimming and hunting with you again."

"So do I," Toma replied, backpedaling toward the gunship. A grin spread across his face. "And next time we race, I will not let you win."

Kypa let out a soft chuckle but quickly wrinkled his brow, unsure if his son was joking. Then, with a playful smile, he replied, "Challenge accepted!"

Aboard Prototype II, Ava headed to the cockpit, noting the subtle differences from her own ship. The interiors were nearly identical, but one crucial omission was the custom wet bath. Her spirits sank. After more than a week without a proper shower, she wanted one desperately. The nanites in her suit might keep her hydrated and clean, but they were no substitute for the bliss of a hot shower.

Then, there was the food menu—or lack thereof.

Stopping by the galley, Ava found herself suddenly famished. Her last meal had been a disgusting ration bar provided by the bounty hunters. She craved a juicy bacon cheeseburger with sweet potato fries doused in ketchup. But again, satisfaction was delayed. The ship's computer had no reference to the dish, but she did find Neil's recipe for Pop-Tarts.

Ava scarfed down her snack while sitting in the pilot's chair, waiting for it to adjust to her body type. Meanwhile, Ten-Tee uploaded its celestial charts to the ship's computer. By the time their tasks were completed, Toma and Nova had arrived.

"How's Neil?" Ava asked. "All squared away?"

"Dr. Garrett is secure below," Nova reported while Toma made his way to the extractor's seat. He promptly directed the ship's computer to generate an additional seat for their crewmate.

"Thank you, Nova," Ava replied as an extra clamshell seat materialized beside Toma. She gestured for him to take his place. "Make yourself comfortable. We've got a long journey ahead."

Nova nodded with appreciation, though his movements were somewhat awkward and restrained. It was clear he felt out of place, grappling with how to fit into this unfamiliar crew.

"Ten-Tee, we good?" Ava asked.

The tiny droid responded with a positive beep, prompting the ship's computer to add, "Celestial charts successfully loaded, Captain."

"Good. Set a course for Starhaven," Ava instructed.

The route appeared instantly on her HUD. Sliding her hands and feet inside the four orbs, Ava took manual control of the ship. A faint smile tugged at her lips as she gazed at the endless sea of stars ahead.

"CAVU," she whispered, a sense of familiarity settling over her—like she was finally herself again.

With a mental command, Ava powered up the twin nacelles and disengaged the ship's moorings. Gently, she manipulated the controls to lift Prototype II off the deck and throttle forward. They departed the Aiwan corvette and veered away from the fleet before jumping to lightspeed and the uncertain fate that awaited.

EPILOGUE

Planet Rogantu

Grawn Krunig stood in solitude on the bridge of his mighty warship, gazing through the main viewport at the volcanic world below. Arms clasped behind his back, he quietly reflected on the recent skirmish. The three Aiwan corvettes had fled, and Prince Kypa's fate remained a mystery, leaving a bitter hunger for vengeance gnawing at him. His gut told him Kypa had survived, for now.

As a consolation, the test of Baroness Shae's Blazecaster had been a success. On the barren world of Rogantu, the devastation had almost seemed like an improvement—a grim beautification. But Krunig knew a similar blast would be cataclysmic if unleashed upon a thriving world.

And you have thirteen more warheads at your disposal, he mused with a sinister grin.

As if on cue, Baroness Shae entered the bridge.

"I trust you are satisfied with the results?" she inquired, her voice brimming with pride.

Krunig turned his head slightly, the planet's dim glow reflecting in his visor. "Indeed," he said approvingly. "The weapon's effectiveness is undeniable. You've outdone yourself."

Shae shrugged modestly. "I do love my work."

"Good," Krunig stated. "Ensure the remaining warheads are ready for deployment. It is time we use them on a bigger scale."

Shae gave a curt nod, anticipation kindling in her gaze.

At the nearby science station, Draxx—acting first officer—leaned over the technician's shoulder, reviewing incoming damage reports following the recent engagement with the Aiwan corvettes. His brow furrowed in concentration until a proximity alarm flashed on the screen. Draxx's eyes widened as a new vessel emerged from hyperspace, its sleek silhouette unmistakable against the backdrop of stars.

"My lord, Aiwan vessel approaching … transport-class," he reported, his voice steady but edged with urgency.

Krunig, unruffled, stepped away from Shae and approached Draxx. "Is it alone?" he asked coolly.

"Yes, my lord," Draxx confirmed, a hint of confusion slipping in his voice. The Aiwan attack was over, and the corvettes had escaped, leaving him to wonder if this transport had arrived by mistake. "It appears to be slowing, sir."

The technician seated beside Draxx touched his earpiece. "Sir, incoming transmission," he reported. "The Aiwan vessel is hailing us."

"On screen," Krunig ordered.

With the flip of a switch, the image of Manta—the Cirran refugee—appeared on a hologram display in the middle of the bridge. He was seated in the pilot's chair of the royal yacht, his expression tense yet composed.

"Aiwan vessel," Draxx commanded with authority. "Power down your engines and lower your shields immediately, or we will open fire."

Manta swallowed hard. "Understood," he replied. "Stand by."

Draxx glanced at the technician, who quickly scanned the yacht and verified compliance.

"Now, state your business," Draxx ordered.

"Tell Grawn Krunig his prize awaits," Manta responded, purposely vague.

Perplexed, Draxx turned to Krunig, his brow knitted. "My lord?"

"No cause for alarm," Krunig said calmly. "They are with us."

He cocked his head sideways, silently signaling Shae. She swiftly reached into her pouch, retrieved a small handheld device, and activated it. A protective shield appeared suddenly, shimmering as it encompassed her entire body.

Krunig responded by tapping a button on his forearm. Instantly, the screens at every terminal flickered for a heartbeat before stabilizing.

"Sir, the main computer has been locked out," the technician reported, his voice rising with urgency.

Draxx leaned in close as the technician attempted to regain access to the ship, but the system remained unresponsive. Realization began to dawn, and he turned sharply to face Krunig, his confusion deepening with alarm.

"What is this? What's happening?" he demanded.

Krunig remained silent, watching impassively as an orange vapor cloud poured from the overhead vents, swirling down to engulf the bridge.

Shae's deadly concoction spread rapidly through the ship. Around her and Krunig, the bridge crew convulsed uncontrollably, collapsing from their stations.

Draxx's eyes grew wide with terror as he clawed desperately at his throat, struggling to draw breath. His voice failed him as the toxin took hold, and with a final, desperate glance at Krunig, his body crumpled to the floor. The bridge fell into an ominous silence, broken only by the steady hum of the ship's systems.

Krunig waited patiently, allowing a few extra moments to ensure the toxin had done its work thoroughly. Satisfied, he addressed the main computer, "Computer, how many life signs are you detecting onboard?"

"Two," the computer responded, flat and emotionless, "Grawn Krunig and Baroness Shae."

"Perfect," Krunig replied without remorse. "Restore all systems and purge the air filtration system. I want every trace of the toxin eliminated."

The ship's computer acknowledged the command. Over the next few minutes, the warship expelled every microbe of the deadly vapor.

"Purge complete," the computer announced. "Toxin levels: zero-point-zero percent."

Shae removed her shield as Krunig approached the science station. With a single, effortless motion, he grabbed the dead technician by the collar and hoisted him out of his chair, tossing the corpse aside.

Leaning forward, Krunig toggled the comm switch. "Manta, proceed to the main hangar."

"Yes, my lord," the Cirran replied dutifully. "We are starting our approach now."

The transmission ended. Krunig stepped over Draxx's remains and said to Shae, "My compliments, Baroness. Exceptional work, as always."

Shae responded with a cold, genial smile. As Krunig departed, she watched him walk purposefully off the bridge, leaving her alone among the dead.

Meanwhile, Manta powered up the royal yacht's main engines and guided the vessel toward Krunig's warship. The yacht passed through the hangar's containment field and touched down on the deck alongside the Reaper.

The boarding ramp lowered, and four armed Cirrans cautiously descended, weapons ready. Stepping onto the deck, they scanned the hangar for any signs of ambush. But what they found was a graveyard—eerily quiet and riddled with the bodies of dead Madreen crew members.

"Clear!" Fara called up the ramp to the others.

More refugees emerged from the yacht, hesitantly descending the ramp, their expressions filled with uncertainty. Nearly a hundred Cirrans debarked in total, pouring out in a steady stream, eying the corpses littering the deck.

At the far end of the hangar, Grawn Krunig appeared, encased in menacing crimson armor that gleamed malevolently under the harsh lights. At the sight of him, the Cirrans instinctively dropped to one knee in reverence—except Seva. She stood tall and resolute among the kneeling crowd, her gaze fixed upon Krunig with a spark of pride.

With bold steps, Seva advanced until she stood directly before the imposing figure. Krunig extended his massive hand; palm upturned in silent expectation. Without hesitation, Seva reached into her cloak and produced the maxixe magnetarite crystal. Its brilliant blue glow pulsated under the lights as she placed it into Krunig's open hand.

A faint smile tugged at her lips. "As promised, my king," she said with pride.

Suddenly, Krunig's crimson armor began to unlock with a series of mechanical hisses and clicks, segments unlocking and retracting. But when it opened to reveal its occupant, it was not a stranger who appeared before Seva, but her betrothed Prince Moorga—the rightful heir to Cirros.

The crowd froze in stunned silence, then erupted into joyous cheers as Moorga abandoned his armor and stepped forth, leaving the crystal cradled in the palm of the now-vacant suit.

Moorga approached Seva, the love of his life. Gently, he placed his forehead against hers, and in that intimate moment, their minds connected, rekindling their telepathic bond. The vows of unity they had exchanged long ago when forces beyond their control tore them apart now rang truer than ever, transcending time and space.

"Well done, my queen," Moorga said softly. "At last, we can be together."

In that poignant reunion, amidst the jubilant cheers of their people, Moorga and Seva turned to face the gathered Cirrans. The prince lifted the glowing crystal high for all to see.

"Behold the key to our salvation!" he proclaimed, his voice echoing in the hangar. "All our suffering, all our sacrifices—they end here. Never again shall Cirrans bow to any master. We will live free and create a new future for ourselves!"

The crowd's response was thunderous, their cheers a resounding chorus of hope and solidarity.

"To our new home," Moorga cried, his voice ringing with unyielding conviction. "To Earth!"

To be concluded in *Beyond the Reaper*.

AUTHOR'S NOTE

As I close the chapter on *Fear the Reaper*, I find myself filled with an overwhelming sense of joy and pride. Writing this book has been a journey of discovery, passion, and perseverance. Each page brought with it a deeper connection to the characters, their struggles, and their triumphs, and I'm thrilled to finally share this story with you.

This book represents not just a story, but a piece of my heart. It's a culmination of countless hours spent crafting twists and turns, exploring the depths of human resilience, and weaving together moments of suspense, action, and heartfelt emotion. Watching the world of *The Reaper Series* take shape has been one of the most rewarding experiences of my life.

Thank you for embarking on this adventure with me. Whether you're new to this world or a returning reader, your support means everything. I hope this story brings you as much excitement, intrigue, and inspiration as it brought me in bringing it to life.

If you enjoyed this book, please consider leaving a review on the retailer's website where you purchased it. Your feedback not only helps me as a writer but also helps other readers discover the story. I'd love to hear your thoughts!

Happy reading,
Todd

APPENDIX

CAST ON EARTH

Ava Tan – Pilot, Captain of the Reaper
Dr. Neil Garrett – Astrophysicist, National Aeronautical Space Administration
Dr. Rose Landry – Pathologist, Centers for Disease Control and Prevention
Lt. Colonel Marlana Nunez – United States Air Force (Husband: Hector)
Jessica Aguri – Deputy Director, National Clandestine Service, CIA
Roger Fitzgerald – President of the United States
Candace Fitzgerald – First Lady of the United States
Cathy Harrington – Vice President of the United States
Ernie Gutierrez – White House Chief of Staff
Ken Hreno – National Security Advisor
Russ Franks – Secretary of Defense
Bill Nguyen – Secretary of State
Admiral Susan Donnelly – Chairman, Joint Chiefs of Staff
Guy Lannister – Director of National Intelligence
Maxine Ratliff – Director, Central Intelligence Agency
Brett Brenham – Director, National Clandestine Service, CIA
General Anthony Garza – Former Chairman, Joint Chiefs of Staff
Gary Sizemore – Former Director, Central Intelligence Agency
Haley Nichols – U.S. Ambassador to the United Nations
Paul Wiggins – CIA Station Chief, Lima, Peru
Dr. M. Edmund Mathias – Founder and CEO, Mathias Industries
Luna – Aiwan engineer from Cirros
Lorenzo "Renzo" Condori – Mathias's henchman
Ms. Daniela Diaz – Mathias's personal assistant
Dr. Gabriel Vlachos – Scientist, Mathias Industries
Colleen Addison (aka Deanna Crowder) – British ULTRA agent

CAST ON AIWA (Ā-wuh)

Prince Kypa (Kī-puh) – Son of King Loka and Queen Qora
Maya (Mī-yuh) – Prince Kypa's mate (Children: Toma, Arya, Fraya)
Queen Qora (Kor-uh) – Queen of the Five Realms
Toma (Tō-muh) – Son of Kypa and Maya
Commodore Boa (Bō-uh) – Lord Commander of the Aiwan Military Forces
Captain Nova (Nō-vuh) – Keeper of the Royal Vault and Commander of the Royal Guards
Lieutenant Vylara (Vī-lair-uh) – Boa's agent investigating Loka's murder

The High Court of the Five Realms
Princess Seva (Sē-vuh) – Acting Warden of Eos
Lord Zefra – Warden of Fonn
Lord Wahla – Warden of Dohrm
Lord Cara – Warden of Maeve (Māv)
Vacant – Warden of Cirros (Sīr-ōs)

Miscellaneous
Grawn Krunig – Underboss, Madreen Crime Syndicate, Aiwan Sector
Vekka – Krunig's trusted aide
Smythe (Smīthe) – Bounty hunter
Gort – Pilot/mechanic (Smythe's business partner)
Hiromi (Hí-rō-mē) – Cyborg slicer
Baroness Shae – Scientest on Madreen
Grawn Supreme – Head of the Madreen Crime Syndicate
Grawn Draven – Underboss, Madreen Crime Syndicate
Ekator (Eck-a-tor) – Grawn Krunig's spaceport within the Mishi Nebula
Maxixe Magnetarite (Max-ice Mag-net-a-rīt) – Rarest of magnetar crystals
Gracylai (Gruh-sill-ī) – Carnivorous creature native to Rogantu
Xipos (Zī-pōz) – Seahorse-like creatures native to Fonn

www.ingramcontent.com/pod-product-compliance
Lightning Source LLC
Chambersburg PA
CBHW030910300726
48970CB00001B/90